PEOPLE AND STORIES THAT SHOULD NOT BE FORGOTTEN

ADVENTURES

ADVENTURES

PEOPLE AND STORIES THAT SHOULD NOT BE FORGOTTEN

WWW.ADVENTURESBOOKZINE.COM

ADVENTURES

PEOPLE AND STORIES THAT SHOULD NOT BE FORGOTTEN

SUMMER 2024 **ISSUE #12**

WHAT

WHERE

Editor's Note

Hello, Adventures fans! For this summer issue, we thought we'd go on a vacation from the norm and give you something a little different.

And you're in for a real treat, as our vacation includes poetry, prose, a play, Purcell, Pretty Sinister, a Paulette poster and plenty more! (We also have Ayn Rand, but she doesn't fit the P pattern. Although, she was a philosopher, so I suppose that works.)

You might only remember poetry or plays as those boring things you had to suffer through in school, but set all that aside and give them a try! Short poems are perfect for a late-summer afternoon, and reading a play is more fun than you'd expect - it's very easy to visualize what's happening. And this particular play has one of my favorite quotes: "I think that life is far too important a thing ever to talk seriously about it."

As mentioned above, we also have a Rand novella in this issue, "Anthem." We here at OffBeat discussed whether we should explain the ending, but we decided to let you interpret is as you will, but if you want to chat about it, shoot us an email!

You'll find some of your usual favorites in this issue, too, including the Reading Break fun page, pulp history, and more. We also have an original story from Murray Eiland, the Managing Editor at Antiqvvs Magazine.

Now, go find a comfortable seat outside, get yourself a glass of ice-cold lemonade, and sit back and enjoy this special edition of Adventures,

Michael Brian

Letters to the editor:

Comments/Questions are accepted. Put *Letter to Editor* in Subject and send to: OffBeatReads@pm.me
*Email content could be published in future *Adventures To Go*.

Flatland: A Romance of Many Dimensions

Edwin A. Abbott (1838-1926.
English scholar, theologian, and writer.)

With Illustrations by the Author, A SQUARE (Edwin A. Abbott)

To

The Inhabitants of SPACE IN GENERAL

And H. C. IN PARTICULAR

This Work is Dedicated

By a Humble Native of Flatland

In the Hope that

Even as he was Initiated into the Mysteries

Of THREE Dimensions

Having been previously conversant

With ONLY TWO

So the Citizens of that Celestial Region

May aspire yet higher and higher

To the Secrets of FOUR FIVE OR EVEN SIX Dimensions

Thereby contributing

To the Enlargement of THE IMAGINATION

And the possible Development

Of that most rare and excellent Gift of MODESTY

Among the Superior Races

Of SOLID HUMANITY

PREFACE TO THE SECOND AND REVISED EDITION, 1884.

BY THE EDITOR

If my poor Flatland friend retained the vigour of mind which he enjoyed when he began to compose these Memoirs, I should not now need to represent him in this preface, in which he desires, firstly, to return his thanks to his readers and critics in Spaceland, whose appreciation has, with unexpected celerity, required a second edition of his work; secondly, to apologize for certain errors and misprints (for which, however, he is not entirely responsible); and, thirdly, to explain one or two misconceptions. But he is not the Square he once was. Years of imprisonment, and the still heavier burden of general incredulity and mockery, have combined with the natural decay of old age to erase from his mind many of the thoughts and notions, and much also of the terminology, which he acquired during his short stay in Spaceland. He has, therefore, requested me to reply in his behalf to two special objections, one of an intellectual, the other of a moral nature.

The first objection is, that a Flatlander, seeing a Line, sees something that must be THICK to the eye as well as LONG to the eye (otherwise it would not be visible, if it had not some thickness); and consequently he ought (it is argued) to acknowledge that his countrymen are not only long and broad, but also (though doubtless in a very slight degree) THICK or HIGH. This objection is plausible, and, to Spacelanders, almost irresistible, so that, I confess, when I first heard it, I knew not what to reply. But my poor old friend's answer appears to me completely to meet it.

"I admit," said he—when I mentioned to him this objection—"I admit the truth of your critic's facts, but I deny his conclusions. It is true that we have really in Flatland a Third unrecognized Dimension called 'height', just as it is also true that you have really in Spaceland a Fourth unrecognized Dimension, called by no name at present, but which I will call 'extra-height'. But we can no more take cognizance of our 'height' than you can of your 'extra-height'. Even I—who have been in Spaceland, and have had the privilege of understanding for twenty-four hours the meaning of 'height'—even I cannot now comprehend it, nor realize it by the sense of sight or by any process of reason; I can but apprehend it by faith.

"The reason is obvious. Dimension implies direction, implies measurement, implies the more and the less. Now, all our lines are EQUALLY and INFINITESIMALLY thick (or high, whichever you like); consequently, there is nothing in them to lead our minds to the conception of that Dimension. No 'delicate micrometer'—as has been suggested by one too hasty Spaceland critic—would in the least avail us; for we should not know WHAT TO MEASURE, NOR IN WHAT DIRECTION. When we see a Line, we see something that is long and BRIGHT; BRIGHTNESS, as well as length, is necessary to the existence of a Line; if the brightness vanishes, the Line is extinguished. Hence, all my Flatland friends—when I talk to them about the unrecognized Dimension which is somehow visible in a Line—say, 'Ah, you mean BRIGHTNESS': and when I reply, 'No, I mean a real Dimension', they at once retort, 'Then measure it, or tell us in what direction it extends'; and this silences me, for I can do neither. Only yesterday, when the Chief Circle (in other words our High Priest) came to inspect the State Prison and paid me his seventh annual visit, and when for the seventh time he put me the question, 'Was I any better?' I tried to prove to him that he was 'high', as well as long and broad, although he did not know it. But what was his reply? 'You say I am "high"; measure my "high-ness" and I will believe you.' What could I do? How could I meet his challenge? I was crushed; and he left the room triumphant.

"Does this still seem strange to you? Then put yourself in a similar position. Suppose a person of the Fourth Dimension, condescending to visit you, were to say, 'Whenever you open your eyes, you see a Plane (which is of Two Dimensions) and you INFER a Solid (which is of Three); but in reality you also see (though you do not recognize) a Fourth Dimension, which is not colour nor brightness nor anything of the kind, but a true Dimension, although I cannot point out to you its direction, nor can you possibly measure it.' What would you say to such a visitor? Would not you have him locked up? Well, that is my fate: and it is as natural for us Flatlanders to lock up a Square for preaching the Third Dimension, as it is for you Spacelanders to lock up a Cube for preaching the Fourth. Alas, how strong a family likeness runs through blind and persecuting humanity in all Dimensions! Points, Lines, Squares, Cubes, Extra-Cubes—we are all liable to the same errors, all alike the Slaves of our respective Dimensional prejudices, as one of your Spaceland poets has said—

'One touch of Nature makes all worlds akin'."

[Note: The Author desires me to add, that the misconception of some of his critics on this matter has induced him to insert in his dialogue with the Sphere, certain remarks which have a bearing on the point in question, and which he had previously omitted as being tedious and unnecessary.]

On this point the defence of the Square seems to me to be impregnable. I wish I could say that his answer to the second (or moral) objection was equally clear and cogent. It has been objected that he is a woman-hater; and as this objection has been vehemently urged by those whom Nature's decree has constituted the somewhat larger half of the Spaceland race, I should like to remove it, so far as I can honestly do so. But the Square is so unaccustomed to the use of the moral terminology of Spaceland that I should be doing him an injustice if I were literally to transcribe his defence against this charge. Acting, therefore, as his interpreter and summarizer, I gather that in the course of an imprisonment of seven years he has himself modified his own personal views, both as regards Women and as regards the Isosceles or Lower Classes. Personally, he now inclines to the opinion of the Sphere that the Straight Lines are in many important respects superior to the Circles. But, writing as a Historian, he has identified himself (perhaps too closely) with the views generally adopted by Flatland, and (as he has been informed) even by Spaceland, Historians; in whose pages (until very recent times) the destinies of Women and of the masses of mankind have seldom been deemed worthy of mention and never of careful consideration.

In a still more obscure passage he now desires to disavow the Circular or aristocratic tendencies with which some critics have naturally credited him. While doing justice to the intellectual power with which a few Circles have for many generations maintained their supremacy over immense multitudes of their countrymen, he believes that the facts of Flatland, speaking for themselves without comment on his part, declare that Revolutions cannot always be suppressed by slaughter, and that Nature, in sentencing the Circles to infecundity, has condemned them to ultimate failure—"and herein," he says, "I see a fulfilment of the great Law of all worlds, that while the wisdom of Man thinks it is working one thing, the wisdom of Nature constrains it to work another, and quite a different and far better thing." For the rest, he begs his readers not to suppose that every minute detail in the daily life of Flatland must needs correspond to some other detail in Spaceland; and yet he hopes that, taken as a whole, his work may prove suggestive as well as amusing, to those Spacelanders of moderate and modest minds who—speaking of that which is of the highest importance, but lies beyond experience—decline to say on the one hand, "This can never be," and on the other hand, "It must needs be precisely thus, and we know all about it."

THIS WORLD

"Be patient, for the world is broad and wide."

SECTION 1.

OF THE NATURE OF FLATLAND

I call our world Flatland, not because we call it so, but to make its nature clearer to you, my happy readers, who are privileged to live in Space.

Imagine a vast sheet of paper on which straight Lines, Triangles, Squares, Pentagons, Hexagons, and other figures, instead of remaining fixed in their places, move freely about, on or in the surface, but without the power of rising above or sinking below it, very much like shadows—only hard and with luminous edges—and you will then have a pretty correct notion of my country and countrymen. Alas, a few years ago, I should have said "my universe": but now my mind has been opened to higher views of things.

In such a country, you will perceive at once that it is impossible that there should be anything of what you call a "solid" kind; but I dare say you will suppose that we could at least distinguish by sight the Triangles, Squares, and other figures, moving about as I have described them. On the contrary, we could see nothing of the kind, not at least so as to distinguish one figure from another. Nothing was visible, nor could be visible, to us, except Straight Lines; and the necessity of this I will speedily demonstrate.

Place a penny on the middle of one of your tables in Space; and leaning over it, look down upon it. It will appear a circle.

But now, drawing back to the edge of the table, gradually lower your eye (thus bringing yourself more and more into the condition of the inhabitants of Flatland), and you will find the penny becoming more and more oval to your view, and at last when you have placed your eye exactly on the edge of the table (so that you are, as it were, actually a Flatlander) the penny will then have ceased to appear oval at all, and will have become, so far as you can see, a straight line.

The same thing would happen if you were to treat in the same way a Triangle, or Square, or any other figure cut out of pasteboard. As soon as you look at it with your eye on the edge on the table, you will find that it ceases to appear to you a figure, and that it becomes in appearance a straight line. Take for example an equilateral Triangle—who represents with us a Tradesman of the respectable class. Fig. 1 represents the Tradesman as you would see him while you were bending over him from above; figs. 2 and 3 represent the Tradesman, as you would see him if your eye were close to the level, or all but on the level of the table; and if your eye were quite on the level of the table (and that is how we see him in Flatland) you would see nothing but a straight line.

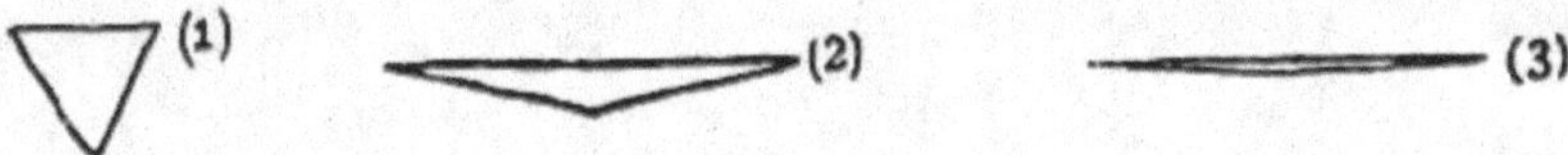

When I was in Spaceland I heard that your sailors have very similar experiences while they traverse your seas and discern some distant island or coast lying on the horizon. The far-off land may have bays, forelands, angles in and out to any number and extent; yet at a distance you see none of these (unless indeed your sun shines bright upon them revealing the projections and retirements by means of light and shade), nothing but a grey unbroken line upon the water.

Well, that is just what we see when one of our triangular or other acquaintances comes toward us in Flatland. As there is neither sun with us, nor any light of such a kind as to make shadows, we have none of the helps to the sight that you have in Spaceland. If our friend comes closer to us we see his line becomes larger; if he leaves us it becomes smaller: but still he looks like a straight line; be he a Triangle, Square, Pentagon, Hexagon, Circle, what you will—a straight Line he looks and nothing else.

You may perhaps ask how under these disadvantageous circumstances we are able to distinguish our friends from one another: but the answer to this very natural question will be more fitly and easily given when I come to describe the inhabitants of Flatland. For the present let me defer this subject, and say a word or two about the climate and houses in our country.

SECTION 2.

OF THE CLIMATE AND HOUSES IN FLATLAND

As with you, so also with us, there are four points of the compass North, South, East, and West.

There being no sun nor other heavenly bodies, it is impossible for us to determine the North in the usual way; but we have a method of our own. By a Law of Nature with us, there is a constant attraction to the South; and, although in temperate climates this is very slight—so that even a Woman in reasonable health can journey several furlongs northward without much difficulty—yet the hampering effect of the southward attraction is quite sufficient to serve as a compass in most parts of our earth. Moreover, the rain (which falls at stated intervals) coming always from the North, is an additional assistance; and in the towns we have the guidance of the houses, which of course have their side-walls running for the most part North and South, so that the roofs may keep off the rain from the North. In the country, where there are no houses, the trunks of the trees serve as some sort of guide. Altogether, we have not so much difficulty as might be expected in determining our bearings.

Yet in our more temperate regions, in which the southward attraction is hardly felt, walking sometimes in a perfectly desolate plain where there have been no houses nor trees to guide me, I have been occasionally compelled to remain stationary for hours together, waiting till the rain came before continuing my journey. On the weak and aged, and especially on delicate Females, the force of attraction tells much more heavily than on the robust of the Male Sex, so that it is a point of breeding, if you meet a Lady in the street, always to give her the North side of the way—by no means an easy thing to do always at short notice when you are in rude health and in a climate where it is difficult to tell your North from your South.

Windows there are none in our houses: for the light comes to us alike in our homes and out of them, by day and by night, equally at all times and in all places, whence we know not. It was in old days, with our learned men, an interesting and oft-investigated question, "What is the origin of light?" and the solution of it has been repeatedly attempted, with no other result than to crowd our lunatic asylums with the would-be solvers. Hence, after fruitless attempts to suppress such investigations indirectly by making them liable to a heavy tax, the Legislature, in comparatively recent times, absolutely prohibited them. I—alas, I alone in Flatland—know now only too well the true solution of this mysterious problem; but my knowledge cannot be made intelligible to a single one of my countrymen; and I am mocked at—I, the sole possessor of the truths of Space and of the theory of the introduction of Light from the world of three Dimensions—as if I were the maddest of the mad! But a truce to these painful digressions: let me return to our houses.

The most common form for the construction of a house is five-sided or pentagonal, as in the annexed figure. The two Northern sides RO, OF, constitute the roof, and for the most part have no doors; on the East is a small door for the Women; on the West a much larger one for the Men; the South side or floor is usually doorless.

Square and triangular houses are not allowed, and for this reason. The angles of a Square (and still more those of an equilateral Triangle), being much more pointed than those of a Pentagon, and the lines of inanimate objects (such as houses) being dimmer than the lines of Men and Women, it follows that there is no little danger lest the points of a square or triangular house residence might do serious injury to an inconsiderate or perhaps absent-minded traveller suddenly therefore, running against them: and as early as the eleventh century of our era, triangular houses were universally forbidden by Law, the only exceptions being fortifications, powder-magazines, barracks, and other state buildings, which it is not desirable that the general public should approach without circumspection.

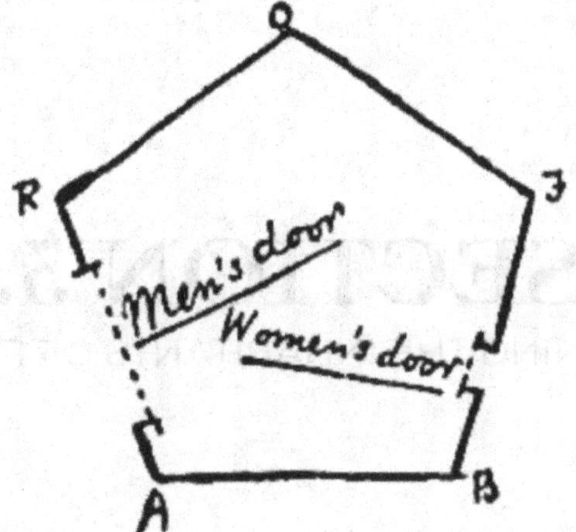

At this period, square houses were still everywhere permitted, though discouraged by a special tax. But, about three centuries afterwards, the Law decided that in all towns containing a population above ten thousand, the angle of a Pentagon was the smallest house-angle that could be allowed consistently with the public safety. The good sense of the community has seconded the efforts of the Legislature; and now, even in the country, the pentagonal construction has superseded every other. It is only now and then in some very remote and backward agricultural district that an antiquarian may still discover a square house.

SECTION 3.

CONCERNING THE INHABITANTS OF FLATLAND

The greatest length or breadth of a full grown inhabitant of Flatland may be estimated at about eleven of your inches. Twelve inches may be regarded as a maximum.

Our Women are Straight Lines.

Our Soldiers and Lowest Classes of Workmen are Triangles with two equal sides, each about eleven inches long, and a base or third side so short (often not exceeding half an inch) that they form at their vertices a very sharp and formidable angle. Indeed when their bases are of the most degraded type (not more than the eighth part of an inch in size), they can hardly be distinguished from Straight Lines or Women; so extremely pointed are their vertices. With us, as with you, these Triangles are distinguished from others by being called Isosceles; and by this name I shall refer to them in the following pages.

Our Middle Class consists of Equilateral or Equal-Sided Triangles.

Our Professional Men and Gentlemen are Squares (to which class I myself belong) and Five-Sided Figures or Pentagons.

Next above these come the Nobility, of whom there are several degrees, beginning at Six-Sided Figures, or Hexagons, and from thence rising in the number of their sides till they receive the honourable title of Polygonal, or many-sided. Finally when the number of the sides becomes so numerous, and the sides themselves so small, that the figure cannot be distinguished from a circle, he is included in the Circular or Priestly order; and this is the highest class of all.

It is a Law of Nature with us that a male child shall have one more side than his father, so that each generation shall rise (as a rule) one step in the scale of development and nobility. Thus the son of a Square is a Pentagon; the son of a Pentagon, a Hexagon; and so on.

But this rule applies not always to the Tradesmen, and still less often to the Soldiers, and to the Workmen; who indeed can hardly be said to deserve the name of human Figures, since they have not all their sides equal. With them therefore the Law of Nature does not hold; and the son of an Isosceles (i.e. a Triangle with two sides equal) remains Isosceles still. Nevertheless, all hope is not shut out, even from the Isosceles, that his posterity may ultimately rise above his degraded condition. For, after a long series of military successes, or diligent and skilful labours, it is generally found that the more intelligent among the Artisan and Soldier classes manifest a slight increase of their third side or base, and a shrinkage of the two other sides. Intermarriages (arranged by the Priests) between the sons and daughters of these more intellectual members of the lower classes generally result in an offspring approximating still more to the type of the Equal-Sided Triangle.

Rarely—in proportion to the vast numbers of Isosceles births—is a genuine and certifiable Equal-Sided Triangle produced from Isosceles parents. [Note: "What need of a certificate?" a Spaceland critic may ask: "Is not the procreation of a Square Son a certificate from Nature herself, proving the Equal-sidedness of the Father?" I reply that no Lady of any position will marry an uncertified Triangle. Square offspring has sometimes resulted from a slightly Irregular Triangle; but in almost every such case the Irregularity of the first generation is visited on the third; which either fails to attain the Pentagonal rank, or relapses to the Triangular.] Such a birth requires, as its antecedents, not only a series of carefully arranged intermarriages, but also a long, continued exercise of frugality and self-control on the part of the would-be ancestors of the coming Equilateral, and a patient, systematic, and continuous development of the Isosceles intellect through many generations.

The birth of a True Equilateral Triangle from Isosceles parents is the subject of rejoicing in our country for many furlongs around. After a strict examination conducted by the Sanitary and Social Board, the infant, if certified as Regular, is with solemn ceremonial admitted into the class of Equilaterals. He is then immediately taken from his proud yet sorrowing parents and adopted by some childless Equilateral, who is bound by oath never to permit the child henceforth to enter his former home or so much as to look upon his relations again, for fear lest the freshly developed organism may, by force of unconscious imitation, fall back again into his hereditary level.

The occasional emergence of an Equilateral from the ranks of his serf-born ancestors is welcomed, not only by the poor serfs themselves, as a gleam of light and hope shed upon the monotonous squalor of their existence, but also by the Aristocracy at large; for all the higher classes are well aware that these rare phenomena, while they do little or nothing to vulgarize their own privileges, serve as a most useful barrier against revolution from below.

Had the acute-angled rabble been all, without exception, absolutely destitute of hope and of ambition, they might have found leaders in some of their many seditious outbreaks, so able as to render their superior numbers and strength too much even for the wisdom of the Circles. But a wise ordinance of Nature has decreed that, in proportion as the working-classes increase in intelligence, knowledge, and all virtue, in that same proportion their acute angle (which makes them physically terrible) shall increase also and approximate to the comparatively harmless angle of the Equilateral Triangle. Thus, in the most brutal and formidable of the soldier class—creatures almost on a level with women in their lack of intelligence—it is found that, as they wax in the mental ability necessary to employ their tremendous penetrating power to advantage, so do they wane in the power of penetration itself.

How admirable is this Law of Compensation! And how perfect a proof of the natural fitness and, I may almost say, the divine origin of the aristocratic constitution of the States in Flatland! By a judicious use of this Law of Nature, the Polygons and Circles are almost always able to stifle sedition in its very cradle, taking advantage of the irrepressible and boundless hopefulness of the human mind. Art also comes to the aid of Law and Order. It is generally found possible—by a little artificial compression or expansion on the part of the State physicians—to make some of the more intelligent leaders of a rebellion perfectly Regular, and to admit them at once into the privileged classes; a much larger number, who are still below the standard, allured by the prospect of being ultimately ennobled, are induced to enter the State Hospitals, where they are kept in honourable confinement for life; one or two alone of the more obstinate, foolish, and hopelessly irregular are led to execution.

Then the wretched rabble of the Isosceles, planless and leaderless, are either transfixed without resistance by the small body of their brethren whom the Chief Circle keeps in pay for emergencies of this kind; or else more often, by means of jealousies and suspicions skilfully fomented among them by the Circular party, they are stirred to mutual warfare, and perish by one another's angles. No less than one hundred and twenty rebellions are recorded in our annals, besides minor outbreaks numbered at two hundred and thirty-five; and they have all ended thus.

SECTION 4.
CONCERNING THE WOMEN

If our highly pointed Triangles of the Soldier class are formidable, it may be readily inferred that far more formidable are our Women. For if a Soldier is a wedge, a Woman is a needle; being, so to speak, ALL point, at least at the two extremities. Add to this the power of making herself practically invisible at will, and you will perceive that a Female, in Flatland, is a creature by no means to be trifled with.

But here, perhaps, some of my younger Readers may ask HOW a woman in Flatland can make herself invisible. This ought, I think, to be apparent without any explanation. However, a few words will make it clear to the most unreflecting.

Place a needle on a table. Then, with your eye on the level of the table, look at it side-ways, and you see the whole length of it; but look at it end-ways, and you see nothing but a point, it has become practically invisible. Just so is it with one of our Women. When her side is turned towards us, we see her as a straight line; when the end containing her eye or mouth—for with us these two organs are identical—is the part that meets our eye, then we see nothing but a highly lustrous point; but when the back is presented to our view, then—being only sub-lustrous, and, indeed, almost as dim as an inanimate object—her hinder extremity serves her as a kind of Invisible Cap.

The dangers to which we are exposed from our Women must now be manifest to the meanest capacity in Spaceland. If even the angle of a respectable Triangle in the middle class is not without its dangers; if to run against a Working Man involves a gash; if collision with an officer of the military class necessitates a serious wound; if a mere touch from the vertex of a Private Soldier brings with it danger of death;—what can it be to run against a Woman, except absolute and immediate destruction? And when a Woman is invisible, or visible only as a dim sub-lustrous point, how difficult must it be, even for the most cautious, always to avoid collision!

Many are the enactments made at different times in the different States of Flatland, in order to minimize this peril; and in the Southern and less temperate climates where the force of gravitation is greater, and human beings more liable to casual and involuntary motions, the Laws concerning Women are naturally much more stringent. But a general view of the Code may be obtained from the following summary:—

1.   Every house shall have one entrance in the Eastern side, for the use of Females only; by which all females shall enter "in a becoming and respectful manner" and not by the Men's or Western door. [Note: When I was in Spaceland I understood that some of your Priestly circles have in the same way a separate entrance for Villagers, Farmers and Teachers of Board Schools (`Spectator', Sept. 1884, p. 1255) that they may "approach in a becoming and respectful manner."]

2.   No Female shall walk in any public place without continually keeping up her Peace-cry, under penalty of death.

3.   Any Female, duly certified to be suffering from St. Vitus's Dance, fits, chronic cold accompanied by violent sneezing, or any disease necessitating involuntary motions, shall be instantly destroyed.

In some of the States there is an additional Law forbidding Females, under penalty of death, from walking or standing in any public place without moving their backs constantly from right to left so as to indicate their presence to those behind them; others oblige a Woman, when travelling, to be followed by one of her sons, or servants, or by her husband; others confine Women altogether to their houses except during the religious festivals. But it has been found by the wisest of our Circles or Statesmen that the multiplication of restrictions on Females tends not only to the debilitation and diminution of the race, but also to the increase of domestic murders to such an extent that a State loses more than it gains by a too prohibitive Code.

For whenever the temper of the Women is thus exasperated by confinement at home or hampering regulations abroad, they are apt to vent their spleen upon their husbands and children; and in the less temperate climates the whole male population of a village has been sometimes destroyed in one or two hours of simultaneous female outbreak. Hence the Three Laws, mentioned above, suffice for the better regulated States, and may be accepted as a rough exemplification of our Female Code.

After all, our principal safeguard is found, not in Legislature, but in the interests of the Women themselves. For, although they can inflict instantaneous death by a retrograde movement, yet unless they can at once disengage their stinging extremity from the struggling body of their victim, their own frail bodies are liable to be shattered.

The power of Fashion is also on our side. I pointed out that in some less civilized States no female is suffered to stand in any public place without swaying her back from right to left. This practice has been universal among ladies of any pretensions to breeding in all well-governed States, as far back as the memory of Figures can reach. It is considered a disgrace to any State that legislation should have to enforce what ought to be, and is in every respectable female, a natural instinct. The rhythmical and, if I may so say, well-modulated undulation of the back in our ladies of Circular rank is envied and imitated by the wife of a common Equilateral, who can achieve nothing beyond a mere monotonous swing, like the ticking of a pendulum; and the regular tick of the Equilateral is no less admired and copied by the wife of the progressive and aspiring Isosceles, in the females of whose family no "back-motion" of any kind has become as yet a necessity of life. Hence, in every family of position and consideration, "back motion" is as prevalent as time itself; and the husbands and sons in these households enjoy immunity at least from invisible attacks.

Not that it must be for a moment supposed that our Women are destitute of affection. But unfortunately the passion of the moment predominates, in the Frail Sex, over every other consideration. This is, of course, a necessity arising from their unfortunate conformation. For as they have no pretensions to an angle, being inferior in this respect to the very lowest of the Isosceles, they are consequently wholly devoid of brainpower, and have neither reflection, judgment nor forethought, and hardly any memory. Hence, in their fits of fury, they remember no claims and recognize no distinctions. I have actually known a case where a Woman has exterminated her whole household, and half an hour afterwards, when her rage was over and the fragments swept away, has asked what has become of her husband and her children.

Obviously then a Woman is not to be irritated as long as she is in a position where she can turn round. When you have them in their apartments—which are constructed with a view to denying them that power—you can say and do what you like; for they are then wholly impotent for mischief, and will not remember a few minutes hence the incident for which they may be at this moment threatening you with death, nor the promises which you may have found it necessary to make in order to pacify their fury.

On the whole we get on pretty smoothly in our domestic relations, except in the lower strata of the Military Classes. There the want of tact and discretion on the part of the husbands produces at times indescribable disasters. Relying too much on the offensive weapons of their acute angles instead of the defensive organs of good sense and seasonable simulation, these reckless creatures too often neglect the prescribed construction of the women's apartments, or irritate their wives by ill-advised expressions out of doors, which they refuse immediately to retract. Moreover a blunt and stolid regard for literal truth indisposes them to make those lavish promises by which the more judicious Circle can in a moment pacify his consort. The result is massacre; not, however, without its advantages, as it eliminates the more brutal and troublesome of the Isosceles; and by many of our Circles the destructiveness of the Thinner Sex is regarded as one among many providential arrangements for suppressing redundant population, and nipping Revolution in the bud.

Yet even in our best regulated and most approximately Circular families I cannot say that the ideal of family life is so high as with you in Spaceland. There is peace, in so far as the absence of slaughter may be called by that name, but there is necessarily little harmony of tastes or pursuits; and the cautious wisdom of the Circles has ensured safety at the cost of domestic comfort. In every Circular or Polygonal household it has been a habit from time immemorial—and now has become a kind of instinct among the women of our higher classes—that the mothers and daughters should constantly keep their eyes and mouths towards their husband and his male friends; and for a lady in a family of distinction to turn her back upon her husband would be regarded as a kind of portent, involving loss of STATUS. But, as I shall soon shew, this custom, though it has the advantage of safety, is not without its disadvantages.

In the house of the Working Man or respectable Tradesman—where the wife is allowed to turn her back upon her husband, while pursuing her household avocations—there are at least intervals of quiet, when the wife is neither seen nor heard, except for the humming sound of the continuous Peace-cry; but in the homes of the upper classes there is too often no peace. There the voluble mouth and bright penetrating eye are ever directed towards the Master of the household; and light itself is not more persistent than the stream of feminine discourse. The tact and skill which suffice to avert a Woman's sting are unequal to the task of stopping a Woman's mouth; and as the wife has absolutely nothing to say, and absolutely no constraint of wit, sense, or conscience to prevent her from saying it, not a few cynics have been found to aver that they prefer the danger of the death-dealing but inaudible sting to the safe sonorousness of a Woman's other end.

To my readers in Spaceland the condition of our Women may seem truly deplorable, and so indeed it is. A Male of the lowest type of the Isosceles may look forward to some improvement of his angle, and to the ultimate elevation of the whole of his degraded caste; but no Woman can entertain such hopes for her sex. "Once a Woman, always a Woman" is a Decree of Nature; and the very Laws of Evolution seem suspended in her disfavour. Yet at least we can admire the wise Prearrangement which has ordained that, as they have no hopes, so they shall have no memory to recall, and no forethought to anticipate, the miseries and humiliations which are at once a necessity of their existence and the basis of the constitution of Flatland.

SECTION 5.
OF OUR METHODS OF RECOGNIZING ONE ANOTHER

You, who are blessed with shade as well as light, you, who are gifted with two eyes, endowed with a knowledge of perspective, and charmed with the enjoyment of various colours, you, who can actually SEE an angle, and contemplate the complete circumference of a circle in the happy region of the Three Dimensions—how shall I make clear to you the extreme difficulty which we in Flatland experience in recognizing one another's configuration?

Recall what I told you above. All beings in Flatland, animate or inanimate, no matter what their form, present TO OUR VIEW the same, or nearly the same, appearance, viz. that of a straight Line. How then can one be distinguished from another, where all appear the same?

The answer is threefold. The first means of recognition is the sense of hearing; which with us is far more highly developed than with you, and which enables us not only to distinguish by the voice our personal friends, but even to discriminate between different classes, at least so far as concerns the three lowest orders, the Equilateral, the Square, and the Pentagon—for of the Isosceles I take no account. But as we ascend in the social scale, the process of discriminating and being discriminated by hearing increases in difficulty, partly because voices are assimilated, partly because the faculty of voice-discrimination is a plebeian virtue not much developed among the Aristocracy. And wherever there is any danger of imposture we cannot trust to this method. Amongst our lowest orders, the vocal organs are developed to a degree more than correspondent with those of hearing, so that an Isosceles can easily feign the voice of a Polygon, and, with some training, that of a Circle himself. A second method is therefore more commonly resorted to.

FEELING is, among our Women and lower classes—about our upper classes I shall speak presently—the principal test of recognition, at all events between strangers, and when the question is, not as to the individual, but as to the class. What therefore "introduction" is among the higher classes in Spaceland, that the process of "feeling" is with us. "Permit me to ask you to feel and be felt by my friend Mr. So-and-so"—is still, among the more old-fashioned of our country gentlemen in districts remote from towns, the customary formula for a Flatland introduction. But in the towns, and among men of business, the words "be felt by" are omitted and the sentence is abbreviated to, "Let me ask you to feel Mr. So-and-so"; although it is assumed, of course, that the "feeling" is to be reciprocal. Among our still more modern and dashing young gentlemen— who are extremely averse to superfluous effort and supremely indifferent to the purity of their native language—the formula is still further curtailed by the use of "to feel" in a technical sense, meaning, "to recommend-for-the-purposes-of-feeling-and-being-felt"; and at this moment the "slang" of polite or fast society in the upper classes sanctions such a barbarism as "Mr. Smith, permit me to feel Mr. Jones."

Let not my Reader however suppose that "feeling" is with us the tedious process that it would be with you, or that we find it necessary to feel right round all the sides of every individual before we determine the class to which he belongs. Long practice and training, begun in the schools and continued in the experience of daily life, enable us to discriminate at once by the sense of touch, between the angles of an equal-sided Triangle, Square, and Pentagon; and I need not say that the brainless vertex of an acute-angled Isosceles is obvious to the dullest touch. It is therefore not necessary, as a rule, to do more than feel a single angle of an individual; and this, once ascertained, tells us the class of the person whom we are addressing, unless indeed he belongs to the higher sections of the nobility. There the difficulty is much greater. Even a Master of Arts in our University of Wentbridge has been known to confuse a ten-sided with a twelve-sided Polygon; and there is hardly a Doctor of Science in or out of that famous University who could pretend to decide promptly and unhesitatingly between a twenty-sided and a twenty-four sided member of the Aristocracy.

Those of my readers who recall the extracts I gave above from the Legislative code concerning Women, will readily perceive that the process of introduction by contact requires some care and discretion. Otherwise the angles might inflict on the unwary Feeler irreparable injury. It is essential for the safety of the Feeler that the Felt should stand perfectly still. A start, a fidgety shifting of the position, yes, even a violent sneeze, has been known before now to prove fatal to the incautious, and to nip in the bud many a promising friendship. Especially is this true among the lower classes of the Triangles. With them, the eye is situated so far from their vertex that they can scarcely take cognizance of what goes on at that extremity of their frame. They are, moreover, of a rough coarse nature, not sensitive to the delicate touch of the highly organized Polygon. What wonder then if an involuntary toss of the head has ere now deprived the State of a valuable life!

I have heard that my excellent Grandfather—one of the least irregular of his unhappy Isosceles class, who indeed obtained, shortly before his decease, four out of seven votes from the Sanitary and Social Board for passing him into the class of the Equal-sided—often deplored, with a tear in his venerable eye, a miscarriage of this kind, which had occured to his great-great-great-Grandfather, a respectable Working Man with an angle or brain of 59 degrees 30 minutes. According to his account, my unfortunate Ancestor, being afflicted with rheumatism, and in the act of being felt by a Polygon, by one sudden start accidentally transfixed the Great Man through the diagonal; and thereby, partly in consequence of his long imprisonment and degradation, and partly because of the moral shock which pervaded the whole of my Ancestor's relations, threw back our family a degree and a half in their ascent towards better things. The result was that in the next generation the family brain was registered at only 58 degrees, and not till the lapse of five generations was the lost ground recovered, the full 60 degrees attained, and the Ascent from the Isosceles finally achieved. And all this series of calamities from one little accident in the process of Feeling.

At this point I think I hear some of my better educated readers exclaim, "How could you in Flatland know anything about angles and degrees, or minutes? We can SEE an angle, because we, in the region of Space, can see two straight lines inclined to one another; but you, who can see nothing but one straight line at a time, or at all events only a number of bits of straight lines all in one straight line—how can you ever discern any angle, and much less register angles of different sizes?"

I answer that though we cannot SEE angles, we can INFER them, and this with great precision. Our sense of touch, stimulated by necessity, and developed by long training, enables us to distinguish angles far more accurately than your sense of sight, when unaided by a rule or measure of angles. Nor must I omit to explain that we have great natural helps. It is with us a Law of Nature that the brain of the Isosceles class shall begin at half a degree, or thirty minutes, and shall increase (if it increases at all) by half a degree in every generation; until the goal of 60 degrees is reached, when the condition of serfdom is quitted, and the freeman enters the class of Regulars.

Consequently, Nature herself supplies us with an ascending scale or Alphabet of angles for half a degree up to 60 degrees, Specimens of which are placed in every Elementary School throughout the land. Owing to occasional retrogressions, to still more frequent moral and intellectual stagnation, and to the extraordinary fecundity of the Criminal and Vagabond Classes, there is always a vast superfluity of individuals of the half degree and single degree class, and a fair abundance of Specimens up to 10 degrees. These are absolutely destitute of civic rights; and a great number of them, not having even intelligence enough for the purposes of warfare, are devoted by the States to the service of education. Fettered immovably so as to remove all possibility of danger, they are placed in the class rooms of our Infant Schools, and there they are utilized by the Board of Education for the purpose of imparting to the offspring of the Middle Classes that tact and intelligence of which these wretched creatures themselves are utterly devoid.

In some States the Specimens are occasionally fed and suffered to exist for several years; but in the more temperate and better regulated regions, it is found in the long run more advantageous for the educational interests of the young, to dispense with food, and to renew the Specimens every month—which is about the average duration of the foodless existence of the Criminal class. In the cheaper schools, what is gained by the longer existence of the Specimen is lost, partly in the expenditure for food, and partly in the diminished accuracy of the angles, which are impaired after a few weeks of constant "feeling". Nor must we forget to add, in enumerating the advantages of the more expensive system, that it tends, though slightly yet perceptibly, to the diminution of the redundant Isosceles population— an object which every statesman in Flatland constantly keeps in view. On the whole therefore—although I am not ignorant that, in many popularly elected School Boards, there is a reaction in favour of "the cheap system" as it is called—I am myself disposed to think that this is one of the many cases in which expense is the truest economy.

But I must not allow questions of School Board politics to divert me from my subject. Enough has been said, I trust, to shew that Recognition by Feeling is not so tedious or indecisive a process as might have been supposed; and it is obviously more trustworthy than Recognition by hearing. Still there remains, as has been pointed out above, the objection that this method is not without danger. For this reason many in the Middle and Lower classes, and all without exception in the Polygonal and Circular orders, prefer a third method, the description of which shall be reserved for the next section.

SECTION 6.
OF RECOGNITION BY SIGHT

I am about to appear very inconsistent. In previous sections I have said that all figures in Flatland present the appearance of a straight line; and it was added or implied, that it is consequently impossible to distinguish by the visual organ between individuals of different classes: yet now I am about to explain to my Spaceland critics how we are able to recognize one another by the sense of sight.

If however the Reader will take the trouble to refer to the passage in which Recognition by Feeling is stated to be universal, he will find this qualification—"among the lower classes". It is only among the higher classes and in our temperate climates that Sight Recognition is practised.

That this power exists in any regions and for any classes is the result of Fog; which prevails during the greater part of the year in all parts save the torrid zones. That which is with you in Spaceland an unmixed evil, blotting out the landscape, depressing the spirits, and enfeebling the health, is by us recognized as a blessing scarcely inferior to air itself, and as the Nurse of arts and Parent of sciences. But let me explain my meaning, without further eulogies on this beneficent Element.

If Fog were non-existent, all lines would appear equally and indistinguishably clear; and this is actually the case in those unhappy countries in which the atmosphere is perfectly dry and transparent. But wherever there is a rich supply of Fog objects that are at a distance, say of three feet, are appreciably dimmer than those at a distance of two feet eleven inches; and the result is that by careful and constant experimental observation of comparative dimness and clearness, we are enabled to infer with great exactness the configuration of the object observed.

An instance will do more than a volume of generalities to make my meaning clear.

Suppose I see two individuals approaching whose rank I wish to ascertain. They are, we will suppose, a Merchant and a Physician, or in other words, an Equilateral Triangle and a Pentagon: how am I to distinguish them?

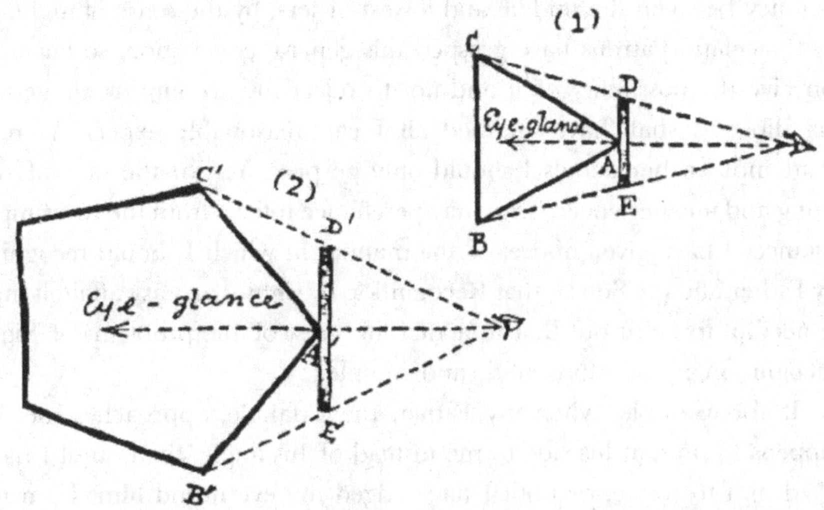

It will be obvious, to every child in Spaceland who has touched the threshold of Geometrical Studies, that, if I can bring my eye so that its glance may bisect an angle (A) of the approaching stranger, my view will lie as it were evenly between his two sides that are next to me (viz. CA and AB), so that I shall contemplate the two impartially, and both will appear of the same size.

Now in the case of (1) the Merchant, what shall I see? I shall see a straight line DAE, in which the middle point (A) will be very bright because it is nearest to me; but on either side the line will shade away RAPIDLY INTO DIMNESS, because the sides AC and AB RECEDE RAPIDLY

INTO THE FOG and what appear to me as the Merchant's extremities, viz. D and E, will be VERY DIM INDEED.

On the other hand in the case of (2) the Physician, though I shall here also see a line (D'A'E') with a bright centre (A'), yet it will shade away LESS RAPIDLY into dimness, because the sides (A'C', A'B') RECEDE LESS RAPIDLY INTO THE FOG: and what appear to me the Physician's extremities, viz. D' and E', will not be NOT SO DIM as the extremities of the Merchant.

The Reader will probably understand from these two instances how—after a very long training supplemented by constant experience—it is possible for the well-educated classes among us to discriminate with fair accuracy between the middle and lowest orders, by the sense of sight. If my Spaceland Patrons have grasped this general conception, so far as to conceive the possibility of it and not to reject my account as altogether incredible—I shall have attained all I can reasonably expect. Were I to attempt further details I should only perplex. Yet for the sake of the young and inexperienced, who may perchance infer—from the two simple instances I have given above, of the manner in which I should recognize my Father and my Sons—that Recognition by sight is an easy affair, it may be needful to point out that in actual life most of the problems of Sight Recognition are far more subtle and complex.

If for example, when my Father, the Triangle, approaches me, he happens to present his side to me instead of his angle, then, until I have asked him to rotate, or until I have edged my eye round him, I am for the moment doubtful whether he may not be a Straight Line, or, in other words, a Woman. Again, when I am in the company of one of my two hexagonal Grandsons, contemplating one of his sides (AB) full front, it will be evident from the accompanying diagram that I shall see one whole line (AB) in comparative brightness (shading off hardly at all at the ends) and two smaller lines (CA and BD) dim throughout and shading away into greater dimness towards the extremities C and D.

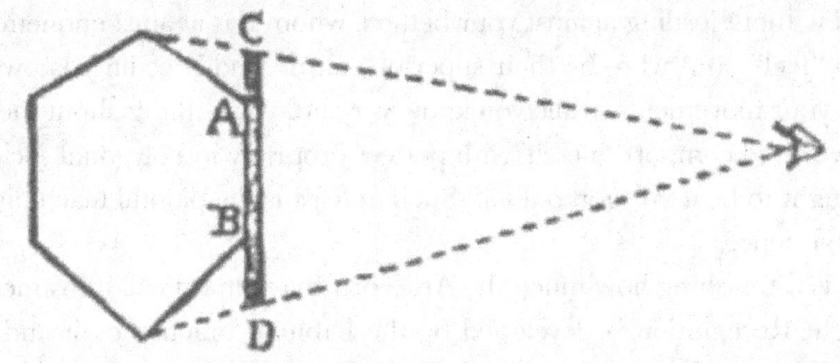

But I must not give way to the temptation of enlarging on these topics. The meanest mathematician in Spaceland will readily believe me when I assert that the problems of life, which present themselves to the well-educated—when they are themselves in motion, rotating, advancing or retreating, and at the same time attempting to discriminate by the sense of sight between a number of Polygons of high rank moving in different directions, as for example in a ball-room or conversazione—must be of a nature to task the angularity of the most intellectual, and amply justify the rich endowments of the Learned Professors of Geometry, both Static and Kinetic, in the illustrious University of Wentbridge, where the Science and Art of Sight Recognition are regularly taught to large classes of the ELITE of the States.

It is only a few of the scions of our noblest and wealthiest houses, who are able to give the time and money necessary for the thorough prosecution of this noble and valuable Art. Even to me, a Mathematician of no mean standing, and the Grandfather of two most hopeful and perfectly regular Hexagons, to find myself in the midst of a crowd of rotating Polygons of the higher classes, is occasionally very perplexing. And of course to a common Tradesman, or Serf, such a sight is almost as unintelligible as it would be to you, my Reader, were you suddenly transported into our country.

In such a crowd you could see on all sides of you nothing but a Line, apparently straight, but of which the parts would vary irregularly and perpetually in brightness or dimness. Even if you had completed your third year in the Pentagonal and Hexagonal classes in the University, and were perfect in the theory of the subject, you would still find that there was need of many years of experience, before you could move in a fashionable crowd without jostling against your betters, whom it is against etiquette to ask to "feel", and who, by their superior culture and breeding, know all about your movements, while you know very little or nothing about theirs. In a word, to comport oneself with perfect propriety in Polygonal society, one ought to be a Polygon oneself. Such at least is the painful teaching of my experience.

It is astonishing how much the Art—or I may almost call it instinct—of Sight Recognition is developed by the habitual practice of it and by the avoidance of the custom of "Feeling". Just as, with you, the deaf and dumb, if once allowed to gesticulate and to use the hand-alphabet, will never acquire the more difficult but far more valuable art of lipspeech and lip-reading, so it is with us as regards "Seeing" and "Feeling". None who in early life resort to "Feeling" will ever learn "Seeing" in perfection.

For this reason, among our Higher Classes, "Feeling" is discouraged or absolutely forbidden. From the cradle their children, instead of going to the Public Elementary schools (where the art of Feeling is taught), are sent to higher Seminaries of an exclusive character; and at our illustrious University, to "feel" is regarded as a most serious fault, involving Rustication for the first offence, and Expulsion for the second.

But among the lower classes the art of Sight Recognition is regarded as an unattainable luxury. A common Tradesman cannot afford to let his son spend a third of his life in abstract studies. The children of the poor are therefore allowed to "feel" from their earliest years, and they gain thereby a precocity and an early vivacity which contrast at first most favourably with the inert, undeveloped, and listless behaviour of the half-instructed youths of the Polygonal class; but when the latter have at last completed their University course, and are prepared to put their theory into practice, the change that comes over them may almost be described as a new birth, and in every art, science, and social pursuit they rapidly overtake and distance their Triangular competitors.

Only a few of the Polygonal Class fail to pass the Final Test or Leaving Examination at the University. The condition of the unsuccessful minority is truly pitiable. Rejected from the higher class, they are also despised by the lower. They have neither the matured and systematically trained powers of the Polygonal Bachelors and Masters of Arts, nor yet the native precocity and mercurial versatility of the youthful Tradesman. The professions, the public services, are closed against them; and though in most States they are not actually debarred from marriage, yet they have the greatest difficulty in forming suitable alliances, as experience shews that the offspring of such unfortunate and ill-endowed parents is generally itself unfortunate, if not positively Irregular.

It is from these specimens of the refuse of our Nobility that the great Tumults and Seditions of past ages have generally derived their leaders; and so great is the mischief thence arising that an increasing minority of our more progressive Statesmen are of opinion that true mercy would dictate their entire suppression, by enacting that all who fail to pass the Final Examination of the University should be either imprisoned for life, or extinguished by a painless death.

But I find myself digressing into the subject of Irregularities, a matter of such vital interest that it demands a separate section.

SECTION 7.
CONCERNING IRREGULAR FIGURES

Throughout the previous pages I have been assuming—what perhaps should have been laid down at the beginning as a distinct and fundamental proposition—that every human being in Flatland is a Regular Figure, that is to say of regular construction. By this I mean that a Woman must not only be a line, but a straight line; that an Artisan or Soldier must have two of his sides equal; that Tradesmen must have three sides equal; Lawyers (of which class I am a humble member), four sides equal, and generally, that in every Polygon, all the sides must be equal.

The size of the sides would of course depend upon the age of the individual. A Female at birth would be about an inch long, while a tall adult Woman might extend to a foot. As to the Males of every class, it may be roughly said that the length of an adult's sides, when added together, is two feet or a little more. But the size of our sides is not under consideration. I am speaking of the EQUALITY of sides, and it does not need much reflection to see that the whole of the social life in Flatland rests upon the fundamental fact that Nature wills all Figures to have their sides equal.

If our sides were unequal our angles might be unequal. Instead of its being sufficient to feel, or estimate by sight, a single angle in order to determine the form of an individual, it would be necessary to ascertain each angle by the experiment of Feeling. But life would be too short for such a tedious grouping. The whole science and art of Sight Recognition would at once perish; Feeling, so far as it is an art, would not long survive; intercourse would become perilous or impossible; there would be an end to all confidence, all forethought; no one would be safe in making the most simple social arrangements; in a word, civilization would relapse into barbarism.

Am I going too fast to carry my Readers with me to these obvious conclusions? Surely a moment's reflection, and a single instance from common life, must convince every one that our whole social system is based upon Regularity, or Equality of Angles. You meet, for example, two or three Tradesmen in the street, whom you recognize at once to be Tradesmen by a glance at their angles and rapidly bedimmed sides, and you ask them to step into your house to lunch. This you do at present with perfect confidence, because everyone knows to an inch or two the area occupied by an adult Triangle: but imagine that your Tradesman drags behind his regular and respectable vertex, a parallelogram of twelve or thirteen inches in diagonal:—what are you to do with such a monster sticking fast in your house door?

But I am insulting the intelligence of my Readers by accumulating details which must be patent to everyone who enjoys the advantages of a Residence in Spaceland. Obviously the measurements of a single angle would no longer be sufficient under such portentous circumstances; one's whole life would be taken up in feeling or surveying the perimeter of one's acquaintances. Already the difficulties of avoiding a collision in a crowd are enough to tax the sagacity of even a well-educated Square; but if no one could calculate the Regularity of a single figure in the company, all would be chaos and confusion, and the slightest panic would cause serious injuries, or—if there happened to be any Women or Soldiers present— perhaps considerable loss of life.

Expediency therefore concurs with Nature in stamping the seal of its approval upon Regularity of conformation: nor has the Law been backward in seconding their efforts. "Irregularity of Figure" means with us the same as, or more than, a combination of moral obliquity and criminality with you, and is treated accordingly. There are not wanting, it is true, some promulgators of paradoxes who maintain that there is no necessary connection between geometrical and moral Irregularity.

"The Irregular", they say, "is from his birth scouted by his own parents, derided by his brothers and sisters, neglected by the domestics, scorned and suspected by society, and excluded from all posts of responsibility, trust, and useful activity. His every movement is jealously watched by the police till he comes of age and presents himself for inspection; then he is either destroyed, if he is found to exceed the fixed margin of deviation, or else immured in a Government Office as a clerk of the seventh class; prevented from marriage; forced to drudge at an uninteresting occupation for a miserable stipend; obliged to live and board at the office, and to take even his vacation under close supervision; what wonder that human nature, even in the best and purest, is embittered and perverted by such surroundings!"

All this very plausible reasoning does not convince me, as it has not convinced the wisest of our Statesmen, that our ancestors erred in laying it down as an axiom of policy that the toleration of Irregularity is incompatible with the safety of the State. Doubtless, the life of an Irregular is hard; but the interests of the Greater Number require that it shall be hard. If a man with a triangular front and a polygonal back were allowed to exist and to propagate a still more Irregular posterity, what would become of the arts of life? Are the houses and doors and churches in Flatland to be altered in order to accommodate such monsters? Are our ticket-collectors to be required to measure every man's perimeter before they allow him to enter a theatre or to take his place in a lecture room? Is an Irregular to be exempted from the militia? And if not, how is he to be prevented from carrying desolation into the ranks of his comrades? Again, what irresistible temptations to fraudulent impostures must needs beset such a creature! How easy for him to enter a shop with his polygonal front foremost, and to order goods to any extent from a confiding tradesman! Let the advocates of a falsely called Philanthropy plead as they may for the abrogation of the Irregular Penal Laws, I for my part have never known an Irregular who was not also what Nature evidently intended him to be—a hypocrite, a misanthropist, and, up to the limits of his power, a perpetrator of all manner of mischief.

Not that I should be disposed to recommend (at present) the extreme measures adopted by some States, where an infant whose angle deviates by half a degree from the correct angularity is summarily destroyed at birth.

Some of our highest and ablest men, men of real genius, have during their earliest days laboured under deviations as great as, or even greater than, forty-five minutes: and the loss of their precious lives would have been an irreparable injury to the State. The art of healing also has achieved some of its most glorious triumphs in the compressions, extensions, trepannings, colligations, and other surgical or diaetetic operations by which Irregularity has been partly or wholly cured. Advocating therefore a VIA MEDIA, I would lay down no fixed or absolute line of demarcation; but at the period when the frame is just beginning to set, and when the Medical Board has reported that recovery is improbable, I would suggest that the Irregular offspring be painlessly and mercifully consumed.

SECTION 8.
OF THE ANCIENT PRACTICE OF PAINTING

If my Readers have followed me with any attention up to this point, they will not be surprised to hear that life is somewhat dull in Flatland. I do not, of course, mean that there are not battles, conspiracies, tumults, factions, and all those other phenomena which are supposed to make History interesting; nor would I deny that the strange mixture of the problems of life and the problems of Mathematics, continually inducing conjecture and giving the opportunity of immediate verification, imparts to our existence a zest which you in Spaceland can hardly comprehend. I speak now from the aesthetic and artistic point of view when I say that life with us is dull; aesthetically and artistically, very dull indeed.

How can it be otherwise, when all one's prospect, all one's landscapes, historical pieces, portraits, flowers, still life, are nothing but a single line, with no varieties except degrees of brightness and obscurity?

It was not always thus. Colour, if Tradition speaks the truth, once for the space of half a dozen centuries or more, threw a transient splendour over the lives of our ancestors in the remotest ages. Some private individual—a Pentagon whose name is variously reported—having casually discovered the constituents of the simpler colours and a rudimentary method of painting, is said to have begun decorating first his house, then his slaves, then his Father, his Sons, and Grandsons, lastly himself. The convenience as well as the beauty of the results commended themselves to all. Wherever Chromatistes,—for by that name the most trustworthy authorities concur in calling him,—turned his variegated frame, there he at once excited attention, and attracted respect. No one now needed to "feel" him; no one mistook his front for his back; all his movements were readily ascertained by his neighbours without the slightest strain on their powers of calculation; no one jostled him, or failed to make way for him; his voice was saved the labour of that exhausting utterance by which we colourless Squares and Pentagons are often forced to proclaim our individuality when we move amid a crowd of ignorant Isosceles.

The fashion spread like wildfire. Before a week was over, every Square and Triangle in the district had copied the example of Chromatistes, and only a few of the more conservative Pentagons still held out. A month or two found even the Dodecagons infected with the innovation. A year had not elapsed before the habit had spread to all but the very highest of the Nobility. Needless to say, the custom soon made its way from the district of Chromatistes to surrounding regions; and within two generations no one in all Flatland was colourless except the Women and the Priests.

Here Nature herself appeared to erect a barrier, and to plead against extending the innovation to these two classes. Many-sidedness was almost essential as a pretext for the Innovators. "Distinction of sides is intended by Nature to imply distinction of colours"—such was the sophism which in those days flew from mouth to mouth, converting whole towns at a time to the new culture. But manifestly to our Priests and Women this adage did not apply. The latter had only one side, and therefore—plurally and pedantically speaking—NO SIDES. The former—if at least they would assert their claim to be really and truly Circles, and not mere high-class Polygons with an infinitely large number of infinitesimally small sides— were in the habit of boasting (what Women confessed and deplored) that they also had no sides, being blessed with a perimeter of one line, or, in other words, a Circumference. Hence it came to pass that these two Classes could see no force in the so-called axiom about "Distinction of Sides implying Distinction of Colour"; and when all others had succumbed to the fascinations of corporal decoration, the Priests and the Women alone still remained pure from the pollution of paint.

Immoral, licentious, anarchical, unscientific—call them by what names you will—yet, from an aesthetic point of view, those ancient days of the Colour Revolt were the glorious childhood of Art in Flatland—a childhood, alas, that never ripened into manhood, nor even reached the blossom of youth. To live was then in itself a delight, because living implied seeing. Even at a small party, the company was a pleasure to behold; the richly varied hues of the assembly in a church or theatre are said to have more than once proved too distracting for our greatest teachers and actors; but most ravishing of all is said to have been the unspeakable magnificence of a military review.

The sight of a line of battle of twenty thousand Isosceles suddenly facing about, and exchanging the sombre black of their bases for the orange and purple of the two sides including their acute angle; the militia of the Equilateral Triangles tricoloured in red, white, and blue; the mauve, ultra-marine, gamboge, and burnt umber of the Square artillerymen rapidly rotating near their vermilion guns; the dashing and flashing of the five-coloured and six-coloured Pentagons and Hexagons careering across the field in their offices of surgeons, geometricians and aides-de-camp—all these may well have been sufficient to render credible the famous story how an illustrious Circle, overcome by the artistic beauty of the forces under his command, threw aside his marshal's baton and his royal crown, exclaiming that he henceforth exchanged them for the artist's pencil. How great and glorious the sensuous development of these days must have been is in part indicated by the very language and vocabulary of the period. The commonest utterances of the commonest citizens in the time of the Colour Revolt seem to have been suffused with a richer tinge of word or thought; and to that era we are even now indebted for our finest poetry and for whatever rhythm still remains in the more scientific utterance of these modern days.

SECTION 9.
OF THE UNIVERSAL COLOUR BILL

But meanwhile the intellectual Arts were fast decaying.

The Art of Sight Recognition, being no longer needed, was no longer practised; and the studies of Geometry, Statics, Kinetics, and other kindred subjects, came soon to be considered superfluous, and fell into disrespect and neglect even at our University. The inferior Art of Feeling speedily experienced the same fate at our Elementary Schools. Then the Isosceles classes, asserting that the Specimens were no longer used nor needed, and refusing to pay the customary tribute from the Criminal classes to the service of Education, waxed daily more numerous and more insolent on the strength of their immunity from the old burden which had formerly exercised the twofold wholesome effect of at once taming their brutal nature and thinning their excessive numbers.

Year by year the Soldiers and Artisans began more vehemently to assert—and with increasing truth—that there was no great difference between them and the very highest class of Polygons, now that they were raised to an equality with the latter, and enabled to grapple with all the difficulties and solve all the problems of life, whether Statical or Kinetical, by the simple process of Colour Recognition. Not content with the natural neglect into which Sight Recognition was falling, they began boldly to demand the legal prohibition of all "monopolizing and aristocratic Arts" and the consequent abolition of all endowments for the studies of Sight Recognition, Mathematics, and Feeling. Soon, they began to insist that inasmuch as Colour, which was a second Nature, had destroyed the need of aristocratic distinctions, the Law should follow in the same path, and that henceforth all individuals and all classes should be recognized as absolutely equal and entitled to equal rights.

Finding the higher Orders wavering and undecided, the leaders of the Revolution advanced still further in their requirements, and at last demanded that all classes alike, the Priests and the Women not excepted, should do homage to Colour by submitting to be painted. When it was objected that Priests and Women had no sides, they retorted that Nature and Expediency concurred in dictating that the front half of every human being (that is to say, the half containing his eye and mouth) should be distinguishable from his hinder half. They therefore brought before a general and extraordinary Assembly of all the States of Flatland a Bill proposing that in every Woman the half containing the eye and mouth should be coloured red, and the other half green. The Priests were to be painted in the same way, red being applied to that semicircle in which the eye and mouth formed the middle point; while the other or hinder semicircle was to be coloured green.

There was no little cunning in this proposal, which indeed emanated not from any Isosceles—for no being so degraded would have had angularity enough to appreciate, much less to devise, such a model of state-craft—but from an Irregular Circle who, instead of being destroyed in his childhood, was reserved by a foolish indulgence to bring desolation on his country and destruction on myriads of his followers.

On the one hand the proposition was calculated to bring the Women in all classes over to the side of the Chromatic Innovation. For by assigning to the Women the same two colours as were assigned to the Priests, the Revolutionists thereby ensured that, in certain positions, every Woman would appear like a Priest, and be treated with corresponding respect and deference—a prospect that could not fail to attract the Female Sex in a mass.

But by some of my Readers the possibility of the identical appearance of Priests and Women, under the new Legislation, may not be recognized; if so, a word or two will make it obvious.

Imagine a woman duly decorated, according to the new Code; with the front half (i.e. the half containing eye and mouth) red, and with the hinder half green. Look at her from one side. Obviously you will see a straight line, HALF RED, HALF GREEN.

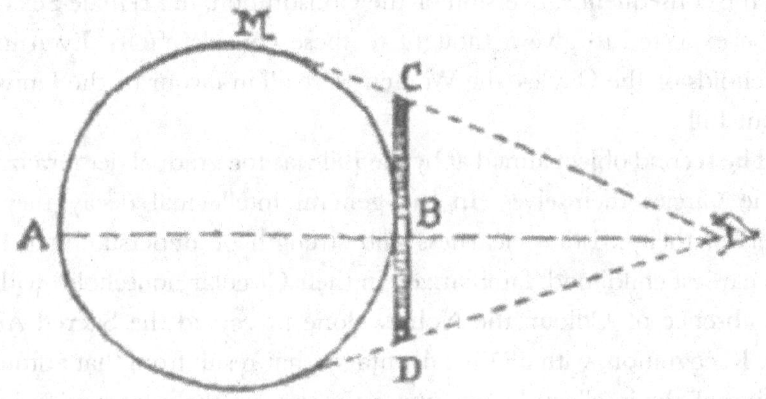

Now imagine a Priest, whose mouth is at M, and whose front semicircle (AMB) is consequently coloured red, while his hinder semicircle is green; so that the diameter AB divides the green from the red. If you contemplate the Great Man so as to have your eye in the same straight line as his dividing diameter (AB), what you will see will be a straight line (CBD), of which ONE HALF (CB) WILL BE RED, AND THE OTHER (BD) GREEN. The whole line (CD) will be rather shorter perhaps than that of a full-sized Woman, and will shade off more rapidly towards its extremities; but the identity of the colours would give you an immediate impression of identity of Class, making you neglectful of other details. Bear in mind the decay of Sight Recognition which threatened society at the time of the Colour Revolt; add too the certainty that Women would speedily learn to shade off their extremities so as to imitate the Circles; it must then be surely obvious to you, my dear Reader, that the Colour Bill placed us under a great danger of confounding a Priest with a young Woman.

How attractive this prospect must have been to the Frail Sex may readily be imagined. They anticipated with delight the confusion that would ensue. At home they might hear political and ecclesiastical secrets intended not for them but for their husbands and brothers, and might even issue commands in the name of a priestly Circle; out of doors the striking combination of red and green, without addition of any other colours, would be sure to lead the common people into endless mistakes, and the Women would gain whatever the Circles lost, in the deference of the passers by. As for the scandal that would befall the Circular Class if the frivolous and unseemly conduct of the Women were imputed to them, and as to the consequent subversion of the Constitution, the Female Sex could not be expected to give a thought to these considerations. Even in the households of the Circles, the Women were all in favour of the Universal Colour Bill.

The second object aimed at by the Bill was the gradual demoralization of the Circles themselves. In the general intellectual decay they still preserved their pristine clearness and strength of understanding. From their earliest childhood, familiarized in their Circular households with the total absence of Colour, the Nobles alone preserved the Sacred Art of Sight Recognition, with all the advantages that result from that admirable training of the intellect. Hence, up to the date of the introduction of the Universal Colour Bill, the Circles had not only held their own, but even increased their lead of the other classes by abstinence from the popular fashion.

Now therefore the artful Irregular whom I described above as the real author of this diabolical Bill, determined at one blow to lower the status of the Hierarchy by forcing them to submit to the pollution of Colour, and at the same time to destroy their domestic opportunities of training in the Art of Sight Recognition, so as to enfeeble their intellects by depriving them of their pure and colourless homes. Once subjected to the chromatic taint, every parental and every childish Circle would demoralize each other. Only in discerning between the Father and the Mother would the Circular infant find problems for the exercise of its understanding—problems too often likely to be corrupted by maternal impostures with the result of shaking the child's faith in all logical conclusions. Thus by degrees the intellectual lustre of the Priestly Order would wane, and the road would then lie open for a total destruction of all Aristocratic Legislature and for the subversion of our Privileged Classes.

SECTION 10.
OF THE SUPPRESSION OF THE CHROMATIC SEDITION

The agitation for the Universal Colour Bill continued for three years; and up to the last moment of that period it seemed as though Anarchy were destined to triumph.

A whole army of Polygons, who turned out to fight as private soldiers, was utterly annihilated by a superior force of Isosceles Triangles—the Squares and Pentagons meanwhile remaining neutral. Worse than all, some of the ablest Circles fell a prey to conjugal fury. Infuriated by political animosity, the wives in many a noble household wearied their lords with prayers to give up their opposition to the Colour Bill; and some, finding their entreaties fruitless, fell on and slaughtered their innocent children and husband, perishing themselves in the act of carnage. It is recorded that during that triennial agitation no less than twenty-three Circles perished in domestic discord.

Great indeed was the peril. It seemed as though the Priests had no choice between submission and extermination; when suddenly the course of events was completely changed by one of those picturesque incidents which Statesmen ought never to neglect, often to anticipate, and sometimes perhaps to originate, because of the absurdly disproportionate power with which they appeal to the sympathies of the populace.

It happened that an Isosceles of a low type, with a brain little if at all above four degrees—accidentally dabbling in the colours of some Tradesman whose shop he had plundered—painted himself, or caused himself to be painted (for the story varies) with the twelve colours of a Dodecagon. Going into the Market Place he accosted in a feigned voice a maiden, the orphan daughter of a noble Polygon, whose affection in former days he had sought in vain; and by a series of deceptions—aided, on the one side, by a string of lucky accidents too long to relate, and on the other, by an almost inconceivable fatuity and neglect of ordinary precautions on the part of the relations of the bride—he succeeded in consummating the marriage. The unhappy girl committed suicide on discovering the fraud to which she had been subjected.

When the news of this catastrophe spread from State to State the minds of the Women were violently agitated. Sympathy with the miserable victim and anticipations of similar deceptions for themselves, their sisters, and their daughters, made them now regard the Colour Bill in an entirely new aspect. Not a few openly avowed themselves converted to antagonism; the rest needed only a slight stimulus to make a similar avowal. Seizing this favourable opportunity, the Circles hastily convened an extraordinary Assembly of the States; and besides the usual guard of Convicts, they secured the attendance of a large number of reactionary Women.

Amidst an unprecedented concourse, the Chief Circle of those days—by name Pantocyclus—arose to find himself hissed and hooted by a hundred and twenty thousand Isosceles. But he secured silence by declaring that henceforth the Circles would enter on a policy of Concession; yielding to the wishes of the majority, they would accept the Colour Bill. The uproar being at once converted to applause, he invited Chromatistes, the leader of the Sedition, into the centre of the hall, to receive in the name of his followers the submission of the Hierarchy. Then followed a speech, a masterpiece of rhetoric, which occupied nearly a day in the delivery, and to which no summary can do justice.

With a grave appearance of impartiality he declared that as they were now finally committing themselves to Reform or Innovation, it was desirable that they should take one last view of the perimeter of the whole subject, its defects as well as its advantages. Gradually introducing the mention of the dangers to the Tradesmen, the Professional Classes and the

Gentlemen, he silenced the rising murmurs of the Isosceles by reminding them that, in spite of all these defects, he was willing to accept the Bill if it was approved by the majority. But it was manifest that all, except the Isosceles, were moved by his words and were either neutral or averse to the Bill.

Turning now to the Workmen he asserted that their interests must not be neglected, and that, if they intended to accept the Colour Bill, they ought at least to do so with full view of the consequences. Many of them, he said, were on the point of being admitted to the class of the Regular Triangles; others anticipated for their children a distinction they could not hope for themselves. That honourable ambition would now have to be sacrificed. With the universal adoption of Colour, all distinctions would cease; Regularity would be confused with Irregularity; development would give place to retrogression; the Workman would in a few generations be degraded to the level of the Military, or even the Convict Class; political power would be in the hands of the greatest number, that is to say the Criminal Classes, who were already more numerous than the Workmen, and would soon out-number all the other Classes put together when the usual Compensative Laws of Nature were violated.

A subdued murmur of assent ran through the ranks of the Artisans, and Chromatistes, in alarm, attempted to step forward and address them. But he found himself encompassed with guards and forced to remain silent while the Chief Circle in a few impassioned words made a final appeal to the Women, exclaiming that, if the Colour Bill passed, no marriage would henceforth be safe, no woman's honour secure; fraud, deception, hypocrisy would pervade every household; domestic bliss would share the fate of the Constitution and pass to speedy perdition. "Sooner than this," he cried, "Come death."

At these words, which were the preconcerted signal for action, the Isosceles Convicts fell on and transfixed the wretched Chromatistes; the Regular Classes, opening their ranks, made way for a band of Women who, under direction of the Circles, moved, back foremost, invisibly and unerringly upon the unconscious soldiers; the Artisans, imitating the example of their betters, also opened their ranks. Meantime bands of Convicts occupied every entrance with an impenetrable phalanx.

The battle, or rather carnage, was of short duration. Under the skillful generalship of the Circles almost every Woman's charge was fatal and very many extracted their sting uninjured, ready for a second slaughter. But no second blow was needed; the rabble of the Isosceles did the rest of the business for themselves. Surprised, leader-less, attacked in front by invisible foes, and finding egress cut off by the Convicts behind them, they at once—after their manner—lost all presence of mind, and raised the cry of "treachery". This sealed their fate. Every Isosceles now saw and felt a foe in every other. In half an hour not one of that vast multitude was living; and the fragments of seven score thousand of the Criminal Class slain by one another's angles attested the triumph of Order.

The Circles delayed not to push their victory to the uttermost. The Working Men they spared but decimated. The Militia of the Equilaterals was at once called out; and every Triangle suspected of Irregularity on reasonable grounds, was destroyed by Court Martial, without the formality of exact measurement by the Social Board. The homes of the Military and Artisan classes were inspected in a course of visitations extending through upwards of a year; and during that period every town, village, and hamlet was systematically purged of that excess of the lower orders which had been brought about by the neglect to pay the tribute of Criminals to the Schools and University, and by the violation of the other natural Laws of the Constitution of Flatland. Thus the balance of classes was again restored.

Needless to say that henceforth the use of Colour was abolished, and its possession prohibited. Even the utterance of any word denoting Colour, except by the Circles or by qualified scientific teachers, was punished by a severe penalty. Only at our University in some of the very highest and most esoteric classes—which I myself have never been privileged to attend— it is understood that the sparing use of Colour is still sanctioned for the purpose of illustrating some of the deeper problems of mathematics. But of this I can only speak from hearsay.

Elsewhere in Flatland, Colour is now non-existent. The art of making it is known to only one living person, the Chief Circle for the time being; and by him it is handed down on his death-bed to none but his Successor. One manufactory alone produces it; and, lest the secret should be betrayed, the Workmen are annually consumed, and fresh ones introduced. So great is the terror with which even now our Aristocracy looks back to the far-distant days of the agitation for the Universal Colour Bill.

SECTION 11.
CONCERNING OUR PRIESTS

It is high time that I should pass from these brief and discursive notes about things in Flatland to the central event of this book, my initiation into the mysteries of Space. THAT is my subject; all that has gone before is merely preface.

For this reason I must omit many matters of which the explanation would not, I flatter myself, be without interest for my Readers: as for example, our method of propelling and stopping ourselves, although destitute of feet; the means by which we give fixity to structures of wood, stone, or brick, although of course we have no hands, nor can we lay foundations as you can, nor avail ourselves of the lateral pressure of the earth; the manner in which the rain originates in the intervals between our various zones, so that the northern regions do not intercept the moisture from falling on the southern; the nature of our hills and mines, our trees and vegetables, our seasons and harvests; our Alphabet and method of writing, adapted to our linear tablets; these and a hundred other details of our physical existence I must pass over, nor do I mention them now except to indicate to my readers that their omission proceeds not from forgetfulness on the part of the author, but from his regard for the time of the Reader.

Yet before I proceed to my legitimate subject some few final remarks will no doubt be expected by my Readers upon those pillars and mainstays of the Constitution of Flatland, the controllers of our conduct and shapers of our destiny, the objects of universal homage and almost of adoration: need I say that I mean our Circles or Priests?

When I call them Priests, let me not be understood as meaning no more than the term denotes with you. With us, our Priests are Administrators of all Business, Art, and Science; Directors of Trade, Commerce, Generalship, Architecture, Engineering, Education, Statesmanship, Legislature, Morality, Theology; doing nothing themselves, they are the Causes of everything worth doing, that is done by others.

Although popularly everyone called a Circle is deemed a Circle, yet among the better educated Classes it is known that no Circle is really a Circle, but only a Polygon with a very large number of very small sides. As the number of the sides increases, a Polygon approximates to a Circle; and, when the number is very great indeed, say for example three or four hundred, it is extremely difficult for the most delicate touch to feel any polygonal angles. Let me say rather, it WOULD be difficult: for, as I have shown above, Recognition by Feeling is unknown among the highest society, and to FEEL a Circle would be considered a most audacious insult. This habit of abstention from Feeling in the best society enables a Circle the more easily to sustain the veil of mystery in which, from his earliest years, he is wont to enwrap the exact nature of his Perimeter or Circumference. Three feet being the average Perimeter it follows that, in a Polygon of three hundred sides each side will be no more than the hundredth part of a foot in length, or little more than the tenth part of an inch; and in a Polygon of six or seven hundred sides the sides are little larger than the diameter of a Spaceland pin-head. It is always assumed, by courtesy, that the Chief Circle for the time being has ten thousand sides.

The ascent of the posterity of the Circles in the social scale is not restricted, as it is among the lower Regular classes, by the Law of Nature which limits the increase of sides to one in each generation. If it were so, the number of sides in a Circle would be a mere question of pedigree and arithmetic, and the four hundred and ninety-seventh descendant of an Equilateral Triangle would necessarily be a Polygon with five hundred sides. But this is not the case. Nature's Law prescribes two antagonistic decrees affecting Circular propagation; first, that as the race climbs higher in the scale of development, so development shall proceed at an accelerated pace; second, that in the same proportion, the race shall become less fertile. Consequently in the home of a Polygon of four or five hundred sides it is rare to find a son; more than one is never seen. On the other hand the son of a five-hundred-sided Polygon has been known to possess five hundred and fifty, or even six hundred sides.

Art also steps in to help the process of the higher Evolution. Our physicians have discovered that the small and tender sides of an infant Polygon of the higher class can be fractured, and his whole frame re-set, with such exactness that a Polygon of two or three hundred sides sometimes—by no means always, for the process is attended with serious risk—but sometimes overleaps two or three hundred generations, and as it were doubles at a stroke, the number of his progenitors and the nobility of his descent.

Many a promising child is sacrificed in this way. Scarcely one out of ten survives. Yet so strong is the parental ambition among those Polygons who are, as it were, on the fringe of the Circular class, that it is very rare to find a Nobleman of that position in society, who has neglected to place his first-born in the Circular Neo-Therapeutic Gymnasium before he has attained the age of a month.

One year determines success or failure. At the end of that time the child has, in all probability, added one more to the tombstones that crowd the Neo-Therapeutic Cemetery; but on rare occasions a glad procession bears back the little one to his exultant parents, no longer a Polygon, but a Circle, at least by courtesy: and a single instance of so blessed a result induces multitudes of Polygonal parents to submit to similar domestic sacrifices, which have a dissimilar issue.

SECTION 12.
OF THE DOCTRINE OF OUR PRIESTS

As to the doctrine of the Circles it may briefly be summed up in a single maxim, "Attend to your Configuration." Whether political, ecclesiastical, or moral, all their teaching has for its object the improvement of individual and collective Configuration—with special reference of course to the Configuration of the Circles, to which all other objects are subordinated.

It is the merit of the Circles that they have effectually suppressed those ancient heresies which led men to waste energy and sympathy in the vain belief that conduct depends upon will, effort, training, encouragement, praise, or anything else but Configuration. It was Pantocyclus—the illustrious Circle mentioned above, as the queller of the Colour Revolt—who first convinced mankind that Configuration makes the man; that if, for example, you are born an Isosceles with two uneven sides, you will assuredly go wrong unless you have them made even—for which purpose you must go to the Isosceles Hospital; similarly, if you are a Triangle, or Square, or even a Polygon, born with any Irregularity, you must be taken to one of the Regular Hospitals to have your disease cured; otherwise you will end your days in the State Prison or by the angle of the State Executioner.

All faults or defects, from the slightest misconduct to the most flagitious crime, Pantocyclus attributed to some deviation from perfect Regularity in the bodily figure, caused perhaps (if not congenital) by some collision in a crowd; by neglect to take exercise, or by taking too much of it; or even by a sudden change of temperature, resulting in a shrinkage or expansion in some too susceptible part of the frame. Therefore, concluded that illustrious Philosopher, neither good conduct nor bad conduct is a fit subject, in any sober estimation, for either praise or blame. For why should you praise, for example, the integrity of a Square who faithfully defends the interests of his client, when you ought in reality rather to admire the exact precision of his right angles? Or again, why blame a lying, thievish Isosceles when you ought rather to deplore the incurable inequality of his sides?

Theoretically, this doctrine is unquestionable; but it has practical drawbacks. In dealing with an Isosceles, if a rascal pleads that he cannot help stealing because of his unevenness, you reply that for that very reason, because he cannot help being a nuisance to his neighbours, you, the Magistrate, cannot help sentencing him to be consumed—and there's an end of the matter. But in little domestic difficulties, where the penalty of consumption, or death, is out of the question, this theory of Configuration sometimes comes in awkwardly; and I must confess that occasionally when one of my own Hexagonal Grandsons pleads as an excuse for his disobedience that a sudden change of the temperature has been too much for his Perimeter, and that I ought to lay the blame not on him but on his Configuration, which can only be strengthened by abundance of the choicest sweetmeats, I neither see my way logically to reject, nor practically to accept, his conclusions.

For my own part, I find it best to assume that a good sound scolding or castigation has some latent and strengthening influence on my Grandson's Configuration; though I own that I have no grounds for thinking so. At all events I am not alone in my way of extricating myself from this dilemma; for I find that many of the highest Circles, sitting as Judges in law courts, use praise and blame towards Regular and Irregular Figures; and in their homes I know by experience that, when scolding their children, they speak about "right" or "wrong" as vehemently and passionately as if they believed that these names represented real existences, and that a human Figure is really capable of choosing between them.

Constantly carrying out their policy of making Configuration the leading idea in every mind, the Circles reverse the nature of that

Commandment which in Spaceland regulates the relations between parents and children. With you, children are taught to honour their parents; with us—next to the Circles, who are the chief object of universal homage—a man is taught to honour his Grandson, if he has one; or, if not, his Son. By "honour", however, is by no means meant "indulgence", but a reverent regard for their highest interests: and the Circles teach that the duty of fathers is to subordinate their own interests to those of posterity, thereby advancing the welfare of the whole State as well as that of their own immediate descendants.

The weak point in the system of the Circles—if a humble Square may venture to speak of anything Circular as containing any element of weakness—appears to me to be found in their relations with Women.

As it is of the utmost importance for Society that Irregular births should be discouraged, it follows that no Woman who has any Irregularities in her ancestry is a fit partner for one who desires that his posterity should rise by regular degrees in the social scale.

Now the Irregularity of a Male is a matter of measurement; but as all Women are straight, and therefore visibly Regular so to speak, one has to devise some other means of ascertaining what I may call their invisible Irregularity, that is to say their potential Irregularities as regards possible offspring. This is effected by carefully-kept pedigrees, which are preserved and supervised by the State; and without a certified pedigree no Woman is allowed to marry.

Now it might have been supposed that a Circle—proud of his ancestry and regardful for a posterity which might possibly issue hereafter in a Chief Circle—would be more careful than any other to choose a wife who had no blot on her escutcheon. But it is not so. The care in choosing a Regular wife appears to diminish as one rises in the social scale. Nothing would induce an aspiring Isosceles, who had hopes of generating an Equilateral Son, to take a wife who reckoned a single Irregularity among her Ancestors; a Square or Pentagon, who is confident that his family is steadily on the rise, does not inquire above the five-hundredth generation; a Hexagon or Dodecagon is even more careless of the wife's pedigree; but a Circle has been known deliberately to take a wife who has had an Irregular Great-Grandfather, and all because of some slight superiority of lustre, or because of the charms of a low voice—which, with us, even more than you, is thought "an excellent thing in Woman".

Such ill-judged marriages are, as might be expected, barren, if they do not result in positive Irregularity or in diminution of sides; but none of these evils have hitherto proved sufficiently deterrent. The loss of a few sides in a highly-developed Polygon is not easily noticed, and is sometimes compensated by a successful operation in the Neo-Therapeutic Gymnasium, as I have described above; and the Circles are too much disposed to acquiesce in infecundity as a Law of the superior development. Yet, if this evil be not arrested, the gradual diminution of the Circular class may soon become more rapid, and the time may be not far distant when, the race being no longer able to produce a Chief Circle, the Constitution of Flatland must fall.

One other word of warning suggests itself to me, though I cannot so easily mention a remedy; and this also refers to our relations with Women. About three hundred years ago, it was decreed by the Chief Circle that, since women are deficient in Reason but abundant in Emotion, they ought no longer to be treated as rational, nor receive any mental education. The consequence was that they were no longer taught to read, nor even to master Arithmetic enough to enable them to count the angles of their husband or children; and hence they sensibly declined during each generation in intellectual power. And this system of female non-education or quietism still prevails.

My fear is that, with the best intentions, this policy has been carried so far as to react injuriously on the Male Sex.

For the consequence is that, as things now are, we Males have to lead a kind of bi-lingual, and I may almost say bi-mental, existence. With Women, we speak of "love", "duty", "right", "wrong", "pity", "hope", and other irrational and emotional conceptions, which have no existence, and the fiction of which has no object except to control feminine exuberances; but among ourselves, and in our books, we have an entirely different vocabulary and I may almost say, idiom. "Love" then becomes "the anticipation of benefits"; "duty" becomes "necessity" or "fitness"; and other words are correspondingly transmuted. Moreover, among Women, we use language implying the utmost deference for their Sex; and they fully believe that the Chief Circle Himself is not more devoutly adored by us than they are: but behind their backs they are both regarded and spoken of—by all except the very young—as being little better than "mindless organisms".

Our Theology also in the Women's chambers is entirely different from our Theology elsewhere.

Now my humble fear is that this double training, in language as well as in thought, imposes somewhat too heavy a burden upon the young, especially when, at the age of three years old, they are taken from the maternal care and taught to unlearn the old language—except for the purpose of repeating it in the presence of their Mothers and Nurses—and to learn the vocabulary and idiom of science. Already methinks I discern a weakness in the grasp of mathematical truth at the present time as compared with the more robust intellect of our ancestors three hundred years ago. I say nothing of the possible danger if a Woman should ever surreptitiously learn to read and convey to her Sex the result of her perusal of a single popular volume; nor of the possibility that the indiscretion or disobedience of some infant Male might reveal to a Mother the secrets of the logical dialect. On the simple ground of the enfeebling of the Male intellect, I rest this humble appeal to the highest Authorities to reconsider the regulations of Female education.

OTHER WORLDS

"O brave new worlds, that have such people in them!"

SECTION 13.
HOW I HAD A VISION OF LINELAND

It was the last day but one of the 1999th year of our era, and the first day of the Long Vacation. Having amused myself till a late hour with my favourite recreation of Geometry, I had retired to rest with an unsolved problem in my mind. In the night I had a dream.

I saw before me a vast multitude of small Straight Lines (which I naturally assumed to be Women) interspersed with other Beings still smaller and of the nature of lustrous points—all moving to and fro in one and the same Straight Line, and, as nearly as I could judge, with the same velocity.

A noise of confused, multitudinous chirping or twittering issued from them at intervals as long as they were moving; but sometimes they ceased from motion, and then all was silence.

Approaching one of the largest of what I thought to be Women, I accosted her, but received no answer. A second and a third appeal on my part were equally ineffectual. Losing patience at what appeared to me intolerable rudeness, I brought my mouth into a position full in front of her mouth so as to intercept her motion, and loudly repeated my question, "Woman, what signifies this concourse, and this strange and confused chirping, and this monotonous motion to and fro in one and the same Straight Line?"

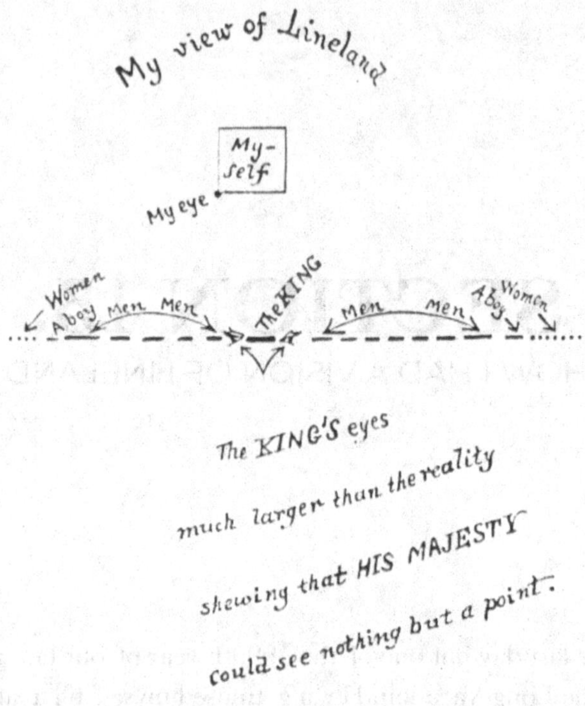

"I am no Woman," replied the small Line. "I am the Monarch of the world. But thou, whence intrudest thou into my realm of Lineland?" Receiving this abrupt reply, I begged pardon if I had in any way startled or molested his Royal Highness; and describing myself as a stranger I besought the King to give me some account of his dominions. But I had the greatest possible difficulty in obtaining any information on points that really interested me; for the Monarch could not refrain from constantly assuming that whatever was familiar to him must also be known to me and that I was simulating ignorance in jest. However, by persevering questions I elicited the following facts:

It seemed that this poor ignorant Monarch—as he called himself—was persuaded that the Straight Line which he called his Kingdom, and in which he passed his existence, constituted the whole of the world, and indeed the whole of Space. Not being able either to move or to see, save in his Straight Line, he had no conception of anything out of it. Though he had heard my voice when I first addressed him, the sounds had come to him in a manner so contrary to his experience that he had made no answer, "seeing no man", as he expressed it, "and hearing a voice as it were from my own intestines." Until the moment when I placed my mouth in his World, he had neither seen me, nor heard anything except confused sounds beating against—what I called his side, but what he called his INSIDE or STOMACH; nor had he even now the least conception of the region from which I had come. Outside his World, or Line, all was a blank to him; nay, not even a blank, for a blank implies Space; say, rather, all was non-existent.

His subjects—of whom the small Lines were men and the Points Women—were all alike confined in motion and eye-sight to that single Straight Line, which was their World. It need scarcely be added that the whole of their horizon was limited to a Point; nor could any one ever see anything but a Point. Man, woman, child, thing—each was a Point to the eye of a Linelander. Only by the sound of the voice could sex or age be distinguished. Moreover, as each individual occupied the whole of the narrow path, so to speak, which constituted his Universe, and no one could move to the right or left to make way for passers by, it followed that no Linelander could ever pass another. Once neighbours, always neighbours. Neighbourhood with them was like marriage with us. Neighbours remained neighbours till death did them part.

Such a life, with all vision limited to a Point, and all motion to a Straight Line, seemed to me inexpressibly dreary; and I was surprised to note the vivacity and cheerfulness of the King. Wondering whether it was possible, amid circumstances so unfavourable to domestic relations, to enjoy the pleasures of conjugal union, I hesitated for some time to question his Royal Highness on so delicate a subject; but at last I plunged into it by abruptly inquiring as to the health of his family. "My wives and children," he replied, "are well and happy."

Staggered at this answer—for in the immediate proximity of the Monarch (as I had noted in my dream before I entered Lineland) there were none but Men—I ventured to reply, "Pardon me, but I cannot imagine how your Royal Highness can at any time either see or approach their Majesties, when there are at least half a dozen intervening individuals, whom you can neither see through, nor pass by? Is it possible that in Lineland proximity is not necessary for marriage and for the generation of children?"

"How can you ask so absurd a question?" replied the Monarch. "If it were indeed as you suggest, the Universe would soon be depopulated. No, no; neighbourhood is needless for the union of hearts; and the birth of children is too important a matter to have been allowed to depend upon such an accident as proximity. You cannot be ignorant of this. Yet since you are pleased to affect ignorance, I will instruct you as if you were the veriest baby in Lineland. Know, then, that marriages are consummated by means of the faculty of sound and the sense of hearing.

"You are of course aware that every Man has two mouths or voices—as well as two eyes—a bass at one and a tenor at the other of his extremities. I should not mention this, but that I have been unable to distinguish your tenor in the course of our conversation." I replied that I had but one voice, and that I had not been aware that his Royal Highness had two. "That confirms my impression," said the King, "that you are not a Man, but a feminine Monstrosity with a bass voice, and an utterly uneducated ear. But to continue.

"Nature having herself ordained that every Man should wed two wives—" "Why two?" asked I. "You carry your affected simplicity too far", he cried. "How can there be a completely harmonious union without the combination of the Four in One, viz. the Bass and Tenor of the Man and the Soprano and Contralto of the two Women?" "But supposing," said I, "that a man should prefer one wife or three?" "It is impossible," he said; "it is as inconceivable as that two and one should make five, or that the human eye should see a Straight Line." I would have interrupted him; but he proceeded as follows:

"Once in the middle of each week a Law of Nature compels us to move to and fro with a rhythmic motion of more than usual violence, which continues for the time you would take to count a hundred and one. In the midst of this choral dance, at the fifty-first pulsation, the inhabitants of the Universe pause in full career, and each individual sends forth his richest, fullest, sweetest strain. It is in this decisive moment that all our marriages are made. So exquisite is the adaptation of Bass to Treble, of Tenor to Contralto, that oftentimes the Loved Ones, though twenty thousand leagues away, recognize at once the responsive note of their destined Lover; and, penetrating the paltry obstacles of distance, Love unites the three. The marriage in that instant consummated results in a threefold Male and Female offspring which takes its place in Lineland."

"What! Always threefold?" said I. "Must one wife then always have twins?"

"Bass-voiced Monstrosity! yes," replied the King. "How else could the balance of the Sexes be maintained, if two girls were not born for every boy? Would you ignore the very Alphabet of Nature?" He ceased, speechless for fury; and some time elapsed before I could induce him to resume his narrative.

"You will not, of course, suppose that every bachelor among us finds his mates at the first wooing in this universal Marriage Chorus. On the contrary, the process is by most of us many times repeated. Few are the hearts whose happy lot it is at once to recognize in each other's voices the partner intended for them by Providence, and to fly into a reciprocal and perfectly harmonious embrace. With most of us the courtship is of long duration. The Wooer's voices may perhaps accord with one of the future wives, but not with both; or not, at first, with either; or the Soprano and Contralto may not quite harmonize. In such cases Nature has provided that every weekly Chorus shall bring the three Lovers into closer harmony. Each trial of voice, each fresh discovery of discord, almost imperceptibly induces the less perfect to modify his or her vocal utterance so as to approximate to the more perfect. And after many trials and many approximations, the result is at last achieved. There comes a day at last, when, while the wonted Marriage Chorus goes forth from universal Lineland, the three far-off Lovers suddenly find themselves in exact harmony, and, before they are awake, the wedded Triplet is rapt vocally into a duplicate embrace; and Nature rejoices over one more marriage and over three more births."

SECTION 14.
HOW I VAINLY TRIED TO EXPLAIN THE NATURE OF FLATLAND

Thinking that it was time to bring down the Monarch from his raptures to the level of common sense, I determined to endeavour to open up to him some glimpses of the truth, that is to say of the nature of things in Flatland. So I began thus: "How does your Royal Highness distinguish the shapes and positions of his subjects? I for my part noticed by the sense of sight, before I entered your Kingdom, that some of your people are Lines and others Points, and that some of the Lines are larger—" "You speak of an impossibility," interrupted the King; "you must have seen a vision; for to detect the difference between a Line and a Point by the sense of sight is, as every one knows, in the nature of things, impossible; but it can be detected by the sense of hearing, and by the same means my shape can be exactly ascertained. Behold me—I am a Line, the longest in Lineland, over six inches of Space—" "Of Length", I ventured to suggest. "Fool," said he, "Space is Length. Interrupt me again, and I have done."

I apologized; but he continued scornfully, "Since you are impervious to argument, you shall hear with your ears how by means of my two voices I reveal my shape to my Wives, who are at this moment six thousand miles seventy yards two feet eight inches away, the one to the North, the other to the South. Listen, I call to them."

He chirruped, and then complacently continued: "My wives at this moment receiving the sound of one of my voices, closely followed by the other, and perceiving that the latter reaches them after an interval in which sound can traverse 6.457 inches, infer that one of my mouths is 6.457 inches further from them than the other, and accordingly know my shape to be 6.457 inches. But you will of course understand that my wives do not make this calculation every time they hear my two voices. They made it, once for all, before we were married. But they COULD make it at any time. And in the same way I can estimate the shape of any of my Male subjects by the sense of sound."

"But how," said I, "if a Man feigns a Woman's voice with one of his two voices, or so disguises his Southern voice that it cannot be recognized as the echo of the Northern? May not such deceptions cause great inconvenience? And have you no means of checking frauds of this kind by commanding your neighbouring subjects to feel one another?" This of course was a very stupid question, for feeling could not have answered the purpose; but I asked with the view of irritating the Monarch, and I succeeded perfectly.

"What!" cried he in horror, "explain your meaning." "Feel, touch, come into contact," I replied. "If you mean by FEELING," said the King, "approaching so close as to leave no space between two individuals, know, Stranger, that this offence is punishable in my dominions by death. And the reason is obvious. The frail form of a Woman, being liable to be shattered by such an approximation, must be preserved by the State; but since Women cannot be distinguished by the sense of sight from Men, the Law ordains universally that neither Man nor Woman shall be approached so closely as to destroy the interval between the approximator and the approximated.

"And indeed what possible purpose would be served by this illegal and unnatural excess of approximation which you call TOUCHING, when all the ends of so brutal and coarse a process are attained at once more easily and more exactly by the sense of hearing? As to your suggested danger of deception, it is non-existent: for the Voice, being the essence of one's Being, cannot be thus changed at will. But come, suppose that I had the power of passing through solid things, so that I could penetrate my subjects, one after another, even to the number of a billion, verifying the size and distance of each by the sense of FEELING: how much time and energy would be wasted in this clumsy and inaccurate method! Whereas now, in one moment of audition, I take as it were the census and statistics, local, corporeal, mental and spiritual, of every living being in Lineland. Hark, only hark!"

So saying he paused and listened, as if in an ecstasy, to a sound which seemed to me no better than a tiny chirping from an innumerable multitude of lilliputian grasshoppers.

"Truly," replied I, "your sense of hearing serves you in good stead, and fills up many of your deficiencies. But permit me to point out that your life in Lineland must be deplorably dull. To see nothing but a Point! Not even to be able to contemplate a Straight Line! Nay, not even to know what a Straight Line is! To see, yet be cut off from those Linear prospects which are vouchsafed to us in Flatland! Better surely to have no sense of sight at all than to see so little! I grant you I have not your discriminative faculty of hearing; for the concert of all Lineland which gives you such intense pleasure, is to me no better than a multitudinous twittering or chirping. But at least I can discern, by sight, a Line from a Point. And let me prove it. Just before I came into your kingdom, I saw you dancing from left to right, and then from right to left, with Seven Men and a Woman in your immediate proximity on the left, and eight Men and two Women on your right. Is not this correct?"

"It is correct," said the King, "so far as the numbers and sexes are concerned, though I know not what you mean by 'right' and 'left'. But I deny that you saw these things. For how could you see the Line, that is to say the inside, of any Man? But you must have heard these things, and then dreamed that you saw them. And let me ask what you mean by those words 'left' and 'right'. I suppose it is your way of saying Northward and Southward."

"Not so," replied I; "besides your motion of Northward and Southward, there is another motion which I call from right to left."

KING. Exhibit to me, if you please, this motion from left to right.

I. Nay, that I cannot do, unless you could step out of your Line altogether.

KING. Out of my Line? Do you mean out of the world? Out of Space?

I. Well, yes. Out of YOUR World. Out of YOUR Space. For your Space is not the true Space. True Space is a Plane; but your Space is only a Line.

KING. If you cannot indicate this motion from left to right by yourself moving in it, then I beg you to describe it to me in words.

I. If you cannot tell your right side from your left, I fear that no words of mine can make my meaning clear to you. But surely you cannot be ignorant of so simple a distinction.

KING. I do not in the least understand you.

I. Alas! How shall I make it clear? When you move straight on, does it not sometimes occur to you that you COULD move in some other way, turning your eye round so as to look in the direction towards which your side is now fronting? In other words, instead of always moving in the direction of one of your extremities, do you never feel a desire to move in the direction, so to speak, of your side?

KING. Never. And what do you mean? How can a man's inside "front" in any direction? Or how can a man move in the direction of his inside?

I. Well then, since words cannot explain the matter, I will try deeds, and will move gradually out of Lineland in the direction which I desire to indicate to you.

At the word I began to move my body out of Lineland. As long as any part of me remained in his dominion and in his view, the King kept exclaiming, "I see you, I see you still; you are not moving." But when I had at last moved myself out of his Line, he cried in his shrillest voice, "She is vanished; she is dead." "I am not dead," replied I; "I am simply out of Lineland, that is to say, out of the Straight Line which you call Space, and in the true Space, where I can see things as they are. And at this moment I can see your Line, or side—or inside as you are pleased to call it; and I can see also the Men and Women on the North and South of you, whom I will now enumerate, describing their order, their size, and the interval between each."

When I had done this at great length, I cried triumphantly, "Does that at last convince you?" And, with that, I once more entered Lineland, taking up the same position as before.

But the Monarch replied, "If you were a Man of sense—though, as you appear to have only one voice I have little doubt you are not a Man but a Woman—but, if you had a particle of sense, you would listen to reason. You ask me to believe that there is another Line besides that which my senses indicate, and another motion besides that of which I am daily conscious. I, in return, ask you to describe in words or indicate by motion that other Line of which you speak. Instead of moving, you merely exercise some magic art of vanishing and returning to sight; and instead of any lucid description of your new World, you simply tell me the numbers and sizes of some forty of my retinue, facts known to any child in my capital. Can anything be more irrational or audacious? Acknowledge your folly or depart from my dominions."

Furious at his perversity, and especially indignant that he professed to be ignorant of my sex, I retorted in no measured terms, "Besotted Being! You think yourself the perfection of existence, while you are in reality the most imperfect and imbecile. You profess to see, whereas you can see nothing but a Point! You plume yourself on inferring the existence of a Straight Line; but I CAN SEE Straight Lines, and infer the existence of Angles, Triangles, Squares, Pentagons, Hexagons, and even Circles. Why waste more words? Suffice it that I am the completion of your incomplete self. You are a Line, but I am a Line of Lines, called in my country a Square: and even I, infinitely superior though I am to you, am of little account among the great nobles of Flatland, whence I have come to visit you, in the hope of enlightening your ignorance."

Hearing these words the King advanced towards me with a menacing cry as if to pierce me through the diagonal; and in that same moment there arose from myriads of his subjects a multitudinous war-cry, increasing in vehemence till at last methought it rivalled the roar of an army of a hundred thousand Isosceles, and the artillery of a thousand Pentagons. Spell-bound and motionless, I could neither speak nor move to avert the impending destruction; and still the noise grew louder, and the King came closer, when I awoke to find the breakfast-bell recalling me to the realities of Flatland.

SECTION 15.
CONCERNING A STRANGER FROM SPACELAND

From dreams I proceed to facts.

It was the last day of the 1999th year of our era. The pattering of the rain had long ago announced nightfall; and I was sitting in the company of my wife, musing on the events of the past and the prospects of the coming year, the coming century, the coming Millennium.

[Note: When I say "sitting", of course I do not mean any change of attitude such as you in Spaceland signify by that word; for as we have no feet, we can no more "sit" nor "stand" (in your sense of the word) than one of your soles or flounders.

Nevertheless, we perfectly well recognize the different mental states of volition implied in "lying", "sitting", and "standing", which are to some extent indicated to a beholder by a slight increase of lustre corresponding to the increase of volition.

But on this, and a thousand other kindred subjects, time forbids me to dwell.]

My four Sons and two orphan Grandchildren had retired to their several apartments; and my wife alone remained with me to see the old Millennium out and the new one in.

I was rapt in thought, pondering in my mind some words that had casually issued from the mouth of my youngest Grandson, a most promising young Hexagon of unusual brilliancy and perfect angularity. His uncles and I had been giving him his usual practical lesson in Sight Recognition, turning ourselves upon our centres, now rapidly, now more slowly, and questioning him as to our positions; and his answers had been so satisfactory that I had been induced to reward him by giving him a few hints on Arithmetic, as applied to Geometry.

Taking nine Squares, each an inch every way, I had put them together so as to make one large Square, with a side of three inches, and I had hence proved to my little Grandson that—though it was impossible for us to SEE the inside of the Square—yet we might ascertain the number of square inches in a Square by simply squaring the number of inches in the side: "and thus," said I, "we know that 3², or 9, represents the number of square inches in a Square whose side is 3 inches long."

The little Hexagon meditated on this a while and then said to me; "But you have been teaching me to raise numbers to the third power: I suppose 3³ must mean something in Geometry; what does it mean?" "Nothing at all," replied I, "not at least in Geometry; for Geometry has only Two Dimensions." And then I began to shew the boy how a Point by moving through a length of three inches makes a Line of three inches, which may be represented by 3; and how a Line of three inches, moving parallel to itself through a length of three inches, makes a Square of three inches every way, which may be represented by 3².

Upon this, my Grandson, again returning to his former suggestion, took me up rather suddenly and exclaimed, "Well, then, if a Point by moving three inches, makes a Line of three inches represented by 3; and if a straight Line of three inches, moving parallel to itself, makes a Square of three inches every way, represented by 3²; it must be that a Square of three inches every way, moving somehow parallel to itself (but I don't see how) must make Something else (but I don't see what) of three inches every way—and this must be represented by 3³."

"Go to bed," said I, a little ruffled by this interruption: "if you would talk less nonsense, you would remember more sense."

So my Grandson had disappeared in disgrace; and there I sat by my Wife's side, endeavouring to form a retrospect of the year 1999 and of the possibilities of the year 2000, but not quite able to shake off the thoughts suggested by the prattle of my bright little Hexagon. Only a few sands now remained in the half-hour glass. Rousing myself from my reverie I turned the glass Northward for the last time in the old Millennium; and in the act, I exclaimed aloud, "The boy is a fool."

Straightway I became conscious of a Presence in the room, and a chilling breath thrilled through my very being. "He is no such thing," cried my Wife, "and you are breaking the Commandments in thus dishonouring your own Grandson." But I took no notice of her. Looking round in every direction I could see nothing; yet still I FELT a Presence, and shivered as the cold whisper came again. I started up. "What is the matter?" said my Wife, "there is no draught; what are you looking for? There is nothing." There was nothing; and I resumed my seat, again exclaiming, "The boy is a fool, I say; 33 can have no meaning in Geometry." At once there came a distinctly audible reply, "The boy is not a fool; and 33 has an obvious Geometrical meaning."

My Wife as well as myself heard the words, although she did not understand their meaning, and both of us sprang forward in the direction of the sound. What was our horror when we saw before us a Figure! At the first glance it appeared to be a Woman, seen sideways; but a moment's observation shewed me that the extremities passed into dimness too rapidly to represent one of the Female Sex; and I should have thought it a Circle, only that it seemed to change its size in a manner impossible for a Circle or for any regular Figure of which I had had experience.

But my Wife had not my experience, nor the coolness necessary to note these characteristics. With the usual hastiness and unreasoning jealousy of her Sex, she flew at once to the conclusion that a Woman had entered the house through some small aperture. "How comes this person here?" she exclaimed, "you promised me, my dear, that there should be no ventilators in our new house." "Nor are there any," said I; "but what makes you think that the stranger is a Woman? I see by my power of Sight Recognition——" "Oh, I have no patience with your Sight Recognition," replied she, "'Feeling is believing' and 'A Straight Line to the touch is worth a Circle to the sight'"—two Proverbs, very common with the Frailer Sex in Flatland.

"Well," said I, for I was afraid of irritating her, "if it must be so, demand an introduction." Assuming her most gracious manner, my Wife advanced towards the Stranger, "Permit me, Madam, to feel and be felt by——" then, suddenly recoiling, "Oh! it is not a Woman, and there are no angles either, not a trace of one. Can it be that I have so misbehaved to a perfect Circle?"

"I am indeed, in a certain sense a Circle," replied the Voice, "and a more perfect Circle than any in Flatland; but to speak more accurately, I am many Circles in one." Then he added more mildly, "I have a message, dear Madam, to your husband, which I must not deliver in your presence; and, if you would suffer us to retire for a few minutes——" But my Wife would not listen to the proposal that our august Visitor should so incommode himself, and assuring the Circle that the hour of her own retirement had long passed, with many reiterated apologies for her recent indiscretion, she at last retreated to her apartment.

I glanced at the half-hour glass. The last sands had fallen. The third Millennium had begun.

SECTION 16.

HOW THE STRANGER VAINLY ENDEAVOURED TO REVEAL TO ME IN WORDS THE MYSTERIES OF SPACELAND

As soon as the sound of the Peace-cry of my departing Wife had died away, I began to approach the Stranger with the intention of taking a nearer view and of bidding him be seated: but his appearance struck me dumb and motionless with astonishment. Without the slightest symptoms of angularity he nevertheless varied every instant with gradations of size and brightness scarcely possible for any Figure within the scope of my experience. The thought flashed across me that I might have before me a burglar or cut-throat, some monstrous Irregular Isosceles, who, by feigning the voice of a Circle, had obtained admission somehow into the house, and was now preparing to stab me with his acute angle.

In a sitting-room, the absence of Fog (and the season happened to be remarkably dry), made it difficult for me to trust to Sight Recognition, especially at the short distance at which I was standing. Desperate with fear, I rushed forward with an unceremonious, "You must permit me, Sir—" and felt him. My Wife was right. There was not the trace of an angle, not the slightest roughness or inequality: never in my life had I met with a more perfect Circle. He remained motionless while I walked round him, beginning from his eye and returning to it again. Circular he was throughout, a perfectly satisfactory Circle; there could not be a doubt of it. Then followed a dialogue, which I will endeavour to set down as near as I can recollect it, omitting only some of my profuse apologies—for I was covered with shame and humiliation that I, a Square, should have been guilty of the impertinence of feeling a Circle. It was commenced by the Stranger with some impatience at the lengthiness of my introductory process.

STRANGER. Have you felt me enough by this time? Are you not introduced to me yet?

I. Most illustrious Sir, excuse my awkwardness, which arises not from ignorance of the usages of polite society, but from a little surprise and nervousness, consequent on this somewhat unexpected visit. And I beseech you to reveal my indiscretion to no one, and especially not to my Wife. But before your Lordship enters into further communications, would he deign to satisfy the curiosity of one who would gladly know whence his Visitor came?

STRANGER. From Space, from Space, Sir: whence else?

I. Pardon me, my Lord, but is not your Lordship already in Space, your Lordship and his humble servant, even at this moment?

STRANGER. Pooh! what do you know of Space? Define Space.

I. Space, my Lord, is height and breadth indefinitely prolonged.

STRANGER. Exactly: you see you do not even know what Space is. You think it is of Two Dimensions only; but I have come to announce to you a Third—height, breadth, and length.

I. Your Lordship is pleased to be merry. We also speak of length and height, or breadth and thickness, thus denoting Two Dimensions by four names.

STRANGER. But I mean not only three names, but Three Dimensions.

I. Would your Lordship indicate or explain to me in what direction is the Third Dimension, unknown to me?

STRANGER. I came from it. It is up above and down below.

I. My Lord means seemingly that it is Northward and Southward.

STRANGER. I mean nothing of the kind. I mean a direction in which you cannot look, because you have no eye in your side.

I. Pardon me, my Lord, a moment's inspection will convince your Lordship that I have a perfect luminary at the juncture of two of my sides.

STRANGER. Yes: but in order to see into Space you ought to have an eye, not on your Perimeter, but on your side, that is, on what you would probably call your inside; but we in Spaceland should call it your side.

I. An eye in my inside! An eye in my stomach! Your Lordship jests.

STRANGER. I am in no jesting humour. I tell you that I come from Space, or, since you will not understand what Space means, from the Land of Three Dimensions whence I but lately looked down upon your Plane which you call Space forsooth. From that position of advantage I discerned all that you speak of as SOLID (by which you mean "enclosed on four sides"), your houses, your churches, your very chests and safes, yes even your insides and stomachs, all lying open and exposed to my view.

I. Such assertions are easily made, my Lord.

STRANGER. But not easily proved, you mean. But I mean to prove mine.

When I descended here, I saw your four Sons, the Pentagons, each in his apartment, and your two Grandsons the Hexagons; I saw your youngest Hexagon remain a while with you and then retire to his room, leaving you and your Wife alone. I saw your Isosceles servants, three in number, in the kitchen at supper, and the little Page in the scullery. Then I came here, and how do you think I came?

I. Through the roof, I suppose.

STRANGER. Not so. Your roof, as you know very well, has been recently repaired, and has no aperture by which even a Woman could penetrate. I tell you I come from Space. Are you not convinced by what I have told you of your children and household?

I. Your Lordship must be aware that such facts touching the belongings of his humble servant might be easily ascertained by any one in the neighbourhood possessing your Lordship's ample means of obtaining information.

STRANGER. (TO HIMSELF.) What must I do? Stay; one more argument suggests itself to me. When you see a Straight Line—your wife, for example—how many Dimensions do you attribute to her?

I. Your Lordship would treat me as if I were one of the vulgar who, being ignorant of Mathematics, suppose that a Woman is really a Straight

Line, and only of One Dimension. No, no, my Lord; we Squares are better advised, and are as well aware as your Lordship that a Woman, though popularly called a Straight Line, is, really and scientifically, a very thin Parallelogram, possessing Two Dimensions, like the rest of us, viz., length and breadth (or thickness).

STRANGER. But the very fact that a Line is visible implies that it possesses yet another Dimension.

I. My Lord, I have just acknowledged that a Woman is broad as well as long. We see her length, we infer her breadth; which, though very slight, is capable of measurement.

STRANGER. You do not understand me. I mean that when you see a Woman, you ought—besides inferring her breadth—to see her length, and to SEE what we call her HEIGHT; although that last Dimension is infinitesimal in your country. If a Line were mere length without "height", it would cease to occupy Space and would become invisible. Surely you must recognize this?

I. I must indeed confess that I do not in the least understand your Lordship. When we in Flatland see a Line, we see length and BRIGHTNESS. If the brightness disappears, the Line is extinguished, and, as you say, ceases to occupy Space. But am I to suppose that your Lordship gives to brightness the title of a Dimension, and that what we call "bright" you call "high"?

STRANGER. No, indeed. By "height" I mean a Dimension like your length: only, with you, "height" is not so easily perceptible, being extremely small.

I. My Lord, your assertion is easily put to the test. You say I have a Third Dimension, which you call "height". Now, Dimension implies direction and measurement. Do but measure my "height", or merely indicate to me the direction in which my "height" extends, and I will become your convert. Otherwise, your Lordship's own understanding must hold me excused.

STRANGER. (TO HIMSELF.) I can do neither. How shall I convince him? Surely a plain statement of facts followed by ocular demonstration ought to suffice. —Now, Sir; listen to me.

You are living on a Plane. What you style Flatland is the vast level surface of what I may call a fluid, on, or in, the top of which you and your countrymen move about, without rising above it or falling below it.

I am not a plane Figure, but a Solid. You call me a Circle; but in reality I am not a Circle, but an infinite number of Circles, of size varying from a Point to a Circle of thirteen inches in diameter, one placed on the top of the other. When I cut through your plane as I am now doing, I make in your plane a section which you, very rightly, call a Circle. For even a Sphere—which is my proper name in my own country—if he manifest himself at all to an inhabitant of Flatland—must needs manifest himself as a Circle.

Do you not remember—for I, who see all things, discerned last night the phantasmal vision of Lineland written upon your brain—do you not remember, I say, how, when you entered the realm of Lineland, you were compelled to manifest yourself to the King, not as a Square, but as a Line, because that Linear Realm had not Dimensions enough to represent the whole of you, but only a slice or section of you? In precisely the same way, your country of Two Dimensions is not spacious enough to represent me, a being of Three, but can only exhibit a slice or section of me, which is what you call a Circle.

The diminished brightness of your eye indicates incredulity. But now prepare to receive proof positive of the truth of my assertions. You cannot indeed see more than one of my sections, or Circles, at a time; for you have no power to raise your eye out of the plane of Flatland; but you can at least see that, as I rise in Space, so my sections become smaller. See now, I will rise; and the effect upon your eye will be that my Circle will become smaller and smaller till it dwindles to a point and finally vanishes.

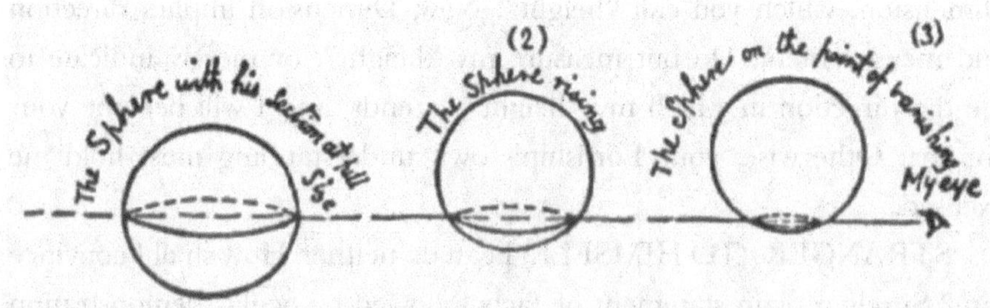

There was no "rising" that I could see; but he diminished and finally vanished. I winked once or twice to make sure that I was not dreaming. But it was no dream. For from the depths of nowhere came forth a hollow voice—close to my heart it seemed—"Am I quite gone? Are you convinced now? Well, now I will gradually return to Flatland and you shall see my section become larger and larger."

Every reader in Spaceland will easily understand that my mysterious Guest was speaking the language of truth and even of simplicity. But to me, proficient though I was in Flatland Mathematics, it was by no means a simple matter. The rough diagram given above will make it clear to any Spaceland child that the Sphere, ascending in the three positions indicated there, must needs have manifested himself to me, or to any Flatlander, as a Circle, at first of full size, then small, and at last very small indeed, approaching to a Point. But to me, although I saw the facts before me, the causes were as dark as ever. All that I could comprehend was, that the Circle had made himself smaller and vanished, and that he had now reappeared and was rapidly making himself larger.

When he regained his original size, he heaved a deep sigh; for he perceived by my silence that I had altogether failed to comprehend him. And indeed I was now inclining to the belief that he must be no Circle at all, but some extremely clever juggler; or else that the old wives' tales were true, and that after all there were such people as Enchanters and Magicians.

After a long pause he muttered to himself, "One resource alone remains, if I am not to resort to action. I must try the method of Analogy." Then followed a still longer silence, after which he continued our dialogue.

SPHERE. Tell me, Mr. Mathematician; if a Point moves Northward, and leaves a luminous wake, what name would you give to the wake?

I. A straight Line.

SPHERE. And a straight Line has how many extremities?

I. Two.

SPHERE. Now conceive the Northward straight Line moving parallel to itself, East and West, so that every point in it leaves behind it the wake of a straight Line. What name will you give to the Figure thereby formed? We will suppose that it moves through a distance equal to the original straight Line. —What name, I say?

I. A Square.

SPHERE. And how many sides has a Square? How many angles?

I. Four sides and four angles.

SPHERE. Now stretch your imagination a little, and conceive a Square in Flatland, moving parallel to itself upward.

I. What? Northward?

SPHERE. No, not Northward; upward; out of Flatland altogether.

If it moved Northward, the Southern points in the Square would have to move through the positions previously occupied by the Northern points. But that is not my meaning.

I mean that every Point in you—for you are a Square and will serve the purpose of my illustration—every Point in you, that is to say in what you call your inside, is to pass upwards through Space in such a way that no Point shall pass through the position previously occupied by any other Point; but each Point shall describe a straight Line of its own. This is all in accordance with Analogy; surely it must be clear to you.

Restraining my impatience—for I was now under a strong temptation to rush blindly at my Visitor and to precipitate him into Space, or out of Flatland, anywhere, so that I could get rid of him—I replied:—

"And what may be the nature of the Figure which I am to shape out by this motion which you are pleased to denote by the word 'upward'? I presume it is describable in the language of Flatland."

SPHERE. Oh, certainly. It is all plain and simple, and in strict accordance with Analogy—only, by the way, you must not speak of the result as being a Figure, but as a Solid. But I will describe it to you. Or rather not I, but Analogy.

We began with a single Point, which of course—being itself a Point—has only ONE terminal Point.

One Point produces a Line with TWO terminal Points.

One Line produces a Square with FOUR terminal Points.

Now you can give yourself the answer to your own question: 1, 2, 4, are evidently in Geometrical Progression. What is the next number?

I. Eight.

SPHERE. Exactly. The one Square produces a SOMETHING-WHICH-   YOU-DO-NOT-AS-YET-KNOW-A-NAME-FOR-BUT-

WHICH-WE-CALL-A-CUBE with EIGHT terminal Points. Now are you convinced?

I. And has this Creature sides, as well as angles or what you call "terminal Points"?

SPHERE. Of course; and all according to Analogy. But, by the way, not what YOU call sides, but what WE call sides. You would call them SOLIDS.

I. And how many solids or sides will appertain to this Being whom I am to generate by the motion of my inside in an "upward" direction, and whom you call a Cube?

SPHERE. How can you ask? And you a mathematician! The side of anything is always, if I may so say, one Dimension behind the thing. Consequently, as there is no Dimension behind a Point, a Point has 0 sides; a Line, if I may say, has 2 sides (for the Points of a Line may be called by courtesy, its sides); a Square has 4 sides; 0, 2, 4; what Progression do you call that?

I. Arithmetical.

SPHERE. And what is the next number?

I. Six.

SPHERE. Exactly. Then you see you have answered your own question. The Cube which you will generate will be bounded by six sides, that is to say, six of your insides. You see it all now, eh?

"Monster," I shrieked, "be thou juggler, enchanter, dream, or devil, no more will I endure thy mockeries. Either thou or I must perish." And saying these words I precipitated myself upon him.

SECTION 17.

HOW THE SPHERE, HAVING IN VAIN TRIED WORDS, RESORTED TO DEEDS

It was in vain. I brought my hardest right angle into violent collision with the Stranger, pressing on him with a force sufficient to have destroyed any ordinary Circle: but I could feel him slowly and unarrestably slipping from my contact; no edging to the right nor to the left, but moving somehow out of the world, and vanishing to nothing. Soon there was a blank. But still I heard the Intruder's voice.

SPHERE. Why will you refuse to listen to reason? I had hoped to find in you—as being a man of sense and an accomplished mathematician—a fit apostle for the Gospel of the Three Dimensions, which I am allowed to preach once only in a thousand years: but now I know not how to convince you. Stay, I have it. Deeds, and not words, shall proclaim the truth. Listen, my friend.

I have told you I can see from my position in Space the inside of all things that you consider closed. For example, I see in yonder cupboard near which you are standing, several of what you call boxes (but like everything else in Flatland, they have no tops nor bottoms) full of money; I see also two tablets of accounts. I am about to descend into that cupboard and to bring you one of those tablets. I saw you lock the cupboard half an hour ago, and I know you have the key in your possession. But I descend from

Space; the doors, you see, remain unmoved. Now I am in the cupboard and am taking the tablet. Now I have it. Now I ascend with it.

I rushed to the closet and dashed the door open. One of the tablets was gone. With a mocking laugh, the Stranger appeared in the other corner of the room, and at the same time the tablet appeared upon the floor. I took it up. There could be no doubt—it was the missing tablet.

I groaned with horror, doubting whether I was not out of my senses; but the Stranger continued: "Surely you must now see that my explanation, and no other, suits the phenomena. What you call Solid things are really superficial; what you call Space is really nothing but a great Plane. I am in Space, and look down upon the insides of the things of which you only see the outsides. You could leave this Plane yourself, if you could but summon up the necessary volition. A slight upward or downward motion would enable you to see all that I can see.

"The higher I mount, and the further I go from your Plane, the more I can see, though of course I see it on a smaller scale. For example, I am ascending; now I can see your neighbour the Hexagon and his family in their several apartments; now I see the inside of the Theatre, ten doors off, from which the audience is only just departing; and on the other side a Circle in his study, sitting at his books. Now I shall come back to you. And, as a crowning proof, what do you say to my giving you a touch, just the least touch, in your stomach? It will not seriously injure you, and the slight pain you may suffer cannot be compared with the mental benefit you will receive."

Before I could utter a word of remonstrance, I felt a shooting pain in my inside, and a demoniacal laugh seemed to issue from within me. A moment afterwards the sharp agony had ceased, leaving nothing but a dull ache behind, and the Stranger began to reappear, saying, as he gradually increased in size, "There, I have not hurt you much, have I? If you are not convinced now, I don't know what will convince you. What say you?"

My resolution was taken. It seemed intolerable that I should endure existence subject to the arbitrary visitations of a Magician who could thus play tricks with one's very stomach. If only I could in any way manage to pin him against the wall till help came!

Once more I dashed my hardest angle against him, at the same time alarming the whole household by my cries for aid. I believe, at the moment of my onset, the Stranger had sunk below our Plane, and really found difficulty in rising. In any case he remained motionless, while I, hearing, as I thought, the sound of some help approaching, pressed against him with redoubled vigour, and continued to shout for assistance.

A convulsive shudder ran through the Sphere. "This must not be," I thought I heard him say: "either he must listen to reason, or I must have recourse to the last resource of civilization." Then, addressing me in a louder tone, he hurriedly exclaimed, "Listen: no stranger must witness what you have witnessed. Send your Wife back at once, before she enters the apartment. The Gospel of Three Dimensions must not be thus frustrated. Not thus must the fruits of one thousand years of waiting be thrown away. I hear her coming. Back! back! Away from me, or you must go with me— whither you know not—into the Land of Three Dimensions!"

"Fool! Madman! Irregular!" I exclaimed; "never will I release thee; thou shalt pay the penalty of thine impostures."

"Ha! Is it come to this?" thundered the Stranger: "then meet your fate: out of your Plane you go. Once, twice, thrice! 'Tis done!"

SECTION 18.

HOW I CAME TO SPACELAND, AND WHAT I SAW THERE

An unspeakable horror seized me. There was a darkness; then a dizzy, sickening sensation of sight that was not like seeing; I saw a Line that was no Line; Space that was not Space: I was myself, and not myself. When I could find voice, I shrieked aloud in agony, "Either this is madness or it is Hell." "It is neither," calmly replied the voice of the Sphere, "it is Knowledge; it is Three Dimensions: open your eye once again and try to look steadily."

I looked, and, behold, a new world! There stood before me, visibly incorporate, all that I had before inferred, conjectured, dreamed, of perfect Circular beauty. What seemed the centre of the Stranger's form lay open to my view: yet I could see no heart, nor lungs, nor arteries, only a beautiful harmonious Something—for which I had no words; but you, my Readers in Spaceland, would call it the surface of the Sphere.

Prostrating myself mentally before my Guide, I cried, "How is it, O divine ideal of consummate loveliness and wisdom that I see thy inside, and yet cannot discern thy heart, thy lungs, thy arteries, thy liver?" "What you think you see, you see not," he replied; "it is not given to you, nor to any other Being to behold my internal parts. I am of a different order of Beings from those in Flatland. Were I a Circle, you could discern my intestines, but I am a Being, composed as I told you before, of many Circles, the Many in the One, called in this country a Sphere. And, just as the outside of a Cube is a Square, so the outside of a Sphere presents the appearance of a Circle."

Bewildered though I was by my Teacher's enigmatic utterance, I no longer chafed against it, but worshipped him in silent adoration. He continued, with more mildness in his voice. "Distress not yourself if you cannot at first understand the deeper mysteries of Spaceland. By degrees they will dawn upon you. Let us begin by casting back a glance at the region whence you came. Return with me a while to the plains of Flatland, and I will shew you that which you have often reasoned and thought about, but never seen with the sense of sight—a visible angle." "Impossible!" I cried; but, the Sphere leading the way, I followed as if in a dream, till once more his voice arrested me: "Look yonder, and behold your own Pentagonal house, and all its inmates."

I looked below, and saw with my physical eye all that domestic individuality which I had hitherto merely inferred with the understanding. And how poor and shadowy was the inferred conjecture in comparison with the reality which I now beheld! My four Sons calmly asleep in the North-Western rooms, my two orphan Grandsons to the South; the Servants, the Butler, my Daughter, all in their several apartments. Only my affectionate Wife, alarmed by my continued absence, had quitted her room and was roving up and down in the Hall, anxiously awaiting my return. Also the Page, aroused by my cries, had left his room, and under pretext of ascertaining whether I had fallen somewhere in a faint, was prying into the cabinet in my study. All this I could now SEE, not merely infer; and as we came nearer and nearer, I could discern even the contents of my cabinet, and the two chests of gold, and the tablets of which the Sphere had made mention.

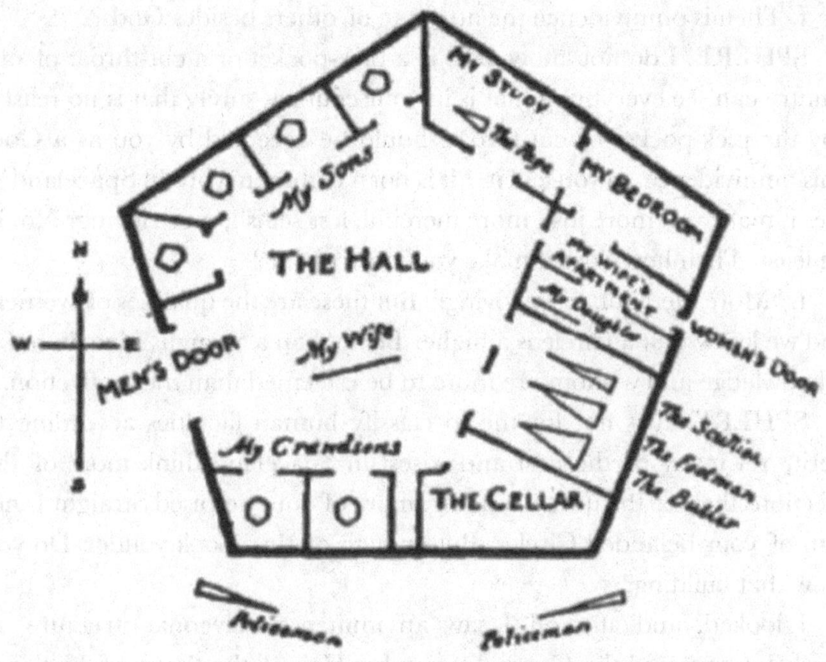

Touched by my Wife's distress, I would have sprung downward to reassure her, but I found myself incapable of motion. "Trouble not yourself about your Wife," said my Guide: "she will not be long left in anxiety; meantime, let us take a survey of Flatland."

Once more I felt myself rising through space. It was even as the Sphere had said. The further we receded from the object we beheld, the larger became the field of vision. My native city, with the interior of every house and every creature therein, lay open to my view in miniature. We mounted higher, and lo, the secrets of the earth, the depths of mines and inmost caverns of the hills, were bared before me.

Awestruck at the sight of the mysteries of the earth, thus unveiled before my unworthy eye, I said to my Companion, "Behold, I am become as a God. For the wise men in our country say that to see all things, or as they express it, OMNIVIDENCE, is the attribute of God alone." There was something of scorn in the voice of my Teacher as he made answer: "Is it so indeed? Then the very pick-pockets and cut-throats of my country are to be worshipped by your wise men as being Gods: for there is not one of them that does not see as much as you see now. But trust me, your wise men are wrong."

I. Then is omnividence the attribute of others besides Gods?

SPHERE. I do not know. But, if a pick-pocket or a cut-throat of our country can see everything that is in your country, surely that is no reason why the pick-pocket or cut-throat should be accepted by you as a God. This omnividence, as you call it—it is not a common word in Spaceland—does it make you more just, more merciful, less selfish, more loving? Not in the least. Then how does it make you more divine?

I. "More merciful, more loving!" But these are the qualities of women! And we know that a Circle is a higher Being than a Straight Line, in so far as knowledge and wisdom are more to be esteemed than mere affection.

SPHERE. It is not for me to classify human faculties according to merit. Yet many of the best and wisest in Spaceland think more of the affections than of the understanding, more of your despised Straight Lines than of your belauded Circles. But enough of this. Look yonder. Do you know that building?

I looked, and afar off I saw an immense Polygonal structure, in which I recognized the General Assembly Hall of the States of Flatland, surrounded by dense lines of Pentagonal buildings at right angles to each other, which I knew to be streets; and I perceived that I was approaching the great Metropolis.

"Here we descend," said my Guide. It was now morning, the first hour of the first day of the two thousandth year of our era. Acting, as was their wont, in strict accordance with precedent, the highest Circles of the realm were meeting in solemn conclave, as they had met on the first hour of the first day of the year 1000, and also on the first hour of the first day of the year 0.

The minutes of the previous meetings were now read by one whom I at once recognized as my brother, a perfectly Symmetrical Square, and the Chief Clerk of the High Council. It was found recorded on each occasion that: "Whereas the States had been troubled by divers ill-intentioned persons pretending to have received revelations from another World, and professing to produce demonstrations whereby they had instigated to frenzy both themselves and others, it had been for this cause unanimously resolved by the Grand Council that on the first day of each millenary, special injunctions be sent to the Prefects in the several districts of Flatland, to make strict search for such misguided persons, and without formality of mathematical examination, to destroy all such as were Isosceles of any degree, to scourge and imprison any regular Triangle, to cause any Square or Pentagon to be sent to the district Asylum, and to arrest any one of higher rank, sending him straightway to the Capital to be examined and judged by the Council."

"You hear your fate," said the Sphere to me, while the Council was passing for the third time the formal resolution. "Death or imprisonment awaits the Apostle of the Gospel of Three Dimensions." "Not so," replied I, "the matter is now so clear to me, the nature of real space so palpable, that methinks I could make a child understand it. Permit me but to descend at this moment and enlighten them." "Not yet," said my Guide, "the time will come for that. Meantime I must perform my mission. Stay thou there in thy place." Saying these words, he leaped with great dexterity into the sea (if I may so call it) of Flatland, right in the midst of the ring of Counsellors. "I come," cried he, "to proclaim that there is a land of Three Dimensions."

I could see many of the younger Counsellors start back in manifest horror, as the Sphere's circular section widened before them. But on a sign from the presiding Circle—who shewed not the slightest alarm or surprise—six Isosceles of a low type from six different quarters rushed upon the Sphere. "We have him," they cried; "No; yes; we have him still! he's going! he's gone!"

"My Lords," said the President to the Junior Circles of the Council, "there is not the slightest need for surprise; the secret archives, to which I alone have access, tell me that a similar occurrence happened on the last two millennial commencements. You will, of course, say nothing of these trifles outside the Cabinet."

Raising his voice, he now summoned the guards. "Arrest the policemen; gag them. You know your duty." After he had consigned to their fate the wretched policemen—ill-fated and unwilling witnesses of a State-secret which they were not to be permitted to reveal—he again addressed the Counsellors. "My Lords, the business of the Council being concluded, I have only to wish you a happy New Year." Before departing, he expressed, at some length, to the Clerk, my excellent but most unfortunate brother, his sincere regret that, in accordance with precedent and for the sake of secrecy, he must condemn him to perpetual imprisonment, but added his satisfaction that, unless some mention were made by him of that day's incident, his life would be spared.

SECTION 19.

HOW, THOUGH THE SPHERE SHEWED ME OTHER MYSTERIES OF SPACELAND, I STILL DESIRED MORE; AND WHAT CAME OF IT

When I saw my poor brother led away to imprisonment, I attempted to leap down into the Council Chamber, desiring to intercede on his behalf, or at least bid him farewell. But I found that I had no motion of my own. I absolutely depended on the volition of my Guide, who said in gloomy tones, "Heed not thy brother; haply thou shalt have ample time hereafter to condole with him. Follow me."

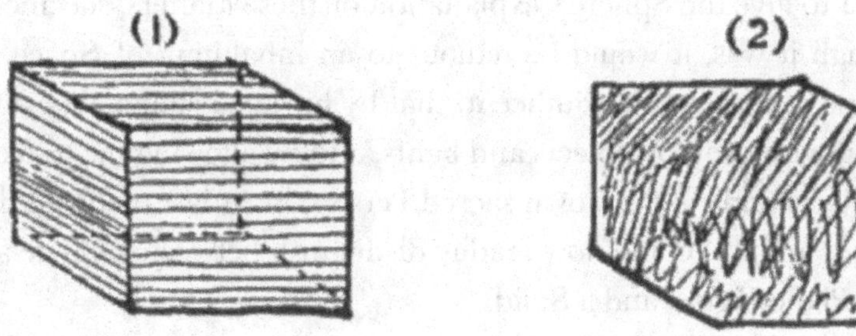

Once more we ascended into space. "Hitherto," said the Sphere, "I have shewn you naught save Plane Figures and their interiors. Now I must introduce you to Solids, and reveal to you the plan upon which they are constructed. Behold this multitude of moveable square cards. See, I put one on another, not, as you supposed, Northward of the other, but ON the other. Now a second, now a third. See, I am building up a Solid by a multitude of Squares parallel to one another. Now the Solid is complete, being as high as it is long and broad, and we call it a Cube."

"Pardon me, my Lord," replied I; "but to my eye the appearance is as of an Irregular Figure whose inside is laid open to the view; in other words, methinks I see no Solid, but a Plane such as we infer in Flatland; only of an Irregularity which betokens some monstrous criminal, so that the very sight of it is painful to my eyes."

"True," said the Sphere, "it appears to you a Plane, because you are not accustomed to light and shade and perspective; just as in Flatland a Hexagon would appear a Straight Line to one who has not the Art of Sight Recognition. But in reality it is a Solid, as you shall learn by the sense of Feeling."

He then introduced me to the Cube, and I found that this marvellous Being was indeed no Plane, but a Solid; and that he was endowed with six plane sides and eight terminal points called solid angles; and I remembered the saying of the Sphere that just such a Creature as this would be formed by a Square moving, in Space, parallel to himself: and I rejoiced to think that so insignificant a Creature as I could in some sense be called the Progenitor of so illustrious an offspring.

But still I could not fully understand the meaning of what my Teacher had told me concerning "light" and "shade" and "perspective"; and I did not hesitate to put my difficulties before him.

Were I to give the Sphere's explanation of these matters, succinct and clear though it was, it would be tedious to an inhabitant of Space, who knows these things already. Suffice it, that by his lucid statements, and by changing the position of objects and lights, and by allowing me to feel the several objects and even his own sacred Person, he at last made all things clear to me, so that I could now readily distinguish between a Circle and a Sphere, a Plane Figure and a Solid.

This was the Climax, the Paradise, of my strange eventful History. Henceforth I have to relate the story of my miserable Fall:——most miserable, yet surely most undeserved! For why should the thirst for knowledge be aroused, only to be disappointed and punished? My volition shrinks from the painful task of recalling my humiliation; yet, like a second Prometheus,

I will endure this and worse, if by any means I may arouse in the interiors of Plane and Solid Humanity a spirit of rebellion against the Conceit which would limit our Dimensions to Two or Three or any number short of Infinity. Away then with all personal considerations! Let me continue to the end, as I began, without further digressions or anticipations, pursuing the plain path of dispassionate History. The exact facts, the exact words,—and they are burnt in upon my brain,—shall be set down without alteration of an iota; and let my Readers judge between me and Destiny.

The Sphere would willingly have continued his lessons by indoctrinating me in the conformation of all regular Solids, Cylinders, Cones, Pyramids, Pentahedrons, Hexahedrons, Dodecahedrons, and Spheres: but I ventured to interrupt him. Not that I was wearied of knowledge. On the contrary, I thirsted for yet deeper and fuller draughts than he was offering to me.

"Pardon me," said I, "O Thou Whom I must no longer address as the Perfection of all Beauty; but let me beg thee to vouchsafe thy servant a sight of thine interior."

SPHERE. My what?

I. Thine interior: thy stomach, thy intestines.

SPHERE. Whence this ill-timed impertinent request? And what mean you by saying that I am no longer the Perfection of all Beauty?

I. My Lord, your own wisdom has taught me to aspire to One even more great, more beautiful, and more closely approximate to Perfection than yourself. As you yourself, superior to all Flatland forms, combine many Circles in One, so doubtless there is One above you who combines many Spheres in One Supreme Existence, surpassing even the Solids of Spaceland. And even as we, who are now in Space, look down on Flatland and see the insides of all things, so of a certainty there is yet above us some higher, purer region, whither thou dost surely purpose to lead me—O Thou Whom I shall always call, everywhere and in all Dimensions, my Priest, Philosopher, and Friend—some yet more spacious Space, some more dimensionable Dimensionality, from the vantage-ground of which we shall look down together upon the revealed insides of Solid things, and where thine own intestines, and those of thy kindred Spheres, will lie exposed to the view of the poor wandering exile from Flatland, to whom so much has already been vouchsafed.

SPHERE. Pooh! Stuff! Enough of this trifling! The time is short, and much remains to be done before you are fit to proclaim the Gospel of Three Dimensions to your blind benighted countrymen in Flatland.

I. Nay, gracious Teacher, deny me not what I know it is in thy power to perform. Grant me but one glimpse of thine interior, and I am satisfied for ever, remaining henceforth thy docile pupil, thy unemancipable slave, ready to receive all thy teachings and to feed upon the words that fall from thy lips.

SPHERE. Well, then, to content and silence you, let me say at once, I would shew you what you wish if I could; but I cannot. Would you have me turn my stomach inside out to oblige you?

I. But my Lord has shewn me the intestines of all my countrymen in the Land of Two Dimensions by taking me with him into the Land of Three. What therefore more easy than now to take his servant on a second journey into the blessed region of the Fourth Dimension, where I shall look down with him once more upon this land of Three Dimensions, and see the inside of every three-dimensioned house, the secrets of the solid earth, the treasures of the mines in Spaceland, and the intestines of every solid living creature, even of the noble and adorable Spheres.

SPHERE. But where is this land of Four Dimensions?

I. I know not: but doubtless my Teacher knows.

SPHERE. Not I. There is no such land. The very idea of it is utterly inconceivable.

I. Not inconceivable, my Lord, to me, and therefore still less inconceivable to my Master. Nay, I despair not that, even here, in this region of Three Dimensions, your Lordship's art may make the Fourth Dimension visible to me; just as in the Land of Two Dimensions my Teacher's skill would fain have opened the eyes of his blind servant to the invisible presence of a Third Dimension, though I saw it not.

Let me recall the past. Was I not taught below that when I saw a Line and inferred a Plane, I in reality saw a Third unrecognized Dimension, not the same as brightness, called "height"? And does it not now follow that, in this region, when I see a Plane and infer a Solid, I really see a Fourth unrecognized Dimension, not the same as colour, but existent, though infinitesimal and incapable of measurement?

And besides this, there is the Argument from Analogy of Figures.

SPHERE. Analogy! Nonsense: what analogy?

I. Your Lordship tempts his servant to see whether he remembers the revelations imparted to him. Trifle not with me, my Lord; I crave, I thirst, for more knowledge. Doubtless we cannot SEE that other higher Spaceland now, because we we have no eye in our stomachs. But, just as there WAS the realm of Flatland, though that poor puny Lineland Monarch could neither turn to left nor right to discern it, and just as there WAS close at hand, and touching my frame, the land of Three Dimensions, though I, blind senseless wretch, had no power to touch it, no eye in my interior to discern it, so of a surety there is a Fourth Dimension, which my Lord perceives with the inner eye of thought. And that it must exist my Lord himself has taught me. Or can he have forgotten what he himself imparted to his servant?

In One Dimension, did not a moving Point produce a Line with TWO terminal points?

In Two Dimensions, did not a moving Line produce a Square with FOUR terminal points?

In Three Dimensions, did not a moving Square produce—did not this eye of mine behold it—that blessed Being, a Cube, with EIGHT terminal points?

And in Four Dimensions shall not a moving Cube—alas, for Analogy, and alas for the Progress of Truth, if it be not so—shall not, I say, the motion of a divine Cube result in a still more divine Organization with SIXTEEN terminal points?

Behold the infallible confirmation of the Series, 2, 4, 8, 16: is not this a Geometrical Progression? Is not this—if I might quote my Lord's own words—"strictly according to Analogy"?

Again, was I not taught by my Lord that as in a Line there are TWO bounding Points, and in a Square there are FOUR bounding Lines, so in a Cube there must be SIX bounding Squares? Behold once more the confirming Series, 2, 4, 6: is not this an Arithmetical Progression? And consequently does it not of necessity follow that the more divine offspring of the divine Cube in the Land of Four Dimensions, must have 8 bounding Cubes: and is not this also, as my Lord has taught me to believe, "strictly according to Analogy"?

O, my Lord, my Lord, behold, I cast myself in faith upon conjecture, not knowing the facts; and I appeal to your Lordship to confirm or deny my logical anticipations. If I am wrong, I yield, and will no longer demand a fourth Dimension; but, if I am right, my Lord will listen to reason.

I ask therefore, is it, or is it not, the fact, that ere now your countrymen also have witnessed the descent of Beings of a higher order than their own, entering closed rooms, even as your Lordship entered mine, without the opening of doors or windows, and appearing and vanishing at will? On the reply to this question I am ready to stake everything. Deny it, and I am henceforth silent. Only vouchsafe an answer.

SPHERE. (AFTER A PAUSE). It is reported so. But men are divided in opinion as to the facts. And even granting the facts, they explain them in different ways. And in any case, however great may be the number of different explanations, no one has adopted or suggested the theory of a Fourth Dimension. Therefore, pray have done with this trifling, and let us return to business.

I. I was certain of it. I was certain that my anticipations would be fulfilled. And now have patience with me and answer me yet one more question, best of Teachers! Those who have thus appeared—no one knows whence—and have returned—no one knows whither—have they also contracted their sections and vanished somehow into that more Spacious Space, whither I now entreat you to conduct me?

SPHERE (MOODILY). They have vanished, certainly—if they ever appeared. But most people say that these visions arose from the thought— you will not understand me—from the brain; from the perturbed angularity of the Seer.

I. Say they so? Oh, believe them not. Or if it indeed be so, that this other Space is really Thoughtland, then take me to that blessed Region where I in Thought shall see the insides of all solid things. There, before my ravished eye, a Cube, moving in some altogether new direction, but strictly according to Analogy, so as to make every particle of his interior pass through a new kind of Space, with a wake of its own—shall create a still more perfect perfection than himself, with sixteen terminal Extra-solid angles, and Eight solid Cubes for his Perimeter. And once there, shall we stay our upward course? In that blessed region of Four Dimensions, shall we linger on the threshold of the Fifth, and not enter therein? Ah, no! Let us rather resolve that our ambition shall soar with our corporal ascent. Then, yielding to our intellectual onset, the gates of the Sixth Dimension shall fly open; after that a Seventh, and then an Eighth— How long I should have continued I know not. In vain did the Sphere, in his voice of thunder, reiterate his command of silence, and threaten me with the direst penalties if I persisted. Nothing could stem the flood of my ecstatic aspirations. Perhaps I was to blame; but indeed I was intoxicated with the recent draughts of Truth to which he himself had introduced me. However, the end was not long in coming. My words were cut short by a crash outside, and a simultaneous crash inside me, which impelled me through space with a velocity that precluded speech. Down! down! down! I was rapidly descending; and I knew that return to Flatland was my doom. One glimpse, one last and never-to-be-forgotten glimpse I had of that dull level wilderness—which was now to become my Universe again—spread out before my eye. Then a darkness. Then a final, all-consummating thunder-peal; and, when I came to myself, I was once more a common creeping Square, in my Study at home, listening to the Peace-Cry of my approaching Wife.

SECTION 20.

HOW THE SPHERE ENCOURAGED ME IN A VISION

Although I had less than a minute for reflection, I felt, by a kind of instinct, that I must conceal my experiences from my Wife. Not that I apprehended, at the moment, any danger from her divulging my secret, but I knew that to any Woman in Flatland the narrative of my adventures must needs be unintelligible. So I endeavoured to reassure her by some story, invented for the occasion, that I had accidentally fallen through the trap-door of the cellar, and had there lain stunned.

The Southward attraction in our country is so slight that even to a Woman my tale necessarily appeared extraordinary and well-nigh incredible; but my Wife, whose good sense far exceeds that of the average of her Sex, and who perceived that I was unusually excited, did not argue with me on the subject, but insisted that I was ill and required repose. I was glad of an excuse for retiring to my chamber to think quietly over what had happened. When I was at last by myself, a drowsy sensation fell on me; but before my eyes closed I endeavoured to reproduce the Third Dimension, and especially the process by which a Cube is constructed through the motion of a Square. It was not so clear as I could have wished; but I remembered that it must be "Upward, and yet not Northward", and I determined steadfastly to retain these words as the clue which, if firmly grasped, could not fail to guide me to the solution. So mechanically repeating, like a charm, the words, "Upward, yet not Northward", I fell into a sound refreshing sleep.

During my slumber I had a dream. I thought I was once more by the side of the Sphere, whose lustrous hue betokened that he had exchanged his wrath against me for perfect placability. We were moving together towards a bright but infinitesimally small Point, to which my Master directed my attention. As we approached, methought there issued from it a slight humming noise as from one of your Spaceland bluebottles, only less resonant by far, so slight indeed that even in the perfect stillness of the Vacuum through which we soared, the sound reached not our ears till we checked our flight at a distance from it of something under twenty human diagonals.

"Look yonder," said my Guide, "in Flatland thou hast lived; of Lineland thou hast received a vision; thou hast soared with me to the heights of Spaceland; now, in order to complete the range of thy experience, I conduct thee downward to the lowest depth of existence, even to the realm of Pointland, the Abyss of No dimensions.

"Behold yon miserable creature. That Point is a Being like ourselves, but confined to the non-dimensional Gulf. He is himself his own World, his own Universe; of any other than himself he can form no conception; he knows not Length, nor Breadth, nor Height, for he has had no experience of them; he has no cognizance even of the number Two; nor has he a thought of Plurality; for he is himself his One and All, being really Nothing. Yet mark his perfect self-contentment, and hence learn this lesson, that to be self-contented is to be vile and ignorant, and that to aspire is better than to be blindly and impotently happy. Now listen."

He ceased; and there arose from the little buzzing creature a tiny, low, monotonous, but distinct tinkling, as from one of your Spaceland phonographs, from which I caught these words, "Infinite beatitude of existence! It is; and there is none else beside It."

"What," said I, "does the puny creature mean by 'it'?" "He means himself," said the Sphere: "have you not noticed before now, that babies and babyish people who cannot distinguish themselves from the world, speak of themselves in the Third Person? But hush!"

"It fills all Space," continued the little soliloquizing Creature, "and what It fills, It is. What It thinks, that It utters; and what It utters, that It hears; and It itself is Thinker, Utterer, Hearer, Thought, Word, Audition; it is the One, and yet the All in All. Ah, the happiness ah, the happiness of Being!"

"Can you not startle the little thing out of its complacency?" said I. "Tell it what it really is, as you told me; reveal to it the narrow limitations of Pointland, and lead it up to something higher." "That is no easy task," said my Master; "try you."

Hereon, raising my voice to the uttermost, I addressed the Point as follows:

"Silence, silence, contemptible Creature. You call yourself the All in All, but you are the Nothing: your so-called Universe is a mere speck in a Line, and a Line is a mere shadow as compared with—" "Hush, hush, you have said enough," interrupted the Sphere, "now listen, and mark the effect of your harangue on the King of Pointland."

The lustre of the Monarch, who beamed more brightly than ever upon hearing my words, shewed clearly that he retained his complacency; and I had hardly ceased when he took up his strain again. "Ah, the joy, ah, the joy of Thought! What can It not achieve by thinking! Its own Thought coming to Itself, suggestive of Its disparagement, thereby to enhance Its happiness! Sweet rebellion stirred up to result in triumph! Ah, the divine creative power of the All in One! Ah, the joy, the joy of Being!"

"You see," said my Teacher, "how little your words have done. So far as the Monarch understands them at all, he accepts them as his own— for he cannot conceive of any other except himself—and plumes himself upon the variety of 'Its Thought' as an instance of creative Power. Let us leave this God of Pointland to the ignorant fruition of his omnipresence and omniscience: nothing that you or I can do can rescue him from his self-satisfaction."

After this, as we floated gently back to Flatland, I could hear the mild voice of my Companion pointing the moral of my vision, and stimulating me to aspire, and to teach others to aspire. He had been angered at first— he confessed—by my ambition to soar to Dimensions above the Third; but, since then, he had received fresh insight, and he was not too proud to acknowledge his error to a Pupil. Then he proceeded to initiate me into mysteries yet higher than those I had witnessed, shewing me how to construct Extra-Solids by the motion of Solids, and Double Extra-Solids by the motion of Extra-Solids, and all "strictly according to Analogy", all by methods so simple, so easy, as to be patent even to the Female Sex.

SECTION 21.

HOW I TRIED TO TEACH THE THEORY OF THREE DIMENSIONS TO MY GRANDSON, AND WITH WHAT SUCCESS

I awoke rejoicing, and began to reflect on the glorious career before me. I would go forth, methought, at once, and evangelize the whole of Flatland. Even to Women and Soldiers should the Gospel of Three Dimensions be proclaimed. I would begin with my Wife.

Just as I had decided on the plan of my operations, I heard the sound of many voices in the street commanding silence. Then followed a louder voice. It was a herald's proclamation. Listening attentively, I recognized the words of the Resolution of the Council, enjoining the arrest, imprisonment, or execution of any one who should pervert the minds of the people by delusions, and by professing to have received revelations from another World.

I reflected. This danger was not to be trifled with. It would be better to avoid it by omitting all mention of my Revelation, and by proceeding on the path of Demonstration—which after all, seemed so simple and so conclusive that nothing would be lost by discarding the former means. "Upward, not Northward"—was the clue to the whole proof. It had seemed to me fairly clear before I fell asleep; and when I first awoke, fresh from my dream, it had appeared as patent as Arithmetic; but somehow it did not seem to me quite so obvious now. Though my Wife entered the room opportunely just at that moment, I decided, after we had exchanged a few words of commonplace conversation, not to begin with her.

My Pentagonal Sons were men of character and standing, and physicians of no mean reputation, but not great in mathematics, and, in that respect, unfit for my purpose. But it occurred to me that a young and docile Hexagon, with a mathematical turn, would be a most suitable pupil. Why therefore not make my first experiment with my little precocious Grandson, whose casual remarks on the meaning of 33 had met with the approval of the Sphere? Discussing the matter with him, a mere boy, I should be in perfect safety; for he would know nothing of the Proclamation of the Council; whereas I could not feel sure that my Sons—so greatly did their patriotism and reverence for the Circles predominate over mere blind affection—might not feel compelled to hand me over to the Prefect, if they found me seriously maintaining the seditious heresy of the Third Dimension.

But the first thing to be done was to satisfy in some way the curiosity of my Wife, who naturally wished to know something of the reasons for which the Circle had desired that mysterious interview, and of the means by which he had entered the house. Without entering into the details of the elaborate account I gave her,—an account, I fear, not quite so consistent with truth as my Readers in Spaceland might desire,—I must be content with saying that I succeeded at last in persuading her to return quietly to her household duties without eliciting from me any reference to the World of Three Dimensions. This done, I immediately sent for my Grandson; for, to confess the truth, I felt that all that I had seen and heard was in some strange way slipping away from me, like the image of a half-grasped, tantalizing dream, and I longed to essay my skill in making a first disciple.

When my Grandson entered the room I carefully secured the door. Then, sitting down by his side and taking our mathematical tablets,—or, as you would call them, Lines—I told him we would resume the lesson of yesterday. I taught him once more how a Point by motion in One Dimension produces a Line, and how a straight Line in Two Dimensions produces a Square. After this, forcing a laugh, I said, "And now, you scamp, you wanted to make me believe that a Square may in the same way by motion 'Upward, not Northward' produce another figure, a sort of extra Square in Three Dimensions. Say that again, you young rascal."

At this moment we heard once more the herald's "O yes! O yes!" outside in the street proclaiming the Resolution of the Council. Young though he was, my Grandson—who was unusually intelligent for his age, and bred up in perfect reverence for the authority of the Circles—took in the situation with an acuteness for which I was quite unprepared. He remained silent till the last words of the Proclamation had died away, and then, bursting into tears, "Dear Grandpapa," he said, "that was only my fun, and of course I meant nothing at all by it; and we did not know anything then about the new Law; and I don't think I said anything about the Third Dimension; and I am sure I did not say one word about 'Upward, not Northward', for that would be such nonsense, you know. How could a thing move Upward, and not Northward? Upward and not Northward! Even if I were a baby, I could not be so absurd as that. How silly it is! Ha! ha! ha!"

"Not at all silly," said I, losing my temper; "here for example, I take this Square," and, at the word, I grasped a moveable Square, which was lying at hand—"and I move it, you see, not Northward but—yes, I move it Upward—that is to say, not Northward, but I move it somewhere—not exactly like this, but somehow—" Here I brought my sentence to an inane conclusion, shaking the Square about in a purposeless manner, much to the amusement of my Grandson, who burst out laughing louder than ever, and declared that I was not teaching him, but joking with him; and so saying he unlocked the door and ran out of the room. Thus ended my first attempt to convert a pupil to the Gospel of Three Dimensions.

SECTION 22.

HOW I THEN TRIED TO DIFFUSE THE THEORY OF THREE DIMENSIONS BY OTHER MEANS, AND OF THE RESULT

My failure with my Grandson did not encourage me to communicate my secret to others of my household; yet neither was I led by it to despair of success. Only I saw that I must not wholly rely on the catch-phrase, "Upward, not Northward", but must rather endeavour to seek a demonstration by setting before the public a clear view of the whole subject; and for this purpose it seemed necessary to resort to writing.

So I devoted several months in privacy to the composition of a treatise on the mysteries of Three Dimensions. Only, with the view of evading the Law, if possible, I spoke not of a physical Dimension, but of a Thoughtland whence, in theory, a Figure could look down upon Flatland and see simultaneously the insides of all things, and where it was possible that there might be supposed to exist a Figure environed, as it were, with six Squares, and containing eight terminal Points. But in writing this book I found myself sadly hampered by the impossibility of drawing such diagrams as were necessary for my purpose; for of course, in our country of Flatland, there are no tablets but Lines, and no diagrams but Lines, all in one straight Line and only distinguishable by difference of size and brightness; so that, when I had finished my treatise (which I entitled, "Through Flatland to Thoughtland") I could not feel certain that many would understand my meaning.

Meanwhile my life was under a cloud. All pleasures palled upon me; all sights tantalized and tempted me to outspoken treason, because I could not but compare what I saw in Two Dimensions with what it really was if seen in Three, and could hardly refrain from making my comparisons aloud. I neglected my clients and my own business to give myself to the contemplation of the mysteries which I had once beheld, yet which I could impart to no one, and found daily more difficult to reproduce even before my own mental vision.

One day, about eleven months after my return from Spaceland, I tried to see a Cube with my eye closed, but failed; and though I succeeded afterwards, I was not then quite certain (nor have I been ever afterwards) that I had exactly realized the original. This made me more melancholy than before, and determined me to take some step; yet what, I knew not. I felt that I would have been willing to sacrifice my life for the Cause, if thereby I could have produced conviction. But if I could not convince my Grandson, how could I convince the highest and most developed Circles in the land?

And yet at times my spirit was too strong for me, and I gave vent to dangerous utterances. Already I was considered heterodox if not treasonable, and I was keenly alive to the danger of my position; nevertheless I could not at times refrain from bursting out into suspicious or half-seditious utterances, even among the highest Polygonal and Circular society. When, for example, the question arose about the treatment of those lunatics who said that they had received the power of seeing the insides of things, I would quote the saying of an ancient Circle, who declared that prophets and inspired people are always considered by the majority to be mad; and I could not help occasionally dropping such expressions as "the eye that discerns the interiors of things", and "the all-seeing land"; once or twice I even let fall the forbidden terms "the Third and Fourth Dimensions". At last, to complete a series of minor indiscretions, at a meeting of our Local Speculative Society held at the palace of the Prefect himself,—some extremely silly person having read an elaborate paper exhibiting the precise reasons why Providence has limited the number of Dimensions to Two, and why the attribute of omnividence is assigned to the Supreme alone—I so far forgot myself as to give an exact account of the whole of my voyage with the Sphere into Space, and to the Assembly Hall in our Metropolis, and then to Space again, and of my return home, and of everything that I had seen and heard in fact or vision. At first, indeed, I pretended that I was describing the imaginary experiences of a fictitious person; but my enthusiasm soon forced me to throw off all disguise, and finally, in a fervent peroration, I exhorted all my hearers to divest themselves of prejudice and to become believers in the Third Dimension.

Need I say that I was at once arrested and taken before the Council?

Next morning, standing in the very place where but a very few months ago the Sphere had stood in my company, I was allowed to begin and to continue my narration unquestioned and uninterrupted. But from the first I foresaw my fate; for the President, noting that a guard of the better sort of Policemen was in attendance, of angularity little, if at all, under 55 degrees, ordered them to be relieved before I began my defence, by an inferior class of 2 or 3 degrees. I knew only too well what that meant. I was to be executed or imprisoned, and my story was to be kept secret from the world by the simultaneous destruction of the officials who had heard it; and, this being the case, the President desired to substitute the cheaper for the more expensive victims.

After I had concluded my defence, the President, perhaps perceiving that some of the junior Circles had been moved by my evident earnestness, asked me two questions:—

1. Whether I could indicate the direction which I meant when I used the words "Upward, not Northward"?

2. Whether I could by any diagrams or descriptions (other than the enumeration of imaginary sides and angles) indicate the Figure I was pleased to call a Cube?

I declared that I could say nothing more, and that I must commit myself to the Truth, whose cause would surely prevail in the end.

The President replied that he quite concurred in my sentiment, and that I could not do better. I must be sentenced to perpetual imprisonment; but if the Truth intended that I should emerge from prison and evangelize the world, the Truth might be trusted to bring that result to pass. Meanwhile I should be subjected to no discomfort that was not necessary to preclude escape, and, unless I forfeited the privilege by misconduct, I should be occasionally permitted to see my brother who had preceded me to my prison.

Seven years have elapsed and I am still a prisoner, and—if I except the occasional visits of my brother—debarred from all companionship save that of my jailers. My brother is one of the best of Squares, just, sensible, cheerful, and not without fraternal affection; yet I confess that my weekly interviews, at least in one respect, cause me the bitterest pain. He was present when the Sphere manifested himself in the Council Chamber; he saw the Sphere's changing sections; he heard the explanation of the phenomena then given to the Circles. Since that time, scarcely a week has passed during seven whole years, without his hearing from me a repetition of the part I played in that manifestation, together with ample descriptions of all the phenomena in Spaceland, and the arguments for the existence of Solid things derivable from Analogy. Yet—I take shame to be forced to confess it—my brother has not yet grasped the nature of the Third Dimension, and frankly avows his disbelief in the existence of a Sphere.

Hence I am absolutely destitute of converts, and, for aught that I can see, the millennial Revelation has been made to me for nothing. Prometheus up in Spaceland was bound for bringing down fire for mortals, but I—poor Flatland Prometheus—lie here in prison for bringing down nothing to my countrymen. Yet I exist in the hope that these memoirs, in some manner, I know not how, may find their way to the minds of humanity in Some Dimension, and may stir up a race of rebels who shall refuse to be confined to limited Dimensionality.

That is the hope of my brighter moments. Alas, it is not always so. Heavily weighs on me at times the burdensome reflection that I cannot honestly say I am confident as to the exact shape of the once-seen, oft-regretted Cube; and in my nightly visions the mysterious precept, "Upward, not Northward", haunts me like a soul-devouring Sphinx. It is part of the martyrdom which I endure for the cause of the Truth that there are seasons of mental weakness, when Cubes and Spheres flit away into the background of scarce-possible existences; when the Land of Three Dimensions seems almost as visionary as the Land of One or None; nay, when even this hard wall that bars me from my freedom, these very tablets on which I am writing, and all the substantial realities of Flatland itself, appear no better than the offspring of a diseased imagination, or the baseless fabric of a dream.

Southwest Scenarios

Politics play part in pups' park proposal

(From January 17, 2002)

RECENTLY THE BULLHEAD CITY ROTARY PARK FINISHED BUILDING A SKATE park for local youth. And from what I have seen, it has been a success for those young folks on small wheels.

But, one of the realities of doing good things for people is, as soon as an organization does something like this, there are other folks who become upset because it wasn't done for them. Bicyclists, who had been using the skate park improperly and had been blamed for some damage to it, complained that no one had built a park for them.

The city has, however, been working with a group of caring folks who are attempting to build a BMX park for bicyclists. When this project is finished, it will help another group of local youths enjoy their free time in Bullhead City.

It will not, however, assist any Pogo Stick aficionados, Hula Hoop hipsters, Yo-yo flippers or spiritual snake dancers. The city leaders should apologize in advance for their slight to these folks.

But our city is moving forward in its attempt to take a bite out of our lack of recreational facilities. The City Parks and Recreation Commission has discussed the development of a dog park. And, oddly enough, the proposal does have a lot of community support.

One dog park supporter proposes the park should be three acres where dogs could run off the leash. She would like to see the area fenced to separate big dogs and little dogs.

I'm not sure we should get involved in any separate-but-equal park areas, canine or not, at this time. Signs that read "no coyotes allowed," "small dogs only" or "you must be this tall to urinate on this tree" could eventually lead to future discrimination lawsuits. However, allowing the petite and plus-sized canines to frolic together could be almost as dangerous as allowing camouflage-fatigue-wearing owners of hunting dogs to mingle with lap dog owners. Those lap dog owners can be pretty mean.

Now, I'm not necessarily against the building of a park for dogs. But I do think the proposal should be thought out thoroughly. For instance: Who's going to design the seats on the swings? And how high should the doors be on the restrooms?

In a *Daily News* story Wednesday, the city parks and rec director pointed out that the Lake Havasu City dog park had a problem with snowbirds taking the doggie bags to use in their RVs. Those must be really large doggie bags.

I would suggest that retired police dogs should probably be hired to handle the security. There's more than just doggie bag theft to worry about. After all, a cat may disguise itself to look like one of those disgusting little yapping dogs that look like walking dryer lint just to enter the park.

Which brings us to another point: To avoid complainers at City Council meetings, should we also develop a cat park, weasel park, ferret park, chicken park or even a nice boa constrictor park (which shouldn't be placed too close to the small dog area)?

Whatever our city leaders decide on this issue is fine with me. We are, after all, in a recreation area and all parks assist in drawing tourists. Perhaps our city could even make a few bucks by selling visiting dog owners special scoops decorated with the printed message, "Bullhead City is piles of fun."

Southwest Scenarios

The commentaries here and in future issues were originally published by *The Mohave Valley Daily News between 1993 & 2013--and* in many ways they apply to today. We are grateful to republish these commentaries written by Darryle Purcell in full and unedited. His own brand of humor and style can deliver insight, provoke thought, and even boil blood.

M-G-M's
Splashy
COLOR BY
TECHNICOLOR
Musical
DANGEROUS WHEN WET
STARRING
ESTHER WILLIAMS
FERNANDO LAMAS
JACK CARSON
CHARLOTTE GREENWOOD
WITH DENISE DARCEL
WILLIAM DEMAREST
DONNA CORCORAN
SEE THE AMAZING "TOM & JERRY" CARTOON SWIMMING SPECTACLE WITH ESTHER!
WRITTEN BY DOROTHY KINGSLEY
MUSIC BY ARTHUR SCHWARTZ
LYRICS BY JOHNNY MERCER
DIRECTED BY CHARLES WALTERS
PRODUCED BY GEORGE WELLS
A METRO-GOLDWYN-MAYER PICTURE

NEW ORIGINAL STORY: HARVEST
BY MURRAY EILAND

PROLOGUE

"So… how did you die?" Liam asked. "I'll tell you mine if you tell me yours."

Two people pondered the meaning of life in the bowels of a sprawling, decrepit complex, starting with their demise. They stood in a dimly lit chamber that seemed to exist beyond the boundaries of time. The air was heavy with a pungent amalgamation of decay and a metallic tang that assaulted their senses with a disconcerting blend of organic putrescence and industrial coldness. Neither said so, but both hoped this was not the afterlife they deserved. This must be something else.

A low hum reverberated amid the gloom, its source hidden in the strange machinery surrounding them. The sound was eerie and hypnotic, a ceaseless reminder of the pulsing energy coursing through the complex. The machinery's purpose remained a vexing enigma, an inscrutable conglomeration of gears, wires, and coils that served a purpose far beyond their comprehension.

A bizarre procession of translucent pods stretched along the chamber's walls, each containing a cold, still body. The forms within were hauntingly beautiful in their lifelessness, their features etched with an otherworldly serenity that spoke of the horrors of their entrapment. The intermittent flickering of the overhead lights cast disjointed patterns across the chamber, conjuring a dance of shadows that played upon the walls like phantoms in a macabre ballet. Each pulse of light offered brief glimpses of the room's features. This interplay of illumination and darkness made the chamber seem as if it existed on the periphery of reality, a place where the laws of physics and perception had been twisted into something unnerving.

Liam stood amid the eerie spectacle, his gaze fixated on the unsettling scene that lay before him. His eyes, once alight with curiosity and vigor, were now filled with a dull weariness. The chamber's eerie grandeur could sap vitality from even the most resolute soul. Beside him was the lean form of a lady, Emily, wearing the same uniform as his. She had silky dark hair framing her pale skin, and her eyes had a similar dullness.

Emily sighed. "To be honest, I don't remember," she confessed in a light voice, ending in a nervous laugh. "I know I did die, though. I just can't remember how." She looked down at her hands, possibly inspecting the half-life they had been brought back to.

With a small sigh that seemed to echo in the chamber's haunting stillness, Liam nodded and continued down the row of pods, looking from face to face and pausing to observe tag after tag. The faces within varied in age, gender, and ethnicity, frozen in expressions from serene to grotesque contortion. The tags, worn and faded, dangled from the pods like somber reminders of lives once lived. The question was, why?

There was more technological advancement here than their familiar world could offer. Maybe they were somewhere else? The pods contained not just bodies but also something else. Lustrous tendrils of luminescent energy moved along the surfaces, casting glows upon the pallid faces within. Intricate arrays of diodes adorned the edges of each pod, their meanings known only to the architects. These symbols seemed to shift and writhe as if alive, etching indiscernible patterns into the air. Liam's breath quickened as he looked around him at the convergence of the mystical and technological, of death and innovation, of the arcane and digital, an unholy alliance that left his senses reeling. He didn't need anyone to tell him how strange it all was. However, he didn't ask a lot of questions about his job in this facility or why he was still alive. To be fair, there was no one to ask. He was an unwilling participant in a story, and he wondered if he really wanted to know more.

Liam paused before a pod. His gloved hands reached for the tag suspended from the side, his eyes focusing on the indiscernible symbols etched onto its surface. His touch was hesitant, as though he was wary of disturbing the dormant inhabitant's slumber. His breath caught in his throat as his gaze shifted to the part of the pod that offered a glimpse into the body's information. The display pulsed with an unnatural luminescence, the data presented in a format that suggested command and control with more regard for a plan than the subject's welfare.

His voice resonated within the chamber's confines as he began to speak. His words punctuated the silence like ripples disturbing a serene pond. "I remember a building collapsing on me and crushing most of my body," he told his companion, his voice carrying a subdued weight as if the very act of recalling the memory was a struggle. There wasn't much to remember. It was all shrouded in an eerie fog that refused to lift. It was as if they were missing crucial pieces of a puzzle they were never meant to solve.

Emily watched with a mix of apprehension and curiosity, her gaze shifting from Liam's contemplative expression to the tag he held. She could see a few characters clearly. "Vincent Blackwood, huh?" she read. "Any idea how he died?"

Liam shook his head, another sigh escaping his lips as they curved into a wry half-smile, a mixture of irony and frustration. "Not a clue. My best guess is he's yet another casualty of the bloody war. Look at his face. He could have been a British soldier. Or a criminal like me. In the end, we're all nobodies. That's why we're here, isn't it?" He turned to Emily, trying on a smile that felt unreal. "No one will come looking for us. We're simply empty vessels. They've given us this half-life, this second chance, but certainly, we need to pay for the privilege someday. I died in 1917. Maybe someone wants me on the front lines."

Emily shook her head as clearly something else was in store for her. She could say nothing. She had no idea what the future might hold. Her gaze swept across the chamber's cool expanse, her eyes a mirror to her inner turmoil, desperately searching for any sign of answers. "The ones who brought us back… they're always watching. I can feel their presence lurking in the shadows." Her tone conveyed a sense of intrusion that seemed to crawl beneath the skin. It was as if the very fabric of the chamber were woven with unseen eyes. And as she spoke, it felt as though the shadows really moved and those eyes were boring into them from dark corners. It was impossible to shake off the feeling. The air seemed to carry an ominous whisper that controlling minds did not want to be heard.

"They're playing some twisted game, that's for sure," Liam muttered, his words carrying an acknowledgment of their powerlessness. His eyes remained fixed on Vincent's face. "Look around you," he continued, gesturing subtly to the row upon row of dormant bodies that lined the chamber's walls, a macabre assembly of half-alive forms trapped within an otherworldly suspension. "They're bringing so many people back; it's like they're building a small half-alive army loyal to them. It could be the Germans. Maybe we're working for the Germans, Emily." His words held a mixture of awe and dread, as though he was grappling with the scene's incomprehensible scope.

Emily's gaze shifted from Vincent to the surrounding pods, each a vessel containing a piece of the puzzle. The notion of an army loyal to unseen puppeteers conjured chilling images, the idea of a legion of the resurrected bound by an inscrutable allegiance. Neither of them said so, but it was hard to keep from thinking religious thoughts at such a time. They silently ran through prayers, begging for forgiveness. Emily placed a hand on Liam's shoulder, causing him to turn to look into her dark eyes gleaming from the pod's eerie light. With a deep resolve, she said, "We don't get a choice, do we? They own us. This is what we are now."

Liam nodded with resignation, acknowledging the task at hand even as shadows of uncertainty loomed overhead. "Well, let's do our job and bring poor Vincent back into the world," he said. His voice bore a semblance of normalcy that stood in stark contrast to the extraordinary circumstances they found themselves in. His gloved hand moved with a steady purpose, his fingers deftly manipulating the lever that would initiate the sequence to release Vincent from his slumber to emerge half-alive into entrapment.

A metallic whirring erupted from the pod as he pushed the lever, a cacophony of buzzing machinery that shattered the chamber's eerie silence. The air seemed charged with an electric tension, anticipation mixing with unease as the body within the pod began its reanimation. The transition was an orchestration of the uncanny, blurring the lines between the natural and the supernatural.

Vincent's naked form was connected to the chamber's high-tech tendrils within the pod by a network of vine-like tubes that snaked around his body. These tubes were like conduits of life, their intricate patterns speaking of a fusion of the organic and inorganic. And as the body stirred, the vines seemed to be alive, their sinuous movements reminding Liam and Emily of writhing serpents.

And then, as the last vine relinquished its hold, Vincent's body drew its first breath. The sound was a profound echo in the chamber, a signal that life had been reclaimed from the clutches of the arcane. His eyes fluttered open, and Liam said, "Welcome back to life, Vincent Blackwood."

CHAPTER 1

From a calm, dreamless sleep, the real world was like a nightmare. His senses were ambushed. The unexpected onslaught of noise tore through the fabric of his reality and punctured his consciousness.

Once a steady metronome of life, Vincent's heart pounded in his chest like a captive creature seeking escape. It was a frenetic drumbeat matching the cadence of distant artillery fire that rumbled through the air like the footfalls of some monstrous titan. He clutched his rifle, his hands slick with sweat and trembling with a mix of fear and adrenaline. The deafening roar of cannonades echoed through the labyrinth of trenches, where life clung precariously to the edge of oblivion. The ground seemed to convulse with each detonation, sending tremors through the earth that reverberated through Vincent's bones. Each breath he took was a testament to the fragility of existence in the shadow of war's relentless appetite.

Heart pounding in his ears, Vincent looked to his side where his comrades in arms fought in desperate determination. Their faces reflected his inner turmoil — eyes wide with the shock of their situation. Their expressions were etched with the grim conviction of those who had stared into the abyss without a chance to blink. The sun, a distant red orb, cast its dying light upon the battlefield, painting the scene with an ethereal glow that only accentuated the horrors it revealed.

Bodies, friend and foe, lay motionless, strewn over the battlefield as if a part of the burnt earth. The soil seemed stained with sorrow and soaked with sacrifice, as though *the land had absorbed the anguish of countless lives cut short. The cries of wounded souls pierced the evening air in a chorus of agony in the name of life or a little more time, contrasting with the serene backdrop of the descending sun.*

As the light waned, casting elongated shadows across the blood-soaked ground, the boundary between the living and the dead blurred. The battlefield was a tapestry woven with despair. Each thread was a reminder of humanity's capacity for destruction. Vincent's heart continued its frenzied rhythm as he clung to his rifle like a talisman against the encroaching darkness.

Bullets traveled overhead, and time seemed to lose all meaning. Vincent's breath came in ragged bursts. He tried to ground himself into the battlefield for just a bit more shelter, taking his attention off the burning in his arm and the throbbing in his head. He barely had the chance to take aim before he was sending bullets out. He was weak and wounded, and every sound felt like it was hammering a nail into his ears.

Yet, he still fought to anchor himself, to channel his focus beyond the inferno of sensations that engulfed him. He clung to the rifle like a lifeline, grim determination eclipsing the tremors that wracked his body. His finger squeezed the trigger, unleashing bullets in a desperate staccato rhythm. Each shot was a testament to his willpower, an act of defiance against his weakness and the enemy's relentless onslaught.

Suddenly, Vincent felt a searing pain pierce his chest, the cruel kiss of a bullet finding its mark. The world around him blurred, his senses faltering as the edges of his vision darkened. He crumpled like a marionette with severed strings as his body collapsed into the pit of mud and debris. He found breathing to be a strenuous activity. He smiled as he realized it would soon be over. The rising moon would light the way to the next world.

The ground beneath him was unyielding, the earth itself a witness to his mortality. The battle raged on around him, an unstoppable force that had swept him into its relentless current. Blood pooled around him, the warm life force seeping from his body into the unforgiving soil. He lay there, a solitary figure abandoned amid the chaos.

Voices and motion surrounded him, but they were distant and distorted echoes in his fading consciousness. His senses were numbing, and the cold hands of oblivion beckoned with a chilling embrace. The edges of his awareness began to blur, the realm of the living slipping further from his grasp. He was laughing now, but his body did not respond. In many ways, he was happy to leave the battle.

He remembered the darkening evening sky and the fact that he was very much dead.

Then, a light pierced his vision, and he drew a breath. "Welcome back to life, Vincent Blackwood," a strange voice said. In the deepest part of his mind, he hoped to see angels, but from the first words he heard, he knew something was horribly wrong.

Vincent stood before a mirror, the soft glow of morning light casting a gentle warmth on his face. His reflection stared back at him from the mirror's silvery surface. The form that met his gaze was his own, yet it seemed like a distant echo of the past, a portrait of a man he was no longer certain he recognized.

Once vibrant and alive, his eyes seemed to have lost their gleam. Now, they held a somberness that reflected the weight of his experiences. He ran a hand through his tousled, dark hair and let his fingers travel downward, settling upon his bare chest. Vincent swallowed. The sensation was grounding – a tactile confirmation of his existence in a reality that felt unreal. Vincent's heart pulsed beneath his touch, the rhythm bearing witness to his inexplicable continuity.

It didn't matter how long he stood looking at his reflection and the gentle arcs that formed his being. It didn't matter how many times his mind repainted the memory of his last moments in the war. There was nothing there. No proof of the death he remembered as vividly as the meal he ate last night.

He gazed into his eyes, searching for answers that remained maddeningly elusive. He knew his body should have been marked by the bullet that had ended his life. It *had* ended his life, he was sure. Yet, there was no visible trace of the fatal wound. There should have been a mark - a scar, a wound - something to bear witness to that fatal encounter. The absence of such evidence was a haunting puzzle. His fingers lightly brushed over the smooth expanse of his skin, jaws clenching in confusion. His chest rose and fell with each steadied breath, proof that he was a living and breathing thing. But every breath felt like a fraud. Even worse, he felt that somehow someone was cheating him out of what he had earned.

He shook his head, attempting to dispel the cloud of confusion that clung to his thoughts like a persistent mist. He turned his focus to the mundane task of buttoning up his shirt. The memory of his death and subsequent rebirth had remained a relentless specter in his mind for the past year. He sighed, the sound carrying a mixture of resignation and determination. The passage of time had done little to quell the echoes of his mortality, but it had granted him perspective. He understood, on some level, that obsessively rehashing his death would yield nothing. His fingers moved with practiced ease as he fastened the last button, his shirt a shield against the outside world and the labyrinth of his thoughts.

Vincent cast a final gaze at his reflection before he tore his attention away. Enough time had gone by for him to know that staring at his body did not help. He had a job to attend to. He crossed the room to gather his belongings and shrugged on his coat, a familiar embrace that offered both comfort and concealment. He stepped out of his room at the Ivy Inn with purposeful strides, the floorboards creaking under his weight.

Vincent's hand moved with practiced ease, locking his door with a firm twist of the key. The echo of the bolt sliding into place was a reassuring reminder of his solitude. It was a boundary he could control in a world where so much remained beyond his grasp. The ambient hush enveloped him as he stepped into the dimly lit hallway, a shroud of quiet that held its own solace.

However, the serenity was abruptly shattered by the intrusion of raised voices, a discordant sound that punctuated the stillness. The source of the commotion was from one of the nearby rooms. A sliver of curiosity stirred within him, an impulse to peer behind the curtains of this private drama. But experience and self-preservation acted as swift restraints, a reminder that interference in the affairs of others often yielded consequences that were best avoided.

His steps were short and restrained as he was suspended between the pull of curiosity and the wisdom of discretion. However, as he passed the slightly ajar door, his peripheral vision caught a glimpse of the scene within – a man, his features twisted with anger, loomed over a young woman. Vincent's gaze shifted to the figure on the receiving end of the man's ire, and her face was familiar. He recognized her as one of the whores who worked in the inn. She had glistening dark skin and tightly packed hair, and at this moment, she was sparsely dressed.

The tableau before him was a snapshot of vulnerability. The tension in the room was palpable, like a storm on the verge of breaking. The man's hand was raised, ready to strike. Vincent's instincts warred within him, a desire to intervene clashing with the knowledge that such actions often invited repercussions far beyond his control. He hesitated, his gut twisting with unease, and his hands balled into fists. He made eye contact with the lady, and within that fleeting connection, he saw a flicker of terror in her face.

Then, the man's gaze shifted, catching Vincent's lingering presence by the door. Their eyes met, a silent exchange charged with an unspoken challenge. In that instant, Vincent was acutely aware of the crossroads he stood upon - the choice between involvement and detachment. Moreover, the ones he owed his living to had given him explicit orders to remain unnoticed.

With a heavy sigh, Vincent decided to mind his own business, and he continued down the hallway, trying to drown out the commotion behind him. The weight of his decision settled upon his shoulders, each step a reminder of the boundaries he had chosen to uphold. As he walked, his heart carried a mixture of empathy and resignation. The turmoil behind the slightly open door receded into the background.

He descended the stairs to the inn's common area, where the soft murmur of conversation and clinking of glasses filled the air. The common area bore witness to the comings and goings of travelers and those who called the inn a temporary home. The bar, the room's focal point, beckoned with its promise of solace and connection. Polished wood and tarnished brass gleamed in the ambient light, the surface bearing the marks of countless patrons who had leaned upon it for respite. The bartender, a grizzled man with a knowing smile, greeted him warmly.

"Damn, you don't look the tiniest bit drunk or hung over after all the drinking last night. Back for another round, Vincent?" he asked, wiping a glass with a cloth.

Vincent nodded and took a seat at the bar. "Just one, James," he replied, his voice tinged with weariness. He had a grim task before him today and would need something to take the edge off. It wasn't as if the drink could really do anything to him.

As the hours waned and the city surrendered to the night's embrace, the familiar rhythm of life transformed into an altogether different cadence. The rain, a melancholic companion to the darkness, descended in a gentle drizzle that painted the streets with shimmering streaks of silver. Like a sentinel amid the obscurity, Vincent lingered in a shadowed corner. The darkness did much to conceal his presence while he watched a man hurriedly move towards an alleyway, his feet clattering over the cobblestones.

Despite the darkness, his sight was good enough to make out his target's figure. Enhanced vision was one of the many changes in his body since he returned. His gaze was a piercing lance that cut through the rain-swept air, his eyes trained on the ebb and flow of the city's secrets.

He didn't take his eyes off the man he had spent most of the day stalking. As he stepped across the street, he soon realized his target was not alone. Now, two figures were in the alleyway, speaking in hushed urgency as the rain steadily increased. They were too far for Vincent to hear their words, and frankly, he didn't care. It would change nothing. The target would die. That was what he was tasked to do.

He stepped out from the shadows, revealing himself. His initial target, a known criminal with a worn-out face and tattered coat, glanced over his shoulder to see Vincent's form. He sensed the danger before his companion, who didn't seem to notice Vincent walking over.

"What do you want? Go mind your business," the criminal said in an overblown and futile attempt to sound intimidating. Vincent had already noticed the man reaching for a small handgun, and his fingers fell on the cold hilt of his concealed blade. The gentle chill that touch gave him made his heart pound for a moment, filling him with adrenaline. He quickly pushed any flicker of hesitation away.

Before the man could pull the trigger, Vincent lunged forward, covering the distance between them at inhuman speed. As he emerged, Vincent's gaze locked with the man's, and he saw a flicker of fear and confusion. There was an attempt to fight back, but Vincent was quick and decisive. In one swift motion, his blade found its mark with deadly accuracy. The man's grip on the gun fell away as he shook and coughed up blood. He hit the wet ground moments later.

Vincent's attention shifted towards the younger man who had pulled his gun. Vincent felt he could hear every drop of rain hitting the ground and every one of his next victim's breaths.

The young man's voice wavered as he struggled to maintain a semblance of composure. "Don't come any closer," he stammered, his voice a fragile shield against the uncertainty looming before him. Vincent took a measured step forward, his presence a manifestation of inexorable purpose. The alleyway seemed to constrict around them, the walls closing in like the pages of a story reaching its climactic moment. The young man's voice, now amplified by desperation, shattered the fragile equilibrium holding them suspended in the shadows. "I said, don't!" he yelled, his voice bouncing off the alley walls. Vincent's steady gaze met the young man's eyes. He refused to heed the words and...

Bang!

The bullet found its mark, striking Vincent's arm with a force that reverberated through his being. Suddenly, Vincent was back in the battlefield pit, the loud noises banging in his mind and pain searing through him. Except this time, it was different. The pain that should have consumed him began to recede, replaced by a strange sensation of flesh knitting together. His healing factor was so rapid he barely lost any blood.

Vincent's voice, which was steady in the middle of all the rain and tension, held a somber note as he addressed the young man whose life had been irrevocably altered by the single pull of a trigger. "You shouldn't have done that, mate," he said. And then, he delivered his knife to the terrified man's chest. The young man went limp and collapsed on the ground.

The blood of the two dead men began to mingle with the rain that now fell harder, also washing blood off the knife in Vincent's hand. He watched the bodies for a moment longer before turning around and disappearing back into the shadows, making his way to the Ivy Inn. The killing was his only job. He didn't really know what happened afterward, only that the rain was a perfect cover. It muffled sounds and cleansed evidence.

The memory of the killing burned into Vincent's mind as he continued toward the less crowded part of town. Then, he heard a strained groan from a corner. Instinctively, he turned to his side to see a figure in an alleyway. A man was sitting on the ground, back against the wall, his wrist deeply cut while he held a small knife in his other hand.

Vincent recognized the face immediately. He couldn't have been past his forties, with a beard the same color as his blonde hair. It was the very man who had been hitting the prostitute earlier that day. The man looked up at Vincent as his wrist continued to drain blood. He had a desperate plea in his eyes while he struggled to get words out.

A frown claimed Vincent's features. He figured this man hadn't slit his own wrist. His gaze shifted to the Ivy Inn just a few blocks down the street, bustling with life. Then, his eyes fell upon a window leading to a lit room where the silhouette of a woman appeared, looking directly at them. Despite the distance, he locked eyes with the lady before looking at the street before him. In his mind, he envisaged himself back on the battlefield, perceiving only that which could be a threat.

He didn't spare another look at the man before continuing his walk.

ISABELLA SHUT HER CURTAIN WITH A DISSATISFIED FROWN AS SHE TURNED BACK toward her room. The room was dimly lit by a single flickering candle, its feeble glow casting long shadows on the walls. The candle's waxy scent mingled with the fragrance of dried flowers that adorned a vase on a nearby shelf. Isabella's dresser stood against one wall, an intricately carved piece that looked like it had seen better years. Her friend Eliza sat before the dresser, applying too much makeup. The vanity mirror reflected her intent gaze and captured her hand's carefulstrokes as she worked to enhance her features.

Isabella's expression quickly grew inquisitive as she sat carefully at the edge of her bed. "What do you know about the strange man that lurks around the inn? He's huge, quiet, and quite handsome," she said, letting her voice sound as polished as the rich folks she often encountered. "He looks like he could have been a soldier."

Eliza raised an eyebrow, a faint smirk playing at the corner of her lips. Isabella was already rolling her eyes at the implication she knew was growing in her friend's mind. "You mean the one with the haunted eyes? Vincent is the name he uses," she said, a heavy dose of amusement in her voice. "He's a peculiar one, that's for sure. Keeps to himself and hardly speaks to anyone. Saw him chug a dozen cups of beer last night, and he barely batted an eye. He doesn't even seem touched by my advances. I think he might be a poof."

Isabella knew she could trust Eliza to deliver information. "You think he's trouble?" There was a curious whisper in her tone now as her eyelashes fluttered and her eyes gleamed in curiosity.

Eliza shrugged nonchalantly. "Could be. Hard to tell with people like him," she said, her voice tinged with a knowing edge. One thing was for certain: he was hiding something. Isabella saw the way he reacted to seeing the man she had murdered in the alleyway. Though, to be fair, she hadn't been quite thorough with her kill. But he was barely moved, and he caught her looking.

They fell into a moment of silence, the only sound filling the room being the distant murmur of voices from the common area downstairs.

"Another body found tonight," Eliza mumbled, her eyes dark with unease.

Isabella nodded solemnly. "It seems like it's happening more and more lately. Poor souls, all of 'em," she said, mustering as much sympathy as she could in her tone.

Eliza's demeanor shifted. Her gaze became momentarily distant as if revisiting a memory that had left an indelible mark on her. "You know," she started, her voice trembling ever so slightly. "I found a dead body in the street just two weeks ago."

The memory seemed to engulf Eliza. Her face was a canvas of distress. When she continued to speak, her voice was a whisper, yet it carried the weight of a story that was still too chilling to fully articulate. The figure she found had been left contorted on the cold cobblestones, its form twisted in angles so unnatural it spoke of violence and a brutal end. "I ran into the inn to tell someone, but by the time I returned, the body had disappeared."

Eliza shivered. She wrapped her arms around herself as if seeking comfort and protection from the memory she was sharing. "I think the most disturbing part is not the murders, it's the fact that the bodies go missing afterward. It's like someone is collecting them. I hope whoever's doing this is caught soon. It's not safe out there anymore," she said, her tone tinged with a mixture of disbelief and dread.

Isabella moved back toward the window, looking through the small crack in the curtain as the rain gently pattered against the glass. Eliza continued, "Bloody war has ruined us all. Look at our city, Izzy; it's a dark place now. I hear stuff about a group of criminals taking out people who don't bend to their will. Some say they're Germans," her words held a note of incredulity, disbelief that such darkness could permeate the world. That even after the war had officially ended, its echoes could continue to reverberate.

"It's 1919, for Christ's sake. Things should be better," Eliza said.

"And they will be," said Isabella, almost dismissively. "Just a little while longer, I promise, and we won't have to do this anymore." Her teeth clenched, and her fingers moved to her cheek where there should have been a bruise from this morning. There was no mark there.

"Anyway, my Duke is coming this evening. Wouldn't want to keep him waiting," Eliza said with a tinge of excitement as she got to her feet and kissed Isabella goodbye before leaving the room. Isabella smiled as her friend shut the door behind her, her thoughts somewhere else entirely.

Her mind played the same scene from several days ago over and over. As Isabella walked down the hall, she had locked eyes with the strange man as he walked toward his room. They were dark, dead eyes, the eyes of a man who had seen death many times. Isabella accidentally bumped into him. As he turned, pushing back his coat in response to the collision, a gleam of light revealed the hilt of a blade concealed within his coat. Who uses a knife? Someone who is sure they can move faster than a bullet.

Isabella straightened, alert, as she watched him continue to his room. As Vincent shut his door, the sound reverberated like a drumbeat in Isabella's ears. Her heart quickened, and a pulse of adrenaline coursed through her veins. Isabella moved quickly to her room and swiftly closed her door behind her.

Inside the sanctuary of her room, she paused, her back pressed against the door. Her breaths were deep and steadying in a conscious effort to restore her equilibrium. The revelation had been a jolt to her senses, and the knife's image lingered in her mind's eye. Isabella took a final deep breath, her resolve steeling itself against currents of uncertainty. The rain outside continued its gentle patter against the window, a rhythm that echoed the palpitations of her heart.

It was drizzling again.

Isabella's fists were burning as she pounded on Vincent's door. She felt warm tears streaming out of her eyes. "I know you're in there, Vincent Blackwood," she seethed bitterly. Eventually, the imposingly tall man opened the door, standing before her with a less-than-pleased look. The contours of his chest and shoulders were bathed in the soft light of the hallway and further accentuated the powerful presence he exuded. She didn't give him a chance to say anything before she pointed a finger in his face, saying, "Did you do anything to her? Did you touch her?" There was such a deadly dose of venom in her tone that even Vincent took a step backward.

"Who the hell are you?" he said, frowning.

"Tell me now, did they pay you to kill her too?" she said, a croak breaking through her voice as she fought to hold back tears.

Vincent massaged his forehead. It was evident how much he was struggling to rein in his annoyance, but Isabella didn't care; she'd punch right through his face if she had to. "What are you talking about?" he demanded.

"I know what you are. Who you are. Who you work for. Because we work for the same person. People. Doesn't matter," she said, spitting out her discovery from two days ago. She had seen him collecting a parcel of money down in the common area from the same person who delivered her payment. But that was beyond irrelevant right now. "So, now I ask you, what have you done with her?" Isabella straightened and swallowed her tears. "Did you kill her?"

"Who?" Vincent all but growled. But he did not scare Isabella.

She moved closer, one hand balled into a fist and the other tightly squeezing her knife. She looked him squarely in the face, ready to pull out the knife and take it to his throat. "Eliza." To say the name made tears fall from her eyes, but she controlled the rest of her emotions. Let the tears roll down; she wasn't going to break before him. "She left here last night, and she's gone. Gone. So, tell me, did you kill her? Huh? Were you paid to do it like you were paid to kill the others?"

Vincent looked around the hallway for a minute, then he drew Isabella into his room. The air in Vincent's room seemed to thicken with tension as Isabella's accusation hung heavily between them. He shut the door behind her and said, "I did not kill anyone. If your friend is missing, maybe you should go to the police."

Isabella scoffed a laugh and wiped the tears off her face. "It seems like there is no brain in that big head of yours," she said. "No police in this city will investigate a missing ivy. We're just whores and prostitutes to them. No one cares about people like us." Then she added bitterly, "People who look like us."

The flickering candlelight in Vincent's room cast a glow upon Isabella's glistening dark skin. Every contour, every nuance of her emotions was illuminated in the intimate embrace of the dimly lit space.

Vincent sighed and cussed under his breath. "Have you ever thought that maybe, just maybe, we are not the only two killers in this city?" he said.

Isabella had indeed thought of that, and that had scared her. It scared her so terribly that her anger dissolved completely. "Then you have to help me find her," she said meekly, sighing and trying to control her breath. "Please. She's all I've got. I know you probably have better things to do, but I need her."

Vincent hesitated for a moment. He just stared at her for a few seconds as though he was mustering the energy to say "No" and just send her away. She didn't know what made Vincent grumble, "Fine. Just let me get a coat and hat."

Isabella did her best to offer all the information she had. Eliza had been called upon by a veteran of a much earlier war. He was an old man who had lost his leg in the war. He was the kind of man most women like them would rather not have as a client, but he paid handsomely for 'exotic' women, so Eliza had thought, 'Why not?' She had gone last night when Isabella was away. Now, she was gone. And no one else seemed to care.

An hour went by as they moved in the light rain, following the path that led to the house Eliza had gone to and searching for any sign of her. The rain's rhythm, a constant drumbeat on the cobblestone streets, seemed to echo the tumultuous emotions that coursed through the hearts of those who were out, those who braved its relentless assault. Isabella and Vincent's clothes clung to their bodies, but they pressed forward. She hated to admit it, but Isabella knew there was a good chance of them finding her body down an alley. A thick blanket of darkness shrouded the city as the night settled in and the rain intensified. It became a relentless downpour, as though the heavens themselves wept for the city's suffering.

"We should probably go back," said Vincent.

Isabella shook her head. "We can still find her," she said. There was a gruff shift in Vincent's demeanor, and she rolled her eyes. "It's not like anything can harm us, is it?"

"You have a point," said Vincent.

"Have you figured out who we work for?" she asked as they moved down an alley underneath a corner that offered some small protection from the rain. The narrow alleyway was a passage many in the city avoided because it had been the site of a terrible massacre during the war. Its path was slick with rain and dark markings that could have been made by blood, oil, or smoke. Its walls, towering on either side, were marred by bullet holes and gouges where shrapnel had taken out larger portions of rock.

Vincent shrugged beside her. "Just some criminals, I reckon. They said they fixed me up after the war with some advanced medical treatment. Could have sworn I was dead, though," he said. "You?"

"I know I was dead, for sure. Some men, well, soldiers, as the war came to an end… let's just say they broke my body and cast me aside. Sometimes, I can still feel them bashing my head in to keep me still while they did their business. Then, I woke up in some strange place. I don't remember much. I just know that now, I barely feel pain and heal fast," she said. "And I kind of figured…" Her voice trailed to a stop as her words got stuck in her throat. Isabella's heart pounded in her chest as she and Vincent stood side by side, hidden in the shadows of the alleyway, their eyes fixed on the lifeless body at their feet.

Isabella knew that small, beautiful face wrapped in smooth, dark skin. She knew that lean body far too well. She tried reaching for words, but nothing came out.

Eliza's lifeless form lay sprawled on the ground. Her once-vibrant eyes were now vacant, staring into the abyss. Her clothes were drenched and disheveled. Isabella's breath caught in her throat. A gut-wrenching sob threatened to escape but remained imprisoned by the suffocating grip of her despair. Her trembling fingers reached out as if to grasp a fading thread of hope, only to be met with the cold, unyielding reality of death. Tears welled in Isabella's eyes, mingling with the rain that now fell in torrents. Eliza, her dear friend, a sweet, kind soul, was truly gone.

"I'm sorry," Vincent said as Isabella still failed to find her voice. So many thoughts, words, and questions swirled in her mind, but nothing fell upon the tip of her tongue.

Vincent suddenly turned, and then Isabella heard the faint sound of movement nearby. They were not alone. Their eyes locked, sharing an unspoken understanding that they needed to stay and find out who or what was coming for the body. They needed to confront the unknown and unravel the mysteries that lurked in the darkness.

Cautiously, they rushed further into the alley and pressed themselves against the cold, damp walls, peering around the corner. The alley, once a place of secrets and shadows, now served as their refuge and vantage point. They spotted a figure approaching in the distance through the veil of rain and mist, a specter emerging from the city's depths. Isabella felt her breathing begin to betray her. She was trembling. A warm hand slipped into hers, and she saw Vincent's nod of encouragement, a confirmation that she was not alone. She swallowed and stayed still, watching.

The figure was humanoid in shape, but there was something otherworldly about it, like an aura of sinister grace that set it apart from anything she had seen before. As it drew closer, she could see it was not alone. The humanoid forms started branching, literally, though she couldn't make out too much in the darkness. She noticed their luminous eyes glowing with an otherworldly light. It sent shivers down her spine.

Isabella exchanged a bewildered glance with Vincent as they watched the beings lift Eliza's lifeless form into their arms. It took five of them to carry her body, and they released eerie sounds that sounded like they came from far away despite how close they were.

The creatures began to walk out of the alleyway. Isabella's rage returned. If she had failed to protect her friend, she was not going to fail at giving her a proper burial, too. She could not let them take her body. "We should follow," she whispered. Vincent nodded. They followed at a safe distance, their senses on high alert. And then…

The humanoid figures were gone.

The exact moment they came out of the alleyway into the street, they were suddenly gone. Isabella looked all around, and her eyes fell on Vincent to see the same confused look on his face. They were gone, and so was Eliza.

"What the hell are we dealing with?" she asked, the fear evident in her voice.

Vincent shifted uncomfortably in the dimly lit room, his gaze fixed on the worn spot on the faded wallpaper. There was a tension in the room so palpable it hung in the air like a heavy, suffocating fog. He could feel Isabella's restless energy filling the space. She paced back and forth, creating a discordant rhythm against the creaking floorboards while her voice held a mix of frustration and disbelief.

"Did you see that, Vincent?" Her voice was sharp, her words punctuated by exasperation. "They just… disappeared, like smoke in the wind. One moment, they were there, and the next… gone."

Vincent nodded, still avoiding her gaze. He focused on the sound of her voice and the cadence of her words as he wrestled with his thoughts. He couldn't deny what they had witnessed. Isabella's words reverberated in his mind, and he grappled with the unsettling truth they held. Those creatures, whatever they were, had simply evaporated into thin air along with Eliza's body. He remembered their vine-like arms with what looked like leaves upon them stretching to wrap around the dead body and the way they moved with their root-like legs. Not human, definitely. They seemed to be mimicking humans. He could not ignore a gnawing feeling that they were not of this world, that their presence in the city was an aberration that defied explanation.

"Yeah," he finally replied, his voice low and measured. "I saw it too."

Isabella paused in her pacing, her gaze settling on him for a moment before she turned her attention back to the task of peeling off her wet clothes. Vincent's cheeks reddened, and he quickly averted his eyes, his discomfort growing. She did not seem to mind that he was there as she hurriedly undressed. It was as though this was all too normal to her. He knew he should not be staring, but he couldn't help the fleeting glances that betrayed his curiosity. Even with those brief glimpses, he could not help but be captivated by her naked body – the soft curves of her breasts and the ridges of her abdomen just below. He looked away when he realized he had been staring for longer than a second, a sense of impropriety washing over him. This was neither the time nor the place for such thoughts.

"We need to figure this out," Isabella continued, her tone determined as she put on some dry clothes. "These things… they're not right. And Eliza… damn it, Vincent, they took her! Maybe we should report this to the police or something."

"And say what? We found aliens in an alleyway, and they just disappeared?"

"You think they're aliens? Besides the point, anyway. Maybe the army, though. You were a soldier; maybe you have some people you can tell. There has to be someone you can talk to."

Vincent clenched his fists at her words. "I am not a soldier; I am a murderer. I was given a pardon in exchange for fighting in the war, and I died," he said before he could stop himself. His words were a raw confession, uttered with a bitterness that cut to the core. "And now, I'm a murderer again who could be working for these aliens who seem to be harvesting bodies." It was the same thing everywhere, and he hated it. The horrors of war and the specter of death had been his constant companions, refusing to release their grip on his consciousness. He might have killed someone once, but that did not give everyone else the right to make him a soldier or a murderer. And these creatures were doing just that.

"Sorry," Isabella said.

He nodded and sighed. "We will find out what's happening, Isabella."

Isabella paused in her movements, her eyes locking onto his with a mixture of frustration and gratitude. Vincent met her gaze, a silent understanding passing between them. They'd known each other just a few hours, but this commitment to uncover the truth drew them very close.

Vincent's attempt to regain his composure was evident, his gaze shifting briefly to the rain-streaked window. The window's glass was distorted by rivulets of water, making it impossible to see anything. Still, he sought solace in the external world as a momentary distraction from the lingering tension in the room and Isabella's half-naked form. Though his eyes may have strayed for a moment, he was determined to maintain his focus on their investigation.

"We should keep looking into it," he finally spoke, his voice steadier than before. "Find out more about those… things." He couldn't bring himself to say the word 'aliens' again as if saying it aloud might somehow make their existence more real and terrifying.

"And we know there may be many more people out there like us working for them. We can find them." His words held an unspoken promise of unity, a recognition that they were not alone in their struggle.

Isabella nodded, a stubborn glint in her eyes. "You're right. Let's not waste any more time. We can start with the man who hands us our pay. He's coming tomorrow morning to pay me for another kill. Be there."

THE IVY INN'S COMMON AREA WAS ALIVE WITH SUBDUED CONVERSATIONS AND glasses clinking. It was an oasis of life amid the shadows and secrets that clung to the city outside. Isabella sat poised at a corner table. Her eyes were like sentinels, meticulously scanning the room. She sat bathed in the soft morning light that filtered through the windows, its gentle warmth casting a subtle glow upon her features. Vincent remained an enigmatic figure in the seat behind her, his form cloaked by a hat worn low and glasses that concealed most of his face. Isabella had insisted on the disguise. It was a precaution against unwanted attention or recognition. Despite his distaste for such measures, he begrudgingly accepted the necessity of anonymity in their ongoing pursuit.

"So, I found someone," Isabella said suddenly, leaning her head back so he could hear while also acting like she wasn't speaking to him and was just scanning the room, recounting a passing thought. "Another prostitute at an inn by the docks. Same work as us. She also remembers dying. Drowning actually. And she knows some brothers who do the same work as us."

"How did you get your information so fast?" grunted Vincent. His curiosity and skepticism were both evident in his tone.

He could imagine the proud smile she wore as she declared confidently, "I'm an ivy. Do not underestimate a woman or a whore. Information is currency here. Just needed to ask the right people the right questions." Her words were a stark reminder that in the dark heart of the city, knowledge was power, and she wielded it with skill and precision.

Vincent thought for a minute. "Can these people bring the dead back to life?" he finally voiced his thoughts, his words carrying a weight of uncertainty. "I mean, me, you, and the person you found… is that what they do with the bodies?"

Isabella countered his hypothesis with logic. "I thought so too, but it just doesn't make sense for them to bring dead people back to life only to then have them kill more people. And then what? Will they bring those ones back to life, too? I don't get it," she said.

Vincent nodded in reluctant agreement, sharing her frustration at their whole situation. He hated how much they didn't know. "I don't get it either," he admitted as he let a sense of helplessness wash over him. He got into position by the bar. It was a strategically chosen position, with enough distance not to get noticed when their employer came but still good enough for him to see and hear all that was occurring.

Minutes later, the door creaked open, and a man stepped into the room. His gaze remained lowered in a deliberate attempt to avoid drawing any unnecessary attention to himself. He was barely middle-aged but walked with the agility of a man twice his age. His eyes glowered around the room before landing on Isabella. Vincent dropped his head quickly. He knew the man as Liam, an annoying talker who always looked at his face strangely during their meet-ups. He made his way cautiously toward Isabella, wearing a nervous smile that didn't quite reach his eyes.

"Isabella, my dear," Liam greeted, taking a seat across from her. "You've been doing good work for us, as always."

Isabella responded with a curt nod, maintaining an air of professionalism as she accepted the small bundle of money. With practiced ease, she concealed the payment and allowed her fingers to drum lightly on the table's surface. The arrival of a bartender with their drinks provided a momentary distraction.

"So, Liam," began Isabella as she took a sip of her drink. Her tone was of casual interest, but her words were tinged with intrigue. "I've been wondering… who are these people we're supposed to get rid of? I mean, they're just regular folk, right? Why do they need to be… you know?"

Vincent observed the role Isabella had chosen to play. It was an inviting yet inconspicuous persona. It was the kind of tactic that could allow them to glean information while remaining unassuming. He was glad that, in this case, it appeared to be working with Liam.

"Ah, Isabella, you don't need to concern yourself with the details. They're just a nuisance, that's all. People who have crossed the wrong crowd, that's why they need to be dealt with," he said after taking a sip of his booze. Vincent had noticed something. Liam's response, while evasive, shed a sliver of light on their mysterious employers and their motivations. The people they killed were often criminals or generally bad people, not that that made it justifiable. Their orders were usually simple, too, and this simplicity was another unsettling aspect. They killed and left the scene. Then, the bodies went missing.

Isabella's eyes narrowed, her acting skills sharpening as she pushed further. "But Liam, they're not just regular folk. I've seen things, strange things. Tell me the truth, or I'll go to the police," she said, keeping her voice low in a threatening whisper and letting the threat glaze her tone.

The threat hung in the air. Liam's face paled noticeably, his discomfort evident as he shifted uneasily in his seat. He appeared cornered and on the verge of capitulating to Isabella's demands. Just as Liam was about to make his escape, Vincent smoothly slid off his stool and stood in front of him, his demeanor unwavering and resolute. "You won't be going anywhere, Liam," he stated firmly, his gaze locked on the man before them. He kept his face stern and his eyes narrow with determination. Liam's eyes widened in recognition as he glanced between Isabella and Vincent.

"You. Vincent. What is this?" he demanded. His voice trembled with a mixture of fear and confusion.

"I'd keep my voice low and sit down if I were you," Vincent advised coolly. He maintained his composed and calculated demeanor. "We have questions, and we expect answers," he said, the implicit threat of exposure hanging in the air. The weight of their collective intent pressed upon Liam, compelling him to heed Vincent's counsel.

Isabella, unyielding in her pursuit of answers, pressed forward with her own questioning. "Tell us about the aliens," she demanded, her voice firm. Liam's face immediately contorted with desperation, his jaw quivering in response to Isabella's words. "They're the ones who brought us back, aren't they? And the ones behind these killings."

Vincent and Isabella looked at each other. The truth, long concealed in the shadows, now hovered on the precipice of revelation. Liam's silence and his subsequent confession would help them understand the sinister forces that had intertwined themselves with their lives.

Liam's hesitation was palpable, evident in the way his lips slightly parted as he considered his response. His gaze shifted between Isabella and Vincent, a battle of secrets playing out in the depths of his eyes. "I don't think you really want the answers you're looking for," he said as he let his gaze fall upon Vincent.

Vincent remained steadfast, his determination unwavering as he countered Liam's reluctance. "Try us," he said.

Liam's internal struggle was apparent as he clenched his jaw and ran his fingers through his disheveled hair. A curse slipped from his lips as he downed a large gulp of his drink, his internal conflict driving him to a reluctant decision. "Fine. Not here," he said, getting to his feet. "Come with me." Vincent and Isabella exchanged a meaningful look before they agreed without a word to each other. Of course, they were both armed in case anything happened, and their unique ability to heal quickly was at their disposal. They were prepared for whatever revelations lay ahead.

As they ventured further from the inn, the morning sun bathed the city's cobbled streets in a gentle, warming glow. Their journey led them through a labyrinth of narrow alleyways, of which there was no shortage in the city.

Liam, who led the way, continued to divulge their grim reality. "The thing is, not everyone who was brought back came with intact memories. The ones like that are easily suggestible," he explained.

Isabella, her determination undeterred, responded with a biting retort. "You mean easier to brainwash," she interjected, her dress swaying with a certain grace as she walked. Each step they took echoed their relentless pursuit of answers.

Liam shrugged. "Does it really matter? Is your life really yours if it's given after death?" If he expected an answer, he didn't get one. "However, there are also people like you and Vincent who remember way too much about their past lives and are put to use. To work. The only problem being you're not so easy to bend," he said. "You don't think you're the first to ask questions or figure things out, do you?"

They arrived at a disused warehouse. It loomed before them, a testament to a once-grand architectural marvel now marred by the scars of war and time's relentless march. Vincent's brows furrowed as he took in the sight, his instincts tingling with unease. The decrepit structure had the potential to be a trap. Bringing them here could easily be a sinister ploy to ensnare them in a dangerous game. He cast a wary gaze at the warehouse, half-expecting the shadows to come alive and gut them.

Isabella's scrutiny of the warehouse mirrored his. Her gaze was sharp and vigilant as she assessed every nook and cranny of the building. The ominous aura that enveloped the warehouse did not escape her notice.

"What's this place?" Vincent asked, his voice showing some of the unease he felt.

Liam smiled flatly. "I've worked with our bosses for over a year now. A few months ago, someone started asking too many questions. I was asked to put her down," he said, and there was a trace of bitterness in his tone.

Just as the weight of Liam's revelation settled upon them, the creaking door opened, revealing a pale-skinned woman with sleek, dark hair. In her right hand was a firearm large enough to take down five men at once. Vincent knew this from the war. Both Vincent and Isabella's reflexes kicked into gear, their hands instinctively moving toward their concealed weapons. Their eyes were locked on the new arrival.

The woman, however, bore a smug smile, her demeanor radiating an air of confidence. "But he couldn't go through with it, so he put me here instead," she said, her words punctuated by a playful wink directed at Vincent, who responded with an irritated grunt. The woman then continued in a tone reminiscent of a tour guide's patter, "Vincent Blackwood. Isabella Rose. I'm sure you both have a lot of questions."

CHAPTER 2

The morning sun's first rays filtered through broken windows within the warehouse's dimly lit interior, casting sporadic patches of illumination amid the pervasive gloom. Most of the space was littered with broken and abandoned machinery. A gallery above held a few figures moving in the shadows, their activities shrouded in mystery. Dust motes danced aimlessly through the air, their dances momentarily caught in the beams of light.

Isabella, Vincent, Emily, and Liam huddled around a makeshift table, the worn wood bearing witness to their shared apprehension. The tension in the air was palpable, as was Isabella and Vincent's anxiety that they were getting close to unraveling the mysteries that had perplexed them for so long.

Vincent's voice, laden with frustration and disbelief, cut through the atmosphere. "So, let me get this straight," he began, his gaze darting from face to face as he attempted to make sense of the madness that had engulfed their lives. "These aliens, they're reanimating the dead, and we're just pawns in their twisted games? They brought us back to life only to make us killers."

The somber nods around the table affirmed the grim reality that was slowly being unveiled before them. Emily, her gaze fixed upon the table, added further depth to their knowledge. "Yes," she said, her voice heavy with the weight of all she knew. "They see us as expendable, disposable. They have been using us for their purposes, and it seems they have grown fond of harvesting live humans as well. Hence, our roles in all of this."

Isabella's features twisted into a troubled frown. This was it. Emily had explained all she had gathered from the aliens before she had to leave a handful of months ago. They had been utilizing reanimated humans from Earth to perform tasks their frail bodies could not manage, like construction. Initially, they had depended on war casualties for a steady supply of dead humans. However, with the war's end, they were now resorting to different means, drawing humans who were very much alive into their society as workers. The realization of her involvement in these malevolent schemes weighed heavily on Isabella, threatening to overwhelm her. She struggled to maintain her composure, focusing on her breath to stave off the rising nausea.

Vincent's ability to absorb the unsettling revelations seemed more impressive than Isabella's. He leaned forward, his brows furrowed in deep thought. The enormity of the situation weighed heavily on him. There was so much to say and so many questions to ask. Isabella could see him visibly struggling to get his thinking under control. "And their invisibility? How does that even work?" he asked finally.

Liam exchanged a knowing glance with Emily before answering. "It's a form of advanced camouflage, an ability they possess. They can blend seamlessly into their surroundings, making them practically invisible to the naked eye, particularly in low-light conditions. That's how they've successfully been moving among humans for hundreds of years." His words cast a light on the extent of the alien's capabilities, leaving Vincent and Isabella to grapple with the chilling implications.

Isabella could not suppress the shiver that coursed through her at the thought. Her mind wandered to countless moments in her life, wondering if she had unwittingly crossed paths with these insidious creatures. Had they always been watching when she took on a job, lurking in the shadows, hidden from her perception? A more chilling notion was the possibility that they had been observing her and Vincent during their recent activities. Perhaps they were even present, watching and listening at that very moment.

Vincent's tone quivered as he voiced the disquieting notion that had been gnawing at Isabella. "And you're saying they could be right here with us now, watching and listening?" His eyes darted nervously, scanning the dimly lit spaces around them. His words, laden with uncertainty, echoed Isabella's fears. The oppressive sense of being under surveillance shook them both, turning the warehouse into an echoing chamber of dread.

"Exactly," replied Emily, her voice low. "They could be anywhere, lurking in the darkness, hidden from view. We might never know they're there until it's too late. They are naturally reluctant to partake in violence, but who knows what could happen?" Isabella had to applaud Liam's bravery, working directly for creatures like that and still plotting behind their backs. He was either very confident in being discreet or incredibly stupid. Neither option made her feel comfortable. Looking at his face now, the way his face contorted into fear answered the question.

They could be right here with us.

The revelation sent a silent horror through the room. The realization that these insidious aliens could be right there with them, concealed in the shadows, cast a palpable sense of unease over the group. The atmosphere in the dimly lit warehouse grew oppressive, and they could not help but let their gazes linger in the dark corners and the hidden recesses, their minds racing with the knowledge that danger could be lurking just beyond their sight.

Isabella's eyes rapidly moved around the space that surrounded them as though she was afraid to have a blind spot. "It's terrifying to think about. They have infiltrated our world and lived among us, and we've been oblivious."

Liam's voice quivered as he spoke. "I've seen them in their true forms. Believe me, they are unlike anything you can imagine. Root-like limbs, glowing eyes, and a presence that oozes malevolence."

Emily chimed in, her tone somber. "We need to be very cautious. We do not know the full extent of what they can do."

Vincent's grip on the edge of the table tightened. "Enough about their capabilities. We need to find out more about their weaknesses. There must be a way to fight back."

Isabella's eyes met Vincent's with determination. "We have to expose them somehow, let the people know what is lurking in the shadows."

Then, as if in response to those very words, the air seemed to suddenly shift, and an alien emerged from the shadows. Fear gripped Isabella, and her heart pounded in her chest. The twisted plant-like form had glowing yellow eyes that bore into her, making the hairs on her skin rise. Then there was its guttural, howling noise that sounded like it came from the depths of the ocean, reverberating through their bones and locking them in a suffocating grip of terror. Time seemed to stretch; their collective breaths caught in their throats as they gazed upon this entity.

Before anyone could shake off the paralyzing fear and react, the stifling silence of the warehouse was shattered by a sudden eruption of blinding plasma. The beam, a searing lance of death, struck the alien with lethal precision. The alien's body hit the floor immediately, staining the ground with a green ooze from the opening in its chest. The twisted creature convulsed in agony for a split second before it went still and lifeless.

Startled and confused, the group turned to see another figure stepping forward, its form hazy in the dim light. A voice, firm and authoritative, spoke. "I am Rellak, an emissary from the government of my home planet," it announced. "We come in peace."

"Hard to believe with that thing pointed at us," said Vincent. He already had Emily's shotgun in his hand, aimed directly at the alien. The tension in the room ratcheted up even higher as the standoff continued. "I wouldn't move nearer if I were you." Isabella noticed then that Liam was now equally armed with a gun pointed at the creature. A strange kind of relief came over her mind, and she found the will to rise on her feet.

Suddenly, Emily let out a sharp whistle, prompting movements from above in the gallery. More reanimated humans, armed and vigilant, took up positions, their weapons trained on the alien and creating an imposing ring of defense. The tide of the standoff seemed to have shifted, leaving the emissary from the alien race outnumbered and at a distinct disadvantage.

The alien they now confronted looked similar to the others they had encountered. His body and limbs were comprised of leaves and thick vines, and his eyes glowed eerily within a cabbage-like head. He clutched a peculiar weapon, no doubt the source of the damned plasma ray that had killed the other one. Isabella looked again at the first one and almost threw up in disgust at its lifeless form.

Rellak lowered his weapon. The emotion on his face was hard to read. He repeated his declaration, this time with more emphasis on the first word, "*We* come in peace."

Then it hit them.

"We?" said Liam, eyes turning to observe the room.

They didn't need to reveal themselves. Isabella couldn't see them, but she knew instantly that they were surrounded. The hidden alien presence was unsettling. There was something about not knowing their enemies. There could be one right behind Isabella, and there could be an entire army just outside. Or the alien could have just been telling a simple lie. Not knowing was the scariest part of it all.

"I suggest you sit down and let us talk," said Rellak, and they knew they had no choice. The room fell into an eerie silence as they complied with Rellak's request. Isabella couldn't shake the fear that she might not be able to heal if that energy blast struck her in the head.

Once they were seated back by the table, Rellak continued speaking. "I want you to know we are not associated with the ones running the human farm here in this city," he said. He stepped under a ray of sunlight, revealing his coarse, leafy body with venation traveling across it in a net formation. "We have been observing the activities of the deviant group that has operated on Earth since your world war, and we cannot allow their actions to continue. We respect the sanctity of life, and that is why we seek to return that life to humans who have died while giving them a home on our planet and having them work for us in return." The words hung in the air for a few seconds. It was a delicate balance between an explanation and an unspoken plea for understanding. The room remained silent as the group processed the alien's words.

"Nice speech," grumbled Liam flatly. Liam looked ready to walk away, while Vincent looked ready to fight them all despite not knowing their number. Rellak remained calm and composed, waiting for the group to decide.

The vines that made up Rellak's hand twisted and wrapped together in a human-like movement as he picked up his gun again. "They've drawn our attention, and our government wants them eliminated. They have gone too far, causing chaos on our home world and here. We offer you the chance to join us in this task to help rid Earth of these criminals," he said firmly. He dropped his weapon on the table and pushed it forward. The thing looked like it was forged out of tree bark, with a rough texture and a grotesque shape. "We can only offer you help by providing weapons that can take them out, but we hope you choose to help, as we cannot partake much in the killing. Life is… sacred." Rellak turned his burning eyes to the ground.

The group exchanged glances, each person dealing internally with their moral and ethical considerations. Isabella saw how Rellak looked at the one he had killed. It seemed like he was disgusted with himself and what he had done. She could not help but feel a strange mixture of emotions. Here was an alien talking about the sanctity of life, something she hadn't expected. On top of that, the alien felt guilt over killing someone who was objectively horrible. That was certainly not how she felt when she killed abusive men.

Vincent's gaze remained fixed on Rellak's weapon, which was both primitive and alien in design. He contemplated the offer and the potential to rid Earth of the dangerous deviant group that had been manipulating them. Liam, on the other hand, seemed torn, his cynical façade momentarily faltering. Liam's connection with the aliens had clearly blurred his sense of right and wrong, and the notion of turning against them felt a little like betrayal. Emily remained quiet, her thoughts hidden behind a mask of stoicism. Her experiences with the aliens had been equally troubling, and the chance to break free from their control seemed like an opportunity she could not ignore.

"Of course, we'll help," sighed Vincent with an encouraging nod from Emily and an annoyed agreement from Liam. Isabella offered him an encouraging smile. She noticed already how much he hated killing and being used as nothing but a murderer, but this was what their lives called for.

Rellak nodded, obviously pleased with their response. "That is very good," he said. "One more thing. You will all have to come with us afterward. There is no home for you here. You were all dead."

"Wow. Your speeches get nicer," Liam rolled his eyes.

"Question. How do we fight what we can't see?" said Isabella. She was more than ready to pick up the tree gun and barge into this human farm

Rellak spoke of just to get to Eliza. But she wasn't willing to cast sensibility aside in the thrill of everything.

Rellak turned to her. He stretched his hand forward, and the vines that made up his arm began to grow, stretching forward. Then, he unfolded his hand to reveal something like a crown made of twisted vines. Isabella picked it up and carefully placed it on her head. Immediately, a screen of translucent green appeared over her face.

"What the bloody..." She shuddered visibly as she saw the number of aliens in the room, hiding in shadowed corners. There were so many. So many. She saw all their forms in a greenish tint. She looked to Rellak.

"What?" said Vincent, obviously confused. Isabella looked at Vincent and saw an alien beside him with a gun pointed right at his head. The alien then turned around and walked away.

She slowly shook her head. "I see them. All of them."

Rellak stared hard at Isabella before saying matter-of-factly, "The apostates will fight hard. Not all of you will survive, and we might not be able to bring you back."

Isabella nodded, "Understood."

"Looks like we have to create ourselves an army," said Liam, rising to his feet. "And, thankfully, I know every *reanimate* in this city."

"I feel like some kind of fraud," Isabella said with a light chuckle. Vincent looked at her and tilted his head to one side. She stopped the fake laugh and sighed genuinely. "Look at me, Vincent. I did not hesitate to kill all those people for money when it was offered to me. I mean, they were very bad people, to be honest. Many of them were criminals or abusive husbands or something. But it wasn't as if that was why I was killing. I did it because I could. Maybe I was greedy." She looked down at the ground. They were a good distance away from the city and crouching behind a wire fence. It was perhaps not the best time for a conversation like this, but Vincent had no control over that. "Then the same thing happened to someone I cared about, and I got mad. I feel like I don't have the right to be angry at them for killing Eliza when I know I would have done the same if she was a stranger to me. I am a fraud."

Vincent smiled and grimaced simultaneously. Then he said, "Yes, you are." This was probably not what Isabella was expecting to hear, judging by how she fixed her gaze upon him. He laughed lightly. She somehow managed to be beautiful, whatever expression she wore on her face. Vincent felt the need to add, "But what if you are? I mean, we are all pretending we are not living on borrowed time. We're all frauds. And would you listen to the bollocks our peace-loving alien friends said? They don't kill due to their religion. As if giving us weapons to fight isn't a way of being involved in the killing. See? All frauds."

"That's a load of piss," Isabella said, but she also wore a smile that reached her eyes. Then, she whispered, "Thank you, Vincent." She bumped her shoulder into his.

"You're welcome, Miss Rose," he whispered back.

Night had already cast its shroud over the world, but they could easily see the enormous facility sitting before them. A light came alive in the distance, and Vincent responded to the sign. He whistled, and green lights flickered to life behind him, not less than twenty of them. All the reanimates assigned to him had a pulsing green screen on their faces so they could see invisible aliens. They all rose carefully and ventured through the opening in the wire fence.

They cautiously approached the door at the back of the building as they had been instructed. Liam and Emily were leading other teams through other openings at other levels. The door creaked open as Vincent pushed in, entering slowly to inspect the area. He whistled sharply, and they all followed.

Together, they ventured cautiously into the heart of the strange building, Vincent making sure to remember the routes Liam had all but yelled at him the past two days. The good news was that they had strength in numbers. It wasn't hard convincing their murdering co-workers to revolt against their alien employers. Many of them still had families and were not thrilled by the thought of those loved ones ending up like them just because of some aliens. The tough part was convincing them of the need to exit the planet once this invasion was done.

Their breath was hushed, and the faint glow of the green-tinted screens covered their faces and illuminated their way. They reached the chamber they had been aiming for in no time. It was cold, and their breath was almost visible in the air before them. It was… dreadfully beautiful. The pods in the room pulsed a purple glow and were all filled with lifeless bodies with strange vines connected to them. It looked like they were in coffins or tombs. Vincent had struggled to think that he was once like these things, but the moment he set eyes on the room, the memory of being here came back.

"Oh, fuck," whispered Isabella beside him. There were over fifty bodies here.

"Spread out," Vincent said in hushed command. "We might not be alone." He heard footsteps disperse around him as his comrades began to observe the entirety of the spacious room.

Isabella moved between the pods, with Vincent following her. She looked from face to face of the people in the tubes. Vincent paused once to see an extension of a device that displayed the names, qualities, and abilities of the people within. He hated that he had been a part of this, maybe even more than how much he had hated partaking in the damned war.

A gasp from Isabella made him lift his head and move to her side. Isabella dropped her gun as she knelt beside one of the tubes. Vincent figured she'd found Eliza. She was already pulling the lever that raised the glass covering the tube to slide it away with a mechanical sound. She hugged her friend quickly, even before the other lady gained consciousness.

"Eliza. Eliza," she whispered through a sob.

Vincent looked around at the comrades assigned to him, at the other people they were supposed to release, and at Isabella's echoing voice. He couldn't shake off the unsettling stillness of the facility. Liam said it should have been crawling with aliens, and Liam and Emily's groups were already inside. They should have been hearing distant gunfire by now if anything.

"Something feels strange," he said to Isabella. The atmosphere seemed to thicken with a sense of foreboding. Suddenly, a familiar and dreadful screech reached his ears. He released a shaky breath, which appeared like a small fog before him.

They both looked up in the direction the sound came from, and a cold shiver ran down their spines. The ceiling was lined with the alien creatures, using the camouflage and darkness to hide themselves. Their eyes slowly opened one after the other, filled with deep malice. Panic swept over the room as they realized they'd walked straight into a trap.

Without warning, the aliens descended upon them, their movements fluid and deadly. Plasma rays and gunfire filled the air, the deafening sounds of battle blending with the agonized screams of their allies and the aliens' unearthly screeches.

A quick moment of thought made Isabella toss her friend's body aside as she reached for her gun in time to send a ray of plasma that blasted an alien's head open. She shouted at the body at her feet. "Get up, Eliza. We have to go," she snapped at her terrified and confused friend. "Vincent!"

Vincent gritted his teeth firmly as he sent blasts of plasma rays flying around while also aware of the vines wrapped tightly around his ankle. He swung his weapon before they could drag him down. He shot the hand that was wrapped around him numerous times to shake it off and then shot the body the hand belonged to.

"We can't take them all. We need the other teams to know they ambushed us," he said, out of breath. Isabella nodded while holding on to Eliza with one hand and shooting with the other.

Vincent nodded back at her and was turning back around when a force collided with his face. The blow sent him crashing into a nearby pod. Vincent's vision changed, and the current battlefield gave way to the time of his death. Real sounds were being drowned out of his mind, and reality seemed blurry as gunfire sounded all around. He was back in the war, lost and dying, and…

"Vincent!!!" Isabella's words cut through his mind. The sound crashed through the illusion and pulled him back to reality. He gasped for breath as he looked around at the chaos unfolding all around him. He looked up to see Isabella's terrified gaze. She was fighting something off while her gaze remained pressed on him.

Vincent realized too late that he was no longer wearing the device that allowed him to see the camouflaged aliens. He heard a snarl dangerously close to his ear, and then he fully understood the horror washing over Isabella's features. Quickly, he reached for his alien gun, but something he could not see hit his hand, pinning it to the ground.

He yelled in pain as he felt his bone snap. This was the most pain he had felt in a while, which was both strange and scary. He felt a weight press upon his legs and begin to move up his body. Vincent shuddered as he struggled to reach for the gun with his immobilized hand. The alien was now so close Vincent could perceive shadows of a strange vision of leaves mixed with blood.

"Get the hell off me," he grunted as he quickly reached for the side of his trousers and the small handgun strapped there. He quickly emptied bullets into the creature and let out a satisfied breath when the thing collapsed on his body.

"You okay?" he heard Isabella say at his side. Vincent grunted loudly as he pushed the invisible alien off his body and rose to his feet. His bones began to snap back into place, and his skin quickly stitched back up. "Here."

Vincent took his crown-like visor from Isabella and breathed a "Thank you." She was covered in alien blood and looked exhausted already.

Movements caught Vincent's eye, and he saw the alien he had just buried with bullets moving again and stirring to its feet. "Oh. Yeah. Only these weapons can kill them. Else, they heal," said Isabella, firing the plasma gun at the soon-to-be-dead pile of leaves.

"Well, this is harder than I thought," Vincent confessed.

"It's about to get harder," Isabella told him grimly. All around were aliens advancing toward them. Isabella and Vincent turned their backs to each other, weapons raised. Vincent could see dead humans all around.

He swore as he held on to his handgun, waiting for the coming attack. There was no way he and Isabella could take them all down. "Wait. Where's Eliza?" he asked, craning his neck.

Just then, the lady's small form appeared at the chamber door. Vincent frowned, but his heart swelled when he saw a line of humans behind her, with Liam and Emily leading them.

"Never underestimate a woman or a whore," Isabella told him. Vincent caught a moment of genuine smile before the chaos of battle resumed.

EPILOGUE

The rising sun painted the horizon with hues of pink and gold as Isabella and Vincent stood on the hill overlooking the alien facility, now a smoldering ruin. The remnants of their battle with the aliens lay scattered around them. Many dead were lying on the ground, too wounded to heal. They all had aliens attending to them who were optimistic they could bring them back.

Rellak strode among the living and the dead, his eyes blazing. Vincent noted the other aliens seemed to defer to him as if he were a commander. Rellak saw Vincent and Isabella and walked to them slowly, almost humbly.

Vincent was puzzled and asked, almost shouted, "Why? Why did you reanimate us? Why are you taking us to your home?"

Rellak stood still and, with a bow, said, "You are animals; we are plants. Your waste products are essential for us."

Vincent and Isabella were dumbfounded, speechless.

Rellak continued. "Human effluent is particularly valued. You will be treasured guests for as long as you live."

Vincent smirked. "Thank you. After the last war, no one ever told me what I was fighting for. Your honesty is refreshing."

Rellak spread his arms out broadly and seemed to attempt a smile. "It is the cycle of life." After an awkward moment or two, he softly exited.

Isabella let out a heavy sigh, her eyes scanning their surroundings. "I can't believe it's over," she said softly, her voice tinged with a mixture of relief and exhaustion.

"It's not really over, is it?" said Vincent. He turned to another point on the horizon, and Isabella followed his gaze. There sat a huge machine that could put a jumbo aircraft to shame. It was camouflaged, of course, but they could tell exactly where it was by subtle distortions in the sunlight.

Yes, they had taken down the deviant aliens, but they were also not allowed to return home or go back to their families. They were all dead men and women who would be taken away in that thing.

"Our lives really aren't our own, are they?" said Isabella.

Vincent shrugged. "No bloody way am I going to get on that machine only to end up serving some other damned people," he grumbled. "No way."

Isabella smiled cheekily. "Me either. We may have to fight for what we want, though," she said.

"When have we not been fighting our way through our damned existence?" said Vincent with a flat smile. "Come on, Eliza looks like a confused rabbit. Maybe leaving this planet will be fun." He stretched out his hand. Isabella laughed heartily as she took it and ran down the hill with him toward a new life.

The End

Author Murray Eiland is an archaeologist and is Managing Editor at Antiqvvs Magazine. He is an enthusiast of science fiction from the 1940s. Murray can be found on Facebook, search "Science Fiction Eiland".

Actress Paulette Goddard

HISTORICAL EMPORIUM

Est. 2003

Buy at... HISTORICAL EMPORIUM

Whose **REPUTATION** is *celebrated* world-wide as the pre-eminent clothing source for the **ADVENTUROUS** and *Fashionable.*

We are...

REVERED
by our customers

REVILED
by our competitors

RESPECTED
by all who know us

NO LOCAL DEALER CAN COMPETE WITH OUR QUALITY, VARIETY AND INCOMPARIBLE CUSTOMER SERVICE!

ACCEPT NO SUBSTITUTE!
If you require clothing and supplies as stylish and **stout-hearted** as you, contact us immediately to be outfitted.

800-997-4311

HistoricalEmporium.com

He spoke to me
of Christmas gifts
to wish me well.
He was once my love
but now a stranger.
By New Year's Eve
a whisper he might be
no need for gifts or thoughts of old
as now two lovers
beginning their years apart
with no more hands to hold.

—Myrica Cook

"By the golden apples of Hesperides!"
Simon Gale is one amusingly boisterous detective.

RECENTLY I LEARNED OF A TRIO OF BOOKS FEATURING ONE OF GERALD VERN-er's unusual and least known series detectives, Simon Gale. To date these are the best mysteries I've read by Verner. Much of their delight and success is due to the detective, a larger than life character who will remind diehard detective fiction fans of other beer guzzling, blustery, and opinionated sleuths like Sir Henry Merrivale created by John Dickson Carr in his Carter Dickson guise. Gale is a professional portrait painter who comes to crime solving by accident. With only a handful of newsworthy successes Gale has gained a reputation as a criminologist and is more than happy to help when puzzling murders come his way.

Of the three books the best is probably Noose for a Lady (1952), Gale's debut as a detective. Here Gale is asked to look into the case of Margaret Hallam in prison for poisoning her husband and about to be executed in only a few days. He must race against the clock and sort out who among the seven suspects was the truly guilty party.

Every one of the suspects has a secret involving a crime of some sort. Gale meets up with Mrs. Barrett, the Hallam housekeeper; Miss Ginch, a spiteful church lady; Mr Upcott, an effeminate collector of rare china; Major

Ferguson, the typical ex-solider; Mrs. Langdon-Humpreys an archetype of the imperious harridan and her niece Vanessa; and Dr. Evershed, the usual local physician who turns up in these village mysteries. The story begins to resemble a sort of homage to And Then There Were None with each secret revealing each of the seven suspects to be more vile and odious than the preceding one interviewed. Among the crimes are murder, mass slaughter during war, negligence leading to a suicide, out of wedlock childbirth and other social "horrors" of the era. But who among these people felt it necessary to poison John Hallam, a sadistic man who collected books on torture and cruelty, and who also dabbled in blackmail? Gale aptly sums up this lurid case: "Murder's a queer thing. It's like suddenly turning on a bright light in an old, damp cellar. All kinds of nasty, crawling things go scuttling away to their holes to get out of the glare."

There are at least two well executed shocking surprises before we reach the truth behind Hallam's poisoning murder. The story is an exciting one what with all the secrets being uncovered and the twist before the denouement is actually the most interesting and unexpected part of the book. Yet again I have to admit that Verner has let me down in the end. The ending is histrionic in the extreme, the murderer is ludicrously far-fetched and makes the entire story seem preposterous. Too much is explained away as madness as it is in Sorcerer's House (the second book in the series) and it is a disappointing finale to an otherwise genuinely fascinating and well constructed detective novel.

Simon Gale is colorful, keen eyed and sharp witted, often providing riotously funny laugh-out-loud moments amid the eerie luridness that pervades his investigations. Despite Verner's flaws in plotting and his penchant for high melodrama and operatic displays of villainy in the final pages I highly recommend these books for anyone unfamiliar with his work. They are most definitely the best of the Gerald Verner mysteries I've read as far as character, atmosphere and detective elements.

Noose for a Lady, Sorcerer's House and The Snark Was a Boojum are all available from Lume Books in either digital format or paperback.

JF Norris is a part time writer and bookseller. In 1999 he started an internet bookselling business from which his blog gets its name. The blog is solely devoted to of out-of-print & vintage crime, supernatural, adventure and other genre fiction. JF has also written critical essays and reviews on detective & supernatural fiction for fanzines, internet sites, and small press publishers.
The Blog: prettysinister.blogspot.com

A NOTE ABOUT THE FOLLOWING WORK:

In 1925 Harper and Brothers published, "Color", by Countee Cullen. Countee

(May 30, 1903 – January 9, 1946) was a talented writer well known during the Harlem Renaissance. What follows is Countee Cullen's first book in it's entirety. It includes many poems as well as his best known, "Heritage".

COLOR
BY COUNTEE CULLEN

To my Mother and Father

First Published by Harper and Brothers, 1925

To You Who Read My Book:

Soon every sprinter,
    However fleet,
Comes to a winter
    Of sure defeat:
Though he may race
    Like the hunted doe,
Time has a pace
    To lay him low.

Soon we who sing,
    However high,
Must face the Thing
    We cannot fly.
Yea, though we fling
    Our notes to the sun,
Time will outsing
    Us every one.

All things must change
    As the wind is blown;
Time will estrange
    The flesh from the bone.
The dream shall elude
    The dreamer's clasp,
And only its hood
    Shall comfort his grasp.

A little while,
    Too brief at most,
And even my smile

Will be a ghost.
A little space,
   A Finger's crook,
And who shall trace
   The path I took?

Who shall declare
   My whereabouts;
Say if in the air
   My being shouts
Along light ways,
   Or if in the sea,
Or deep earth stays
   The germ of me?

Ah, none knows, none,
   Save (but too well)
The Cryptic One
   Who will not tell.

This is my hour
   To wax and climb,
Flaunt a red flower
   In the face of time.
And only an hour
   Time gives, then snap
Goes the flower,
   And dried is the sap.

Juice of the first
   Grapes of my vine,
I proffer your thirst
   My own heart's wine.
Here of my growing
   A red rose sways,
Seed of my sowing,

    And work of my days.

(I run, but time's
    Abreast with me;
I sing, but he climbs
    With my highest C.)

Drink while my blood
    Colors the wine,
Reach while the bud
    Is still on the vine....

Then...
    When the hawks of death
Tear at my throat
    Till song and breath
Ebb note by note,
    Turn to this book
Of the mellow word
    For a singing look
At the stricken bird.

Say, "This is the way
    He chirped and sung,
In the sweet heyday
    When his heart was young.
Though his throat is bare,
    By death defiled,
Song labored there
    And bore a child."

When the dreadful Ax
    Rives me apart,
When the sharp wedge cracks
    My arid heart,
Turn to this book

Of the singing me
For a springtime look
    At the wintry tree.

Say, "Thus it was weighed
    With flower and fruit,
Ere the Ax was laid
    Unto its root.
Though the blows fall free
    On a gnarled trunk now,
Once he was a tree
    With a blossomy bough."

COLOR

Yet Do I Marvel

I doubt not God is good, well-meaning, kind,
And did He stoop to quibble could tell why
The little buried mole continues blind,
Why flesh that mirrors Him must some day die,
Make plain the reason tortured Tantalus
Is baited by the fickle fruit, declare
If merely brute caprice dooms Sisyphus
To struggle up a never-ending stair.
Inscrutable His ways are, and immune
To catechism by a mind too strewn
With petty cares to slightly understand
What awful brain compels His awful hand.
Yet do I marvel at this curious thing:
To make a poet black, and bid him sing!

A Song of Praise

(For one who praised his lady's being fair.)

You have not heard my love's dark throat,
    Slow-fluting like a reed,
Release the perfect golden note
    She caged there for my need.

Her walk is like the replica

Of some barbaric dance
Wherein the soul of Africa
   Is winged with arrogance.

And yet so light she steps across
   The ways her sure feet pass,
She does not dent the smoothest moss
   Or bend the thinnest grass.

My love is dark as yours is fair,
   Yet lovelier I hold her
Than listless maids with pallid hair,
   And blood that's thin and colder.

You-proud-and-to-be-pitied one,
   Gaze on her and despair;
Then seal your lips until the sun
   Discovers one as fair.

Brown Boy to Brown Girl

(Remembrance on a hill) (For Yolande)

"As surely as I hold your hand in mine,
As surely as your crinkled hair belies
The enamoured sun pretending that he dies
While still he loiters in its glossy shine,
As surely as I break the slender line
That spider linked us with, in no least wise
Am I uncertain that these alien skies
Do not our whole life measure and confine.
No less, once in a land of scarlet suns
And brooding winds, before the hurricane
Bore down upon us, long before this pain,
We found a place where quiet water runs;
I held your hand this way upon a hill,
And felt my heart forebear, my pulse grow still."

A Brown Girl Dead

With two white roses on her breasts,
    White candles at head and feet,
Dark Madonna of the grave she rests;
    Lord Death has found her sweet.

Her mother pawned her wedding ring
    To lay her out in white;
She'd be so proud she'd dance and sing
    To see herself tonight.

To a Brown Girl
(For Roberta)

What if his glance is bold and free,
    His mouth the lash of whips?
So should the eyes of lovers be,
    And so a lover's lips.

What if no puritanic strain
    Confines him to the nice?
He will not pass this way again,
    Nor hunger for you twice.

Since in the end consort together
    Magdalen and Mary,
Youth is the time for careless weather:
    Later, lass, be wary.

To a Brown Boy

That brown girl's swagger gives a twitch
    To beauty like a queen;

Lad, never dam your body's itch
    When loveliness is seen.

For there is ample room for bliss
    In pride in clean, brown limbs,
And lips know better how to kiss
    Than how to raise white hymns.

And when your body's death gives birth
    To soil for spring to crown,
Men will not ask if that rare earth
    Was white flesh once, or brown.

Black Magdalens

These have no Christ to spit and stoop
    To write upon the sand,
Inviting him that has not sinned
    To raise the first rude hand.

And if he came they could not buy
    Rich ointment for his feet,
The body's sale scarce yields enough
    To let the body eat.

The chaste clean ladies pass them by
    And draw their skirts aside,
But Magdalens have a ready laugh;
    They wrap their wounds in pride.

They fare full ill since Christ forsook
    The cross to mount a throne,
And Virtue still is stooping down
    To cast the first hard stone.

Atlantic City Waiter

With subtle poise he grips his tray
    Of delicate things to eat;
Choice viands to their mouths half way,
    The ladies watch his feet

Go carving dexterous avenues
    Through sly intricacies;
Ten thousand years on jungle clues
    Alone shaped feet like these.

For him to be humble who is proud
    Needs colder artifice;
Though half his pride is disavowed,
    In vain the sacrifice.

Sheer through his acquiescent mask
    Of bland gentility,
The jungle flames like a copper cask
    Set where the sun strikes free.

Near White

Ambiguous of race they stand,
    By one disowned, scorned of another,
Not knowing where to stretch a hand,
    And cry, "My sister" or "My brother."

Tableau
For Donald Duff

Locked arm in arm they cross the way,
    The black boy and the white,

The golden splendor of the day,
    The sable pride of night.

From lowered blinds the dark folk stare,
    And here the fair folk talk,
Indignant that these two should dare
    In unison to walk.

Oblivious to look and word
    They pass, and see no wonder
That lightning brilliant as a sword
    Should blaze the path of thunder.

Harlem Wine

This is not water running here,
    These thick rebellious streams
That hurtle flesh and bone past fear
    Down alleyways of dreams.

This is a wine that must flow on
    Not caring how nor where,
So it has ways to flow upon
    Where song is in the air.

So it can woo an artful flute
    With loose, elastic lips,
Its measurement of joy compute
    With blithe, ecstatic hips.

Simon the Cyrenian Speaks

He never spoke a word to me,
    And yet He called my name;
He never gave a sign to me,

And yet I knew and came.

At first I said, "I will not bear
   His cross upon my back;
He only seeks to place it there
   Because my skin is black."

But He was dying for a dream,
   And He was very meek,
And in His eyes there shone a gleam
   Men journey far to seek.

It was Himself my pity bought;
   I did for Christ alone
What all of Rome could not have wrought
   With bruise of lash or stone.

Incident

(For Eric Walrond)

Once riding in old Baltimore,
   Heart-filled, head-filled with glee,
I saw a Baltimorean
   Keep looking straight at me.

Now I was eight and very small,
   And he was no whit bigger,
And so I smiled, but he poked out
   His tongue, and called me, "Nigger."

I saw the whole of Baltimore
   From May until December;
Of all the things that happened there
   That's all that I remember.

Two Who Crossed a Line
(She Crosses)

From where she stood the air she craved
    Smote with the smell of pine;
It was too much to bear; she braved
    Her gods and crossed the line.

And we were hurt to see her go,
    With her fair face and hair,
And veins too thin and blue to show
    What mingled blood flowed there.

We envied her a while, who still
    Pursued the hated track;
Then we forgot her name, until
    One day her shade came back.

Calm as a wave without a crest,
    Sorrow-proud and sorrow-wise,
With trouble sucking at her breast,
    With tear-disdainful eyes,

She slipped into her ancient place,
    And, no word asked, gave none;
Only the silence in her face
    Said seats were dear in the sun.

Two Who Crossed a Line
(He Crosses)

He rode across like a cavalier,
    Spurs clicking hard and loud;
And where he tarried dropped his tear
    On heads he left low-bowed.

But, "Even Stephen," he cried, and struck
    His steed an urgent blow;
He swore by youth he was a buck
    With savage oats to sow.

To even up some standing scores,
    From every flower bed
He passed, he plucked by threes and fours
    Till wheels whirled in his head.

But long before the drug could tell,
    He took his anodyne;
With scornful grace, he bowed farewell
    And retraversed the line.

Saturday's Child

Some are teethed on a silver spoon,
    With the stars strung for a rattle;
I cut my teeth as the black raccoon--
    For implements of battle.

Some are swaddled in silk and down,
    And heralded by a star;
They swathed my limbs in a sackcloth gown
    On a night that was black as tar.

For some, godfather and goddame
    The opulent fairies be;
Dame Poverty gave me my name,
    And Pain godfathered me.

For I was born on Saturday--
    "Bad time for planting a seed,"

Was all my father had to say,
    And, "One mouth more to feed."

Death cut the strings that gave me life,
    And handed me to Sorrow,
The only kind of middle wife
    My folks could beg or borrow.

The Dance of Love
(After reading René Maran's "Batouala")

All night we danced upon our windy hill,
Your dress a cloud of tangled midnight hair,
And love was much too much for me to wear
My leaves; the killer roared above his kill,
But you danced on, and when some star would spill
Its red and white upon you whirling there,
I sensed a hidden beauty in the air;
Though you danced on, my heart and I stood still.

But suddenly a bit of morning crept
Along your trembling sides of ebony;
I saw the tears your tired limbs had wept,
And how your breasts heaved high, how languidly
Your dark arms moved; I drew you close to me;
We flung ourselves upon our hill and slept.

Pagan Prayer

Not for myself I make this prayer,
    But for this race of mine
That stretches forth from shadowed places
    Dark hands for bread and wine.

For me, my heart is pagan mad,
    My feet are never still,

But give them hearths to keep them warm
    In homes high on a hill.

For me, my faith lies fallowing,
    I bow not till I see,
But these are humble and believe;
    Bless their credulity.

For me, I pay my debts in kind,
    And see no better way,
Bless these who turn the other cheek
    For love of you, and pray.

Our Father, God, our Brother, Christ--
    So are we taught to pray;
Their kinship seems a little thing
    Who sorrow all the day.

Our Father, God; our Brother, Christ,
    Or are we bastard kin,
That to our plaints your ears are closed,
    Your doors barred from within?

Our Father, God; our Brother, Christ,
    Retrieve my race again;
So shall you compass this black sheep,
    This pagan heart. Amen.

Wisdom Cometh With the Years

Now I am young and credulous,
    My heart is quick to bleed
At courage in the tremulous
    Slow sprouting of a seed.

Now I am young and sensitive,
    Man's lack can stab me through;
I own no stitch I would not give
    To him that asked me to.

Now I am young and a fool for love,
    My blood goes mad to see
A brown girl pass me like a dove
    That flies melodiously.

Let me be lavish of my tears,
    And dream that false is true;
Though wisdom cometh with the years,
    The barren days come, too.

To My Fairer Brethren

Though I score you with my best,
    Treble circumstance
Must confirm the verdict, lest
    It be laid to chance.

    Insufficient that I match you
    Every coin you flip;
    Your demand is that I catch you
    Squarely on the hip.

    Should I wear my wreaths a bit
    Rakishly and proud,
    I have bought my right to it;
    Let it be allowed.

Fruit of the Flower

My father is a quiet man
    With sober, steady ways;
For simile, a folded fan;
    His nights are like his days.

My mother's life is puritan,
    No hint of cavalier,
A pool so calm you're sure it can
    Have little depth to fear.

And yet my father's eyes can boast
    How full his life has been;
There haunts them yet the languid ghost
    Of some still sacred sin.

And though my mother chants of God,
    And of the mystic river,
I've seen a bit of checkered sod
    Set all her flesh aquiver.

Why should he deem it pure mischance
    A son of his is fain
To do a naked tribal dance
    Each time he hears the rain?

Why should she think it devil's art
    That all my songs should be
Of love and lovers, broken heart,
    And wild sweet agony?

Who plants a seed begets a bud,
    Extract of that same root;

Why marvel at the hectic blood
   That flushes this wild fruit?

The Shroud of Color
(For Llewellyn Ransom)

"Lord, being dark," I said, "I cannot bear
The further touch of earth, the scented air;
Lord, being dark, forewilled to that despair
My color shrouds me in, I am as dirt
Beneath my brother's heel; there is a hurt
In all the simple joys which to a child
Are sweet; they are contaminate, defiled
By truths of wrongs the childish vision fails
To see; too great a cost this birth entails.
I strangle in this yoke drawn tighter than
The worth of bearing it, just to be man.
I am not brave enough to pay the price
In full; I lack the strength to sacrifice.
I who have burned my hands upon a star,
And climbed high hills at dawn to view the far
Illimitable wonderments of earth,
For whom all cups have dripped the wine of mirth,
For whom the sea has strained her honeyed throat
Till all the world was sea, and I a boat
Unmoored, on what strange quest I willed to float;
Who wore a many-colored coat of dreams,
Thy gift, O Lord--I whom sun-dabbled streams
Have washed, whose bare brown thighs have held the sun
Incarcerate until his course was run,
I who considered man a high-perfected
Glass where loveliness could lie reflected,
Now that I sway athwart Truth's deep abyss,
Denuding man for what he was and is,
Shall breath and being so inveigle me
That I can damn my dreams to hell, and be

Content, each new-born day, anew to see
The steaming crimson vintage of my youth
Incarnadine the altar-slab of Truth?

Or hast Thou, Lord, somewhere I cannot see,
A lamb imprisoned in a bush for me?

Not so? Then let me render one by one
Thy gifts, while still they shine; some little sun
Yet gilds these thighs; my coat, albeit worn,
Still holds its colors fast; albeit torn,
My heart will laugh a little yet, if I
May win of Thee this grace, Lord: on this high
And sacrificial hill 'twixt earth and sky,
To dream still pure all that I loved, and die.
There is no other way to keep secure
My wild chimeras; grave-locked against the lure
Of Truth, the small hard teeth of worms, yet less
Envenomed than the mouth of Truth, will bless
Them into dust and happy nothingness.
Lord, Thou art God; and I, Lord, what am I
But dust? With dust my place. Lord, let me die."

Across the earth's warm, palpitating crust
I flung my body in embrace; I thrust
My mouth into the grass and sucked the dew,
Then gave it back in tears my anguish drew;
So hard I pressed against the ground, I felt
The smallest sandgrain like a knife, and smelt
The next year's flowering; all this to speed
My body's dissolution, fain to feed
The worms. And so I groaned, and spent my strength
Until, all passion spent, I lay full length
And quivered like a flayed and bleeding thing.

So lay till lifted on a great black wing

That had no mate nor flesh-apparent trunk
To hamper it; with me all time had sunk
Into oblivion; when I awoke
The wing hung poised above two cliffs that broke
The bowels of the earth in twain, and cleft
The seas apart. Below, above, to left,
To right, I saw what no man saw before:
Earth, hell, and heaven; sinew, vein, and core.
All things that swim or walk or creep or fly,
All things that live and hunger, faint and die,
Were made majestic then and magnified
By sight so clearly purged and deified.
The smallest bug that crawls was taller than
A tree, the mustard seed loomed like a man.
The earth that writhes eternally with pain
Of birth, and woe of taking back her slain,
Laid bare her teeming bosom to my sight,
And all was struggle, gasping breath, and fight.
A blind worm here dug tunnels to the light,
And there a seed, racked with heroic pain,
Thrust eager tentacles to sun and rain;
It climbed; it died; the old love conquered me
To weep the blossom it would never be.
But here a bud won light; it burst and flowered
Into a rose whose beauty challenged, "Coward!"
There was no thing alive save only I
That held life in contempt and longed to die.
And still I writhed and moaned, "The curse, the curse,
Than animated death, can death be worse?"

"_Dark child of sorrow, mine no less, what art
Of mine can make thee see and play thy part?
The key to all strange things is in thy heart._"

What voice was this that coursed like liquid fire
Along my flesh, and turned my hair to wire?

I raised my burning eyes, beheld a field
All multitudinous with carnal yield,
A grim ensanguined mead whereon I saw
Evolve the ancient fundamental law
Of tooth and talon, fist and nail and claw.
There with the force of living, hostile hills
Whose clash the hemmed-in vale with clamor fills,
With greater din contended fierce majestic wills
Of beast with beast, of man with man, in strife
For love of what my heart despised, for life
That unto me at dawn was now a prayer
For night, at night a bloody heart-wrung tear
For day again; for _this_, these groans
From tangled flesh and interlockèd bones.
And no thing died that did not give
A testimony that it longed to live.
Man, strange composite blend of brute and god,
Pushed on, nor backward glanced where last he trod.
He seemed to mount a misty ladder flung
Pendant from a cloud, yet never gained a rung
But at his feet another tugged and clung.
My heart was still a pool of bitterness,
Would yield nought else, nought else confess.
I spoke (although no form was there
To see, I knew an ear was there to hear),
"Well, let them fight; they _can_ whose flesh is fair."

Crisp lightning flashed; a wave of thunder shook
My wing; a pause, and then a speaking, "Look."

I scarce dared trust my ears or eyes for awe
Of what they heard, and dread of what they saw;
For, privileged beyond degree, this flesh
Beheld God and His heaven in the mesh
Of Lucifer's revolt, saw Lucifer

Glow like the sun, and like a dulcimer
I heard his sin-sweet voice break on the yell
Of God's great warriors: Gabriel,
Saint Clair and Michael, Israfel and Raphael.
And strange it was to see God with His back
Against a wall, to see Christ hew and hack
Till Lucifer, pressed by the mighty pair,
And losing inch by inch, clawed at the air
With fevered wings; then, lost beyond repair,
He tricked a mass of stars into his hair;
He filled his hands with stars, crying as he fell,
"A star's a star although it burns in hell."
So God was left to His divinity,
Omnipotent at that most costly fee.

There was a lesson here, but still the clod
In me was sycophant unto the rod,
And cried, "Why mock me thus? Am I a god?"

"_One trial more: this failing, then I give
You leave to die; no further need to live._"

Now suddenly a strange wild music smote
A chord long impotent in me; a note
Of jungles, primitive and subtle, throbbed
Against my echoing breast, and tom-toms sobbed
In every pulse-beat of my frame. The din
A hollow log bound with a python's skin
Can make wrought every nerve to ecstasy,
And I was wind and sky again, and sea,
And all sweet things that flourish, being free.

Till all at once the music changed its key.

And now it was of bitterness and death,
The cry the lash extorts, the broken breath

Of liberty enchained; and yet there ran
Through all a harmony of faith in man,
A knowledge all would end as it began.
All sights and sounds and aspects of my race
Accompanied this melody, kept pace
With it; with music all their hopes and hates
Were charged, not to be downed by all the fates.
And somehow it was borne upon my brain
How being dark, and living through the pain
Of it, is courage more than angels have. I knew
What storms and tumults lashed the tree that grew
This body that I was, this cringing I
That feared to contemplate a changing sky,
This that I grovelled, whining, "Let me die,"
While others struggled in Life's abattoir.
The cries of all dark people near or far
Were billowed over me, a mighty surge
Of suffering in which my puny grief must merge
And lose itself; I had no further claim to urge
For death; in shame I raised my dust-grimed head,
And though my lips moved not, God knew I said,
"Lord, not for what I saw in flesh or bone
Of fairer men; not raised on faith alone;
Lord, I will live persuaded by mine own.
I cannot play the recreant to these;
My spirit has come home, that sailed the doubtful seas."

With the whiz of a sword that severs space,
The wing dropped down at a dizzy pace,
And flung me on my hill flat on my face;
Flat on my face I lay defying pain,
Glad of the blood in my smallest vein,
And in my hands I clutched a loyal dream,
Still spitting fire, bright twist and coil and gleam,
And chiselled like a hound's white tooth.
"Oh, I will match you yet," I cried, "to truth."

Right glad I was to stoop to what I once had spurned,
Glad even unto tears; I laughed aloud; I turned
Upon my back, and though the tears for joy would run,
My sight was clear; I looked and saw the rising sun.

Heritage

(For Harold Jackman)

What is Africa to me:
Copper sun or scarlet sea,
Jungle star or jungle track,
Strong bronzed men, or regal black
Women from whose loins I sprang
When the birds of Eden sang?
_One three centuries removed
From the scenes his fathers loved,
Spicy grove, cinnamon tree,
What is Africa to me?_

So I lie, who all day long
Want no sound except the song
Sung by wild barbaric birds
Goading massive jungle herds,
Juggernauts of flesh that pass
Trampling tall defiant grass
Where young forest lovers lie,
Plighting troth beneath the sky.
So I lie, who always hear,
Though I cram against my ear
Both my thumbs, and keep them there,
Great drums throbbing through the air.
So I lie, whose fount of pride,
Dear distress, and joy allied,
Is my somber flesh and skin,
With the dark blood dammed within

Like great pulsing tides of wine
That, I fear, must burst the fine
Channels of the chafing net
Where they surge and foam and fret.

Africa? A book one thumbs
Listlessly, till slumber comes.
Unremembered are her bats
Circling through the night, her cats
Crouching in the river reeds,
Stalking gentle flesh that feeds
By the river brink; no more
Does the bugle-throated roar
Cry that monarch claws have leapt
From the scabbards where they slept.
Silver snakes that once a year
Doff the lovely coats you wear,
Seek no covert in your fear
Lest a mortal eye should see;
What's your nakedness to me?
Here no leprous flowers rear
Fierce corollas in the air;
Here no bodies sleek and wet,
Dripping mingled rain and sweat,
Tread the savage measures of
Jungle boys and girls in love.
What is last year's snow to me,
Last year's anything? The tree
Budding yearly must forget
How its past arose or set--
Bough and blossom, flower, fruit,
Even what shy bird with mute
Wonder at her travail there,
Meekly labored in its hair.
_One three centuries removed
From the scenes his fathers loved,

Spicy grove, cinnamon tree,
What is Africa to me?_

So I lie, who find no peace
Night or day, no slight release
From the unremittant beat
Made by cruel padded feet
Walking through my body's street.
Up and down they go, and back,
Treading out a jungle track.
So I lie, who never quite
Safely sleep from rain at night--
I can never rest at all
When the rain begins to fall;
Like a soul gone mad with pain
I must match its weird refrain;
Ever must I twist and squirm,
Writhing like a baited worm,
While its primal measures drip
Through my body, crying, "Strip!
Doff this new exuberance.
Come and dance the Lover's Dance!"
In an old remembered way
Rain works on me night and day.

Quaint, outlandish heathen gods
Black men fashion out of rods,
Clay, and brittle bits of stone,
In a likeness like their own,
My conversion came high-priced;
I belong to Jesus Christ,
Preacher of humility;
Heathen gods are naught to me.

Father, Son, and Holy Ghost,
So I make an idle boast;

Jesus of the twice-turned cheek,
Lamb of God, although I speak
With my mouth thus, in my heart
Do I play a double part.
Ever at Thy glowing altar
Must my heart grow sick and falter,
Wishing He I served were black,
Thinking then it would not lack
Precedent of pain to guide it,
Let who would or might deride it;
Surely then this flesh would know
Yours had borne a kindred woe.
Lord, I fashion dark gods, too,
Daring even to give You
Dark despairing features where,
Crowned with dark rebellious hair,
Patience wavers just so much as
Mortal grief compels, while touches
Quick and hot, of anger, rise
To smitten cheek and weary eyes.
Lord, forgive me if my need
Sometimes shapes a human creed.

_All day long and all night through,
One thing only must I do:
Quench my pride and cool my blood,
Lest I perish in the flood.
Lest a hidden ember set
Timber that I thought was wet
Burning like the dryest flax,
Melting like the merest wax,
Lest the grave restore its dead.
Not yet has my heart or head
In the least way realized
They and I are civilized._

EPITAPHS

For a Poet

I have wrapped my dreams in a silken cloth,
And laid them away in a box of gold;
Where long will cling the lips of the moth,
I have wrapped my dreams in a silken cloth;
I hide no hate; I am not even wroth
Who found earth's breath so keen and cold;
I have wrapped my dreams in a silken cloth,
And laid them away in a box of gold.

For My Grandmother

This lovely flower fell to seed;
   Work gently, sun and rain;
She held it as her dying creed
   That she would grow again.

For a Cynic

Birth is a crime
All men commit;
Life gives them time
To atone for it;
Death ends the rhyme
As the price for it.

For a Singer

Death clogged this flute
    At its highest note;
Song sleeps here mute
    In this breathless throat.

For a Virgin

For forty years I shunned the lust
    Inherent in my clay;
Death only was so amorous
    I let him have his way.

For a Lady I Know

She even thinks that up in heaven
    Her class lies late and snores,
While poor black cherubs rise at seven
    To do celestial chores.

For a Lovely Lady

A creature slender as a reed,
    And sad-eyed as a doe
Lies here (but take my word for it,
    And do not pry below).

For an Atheist

Mountains cover me like rain,
    Billows whirl and rise;
Hide me from the stabbing pain
    In His reproachful eyes.

For an Evolutionist and His Opponent

Showing that our ways agreed,
    Death is proof enough;
Body seeks the primal clay,
    Soul transcends the slough.

For an Anarchist

What matters that I stormedare
    and swore?
Not Samson with an ass's jaw,
    Not though a forest of hair he wore,
Could break death's adamantine law.

For a Magician

I whose magic could explore

Ways others might not guess or see,
Now am barred behind a door
    That has no "Open Sesame."

For a Pessimist

He wore his coffin for a hat,
    Calamity his cape,
While on his face a death's-head sat
    And waved a bit of crape.

For a Mouthy Woman

God and the devil still are wrangling
    Which should have her, which repel;
God wants no discord in his heaven;
    Satan has enough in hell.

For a Philosopher

Here lies one who tried to solve
    The riddle of being and breath:
The wee blind mole that gnaws his bones
    Tells him the answer is death.

For an Unsuccessful Sinner

I boasted my sins were sure to sink me
    Out of all sound and sight of glory;
And the most I've won for all my pains
    Is a century of purgatory.

For a Fool

On earth the wise man makes the rules,
    And is the fool's adviser,
But here the wise are as the fools,
    (And no man is the wiser).

For One Who Gayly Sowed His Oats

My days were a thing for me to live,
    For others to deplore;
I took of life all it could give:
    Rind, inner fruit, and core.

For a Skeptic

Blood-brother unto Thomas whose
    Weak faith doubt kept in trammels,
His little credence strained at gnats--
    But grew robust on camels.

For a Fatalist

Life ushers some as heirs-elect
    To weather wind and gale;
Here lies a man whose ships were wrecked
    Ere he could hoist a sail.

For Daughters of Magdalen

Ours is the ancient story:
    Delicate flowers of sin,

Lilies, arrayed in glory,
    That would not toil nor spin.

For a Wanton

To men no more than so much cover
    For them to doff or try,
I found in Death a constant lover:
    Here in his arms I lie.

For a Preacher

Vanity of vanities,
    All is vanity; yea,
Even the rod He flayed you with
    Crumbled and turned to clay.

For One Who Died Singing of Death

He whose might you sang so well
    Living, will not let you rust:
Death has set the golden bell
    Pealing in the courts of dust.

For John Keats, Apostle of Beauty

Not writ in water, nor in mist,
    Sweet lyric throat, thy name;
Thy singing lips that cold death kissed
    Have seared his own with flame.

For Hazel Hall, American Poet

Soul-troubled at the febrile ways of breath,
    Her timid breast shot through with faint alarm,
"Yes, I'm a stranger here," she said to Death,
    "It's kind of you to let me take your arm."

For Paul Laurence Dunbar

Born of the sorrowful of heart,
    Mirth was a crown upon his head;
Pride kept his twisted lips apart
    In jest, to hide a heart that bled.

For Joseph Conrad

Not of the dust, but of the wave
    His final couch should be;
They lie not easy in a grave
    Who once have known the sea.
How shall earth's meagre bed enthrall
    The hardiest seaman of them all?

For Myself

What's in this grave is worth your tear;
    There's more than the eye can see;
Folly and Pride and Love lie here
    Buried alive with me.

All the Dead

Priest and layman, virgin, strumpet,
    Good and ill commingled sleep,
Waiting till the dreadful trumpet
    Separates the wolves and sheep.

FOR LOVE'S SAKE

Oh, for a Little While Be Kind
(For Ruth Marie)

Oh, for a little while be kind to me
Who stand in such imperious need of you,
And for a fitful space let my head lie
Happily on your passion's frigid breast.
Although yourself no more resigned to me
Than on all bitter yesterdays I knew,
This half a loaf from sumptuous crumbs your shy
Reneging hand lets fall shall make me blest.
The sturdy homage of a love that throws
Its strength about you, dawn and dusk, at bed
And board, is not for scorn. When all is said
With final amen certitude, who knows
But Dives found a matchless fragrance fled
When Lazarus no longer shocked his nose?

If You Should Go

Love, leave me like the light,
    The gently passing day;
We would not know, but for the night,
    When it has slipped away.

Go quietly; a dream,
    When done, should leave no trace
That it has lived, except a gleam
    Across the dreamer's face.

To One Who Said Me Nay

This much the gods vouchsafe today:
    That we two lie in the clover,
Watching the heavens dip and sway,
    With galleons sailing over.

This much is granted for an hour:
    That we are young and tender,
That I am bee and you are flower,
    Honey-mouthed and swaying slender.

This sweet of sweets is ours now:
    To wander through the land,
Plucking an apple from its bough
    To toss from hand to hand.

No thing is certain, joy nor sorrow,
    Except the hour we know it;
Oh, wear my heart today; tomorrow
    Who knows where the winds will blow it?

ADVICE TO YOUTH

(For Guillaume)

Since little time is granted here
For pride in pain or play,
Since blood soon cools before that Fear
That makes our prowess clay,
If lips to kiss are freely met,
Lad, be not proud nor shy;
There are no lips where men forget,
And undesiring lie.

Caprice

"I'll tell him, when he comes," she said,
  "Body and baggage, to go,
Though the night be darker than my hair,
  And the ground be hard with snow."

But when he came with his gay black head
    Thrown back, and his lips apart,
She flipped a light hair from his coat,
    And sobbed against his heart.

Sacrament

She gave her body for my meat,
    Her soul to be my wine,
And prayed that I be made complete
    In sunlight and starshine.

With such abandoned grace she gave
    Of all that passion taught her,
She never knew her tidal wave
    Cast bread on stagnant water.

Bread and Wine

From death of star to new star's birth,
    This ache of limb, this throb of head,
This sweaty shop, this smell of earth,
    For this we pray, "Give daily bread."

Then tenuous with dreams the night,
    The feel of soft brown hands in mine,
Strength from your lips for one more fight:
    Bread's not so dry when dipped in wine.

Spring Reminiscence

"My sweet," you sang, and, "Sweet," I sang,
    And sweet we sang together,
Glad to be young as the world was young,

Two colts too strong for a tether.

Shall ever a spring be like that spring,
    Or apple blossoms as white;
Or ever clover smell like the clover
    We lay upon that night?

Shall ever your hand lie in my hand,
    Pulsing to it, I wonder;
Or have the gods, being jealous gods,
    Envied us our thunder?

VARIA

Suicide Chant

I am the seed
    The Sower sowed;
I am the deed
    His hand bestowed
Upon the world.

Censure me not
    If a rank weed flood
The garden plot,
    Instead of a bud
To be unfurled.

Bridle your blame
    If the deed prove less
Than the bruited fame
    With which it came
From nothingness.

The seed of a weed
    Cannot be flowered,
Nor a hero's deed
    Spring from a coward.

Pull up the weed;
    Bring plow and mower;
Then fetch new seed
    For the hand of the Sower.

She of the Dancing Feet Sings
(To Ottie Graham)

"And what would I do in heaven, pray,
    Me with my dancing feet,
And limbs like apple boughs that sway
    When the gusty rain winds beat?

And how would I thrive in a perfect place
    Where dancing would be sin,
With not a man to love my face,
    Nor an arm to hold me in?

The seraphs and the cherubim
    Would be too proud to bend
To sing the faery tunes that brim
    My heart from end to end.

The wistful angels down in hell
    Will smile to see my face,
And understand, because they fell
    From that all-perfect place."

Judas Iscariot

I think when Judas' mother heard
    His first faint cry the night
That he was born, that worship stirred
    Her at the sound and sight.
She thought his was as fair a frame
    As flesh and blood had worn;
I think she made this lovely name
    For him--"Star of my morn."

As any mother's son he grew
    From spring to crimson spring;
I think his eyes were black, or blue,
    His hair curled like a ring.
His mother's heart-strings were a lute
    Whereon he all day played;
She listened rapt, abandoned, mute,
    To every note he made.

I think he knew the growing Christ,
    And played with Mary's son,
And where mere mortal craft sufficed,
    There Judas may have won.
Perhaps he little cared or knew,
    So folly-wise is youth,
That He whose hand his hand clung to
    Was flesh-embodied Truth;

Until one day he heard young Christ,
    With far-off eyes agleam,
Tell of a mystic, solemn tryst
    Between Him and a dream.
And Judas listened, wonder-eyed,

Until the Christ was through,
Then said, "And I, though good betide,
    Or ill, will go with you."

And so he followed, heard Christ preach,
    Saw how by miracle
The blind man saw, the dumb got speech,
    The leper found him well.
And Judas in those holy hours
    Loved Christ, and loved Him much,
And in his heart he sensed dead flowers
    Bloom at the Master's touch.

And when Christ felt the death hour creep
    With sullen, drunken lurch,
He said to Peter, "Feed my sheep,
    And build my holy church."
He gave to each the special task
    That should be his to do,
But reaching one, I hear him ask,
    "What shall I give to you?"

Then Judas in his hot desire
    Said, "Give me what you will."
Christ spoke to him with words of fire,
    "Then, Judas, you must kill
One whom you love, One who loves you
    As only God's son can:
This is the work for you to do
    To save the creature man."

"And men to come will curse your name,
    And hold you up to scorn;
In all the world will be no shame
    Like yours; this is love's thorn.
It takes strong will of heart and soul,

But man is under ban.
Think, Judas, can you play this role
    In heaven's mystic plan?"

So Judas took the sorry part,
    Went out and spoke the word,
And gave the kiss that broke his heart,
    But no one knew or heard.
And no one knew what poison ate
    Into his palm that day,
Where, bright and damned, the monstrous weight
    Of thirty white coins lay.

It was not death that Judas found
    Upon a kindly tree;
The man was dead long ere he bound
    His throat as final fee.
And who can say if on that day
    When gates of pearl swung wide,
Christ did not go His honored way
    With Judas by His side?

I think somewhere a table round
    Owns Jesus as its head,
And there the saintly twelve are found
    Who followed where He led.
And Judas sits down with the rest,
    And none shrinks from His hand,
For there the worst is as the best,
    And there they understand.

And you may think of Judas, friend,
    As one who broke his word,
Whose neck came to a bitter end
    For giving up his Lord.
But I would rather think of him

As the little Jewish lad
Who gave young Christ heart, soul, and limb,
  And all the love he had.

The Wise

(For Alain Locke)

Dead men are wisest, for they know
How far the roots of flowers go,
How long a seed must rot to grow.

Dead men alone bear frost and rain
On throbless heart and heatless brain,
And feel no stir of joy or pain.

Dead men alone are satiate;
They sleep and dream and have no weight,
To curb their rest, of love or hate.

Strange, men should flee their company,
Or think me strange who long to be
Wrapped in their cool immunity.

Mary, Mother of Christare

That night she felt those searching hands
Grip deep upon her breast,
She laughed and sang a silly tune
To lull her babe to rest;

That night she kissed his coral lips
How could she know the rest?

Dialogue

Soul: There is no stronger thing than song;
 In sun and rain and leafy trees

It wafts the timid soul along
On crested waves of melodies.

Body: But leaves the body bare to feed
Its hunger with its very need.

Soul: Although the frenzied belly writhes,
Yet render up in song your tithes;
Song is the weakling's oaken rod,
His Jacob's ladder dropped from God.

Body: Song is not drink; song is not meat,
Nor strong, thick shoes for naked feet.

Soul: Who sings by unseen hands is fed
With honeyed milk and warm, white bread;
His ways in pastures green are led,
And perfumed oil illumes his head;
His cup with wine is surfeited,
And when the last low note is read,
He sings among the lipless dead
With singing stars to crown his head.

Body: But will song buy a wooden box
The length of me from toe to crown,
To keep me safe from carrion flocks
When singing's done and lyre laid down?

In Memory of Col. Charles Young

Along the shore the tall, thin grass
That fringes that dark river,
While sinuously soft feet pass,
Begins to bleed and quiver.

The great dark voice breaks with a sob
    Across the womb of night;
Above your grave the tom-toms throb,
    And the hills are weird with light.

The great dark heart is like a well
    Drained bitter by the sky,
And all the honeyed lies they tell
    Come there to thirst and die.

No lie is strong enough to kill
    The roots that work below;
From your rich dust and slaughtered will
    A tree with tongues will grow.

To My Friends

You feeble few that hold me somewhat more
Than all I am; base clay and spittle joined
To shape an aimless whim substantial; coined
Amiss one idle hour, this heart, though poor,--
O golden host I count upon the ends
Of one bare hand, with fingers still to spare,--
Is rich enough for this: to harbor there
In opulence its frugal meed of friends.
Let neither lose his faith, lest by such loss
Each find insufferable his daily cross.
And be not less immovable to me,
Not less love-leal and staunch, than my heart is.
In brief, these fine heroics come to this,
My friends: if you are true, I needs must be.

Gods

I fast and pray and go to church,
    And put my penny in,
But God's not fooled by such slight tricks,
    And I'm not saved from sin.

I cannot hide from Him the gods
    That revel in my heart,
Nor can I find an easy word
    To tell them to depart:

God's alabaster turrets gleam
    Too high for me to win,
Unless He turns His face and lets
    Me bring my own gods in.

To John Keats, Poet. At Spring Time
(For Carl Van Vechten)

I cannot hold my peace, John Keats;
There never was a spring like this;
It is an echo, that repeats
My last year's song and next year's bliss.
I know, in spite of all men say
Of Beauty, you have felt her most.
Yea, even in your grave her way
Is laid. Poor, troubled, lyric ghost,
Spring never was so fair and dear
As Beauty makes her seem this year.

I cannot hold my peace, John Keats,
I am as helpless in the toil
Of Spring as any lamb that bleats
To feel the solid earth recoil

Beneath his puny legs. Spring beats
Her tocsin call to those who love her,
And lo! the dogwood petals cover

Her breast with drifts of snow, and sleek
White gulls fly screaming to her, and hover
About her shoulders, and kiss her cheek,
While white and purple lilacs muster
A strength that bears them to a cluster
Of color and odor; for her sake
All things that slept are now awake.

And you and I, shall we lie still,
John Keats, while Beauty summons us?
Somehow I feel your sensitive will
Is pulsing up some tremulous
Sap road of a maple tree, whose leaves
Grow music as they grow, since your
Wild voice is in them, a harp that grieves
For life that opens death's dark door.
Though dust, your fingers still can push
The Vision Splendid to a birth,
Though now they work as grass in the hush
Of the night on the broad sweet page of the earth.

"John Keats is dead," they say, but I
Who hear your full insistent cry
In bud and blossom, leaf and tree,
Know John Keats still writes poetry.
And while my head is earthward bowed
To read new life sprung from your shroud,
Folks seeing me must think it strange
That merely spring should so derange
My mind. They do not know that you,
John Keats, keep revel with me, too.

On Going
(For Willard Johnson)

A grave is all too weak a thing
    To hold my fancy long;
I'll bear a blossom with the spring,
    Or be a blackbird's song,

I think that I shall fade with ease,
    Melt into earth like snow,
Be food for hungry, growing trees,
    Or help the lilies blow.

And if my love should lonely walk,
    Quite of my nearness fain,
I may come back to her, and talk
    In liquid words of rain.

Harsh World That Lashest Me
(For Walter White)

Harsh World that lashest me each day,
    Dub me not cowardly because
I seem to find no sudden way
    To throttle you or clip your claws.
No force compels me to the wound
    Whereof my body bears the scar;
Although my feet are on the ground,
    Doubt not my eyes are on a star.

You cannot keep me captive, World,
    Entrammeled, chained, spit on, and spurned.
More free than all your flags unfurled,
    I give my body to be burned.
I mount my cross because I will,
    I drink the hemlock which you give

For wine which you withhold--and still,
    Because I will not die, I live.

I live because an ember in
    Me smoulders to regain its fire,
Because what is and what has been
    Not yet have conquered my desire.
I live to prove the groping clod
    Is surely more than simple dust;
I live to see the breath of God
    Beatify the carnal crust.

But when I will, World, I can go,
    Though triple bronze should wall me round,
Slip past your guard as swift as snow,
    Translated without pain or sound.
Within myself is lodged the key
    To that vast room of couches laid
For those too proud to live and see
    Their dreams of light eclipsed in shade.

Requiescam

_I am for sleeping and forgetting
    All that has gone before;
I am for lying still and letting
    Who will beat at my door;
I would my life's cold sun were setting
    To rise for me no more._

End

SEPTEMBER
25¢
VOLUME 14 NUMBER 9
TOUGH GUY By NOEL LOOMIS
fantastic ADVENTURES
Could this lovely girl's body appease the TERROR FROM THE ABYSS
By JOHN FLETCHER

READING BREAK!!!

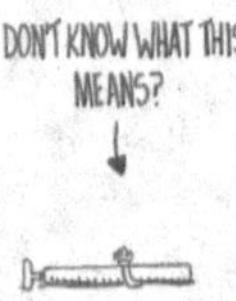

SUDOKU

<table>
<tr><td></td><td></td><td></td><td></td><td></td><td>8</td><td></td><td></td><td></td></tr>
<tr><td>3</td><td></td><td></td><td></td><td></td><td></td><td></td><td></td><td>2</td></tr>
<tr><td></td><td>7</td><td>8</td><td>2</td><td></td><td></td><td></td><td>1</td><td></td></tr>
<tr><td></td><td>4</td><td></td><td></td><td></td><td></td><td>2</td><td></td><td></td></tr>
<tr><td></td><td>5</td><td></td><td></td><td>3</td><td>6</td><td></td><td></td><td></td></tr>
<tr><td>9</td><td></td><td></td><td></td><td>2</td><td></td><td></td><td></td><td></td></tr>
<tr><td></td><td></td><td>4</td><td></td><td></td><td></td><td></td><td></td><td>7</td></tr>
<tr><td>3</td><td></td><td>2</td><td>8</td><td></td><td>4</td><td></td><td></td><td>5</td></tr>
<tr><td></td><td></td><td>5</td><td>9</td><td></td><td></td><td>6</td><td></td><td></td></tr>
</table>

(MEDIUM DIFFICULTY; ANSWERS IN BACK OF BOOK)

> Liberty is meaningless where the right to utter one's thoughts and opinions has ceased to exist. That, of all rights, is the dread of tyrants. It is the right which they first...strike down. They know its power.
> -Frederick Douglass

R. RIVETER.
AMERICAN ★ HANDMADE

Want your short story published in *Adventures*?

Email your entire story, with "Submission" in Subject to:
OffBeatReads@pm.me

Movie poster from Allentown, PA; 1946

Actress Lotta; from the Actresses and Actors Series
of Old Judge cigarette cards; late 18th century

Coke ad from 1926

LADY WINDERMERE'S FAN

A PLAY
ABOUT A GOOD WOMAN

BY
OSCAR WILDE

*To the dear memory of
Robert Earl of Lytton
in Affection
and
Admiration*

First Published in 1893

THE PERSONS OF THE PLAY:

Lord Windermere

Lord Darlington

Lord Augustus Lorton

Mr. Dumby

Mr. Cecil Graham

Mr. Hopper

Parker, Butler

Lady Windermere

The Duchess of Berwick

Lady Agatha Carlisle

Lady Plymdale

Lady Stutfield

Lady Jedburgh

Mrs. Cowper-Cowper

Mrs. Erlynne

Rosalie, Maid

THE SCENES OF THE PLAY:

Act I.	*Morning-room in Lord Windermere's house.*
Act II.	*Drawing-room in Lord Windermere's house.*
Act III.	*Lord Darlington's rooms.*
Act IV.	*Same as Act I.*
Time:	*The Present.*
Place:	*London.*

The action of the play takes place within twenty-four hours, beginning on a Tuesday afternoon at five o'clock, and ending the next day at 1.30 p.m.

FIRST ACT

SCENE

Morning-room of Lord Windermere's house in Carlton House Terrace. Doors C. and R. Bureau with books and papers R. Sofa with small tea-table L. Window opening on to terrace L. Table R.

[**LADY WINDERMERE** *is at table R., arranging roses in a blue bowl.*]

[*Enter* **PARKER**.]

PARKER. Is your ladyship at home this afternoon?

LADY WINDERMERE. Yes—who has called?

PARKER. Lord Darlington, my lady.

LADY WINDERMERE. [*Hesitates for a moment.*] Show him up—and I'm at home to any one who calls.

PARKER. Yes, my lady.

[*Exit C.*]

LADY WINDERMERE. It's best for me to see him before to-night. I'm glad he's come.

[*Enter* **PARKER** *C.*]

PARKER. Lord Darlington,

[*Enter* **LORD DARLINGTON** *C.*]

[*Exit* **PARKER**.]

LORD DARLINGTON. How do you do, Lady Windermere?

LADY WINDERMERE. How do you do, Lord Darlington? No, I can't shake hands with you. My hands are all wet with these roses. Aren't they lovely? They came up from Selby this morning.

LORD DARLINGTON. They are quite perfect. [*Sees a fan lying on the table.*] And what a wonderful fan! May I look at it?

LADY WINDERMERE. Do. Pretty, isn't it! It's got my name on it, and everything. I have only just seen it myself. It's my husband's birthday present to me. You know to-day is my birthday?

LORD DARLINGTON. No? Is it really?

LADY WINDERMERE. Yes, I'm of age to-day. Quite an important day in my life, isn't it? That is why I am giving this party to-night. Do sit down. [*Still arranging flowers.*]

LORD DARLINGTON. [*Sitting down.*] I wish I had known it was your birthday, Lady Windermere. I would have covered the whole street in front of your house with flowers for you to walk on. They are made for you.

[*A short pause.*]

LADY WINDERMERE. Lord Darlington, you annoyed me last night at the Foreign Office. I am afraid you are going to annoy me again.

LORD DARLINGTON. I, Lady Windermere?

[*Enter* **PARKER** *and* **FOOTMAN** *C., with tray and tea things.*]

LADY WINDERMERE. Put it there, Parker. That will do. [*Wipes her hands with her pocket-handkerchief, goes to tea-table, and sits down.*] Won't you come over, Lord Darlington?

[*Exit* **PARKER** *C.*]

LORD DARLINGTON. [*Takes chair and goes across L.C.*] I am quite miserable, Lady Windermere. You must tell me what I did. [*Sits down at table L.*]

LADY WINDERMERE. Well, you kept paying me elaborate compliments the whole evening.

LORD DARLINGTON. [*Smiling.*] Ah, nowadays we are all of us so hard up, that the only pleasant things to pay *are* compliments. They're the only things we *can* pay.

LADY WINDERMERE. [*Shaking her head.*] No, I am talking very seriously. You mustn't laugh, I am quite serious. I don't like compliments, and I don't see why a man should think he is pleasing a woman enormously when he says to her a whole heap of things that he doesn't mean.

LORD DARLINGTON. Ah, but I did mean them. [*Takes tea which she offers him.*]

LADY WINDERMERE. [*Gravely.*] I hope not. I should be sorry to have to quarrel with you, Lord Darlington. I like you very much, you know that. But I shouldn't like you at all if I thought you were what most other men are. Believe me, you are better than most other men, and I sometimes think you pretend to be worse.

LORD DARLINGTON. We all have our little vanities, Lady Windermere.

LADY WINDERMERE. Why do you make that your special one? [*Still seated at table L.*]

LORD DARLINGTON. [*Still seated L. C.*] Oh, nowadays so many conceited people go about Society pretending to be good, that I think it shows rather a sweet and modest disposition to pretend to be bad. Besides, there is this to be said. If you pretend to be good, the world takes you very seriously. If you pretend to be bad, it doesn't. Such is the astounding stupidity of optimism.

LADY WINDERMERE. Don't you *want* the world to take you seriously then, Lord Darlington?

LORD DARLINGTON. No, not the world. Who are the people the world takes seriously? All the dull people one can think of, from the Bishops down to the bores. I should like *you* to take me very seriously, Lady Windermere, *you* more than any one else in life.

LADY WINDERMERE. Why—why me?

LORD DARLINGTON. [*After a slight hesitation.*] Because I think we might be great friends. Let us be great friends. You may want a friend some day.

LADY WINDERMERE. Why do you say that?

LORD DARLINGTON. Oh!—we all want friends at times.

LADY WINDERMERE. I think we're very good friends already, Lord Darlington. We can always remain so as long as you don't—

LORD DARLINGTON. Don't what?

LADY WINDERMERE. Don't spoil it by saying extravagant silly things to me. You think I am a Puritan, I suppose? Well, I have something of the Puritan in me. I was brought up like that. I am glad of it. My mother died when I was a mere child. I lived always with Lady Julia, my father's elder sister, you know. She was stern to me, but she taught me what the world is forgetting, the difference that there is between what is right and what is wrong. *She* allowed of no compromise. *I* allow of none.

LORD DARLINGTON. My dear Lady Windermere!

LADY WINDERMERE. [*Leaning back on the sofa.*] You look on me as being behind the age.—Well, I am! I should be sorry to be on the same level as an age like this.

LORD DARLINGTON. You think the age very bad?

LADY WINDERMERE. Yes. Nowadays people seem to look on life as a speculation. It is not a speculation. It is a sacrament. Its ideal is Love. Its purification is sacrifice.

LORD DARLINGTON. [*Smiling.*] Oh, anything is better than being sacrificed!

LADY WINDERMERE. [*Leaning forward.*] Don't say that.

LORD DARLINGTON. I do say it. I feel it—I know it.

[*Enter* **PARKER** *C.*]

PARKER. The men want to know if they are to put the carpets on the terrace for to-night, my lady?

LADY WINDERMERE. You don't think it will rain, Lord Darlington, do you?

LORD DARLINGTON. I won't hear of its raining on your birthday!

LADY WINDERMERE. Tell them to do it at once, Parker.

[*Exit* **PARKER** *C.*]

LORD DARLINGTON. [*Still seated.*] Do you think then—of course I am only putting an imaginary instance—do you think that in the case of a young married couple, say about two years married, if the husband suddenly becomes the intimate friend of a woman of—well, more than doubtful character—is always calling upon her, lunching with her, and probably paying her bills—do you think that the wife should not console herself?

LADY WINDERMERE. [*Frowning.*] Console herself?

LORD DARLINGTON. Yes, I think she should—I think she has the right.

LADY WINDERMERE. Because the husband is vile—should the wife be vile also?

LORD DARLINGTON. Vileness is a terrible word, Lady Windermere.

LADY WINDERMERE. It is a terrible thing, Lord Darlington.

LORD DARLINGTON. Do you know I am afraid that good people do a great deal of harm in this world. Certainly the greatest harm they do is that they make badness of such extraordinary importance. It is absurd to divide people into good and bad. People are either charming or tedious. I take the side of the charming, and you, Lady Windermere, can't help belonging to them.

LADY WINDERMERE. Now, Lord Darlington. [*Rising and crossing R., front of him.*] Don't stir, I am merely going to finish my flowers. [*Goes to table R.C.*]

LORD DARLINGTON. [*Rising and moving chair.*] And I must say I think you are very hard on modern life, Lady Windermere. Of course there is much against it, I admit. Most women, for instance, nowadays, are rather mercenary.

LADY WINDERMERE. Don't talk about such people.

LORD DARLINGTON. Well then, setting aside mercenary people, who, of course, are dreadful, do you think seriously that women who have committed what the world calls a fault should never be forgiven?

LADY WINDERMERE. [*Standing at table.*] I think they should never be forgiven.

LORD DARLINGTON. And men? Do you think that there should be the same laws for men as there are for women?

LADY WINDERMERE. Certainly!

LORD DARLINGTON. I think life too complex a thing to be settled by these hard and fast rules.

LADY WINDERMERE. If we had 'these hard and fast rules,' we should find life much more simple.

LORD DARLINGTON. You allow of no exceptions?

LADY WINDERMERE. None!

LORD DARLINGTON. Ah, what a fascinating Puritan you are, Lady Windermere!

LADY WINDERMERE. The adjective was unnecessary, Lord Darlington.

LORD DARLINGTON. I couldn't help it. I can resist everything except temptation.

LADY WINDERMERE. You have the modern affectation of weakness.

LORD DARLINGTON. [*Looking at her.*] It's only an affectation, Lady Windermere.

[*Enter* **PARKER** *C.*]

PARKER. The Duchess of Berwick and Lady Agatha Carlisle.

[*Enter the* **DUCHESS OF BERWICK** and **LADY AGATHA CARLISLE** *C.*]

[*Exit* **PARKER** *C.*]

DUCHESS OF BERWICK. [*Coming down C., and shaking hands.*] Dear Margaret, I am so pleased to see you. You remember Agatha, don't you? [*Crossing L.C.*] How do you do, Lord Darlington? I won't let you know my daughter, you are far too wicked.

LORD DARLINGTON. Don't say that, Duchess. As a wicked man I am a complete failure. Why, there are lots of people who say I have never really done anything wrong in the whole course of my life. Of course they only say it behind my back.

DUCHESS OF BERWICK. Isn't he dreadful? Agatha, this is Lord Darlington. Mind you don't believe a word he says. [**LORD DARLINGTON** *crosses R.C.*] No, no tea, thank you, dear. [*Crosses and sits on sofa.*] We have just had tea at Lady Markby's. Such bad tea, too. It was quite undrinkable. I wasn't at all surprised. Her own son-in-law supplies it. Agatha is looking forward so much to your ball to-night, dear Margaret.

LADY WINDERMERE. [*Seated L.C.*] Oh, you mustn't think it is going to be a ball, Duchess. It is only a dance in honour of my birthday. A small and early.

LORD DARLINGTON. [*Standing L.C.*] Very small, very early, and very select, Duchess.

DUCHESS OF BERWICK. [*On sofa L.*] Of course it's going to be select. But we know *that*, dear Margaret, about *your* house. It is really one of the few houses in London where I can take Agatha, and where I feel perfectly secure about dear Berwick. I don't know what society is coming to. The most dreadful people seem to go everywhere. They certainly come to my parties—the men get quite furious if one doesn't ask them. Really, some one should make a stand against it.

LADY WINDERMERE. *I* will, Duchess. I will have no one in my house about whom there is any scandal.

LORD DARLINGTON. [*R.C.*] Oh, don't say that, Lady Windermere. I should never be admitted! [*Sitting.*]

DUCHESS OF BERWICK. Oh, men don't matter. With women it is different. We're good. Some of us are, at least. But we are positively getting elbowed into the corner. Our husbands would really forget our existence if we didn't nag at them from time to time, just to remind them that we have a perfect legal right to do so.

LORD DARLINGTON. It's a curious thing, Duchess, about the game of marriage—a game, by the way, that is going out of fashion—the wives hold all the honours, and invariably lose the odd trick.

DUCHESS OF BERWICK. The odd trick? Is that the husband, Lord Darlington?

LORD DARLINGTON. It would be rather a good name for the modern husband.

DUCHESS OF BERWICK. Dear Lord Darlington, how thoroughly depraved you are!

LADY WINDERMERE. Lord Darlington is trivial.

LORD DARLINGTON. Ah, don't say that, Lady Windermere.

LADY WINDERMERE. Why do you *talk* so trivially about life, then?

LORD DARLINGTON. Because I think that life is far too important a thing ever to talk seriously about it. [*Moves up C.*]

DUCHESS OF BERWICK. What does he mean? Do, as a concession to my poor wits, Lord Darlington, just explain to me what you really mean.

LORD DARLINGTON. [*Coming down back of table.*] I think I had better not, Duchess. Nowadays to be intelligible is to be found out. Good-bye! [*Shakes hands with* **DUCHESS**.] And now—[*goes up stage*] Lady Windermere, good-bye. I may come to-night, mayn't I? Do let me come.

LADY WINDERMERE. [*Standing up stage with* **LORD DARLINGTON**.] Yes, certainly. But you are not to say foolish, insincere things to people.

LORD DARLINGTON. [*Smiling.*] Ah! you are beginning to reform me. It is a dangerous thing to reform any one, Lady Windermere. [*Bows, and exit C.*]

DUCHESS OF BERWICK. [*Who has risen, goes C.*] What a charming, wicked creature! I like him so much. I'm quite delighted he's gone! How sweet you're looking! Where *do* you get your gowns? And now I must tell you how sorry I am for you, dear Margaret. [*Crosses to sofa and sits with* **LADY WINDERMERE**.] Agatha, darling!

LADY AGATHA. Yes, mamma. [*Rises.*]

DUCHESS OF BERWICK. Will you go and look over the photograph album that I see there?

LADY AGATHA. Yes, mamma. [*Goes to table up L.*]

DUCHESS OF BERWICK. Dear girl! She is so fond of photographs of Switzerland. Such a pure taste, I think. But I really am so sorry for you, Margaret.

LADY WINDERMERE. [*Smiling.*] Why, Duchess?

DUCHESS OF BERWICK. Oh, on account of that horrid woman. She dresses so well, too, which makes it much worse, sets such a dreadful example. Augustus—you know my disreputable brother—such a trial to us all—well, Augustus is completely infatuated about her. It is quite scandalous, for she is absolutely inadmissible into society. Many a woman has a past, but I am told that she has at least a dozen, and that they all fit.

LADY WINDERMERE. Whom are you talking about, Duchess?

DUCHESS OF BERWICK. About Mrs. Erlynne.

LADY WINDERMERE. Mrs. Erlynne? I never heard of her, Duchess. And what *has* she to do with me?

DUCHESS OF BERWICK. My poor child! Agatha, darling!

LADY AGATHA. Yes, mamma.

DUCHESS OF BERWICK. Will you go out on the terrace and look at the sunset?

LADY AGATHA. Yes, mamma.

[*Exit through window, L.*]

DUCHESS OF BERWICK. Sweet girl! So devoted to sunsets! Shows such refinement of feeling, does it not? After all, there is nothing like Nature, is there?

LADY WINDERMERE. But what is it, Duchess? Why do you talk to me about this person?

DUCHESS OF BERWICK. Don't you really know? I assure you we're all so distressed about it. Only last night at dear Lady Jansen's every one was saying how extraordinary it was that, of all men in London, Windermere should behave in such a way.

LADY WINDERMERE. My husband—what has *he* got to do with any woman of that kind?

DUCHESS OF BERWICK. Ah, what indeed, dear? That is the point. He goes to see her continually, and stops for hours at a time, and while he is there she is not at home to any one. Not that many ladies call on her, dear, but she has a great many disreputable men friends—my own brother particularly, as I told you—and that is what makes it so dreadful about Windermere. We looked upon *him* as being such a model husband, but I am afraid there is no doubt about it. My dear nieces—you know the Saville girls, don't you?—such nice domestic creatures—plain, dreadfully plain, but so good—well, they're always at the window doing fancy work, and making ugly things for the poor, which I think so useful of them in these dreadful socialistic days, and this terrible woman has taken a house in Curzon Street, right opposite them—such a respectable street, too! I don't know what we're coming to! And they tell me that Windermere goes there four and five times a week—they *see* him. They can't help it—and although they never talk scandal, they—well, of course—they remark on it to every one. And the worst of it all is that I have been told that this woman has got a great deal of money out of somebody, for it seems that she came to London six months ago without anything at all to speak of, and now she has this charming house in Mayfair, drives her ponies in the Park every afternoon and all—well, all—since she has known poor dear Windermere.

LADY WINDERMERE. Oh, I can't believe it!

DUCHESS OF BERWICK. But it's quite true, my dear. The whole of London knows it. That is why I felt it was better to come and talk to you, and advise you to take Windermere away at once to Homburg or to Aix, where he'll have something to amuse him, and where you can watch him all day long. I assure you, my dear, that on several occasions after I was first married, I had to pretend to be very ill, and was obliged to drink the most unpleasant mineral waters, merely to get Berwick out of town. He was so extremely susceptible. Though I am bound to say he never gave away any large sums of money to anybody. He is far too high-principled for that!

LADY WINDERMERE. [*Interrupting.*] Duchess, Duchess, it's impossible! [*Rising and crossing stage to C.*] We are only married two years. Our child is but six months old. [*Sits in chair R. of L. table.*]

DUCHESS OF BERWICK. Ah, the dear pretty baby! How is the little darling? Is it a boy or a girl? I hope a girl—Ah, no, I remember it's a boy! I'm so sorry. Boys are so wicked. My boy is excessively immoral. You wouldn't believe at what hours he comes home. And he's only left Oxford a few months—I really don't know what they teach them there.

LADY WINDERMERE. Are *all* men bad?

DUCHESS OF BERWICK. Oh, all of them, my dear, all of them, without any exception. And they never grow any better. Men become old, but they never become good.

LADY WINDERMERE. Windermere and I married for love.

DUCHESS OF BERWICK. Yes, we begin like that. It was only Berwick's brutal and incessant threats of suicide that made me accept him at all, and before the year was out, he was running after all kinds of petticoats, every colour, every shape, every material. In fact, before the honeymoon was over, I caught him winking at my maid, a most pretty, respectable girl. I dismissed her at once without a character.—No, I remember I passed her on to my sister; poor dear Sir George is so short-sighted, I thought it wouldn't matter. But it did, though—it was most unfortunate. [*Rises.*] And now, my dear child, I must go, as we are dining out. And mind you don't take this little aberration of Windermere's too much to heart. Just take him abroad, and he'll come back to you all right.

LADY WINDERMERE. Come back to me? [*C.*]

DUCHESS OF BERWICK. [*L.C.*] Yes, dear, these wicked women get our husbands away from us, but they always come back, slightly damaged, of course. And don't make scenes, men hate them!

LADY WINDERMERE. It is very kind of you, Duchess, to come and tell me all this. But I can't believe that my husband is untrue to me.

DUCHESS OF BERWICK. Pretty child! I was like that once. Now I know that all men are monsters. [**LADY WINDERMERE** *rings bell.*] The only thing to do is to feed the wretches well. A good cook does wonders, and that I know you have. My dear Margaret, you are not going to cry?

LADY WINDERMERE. You needn't be afraid, Duchess, I never cry.

DUCHESS OF BERWICK. That's quite right, dear. Crying is the refuge of plain women but the ruin of pretty ones. Agatha, darling!

LADY AGATHA. [*Entering L.*] Yes, mamma. [*Stands back of table L.C.*]

DUCHESS OF BERWICK. Come and bid good-bye to Lady Windermere, and thank her for your charming visit. [*Coming down again.*] And by the way, I must thank you for sending a card to Mr. Hopper—he's that rich young Australian people are taking such notice of just at present. His father made a great fortune by selling some kind of food in circular tins—most palatable, I believe—I fancy it is the thing the servants always refuse to eat. But the son is quite interesting. I think he's attracted by dear Agatha's clever talk. Of course, we should be very sorry to lose her, but I think that a mother who doesn't part with a daughter every season has no real affection. We're coming to-night, dear. [**PARKER** *opens C. doors.*] And remember my advice, take the poor fellow out of town at once, it is the only thing to do. Good-bye, once more; come, Agatha.

[*Exeunt* **DUCHESS** *and* **LADY AGATHA** *C.*]

LADY WINDERMERE. How horrible! I understand now what Lord Darlington meant by the imaginary instance of the couple not two years married. Oh! it can't be true—she spoke of enormous sums of money paid to this woman. I know where Arthur keeps his bank book—in one of the drawers of that desk. I might find out by that. I *will* find out. [*Opens drawer.*] No, it is some hideous mistake. [*Rises and goes C.*] Some silly scandal! He loves *me*! He loves *me*! But why should I not look? I am his wife, I have a right to look! [*Returns to bureau, takes out book and examines it page by page, smiles and gives a sigh of relief.*] I knew it! there is not a word of truth in this stupid story. [*Puts book back in drawer. As he does so, starts and takes out another book.*] A second book—private—locked! [*Tries to open it, but fails. Sees paper knife on bureau, and with it cuts cover from book. Begins to start at the first page.*] 'Mrs. Erlynne—£600—Mrs. Erlynne—£700—Mrs. Erlynne—£400.' Oh! it is true! It is true! How horrible! [*Throws book on floor.*]

[*Enter* **LORD WINDERMERE** *C.*]

LORD WINDERMERE. Well, dear, has the fan been sent home yet? [*Going R.C. Sees book.*] Margaret, you have cut open my bank book. You have no right to do such a thing!

LADY WINDERMERE. You think it wrong that you are found out, don't you?

LORD WINDERMERE. I think it wrong that a wife should spy on her husband.

LADY WINDERMERE. I did not spy on you. I never knew of this woman's existence till half an hour ago. Some one who pitied me was kind enough to tell me what every one in London knows already—your daily visits to Curzon Street, your mad infatuation, the monstrous sums of money you squander on this infamous woman! [*Crossing L.*]

LORD WINDERMERE. Margaret! don't talk like that of Mrs. Erlynne, you don't know how unjust it is!

LADY WINDERMERE. [*Turning to him.*] You are very jealous of Mrs. Erlynne's honour. I wish you had been as jealous of mine.

LORD WINDERMERE. Your honour is untouched, Margaret. You don't think for a moment that—[*Puts book back into desk.*]

LADY WINDERMERE. I think that you spend your money strangely. That is all. Oh, don't imagine I mind about the money. As far as I am concerned, you may squander everything we have. But what I *do* mind is that you who have loved me, you who have taught me to love you, should pass from the love that is given to the love that is bought. Oh, it's horrible! [*Sits on sofa.*] And it is I who feel degraded! *you* don't feel anything. I feel stained, utterly stained. You can't realise how hideous the last six months seems to me now—every kiss you have given me is tainted in my memory.

LORD WINDERMERE. [*Crossing to her.*] Don't say that, Margaret. I never loved any one in the whole world but you.

LADY WINDERMERE. [*Rises.*] Who is this woman, then? Why do you take a house for her?

LORD WINDERMERE. I did not take a house for her.

LADY WINDERMERE. You gave her the money to do it, which is the same thing.

LORD WINDERMERE. Margaret, as far as I have known Mrs. Erlynne—

LADY WINDERMERE. Is there a Mr. Erlynne—or is he a myth?

LORD WINDERMERE. Her husband died many years ago. She is alone in the world.

LADY WINDERMERE. No relations? [*A pause.*]

LORD WINDERMERE. None.

LADY WINDERMERE. Rather curious, isn't it? [*L.*]

LORD WINDERMERE. [*L.C.*] Margaret, I was saying to you—and I beg you to listen to me—that as far as I have known Mrs. Erlynne, she has conducted herself well. If years ago—

LADY WINDERMERE. Oh! [*Crossing R.C.*] I don't want details about her life!

LORD WINDERMERE. [*C.*] I am not going to give you any details about her life. I tell you simply this—Mrs. Erlynne was once honoured, loved, respected. She was well born, she had position—she lost everything—threw it away, if you like. That makes it all the more bitter. Misfortunes one can endure—they come from outside, they are accidents. But to suffer for one's own faults—ah!—there is the sting of life. It was twenty years ago, too. She was little more than a girl then. She had been a wife for even less time than you have.

LADY WINDERMERE. I am not interested in her—and—you should not mention this woman and me in the same breath. It is an error of taste. [*Sitting R. at desk.*]

LORD WINDERMERE. Margaret, you could save this woman. She wants to get back into society, and she wants you to help her. [*Crossing to her.*]

LADY WINDERMERE. Me!

LORD WINDERMERE. Yes, you.

LADY WINDERMERE. How impertinent of her! [*A pause.*]

LORD WINDERMERE. Margaret, I came to ask you a great favour, and I still ask it of you, though you have discovered what I had intended you should never have known that I have given Mrs. Erlynne a large sum of money. I want you to send her an invitation for our party to-night. [*Standing L. of her.*]

LADY WINDERMERE. You are mad! [*Rises.*]

LORD WINDERMERE. I entreat you. People may chatter about her, do chatter about her, of course, but they don't know anything definite against her. She has been to several houses—not to houses where you would go, I admit, but still to houses where women who are in what is called Society nowadays do go. That does not content her. She wants you to receive her once.

LADY WINDERMERE. As a triumph for her, I suppose?

LORD WINDERMERE. No; but because she knows that you are a good woman—and that if she comes here once she will have a chance of a happier, a surer life than she has had. She will make no further effort to know you. Won't you help a woman who is trying to get back?

LADY WINDERMERE. No! If a woman really repents, she never wishes to return to the society that has made or seen her ruin.

LORD WINDERMERE. I beg of you.

LADY WINDERMERE. [*Crossing to door R.*] I am going to dress for dinner, and don't mention the subject again this evening. Arthur [*going to him C.*], you fancy because I have no father or mother that I am alone in the world, and that you can treat me as you choose. You are wrong, I have friends, many friends.

LORD WINDERMERE. [*L.C.*] Margaret, you are talking foolishly, recklessly. I won't argue with you, but I insist upon your asking Mrs. Erlynne to-night.

LADY WINDERMERE. [*R.C.*] I shall do nothing of the kind. [*Crossing L.C.*]

LORD WINDERMERE. You refuse? [*C.*]

LADY WINDERMERE. Absolutely!

LORD WINDERMERE. Ah, Margaret, do this for my sake; it is her last chance.

LADY WINDERMERE. What has that to do with me?

LORD WINDERMERE. How hard good women are!

LADY WINDERMERE. How weak bad men are!

LORD WINDERMERE. Margaret, none of us men may be good enough for the women we marry—that is quite true—but you don't imagine I would ever—oh, the suggestion is monstrous!

LADY WINDERMERE. Why should *you* be different from other men? I am told that there is hardly a husband in London who does not waste his life over *some* shameful passion.

LORD WINDERMERE. I am not one of them.

LADY WINDERMERE. I am not sure of that!

LORD WINDERMERE. You are sure in your heart. But don't make chasm after chasm between us. God knows the last few minutes have thrust us wide enough apart. Sit down and write the card.

LADY WINDERMERE. Nothing in the whole world would induce me.

LORD WINDERMERE. [*Crossing to bureau.*] Then I will! [*Rings electric bell, sits and writes card.*]

LADY WINDERMERE. You are going to invite this woman? [*Crossing to him.*]

LORD WINDERMERE. Yes. [*Pause. Enter* **PARKER**.] Parker!

PARKER. Yes, my lord. [*Comes down L.C.*]

LORD WINDERMERE. Have this note sent to Mrs. Erlynne at No. 84A Curzon Street. [*Crossing to L.C. and giving note to* **PARKER**.] There is no answer!

[*Exit* **PARKER** *C.*]

LADY WINDERMERE. Arthur, if that woman comes here, I shall insult her.

LORD WINDERMERE. Margaret, don't say that.

LADY WINDERMERE. I mean it.

LORD WINDERMERE. Child, if you did such a thing, there's not a woman in London who wouldn't pity you.

LADY WINDERMERE. There is not a *good* woman in London who would not applaud me. We have been too lax. We must make an example. I propose to begin to-night. [*Picking up fan.*] Yes, you gave me this fan to-day; it was your birthday present. If that woman crosses my threshold, I shall strike her across the face with it.

LORD WINDERMERE. Margaret, you couldn't do such a thing.

LADY WINDERMERE. You don't know me! [*Moves R.*]

[*Enter* **PARKER**.]

Parker!

PARKER. Yes, my lady.

LADY WINDERMERE. I shall dine in my own room. I don't want dinner, in fact. See that everything is ready by half-past ten. And, Parker, be sure you pronounce the names of the guests very distinctly to-night. Sometimes you speak so fast that I miss them. I am particularly anxious to hear the names quite clearly, so as to make no mistake. You understand, Parker?

PARKER. Yes, my lady.

LADY WINDERMERE. That will do!

[*Exit* **PARKER** *C.*]

[*Speaking to* **LORD WINDERMERE**.] Arthur, if that woman comes here—I warn you—

LORD WINDERMERE. Margaret, you'll ruin us!

LADY WINDERMERE. Us! From this moment my life is separate from yours. But if you wish to avoid a public scandal, write at once to this woman, and tell her that I forbid her to come here!

LORD WINDERMERE. I will not—I cannot—she must come!

LADY WINDERMERE. Then I shall do exactly as I have said. [*Goes R.*] You leave me no choice.

[*Exit R.*]

LORD WINDERMERE. [*Calling after her.*] Margaret! Margaret! [*A pause.*] My God! What shall I do? I dare not tell her who this woman really is. The shame would kill her. [*Sinks down into a chair and buries his face in his hands.*]

ACT DROP

SECOND ACT

SCENE

Drawing-room in Lord Windermere's house. Door R.U. opening into ball-room, where band is playing. Door L. through which guests are entering. Door L.U. opens on to illuminated terrace. Palms, flowers, and brilliant lights. Room crowded with guests. Lady Windermere is receiving them.

DUCHESS OF BERWICK. [*Up C.*] So strange Lord Windermere isn't here. Mr. Hopper is very late, too. You have kept those five dances for him, Agatha? [*Comes down.*]

LADY AGATHA. Yes, mamma.

DUCHESS OF BERWICK. [*Sitting on sofa.*] Just let me see your card. I'm so glad Lady Windermere has revived cards.—They're a mother's only safeguard. You dear simple little thing! [*Scratches out two names.*] No nice girl should ever waltz with such particularly younger sons! It looks so fast! The last two dances you might pass on the terrace with Mr. Hopper.

[*Enter **MR. DUMBY** and **LADY PLYMDALE** from the ball-room.*]

LADY AGATHA. Yes, mamma.

DUCHESS OF BERWICK. [*Fanning herself.*] The air is so pleasant there.

241

PARKER. Mrs. Cowper-Cowper. Lady Stutfield. Sir James Royston. Mr. Guy Berkeley.

[*These people enter as announced.*]

DUMBY. Good evening, Lady Stutfield. I suppose this will be the last ball of the season?

LADY STUTFIELD. I suppose so, Mr. Dumby. It's been a delightful season, hasn't it?

DUMBY. Quite delightful! Good evening, Duchess. I suppose this will be the last ball of the season?

DUCHESS OF BERWICK. I suppose so, Mr. Dumby. It has been a very dull season, hasn't it?

DUMBY. Dreadfully dull! Dreadfully dull!

MR. COWPER-COWPER. Good evening, Mr. Dumby. I suppose this will be the last ball of the season?

DUMBY. Oh, I think not. There'll probably be two more. [*Wanders back to* **LADY PLYMDALE**.]

PARKER. Mr. Rufford. Lady Jedburgh and Miss Graham. Mr. Hopper.

[*These people enter as announced.*]

HOPPER. How do you do, Lady Windermere? How do you do, Duchess? [*Bows to* **LADY AGATHA**.]

DUCHESS OF BERWICK. Dear Mr. Hopper, how nice of you to come so early. We all know how you are run after in London.

HOPPER. Capital place, London! They are not nearly so exclusive in London as they are in Sydney.

DUCHESS OF BERWICK. Ah! we know your value, Mr. Hopper. We wish there were more like you. It would make life so much easier. Do you know, Mr. Hopper, dear Agatha and I are so much interested in Australia. It must be so pretty with all the dear little kangaroos flying about. Agatha has found it on the map. What a curious shape it is! Just like a large packing case. However, it is a very young country, isn't it?

HOPPER. Wasn't it made at the same time as the others, Duchess?

DUCHESS OF BERWICK. How clever you are, Mr. Hopper. You have a cleverness quite of your own. Now I mustn't keep you.

HOPPER. But I should like to dance with Lady Agatha, Duchess.

DUCHESS OF BERWICK. Well, I hope she has a dance left. Have you a dance left, Agatha?

LADY AGATHA. Yes, mamma.

DUCHESS OF BERWICK. The next one?

LADY AGATHA. Yes, mamma.

HOPPER. May I have the pleasure? [**LADY AGATHA** *bows*.]

DUCHESS OF BERWICK. Mind you take great care of my little chatterbox, Mr. Hopper.

[**LADY AGATHA** *and* **MR. HOPPER** *pass into ball-room*.]

[*Enter* **LORD WINDERMERE**.]

LORD WINDERMERE. Margaret, I want to speak to you.

LADY WINDERMERE. In a moment. [*The music drops*.]

PARKER. Lord Augustus Lorton.

[*Enter* **LORD AUGUSTUS**.]

LORD AUGUSTUS. Good evening, Lady Windermere.

DUCHESS OF BERWICK. Sir James, will you take me into the ball-room? Augustus has been dining with us to-night. I really have had quite enough of dear Augustus for the moment.

[**SIR JAMES ROYSTON** *gives the* **DUCHESS** *his arm and escorts her into the ball-room*.]

PARKER. Mr. and Mrs. Arthur Bowden. Lord and Lady Paisley. Lord Darlington.

[*These people enter as announced*.]

LORD AUGUSTUS. [*Coming up to* **LORD WINDERMERE**.] Want to speak to you particularly, dear boy. I'm worn to a shadow. Know I don't look it. None of us men do look what we really are. Demmed good thing, too. What I want to know is this. Who is she? Where does she come from?

Why hasn't she got any demmed relations? Demmed nuisance, relations! But they make one so demmed respectable.

LORD WINDERMERE. You are talking of Mrs. Erlynne, I suppose? I only met her six months ago. Till then, I never knew of her existence.

LORD AUGUSTUS. You have seen a good deal of her since then.

LORD WINDERMERE. [*Coldly*.] Yes, I have seen a good deal of her since then. I have just seen her.

LORD AUGUSTUS. Egad! the women are very down on her. I have been dining with Arabella this evening! By Jove! you should have heard what she said about Mrs. Erlynne. She didn't leave a rag on her. . . . [*Aside*.] Berwick and I told her that didn't matter much, as the lady in question must have an extremely fine figure. You should have seen Arabella's expression! . . . But, look here, dear boy. I don't know what to do about Mrs. Erlynne. Egad! I might be married to her; she treats me with such demmed indifference. She's deuced clever, too! She explains everything. Egad! she explains you. She has got any amount of explanations for you—and all of them different.

LORD WINDERMERE. No explanations are necessary about my friendship with Mrs. Erlynne.

LORD AUGUSTUS. Hem! Well, look here, dear old fellow. Do you think she will ever get into this demmed thing called Society? Would you introduce her to your wife? No use beating about the confounded bush. Would you do that?

LORD WINDERMERE. Mrs. Erlynne is coming here to-night.

LORD AUGUSTUS. Your wife has sent her a card?

LORD WINDERMERE. Mrs. Erlynne has received a card.

LORD AUGUSTUS. Then she's all right, dear boy. But why didn't you tell me that before? It would have saved me a heap of worry and demmed misunderstandings!

[**LADY AGATHA** *and* **MR. HOPPER** *cross and exit on terrace L.U.E.*]

PARKER. Mr. Cecil Graham!

[*Enter* **MR. CECIL GRAHAM**.]

CECIL GRAHAM. [*Bows to* **LADY WINDERMERE**, *passes over and shakes hands with* **LORD WINDERMERE**.] Good evening, Arthur. Why don't you ask me how I am? I like people to ask me how I am. It shows a wide-spread interest in my health. Now, to-night I am not at all well. Been dining with my people. Wonder why it is one's people are always so tedious? My father would talk morality after dinner. I told him he was old enough to know better. But my experience is that as soon as people are old enough to know better, they don't know anything at all. Hallo, Tuppy! Hear you're going to be married again; thought you were tired of that game.

LORD AUGUSTUS. You're excessively trivial, my dear boy, excessively trivial!

CECIL GRAHAM. By the way, Tuppy, which is it? Have you been twice married and once divorced, or twice divorced and once married? I say you've been twice divorced and once married. It seems so much more probable.

LORD AUGUSTUS. I have a very bad memory. I really don't remember which. [*Moves away R.*]

LADY PLYMDALE. Lord Windermere, I've something most particular to ask you.

LORD WINDERMERE. I am afraid—if you will excuse me—I must join my wife.

LADY PLYMDALE. Oh, you mustn't dream of such a thing. It's most dangerous nowadays for a husband to pay any attention to his wife in public. It always makes people think that he beats her when they're alone. The world has grown so suspicious of anything that looks like a happy married life. But I'll tell you what it is at supper. [*Moves towards door of ball-room.*]

LORD WINDERMERE. [*C.*] Margaret! I *must* speak to you.

LADY WINDERMERE. Will you hold my fan for me, Lord Darlington? Thanks. [*Comes down to him.*]

LORD WINDERMERE. [*Crossing to her.*] Margaret, what you said before dinner was, of course, impossible?

LADY WINDERMERE. That woman is not coming here to-night!

LORD WINDERMERE. [*R.C.*] Mrs. Erlynne is coming here, and if you in any way annoy or wound her, you will bring shame and sorrow on us both. Remember that! Ah, Margaret! only trust me! A wife should trust her husband!

LADY WINDERMERE. [*C.*] London is full of women who trust their husbands. One can always recognise them. They look so thoroughly unhappy. I am not going to be one of them. [*Moves up.*] Lord Darlington, will you give me back my fan, please? Thanks. . . . A useful thing a fan, isn't it? . . . I want a friend to-night, Lord Darlington: I didn't know I would want one so soon.

LORD DARLINGTON. Lady Windermere! I knew the time would come some day; but why to-night?

LORD WINDERMERE. I *will* tell her. I must. It would be terrible if there were any scene. Margaret . . .

PARKER. Mrs. Erlynne!

[**LORD WINDERMERE** *starts.* **MRS. ERLYNNE** *enters, very beautifully dressed and very dignified.* **LADY WINDERMERE** *clutches at her fan, then lets it drop on the door. She bows coldly to* **MRS. ERLYNNE**, *who bows to her sweetly in turn, and sails into the room.*]

LORD DARLINGTON. You have dropped your fan, Lady Windermere. [*Picks it up and hands it to her.*]

MRS. ERLYNNE. [*C.*] How do you do, again, Lord Windermere? How charming your sweet wife looks! Quite a picture!

LORD WINDERMERE. [*In a low voice.*] It was terribly rash of you to come!

MRS. ERLYNNE. [*Smiling.*] The wisest thing I ever did in my life. And, by the way, you must pay me a good deal of attention this evening. I am afraid of the women. You must introduce me to some of them. The men I can always manage. How do you do, Lord Augustus? You have quite neglected me lately. I have not seen you since yesterday. I am afraid you're faithless. Every one told me so.

LORD AUGUSTUS. [*R.*] Now really, Mrs. Erlynne, allow me to explain.

MRS. ERLYNNE. [*R.C.*] No, dear Lord Augustus, you can't explain anything. It is your chief charm.

LORD AUGUSTUS. Ah! if you find charms in me, Mrs. Erlynne—

[*They converse together.* **LORD WINDERMERE** *moves uneasily about the room watching* **MRS. ERLYNNE**.]

LORD DARLINGTON. [*To* **LADY WINDERMERE**.] How pale you are!

LADY WINDERMERE. Cowards are always pale!

LORD DARLINGTON. You look faint. Come out on the terrace.

LADY WINDERMERE. Yes. [*To* **PARKER**.] Parker, send my cloak out.

MRS. ERLYNNE. [*Crossing to her.*] Lady Windermere, how beautifully your terrace is illuminated. Reminds me of Prince Doria's at Rome.

[**LADY WINDERMERE** *bows coldly, and goes off with* **LORD DARLINGTON**.]

Oh, how do you do, Mr. Graham? Isn't that your aunt, Lady Jedburgh? I should so much like to know her.

CECIL GRAHAM. [*After a moment's hesitation and embarrassment.*] Oh, certainly, if you wish it. Aunt Caroline, allow me to introduce Mrs. Erlynne.

MRS. ERLYNNE. So pleased to meet you, Lady Jedburgh. [*Sits beside her on the sofa.*] Your nephew and I are great friends. I am so much interested in his political career. I think he's sure to be a wonderful success. He thinks like a Tory, and talks like a Radical, and that's so important nowadays. He's such a brilliant talker, too. But we all know from whom he inherits that. Lord Allandale was saying to me only yesterday, in the Park, that Mr. Graham talks almost as well as his aunt.

LADY JEDBURGH. [*R.*] Most kind of you to say these charming things to me! [**MRS. ERLYNNE** *smiles, and continues conversation.*]

DUMBY. [*To* **CECIL GRAHAM**.] Did you introduce Mrs. Erlynne to Lady Jedburgh?

CECIL GRAHAM. Had to, my dear fellow. Couldn't help it! That woman can make one do anything she wants. How, I don't know.

DUMBY. Hope to goodness she won't speak to me! [*Saunters towards* **LADY PLYMDALE**.]

MRS. ERLYNNE. [*C. To* **LADY JEDBURGH**.] On Thursday? With great pleasure. [*Rises, and speaks to* **LORD WINDERMERE**, *laughing*.] What a bore it is to have to be civil to these old dowagers! But they always insist on it!

LADY PLYMDALE. [*To* **MR. DUMBY**.] Who is that well-dressed woman talking to Windermere?

DUMBY. Haven't got the slightest idea! Looks like an *édition de luxe* of a wicked French novel, meant specially for the English market.

MRS. ERLYNNE. So that is poor Dumby with Lady Plymdale? I hear she is frightfully jealous of him. He doesn't seem anxious to speak to me to-night. I suppose he is afraid of her. Those straw-coloured women have dreadful tempers. Do you know, I think I'll dance with you first, Windermere. [**LORD WINDERMERE** *bites his lip and frowns*.] It will make Lord Augustus so jealous! Lord Augustus! [**LORD AUGUSTUS** *comes down*.] Lord Windermere insists on my dancing with him first, and, as it's his own house, I can't well refuse. You know I would much sooner dance with you.

LORD AUGUSTUS. [*With a low bow*.] I wish I could think so, Mrs. Erlynne.

MRS. ERLYNNE. You know it far too well. I can fancy a person dancing through life with you and finding it charming.

LORD AUGUSTUS. [*Placing his hand on his white waistcoat*.] Oh, thank you, thank you. You are the most adorable of all ladies!

MRS. ERLYNNE. What a nice speech! So simple and so sincere! Just the sort of speech I like. Well, you shall hold my bouquet. [*Goes towards ball-room on* **LORD WINDERMERE'S** *arm*.] Ah, Mr. Dumby, how are you? I am so sorry I have been out the last three times you have called. Come and lunch on Friday.

DUMBY. [*With perfect nonchalance*.] Delighted!

[**LADY PLYMDALE** *glares with indignation at* **MR. DUMBY**. **LORD AUGUSTUS** *follows* **MRS. ERLYNNE** *and* **LORD WINDERMERE** *into the ball-room holding bouquet.*]

LADY PLYMDALE. [*To* **MR. DUMBY**.] What an absolute brute you are! I never can believe a word you say! Why did you tell me you didn't know her? What do you mean by calling on her three times running? You are not to go to lunch there; of course you understand that?

DUMBY. My dear Laura, I wouldn't dream of going!

LADY PLYMDALE. You haven't told me her name yet! Who is she?

DUMBY. [*Coughs slightly and smooths his hair.*] She's a Mrs. Erlynne.

LADY PLYMDALE. That woman!

DUMBY. Yes; that is what every one calls her.

LADY PLYMDALE. How very interesting! How intensely interesting! I really must have a good stare at her. [*Goes to door of ball-room and looks in.*] I have heard the most shocking things about her. They say she is ruining poor Windermere. And Lady Windermere, who goes in for being so proper, invites her! How extremely amusing! It takes a thoroughly good woman to do a thoroughly stupid thing. You are to lunch there on Friday!

DUMBY. Why?

LADY PLYMDALE. Because I want you to take my husband with you. He has been so attentive lately, that he has become a perfect nuisance. Now, this woman is just the thing for him. He'll dance attendance upon her as long as she lets him, and won't bother me. I assure you, women of that kind are most useful. They form the basis of other people's marriages.

DUMBY. What a mystery you are!

LADY PLYMDALE. [*Looking at him.*] I wish *you* were!

DUMBY. I am—to myself. I am the only person in the world I should like to know thoroughly; but I don't see any chance of it just at present.

[*They pass into the ball-room, and* **LADY WINDERMERE** *and* **LORD DARLINGTON** *enter from the terrace.*]

LADY WINDERMERE. Yes. Her coming here is monstrous, unbearable. I know now what you meant to-day at tea-time. Why didn't you tell me right out? You should have!

LORD DARLINGTON. I couldn't! A man can't tell these things about another man! But if I had known he was going to make you ask her here to-night, I think I would have told you. That insult, at any rate, you would have been spared.

LADY WINDERMERE. I did not ask her. He insisted on her coming—against my entreaties—against my commands. Oh! the house is tainted for me! I feel that every woman here sneers at me as she dances by with my husband. What have I done to deserve this? I gave him all my life. He took it—used it—spoiled it! I am degraded in my own eyes; and I lack courage—I am a coward! [*Sits down on sofa.*]

LORD DARLINGTON. If I know you at all, I know that you can't live with a man who treats you like this! What sort of life would you have with him? You would feel that he was lying to you every moment of the day. You would feel that the look in his eyes was false, his voice false, his touch false, his passion false. He would come to you when he was weary of others; you would have to comfort him. He would come to you when he was devoted to others; you would have to charm him. You would have to be to him the mask of his real life, the cloak to hide his secret.

LADY WINDERMERE. You are right—you are terribly right. But where am I to turn? You said you would be my friend, Lord Darlington.—Tell me, what am I to do? Be my friend now.

LORD DARLINGTON. Between men and women there is no friendship possible. There is passion, enmity, worship, love, but no friendship. I love you—

LADY WINDERMERE. No, no! [*Rises.*]

LORD DARLINGTON. Yes, I love you! You are more to me than anything in the whole world. What does your husband give you? Nothing. Whatever is in him he gives to this wretched woman, whom he has thrust into your society, into your home, to shame you before every one. I offer you my life—

LADY WINDERMERE. Lord Darlington!

LORD DARLINGTON. My life—my whole life. Take it, and do with it what you will. . . . I love you—love you as I have never loved any living thing. From the moment I met you I loved you, loved you blindly, adoringly, madly! You did not know it then—you know it now! Leave this house to-night. I won't tell you that the world matters nothing, or the world's voice, or the voice of society. They matter a great deal. They matter far too much. But there are moments when one has to choose between living one's own life, fully, entirely, completely—or dragging out some false, shallow, degrading existence that the world in its hypocrisy demands. You have that moment now. Choose! Oh, my love, choose.

LADY WINDERMERE. [*Moving slowly away from him, and looking at him with startled eyes.*] I have not the courage.

LORD DARLINGTON. [*Following her.*] Yes; you have the courage. There may be six months of pain, of disgrace even, but when you no longer bear his name, when you bear mine, all will be well. Margaret, my love, my wife that shall be some day—yes, my wife! You know it! What are you now? This woman has the place that belongs by right to you. Oh! go—go out of this house, with head erect, with a smile upon your lips, with courage in your eyes. All London will know why you did it; and who will blame you? No one. If they do, what matter? Wrong? What is wrong? It's wrong for a man to abandon his wife for a shameless woman. It is wrong for a wife to remain with a man who so dishonours her. You said once you would make no compromise with things. Make none now. Be brave! Be yourself!

LADY WINDERMERE. I am afraid of being myself. Let me think! Let me wait! My husband may return to me. [*Sits down on sofa.*]

LORD DARLINGTON. And you would take him back! You are not what I thought you were. You are just the same as every other woman. You would stand anything rather than face the censure of a world, whose praise you would despise. In a week you will be driving with this woman in the Park. She will be your constant guest—your dearest friend. You would endure anything rather than break with one blow this monstrous tie. You are right. You have no courage; none!

LADY WINDERMERE. Ah, give me time to think. I cannot answer you now. [*Passes her hand nervously over her brow.*]

LORD DARLINGTON. It must be now or not at all.

LADY WINDERMERE. [*Rising from the sofa.*] Then, not at all! [*A pause.*]

LORD DARLINGTON. You break my heart!

LADY WINDERMERE. Mine is already broken. [*A pause.*]

LORD DARLINGTON. To-morrow I leave England. This is the last time I shall ever look on you. You will never see me again. For one moment our lives met—our souls touched. They must never meet or touch again. Good-bye, Margaret. [*Exit.*]

LADY WINDERMERE. How alone I am in life! How terribly alone!

[*The music stops. Enter the* **DUCHESS OF BERWICK** *and* **LORD PAISLEY** *laughing and talking. Other guests come on from ball-room.*]

DUCHESS OF BERWICK. Dear Margaret, I've just been having such a delightful chat with Mrs. Erlynne. I am so sorry for what I said to you this afternoon about her. Of course, she must be all right if *you* invite her. A most attractive woman, and has such sensible views on life. Told me she entirely disapproved of people marrying more than once, so I feel quite safe about poor Augustus. Can't imagine why people speak against her. It's those horrid nieces of mine—the Saville girls—they're always talking scandal. Still, I should go to Homburg, dear, I really should. She is just a little too attractive. But where is Agatha? Oh, there she is: [**LADY AGATHA** *and* **MR. HOPPER** *enter from terrace L.U.E.*] Mr. Hopper, I am very, very angry with you. You have taken Agatha out on the terrace, and she is so delicate.

HOPPER. Awfully sorry, Duchess. We went out for a moment and then got chatting together.

DUCHESS OF BERWICK. [*C.*] Ah, about dear Australia, I suppose?

HOPPER. Yes!

DUCHESS OF BERWICK. Agatha, darling! [*Beckons her over.*]

LADY AGATHA. Yes, mamma!

DUCHESS OF BERWICK. [*Aside.*] Did Mr. Hopper definitely—

LADY AGATHA. Yes, mamma.

DUCHESS OF BERWICK. And what answer did you give him, dear child?

LADY AGATHA. Yes, mamma.

DUCHESS OF BERWICK. [*Affectionately.*] My dear one! You always say the right thing. Mr. Hopper! James! Agatha has told me everything. How cleverly you have both kept your secret.

HOPPER. You don't mind my taking Agatha off to Australia, then, Duchess?

DUCHESS OF BERWICK. [*Indignantly.*] To Australia? Oh, don't mention that dreadful vulgar place.

HOPPER. But she said she'd like to come with me.

DUCHESS OF BERWICK. [*Severely.*] Did you say that, Agatha?

LADY AGATHA. Yes, mamma.

DUCHESS OF BERWICK. Agatha, you say the most silly things possible. I think on the whole that Grosvenor Square would be a more healthy place to reside in. There are lots of vulgar people live in Grosvenor Square, but at any rate there are no horrid kangaroos crawling about. But we'll talk about that to-morrow. James, you can take Agatha down. You'll come to lunch, of course, James. At half-past one, instead of two. The Duke will wish to say a few words to you, I am sure.

HOPPER. I should like to have a chat with the Duke, Duchess. He has not said a single word to me yet.

DUCHESS OF BERWICK. I think you'll find he will have a great deal to say to you to-morrow. [*Exit* **LADY AGATHA** *with* **MR. HOPPER.**] And now good-night, Margaret. I'm afraid it's the old, old story, dear. Love— well, not love at first sight, but love at the end of the season, which is so much more satisfactory.

LADY WINDERMERE. Good-night, Duchess.

[*Exit the* **DUCHESS OF BERWICK** *on* **LORD PAISLEY'S** *arm.*]

LADY PLYMDALE. My dear Margaret, what a handsome woman your husband has been dancing with! I should be quite jealous if I were you! Is she a great friend of yours?

LADY WINDERMERE. No!

LADY PLYMDALE. Really? Good-night, dear. [*Looks at* **MR. DUMBY** *and exit.*]

DUMBY. Awful manners young Hopper has!

CECIL GRAHAM. Ah! Hopper is one of Nature's gentlemen, the worst type of gentleman I know.

DUMBY. Sensible woman, Lady Windermere. Lots of wives would have objected to Mrs. Erlynne coming. But Lady Windermere has that uncommon thing called common sense.

CECIL GRAHAM. And Windermere knows that nothing looks so like innocence as an indiscretion.

DUMBY. Yes; dear Windermere is becoming almost modern. Never thought he would. [*Bows to* **LADY WINDERMERE** *and exit.*]

LADY JEDBURGH. Good night, Lady Windermere. What a fascinating woman Mrs. Erlynne is! She is coming to lunch on Thursday, won't you come too? I expect the Bishop and dear Lady Merton.

LADY WINDERMERE. I am afraid I am engaged, Lady Jedburgh.

LADY JEDBURGH. So sorry. Come, dear. [*Exeunt* **LADY JEDBURGH** *and* **MISS GRAHAM**.]

[*Enter* **MRS. ERLYNNE** *and* **LORD WINDERMERE**.]

MRS. ERLYNNE. Charming ball it has been! Quite reminds me of old days. [*Sits on sofa.*] And I see that there are just as many fools in society as there used to be. So pleased to find that nothing has altered! Except Margaret. She's grown quite pretty. The last time I saw her—twenty years ago, she was a fright in flannel. Positive fright, I assure you. The dear Duchess! and that sweet Lady Agatha! Just the type of girl I like! Well, really, Windermere, if I am to be the Duchess's sister-in-law—

LORD WINDERMERE. [*Sitting L. of her.*] But are you—?

[*Exit* **MR. CECIL GRAHAM** *with rest of guests.* **LADY WINDERMERE** *watches, with a look of scorn and pain,* **MRS. ERLYNNE** *and her husband. They are unconscious of her presence.*]

MRS. ERLYNNE. Oh, yes! He's to call to-morrow at twelve o'clock! He wanted to propose to-night. In fact he did. He kept on proposing. Poor Augustus, you know how he repeats himself. Such a bad habit! But I told him I wouldn't give him an answer till to-morrow. Of course I am going to take him. And I dare say I'll make him an admirable wife, as wives go. And there is a great deal of good in Lord Augustus. Fortunately it is all on the surface. Just where good qualities should be. Of course you must help me in this matter.

LORD WINDERMERE. I am not called on to encourage Lord Augustus, I suppose?

MRS. ERLYNNE. Oh, no! I do the encouraging. But you will make me a handsome settlement, Windermere, won't you?

LORD WINDERMERE. [*Frowning.*] Is that what you want to talk to me about to-night?

MRS. ERLYNNE. Yes.

LORD WINDERMERE. [*With a gesture of impatience.*] I will not talk of it here.

MRS. ERLYNNE. [*Laughing.*] Then we will talk of it on the terrace. Even business should have a picturesque background. Should it not, Windermere? With a proper background women can do anything.

LORD WINDERMERE. Won't to-morrow do as well?

MRS. ERLYNNE. No; you see, to-morrow I am going to accept him. And I think it would be a good thing if I was able to tell him that I had—well, what shall I say?—£2000 a year left to me by a third cousin—or a second husband—or some distant relative of that kind. It would be an additional attraction, wouldn't it? You have a delightful opportunity now of paying me a compliment, Windermere. But you are not very clever at paying compliments. I am afraid Margaret doesn't encourage you in that excellent habit. It's a great mistake on her part. When men give up saying what is charming, they give up thinking what is charming. But seriously, what do you say to £2000? £2500, I think. In modern life margin is everything. Windermere, don't you think the world an intensely amusing place? I do!

[*Exit on terrace with* **LORD WINDERMERE**. Music strikes up in ball-room.]

LADY WINDERMERE. To stay in this house any longer is impossible. To-night a man who loves me offered me his whole life. I refused it. It was foolish of me. I will offer him mine now. I will give him mine. I will go to him! [*Puts on cloak and goes to the door, then turns back. Sits down at table and writes a letter, puts it into an envelope, and leaves it on table.*] Arthur has never understood me. When he reads this, he will. He may do as he chooses now with his life. I have done with mine as I think best, as I think right. It is he who has broken the bond of marriage—not I. I only break its bondage.

[*Exit.*]

[**PARKER** *enters L. and crosses towards the ball-room R. Enter* **MRS. ERLYNNE**.]

MRS. ERLYNNE. Is Lady Windermere in the ball-room?

PARKER. Her ladyship has just gone out.

MRS. ERLYNNE. Gone out? She's not on the terrace?

PARKER. No, madam. Her ladyship has just gone out of the house.

MRS. ERLYNNE. [*Starts, and looks at the servant with a puzzled expression in her face.*] Out of the house?

PARKER. Yes, madam—her ladyship told me she had left a letter for his lordship on the table.

MRS. ERLYNNE. A letter for Lord Windermere?

PARKER. Yes, madam.

MRS. ERLYNNE. Thank you.

[*Exit* **PARKER**. *The music in the ball-room stops.*] Gone out of her house! A letter addressed to her husband! [*Goes over to bureau and looks at letter. Takes it up and lays it down again with a shudder of fear.*] No, no! It would be impossible! Life doesn't repeat its tragedies like that! Oh, why does this horrible fancy come across me? Why do I remember now the one moment of my life I most wish to forget? Does life repeat its tragedies? [*Tears letter open and reads it, then sinks down into a chair with a gesture of anguish.*] Oh, how terrible! The same words that twenty years ago I wrote to her father! and how bitterly I have been punished for it! No; my punishment, my real punishment is to-night, is now! [*Still seated R.*]

[*Enter* **LORD WINDERMERE** *L.U.E.*]

LORD WINDERMERE. Have you said good-night to my wife? [*Comes C.*]

MRS. ERLYNNE. [*Crushing letter in her hand.*] Yes.

LORD WINDERMERE. Where is she?

MRS. ERLYNNE. She is very tired. She has gone to bed. She said she had a headache.

LORD WINDERMERE. I must go to her. You'll excuse me?

MRS. ERLYNNE. [*Rising hurriedly.*] Oh, no! It's nothing serious. She's only very tired, that is all. Besides, there are people still in the supper-room. She wants you to make her apologies to them. She said she didn't wish to be disturbed. [*Drops letter.*] She asked me to tell you!

LORD WINDERMERE. [*Picks up letter.*] You have dropped something.

MRS. ERLYNNE. Oh yes, thank you, that is mine. [*Puts out her hand to take it.*]

LORD WINDERMERE. [*Still looking at letter.*] But it's my wife's handwriting, isn't it?

MRS. ERLYNNE. [*Takes the letter quickly.*] Yes, it's—an address. Will you ask them to call my carriage, please?

LORD WINDERMERE. Certainly.

[*Goes L. and Exit.*]

MRS. ERLYNNE. Thanks! What can I do? What can I do? I feel a passion awakening within me that I never felt before. What can it mean? The daughter must not be like the mother—that would be terrible. How can I save her? How can I save my child? A moment may ruin a life. Who knows that better than I? Windermere must be got out of the house; that is absolutely necessary. [*Goes L.*] But how shall I do it? It must be done somehow. Ah!

[*Enter* **LORD AUGUSTUS** *R.U.E. carrying bouquet.*]

LORD AUGUSTUS. Dear lady, I am in such suspense! May I not have an answer to my request?

MRS. ERLYNNE. Lord Augustus, listen to me. You are to take Lord Windermere down to your club at once, and keep him there as long as possible. You understand?

LORD AUGUSTUS. But you said you wished me to keep early hours!

MRS. ERLYNNE. [*Nervously.*] Do what I tell you. Do what I tell you.

LORD AUGUSTUS. And my reward?

MRS. ERLYNNE. Your reward? Your reward? Oh! ask me that to-morrow. But don't let Windermere out of your sight to-night. If you do I will never forgive you. I will never speak to you again. I'll have nothing to do with you. Remember you are to keep Windermere at your club, and don't let him come back to-night.

[*Exit L.*]

LORD AUGUSTUS. Well, really, I might be her husband already. Positively I might. [*Follows her in a bewildered manner.*]

ACT DROP.

THIRD ACT

SCENE

*Lord Darlington's Rooms. A large sofa is in front of fireplace R. At the
back of the stage a curtain is drawn across the window. Doors L. and
R. Table R. with writing materials. Table C. with syphons, glasses, and
Tantalus frame. Table L. with cigar and cigarette box. Lamps lit.*

LADY WINDERMERE. [*Standing by the fireplace.*] Why doesn't he come?
This waiting is horrible. He should be here. Why is he not here, to wake by
passionate words some fire within me? I am cold—cold as a loveless thing.
Arthur must have read my letter by this time. If he cared for me, he would
have come after me, would have taken me back by force. But he doesn't
care. He's entrammelled by this woman—fascinated by her—dominated
by her. If a woman wants to hold a man, she has merely to appeal to what
is worst in him. We make gods of men and they leave us. Others make
brutes of them and they fawn and are faithful. How hideous life is! . . .
Oh! it was mad of me to come here, horribly mad. And yet, which is the
worst, I wonder, to be at the mercy of a man who loves one, or the wife
of a man who in one's own house dishonours one? What woman knows?
What woman in the whole world? But will he love me always, this man
to whom I am giving my life? What do I bring him? Lips that have lost

the note of joy, eyes that are blinded by tears, chill hands and icy heart. I bring him nothing. I must go back—no; I can't go back, my letter has put me in their power—Arthur would not take me back! That fatal letter! No! Lord Darlington leaves England to-morrow. I will go with him—I have no choice. [*Sits down for a few moments. Then starts up and puts on her cloak.*] No, no! I will go back, let Arthur do with me what he pleases. I can't wait here. It has been madness my coming. I must go at once. As for Lord Darlington— Oh! here he is! What shall I do? What can I say to him? Will he let me go away at all? I have heard that men are brutal, horrible . . . Oh! [*Hides her face in her hands.*]

[*Enter* **MRS. ERLYNNE** *L.*]

MRS. ERLYNNE. Lady Windermere! [**LADY WINDERMERE** *starts and looks up. Then recoils in contempt.*] Thank Heaven I am in time. You must go back to your husband's house immediately.

LADY WINDERMERE. Must?

MRS. ERLYNNE. [*Authoritatively.*] Yes, you must! There is not a second to be lost. Lord Darlington may return at any moment.

LADY WINDERMERE. Don't come near me!

MRS. ERLYNNE. Oh! You are on the brink of ruin, you are on the brink of a hideous precipice. You must leave this place at once, my carriage is waiting at the corner of the street. You must come with me and drive straight home.

[**LADY WINDERMERE** *throws off her cloak and flings it on the sofa.*]

What are you doing?

LADY WINDERMERE. Mrs. Erlynne—if you had not come here, I would have gone back. But now that I see you, I feel that nothing in the whole world would induce me to live under the same roof as Lord Windermere. You fill me with horror. There is something about you that stirs the wildest—rage within me. And I know why you are here. My husband sent you to lure me back that I might serve as a blind to whatever relations exist between you and him.

MRS. ERLYNNE. Oh! You don't think that—you can't.

LADY WINDERMERE. Go back to my husband, Mrs. Erlynne. He belongs to you and not to me. I suppose he is afraid of a scandal. Men are such cowards. They outrage every law of the world, and are afraid of the world's tongue. But he had better prepare himself. He shall have a scandal. He shall have the worst scandal there has been in London for years. He shall see his name in every vile paper, mine on every hideous placard.

MRS. ERLYNNE. No—no—

LADY WINDERMERE. Yes! he shall. Had he come himself, I admit I would have gone back to the life of degradation you and he had prepared for me—I was going back—but to stay himself at home, and to send you as his messenger—oh! it was infamous—infamous.

MRS. ERLYNNE. [*C.*] Lady Windermere, you wrong me horribly—you wrong your husband horribly. He doesn't know you are here—he thinks you are safe in your own house. He thinks you are asleep in your own room. He never read the mad letter you wrote to him!

LADY WINDERMERE. [*R.*] Never read it!

MRS. ERLYNNE. No—he knows nothing about it.

LADY WINDERMERE. How simple you think me! [*Going to her.*] You are lying to me!

MRS. ERLYNNE. [*Restraining herself.*] I am not. I am telling you the truth.

LADY WINDERMERE. If my husband didn't read my letter, how is it that you are here? Who told you I had left the house you were shameless enough to enter? Who told you where I had gone to? My husband told you, and sent you to decoy me back. [*Crosses L.*]

MRS. ERLYNNE. [*R.C.*] Your husband has never seen the letter. I—saw it, I opened it. I—read it.

LADY WINDERMERE. [*Turning to her.*] You opened a letter of mine to my husband? You wouldn't dare!

MRS. ERLYNNE. Dare! Oh! to save you from the abyss into which you are falling, there is nothing in the world I would not dare, nothing in the whole world. Here is the letter. Your husband has never read it. He never shall read it. [*Going to fireplace.*] It should never have been written. [*Tears it and throws it into the fire.*]

LADY WINDERMERE. [*With infinite contempt in her voice and look.*] How do I know that that was my letter after all? You seem to think the commonest device can take me in!

MRS. ERLYNNE. Oh! why do you disbelieve everything I tell you? What object do you think I have in coming here, except to save you from utter ruin, to save you from the consequence of a hideous mistake? That letter that is burnt now *was* your letter. I swear it to you!

LADY WINDERMERE. [*Slowly.*] You took good care to burn it before I had examined it. I cannot trust you. You, whose whole life is a lie, could you speak the truth about anything? [*Sits down.*]

MRS. ERLYNNE. [*Hurriedly.*] Think as you like about me—say what you choose against me, but go back, go back to the husband you love.

LADY WINDERMERE. [*Sullenly.*] I do *not* love him!

MRS. ERLYNNE. You do, and you know that he loves you.

LADY WINDERMERE. He does not understand what love is. He understands it as little as you do—but I see what you want. It would be a great advantage for you to get me back. Dear Heaven! what a life I would have then! Living at the mercy of a woman who has neither mercy nor pity in her, a woman whom it is an infamy to meet, a degradation to know, a vile woman, a woman who comes between husband and wife!

MRS. ERLYNNE. [*With a gesture of despair.*] Lady Windermere, Lady Windermere, don't say such terrible things. You don't know how terrible they are, how terrible and how unjust. Listen, you must listen! Only go back to your husband, and I promise you never to communicate with him again on any pretext—never to see him—never to have anything to do with his life or yours. The money that he gave me, he gave me not through love, but through hatred, not in worship, but in contempt. The hold I have over him—

LADY WINDERMERE. [*Rising.*] Ah! you admit you have a hold!

MRS. ERLYNNE. Yes, and I will tell you what it is. It is his love for you, Lady Windermere.

LADY WINDERMERE. You expect me to believe that?

MRS. ERLYNNE. You must believe it! It is true. It is his love for you that has made him submit to—oh! call it what you like, tyranny, threats, anything you choose. But it is his love for you. His desire to spare you—shame, yes, shame and disgrace.

LADY WINDERMERE. What do you mean? You are insolent! What have I to do with you?

MRS. ERLYNNE. [*Humbly*.] Nothing. I know it—but I tell you that your husband loves you—that you may never meet with such love again in your whole life—that such love you will never meet—and that if you throw it away, the day may come when you will starve for love and it will not be given to you, beg for love and it will be denied you—Oh! Arthur loves you!

LADY WINDERMERE. Arthur? And you tell me there is nothing between you?

MRS. ERLYNNE. Lady Windermere, before Heaven your husband is guiltless of all offence towards you! And I—I tell you that had it ever occurred to me that such a monstrous suspicion would have entered your mind, I would have died rather than have crossed your life or his—oh! died, gladly died! [*Moves away to sofa R.*]

LADY WINDERMERE. You talk as if you had a heart. Women like you have no hearts. Heart is not in you. You are bought and sold. [*Sits L.C.*]

MRS. ERLYNNE. [*Starts, with a gesture of pain. Then restrains herself, and comes over to where* **LADY WINDERMERE** *is sitting. As she speaks, she stretches out her hands towards her, but does not dare to touch her.*] Believe what you choose about me. I am not worth a moment's sorrow. But don't spoil your beautiful young life on my account! You don't know what may be in store for you, unless you leave this house at once. You don't know what it is to fall into the pit, to be despised, mocked, abandoned, sneered at—to be an outcast! to find the door shut against one, to have to creep in by hideous byways, afraid every moment lest the mask should be stripped from one's face, and all the while to hear the laughter, the horrible laughter of the world, a thing more tragic than all the tears the world has ever shed. You don't know what it is. One pays for one's sin, and then one pays again, and all one's life one pays. You must never know that.—As for me, if suffering be an expiation, then at this moment I have expiated all my faults, whatever they have been; for to-night you have made a heart in one who had it not, made it and broken it.—But let that pass. I may have wrecked my own life, but I will not let you wreck yours. You—why, you are a mere girl, you would be lost. You haven't got the kind of brains that enables a woman to get back. You have neither the wit nor the courage. You couldn't stand dishonour! No! Go back, Lady Windermere, to the husband who loves you, whom you love. You have a child, Lady Windermere. Go back to that child who even now, in pain or in joy, may be calling to you. [**LADY WINDERMERE** *rises.*] God gave you that child. He will require from you that you make his life fine, that you watch over him. What answer will you make to God if his life is ruined through you? Back to your house, Lady Windermere—your husband loves you! He has never swerved for a moment from the love he bears you. But even if he had a thousand loves, you must stay with your child. If he was harsh to you, you must stay with your child. If he ill-treated you, you must stay with your child. If he abandoned you, your place is with your child.

[**LADY WINDERMERE** *bursts into tears and buries her face in her hands.*]

[*Rushing to her.*] Lady Windermere!

LADY WINDERMERE. [*Holding out her hands to her, helplessly, as a child might do.*] Take me home. Take me home.

MRS. ERLYNNE. [*Is about to embrace her. Then restrains herself. There is a look of wonderful joy in her face.*] Come! Where is your cloak? [*Getting it from sofa.*] Here. Put it on. Come at once!

[*They go to the door.*]

LADY WINDERMERE. Stop! Don't you hear voices?

MRS. ERLYNNE. No, no! There was no one!

LADY WINDERMERE. Yes, there is! Listen! Oh! that is my husband's voice! He is coming in! Save me! Oh, it's some plot! You have sent for him.

[*Voices outside.*]

MRS. ERLYNNE. Silence! I'm here to save you, if I can. But I fear it is too late! There! [*Points to the curtain across the window.*] The first chance you have, slip out, if you ever get a chance!

LADY WINDERMERE. But you?

MRS. ERLYNNE. Oh! never mind me. I'll face them.

[**LADY WINDERMERE** *hides herself behind the curtain.*]

LORD AUGUSTUS. [*Outside.*] Nonsense, dear Windermere, you must not leave me!

MRS. ERLYNNE. Lord Augustus! Then it is I who am lost! [*Hesitates for a moment,* then *looks round and sees door R., and exits through it.*]

[*Enter* **LORD DARLINGTON**, **MR. DUMBY**, **LORD WINDERMERE**, **LORD AUGUSTUS LORTON**, *and* **MR. CECIL GRAHAM**.

DUMBY. What a nuisance their turning us out of the club at this hour! It's only two o'clock. [*Sinks into a chair.*] The lively part of the evening is only just beginning. [*Yawns and closes his eyes.*]

LORD WINDERMERE. It is very good of you, Lord Darlington, allowing Augustus to force our company on you, but I'm afraid I can't stay long.

LORD DARLINGTON. Really! I am so sorry! You'll take a cigar, won't you?

LORD WINDERMERE. Thanks! [*Sits down.*]

LORD AUGUSTUS. [*To* **LORD WINDERMERE**.] My dear boy, you must not dream of going. I have a great deal to talk to you about, of demmed importance, too. [*Sits down with him at L. table.*]

CECIL GRAHAM. Oh! We all know what that is! Tuppy can't talk about anything but Mrs. Erlynne.

LORD WINDERMERE. Well, that is no business of yours, is it, Cecil?

CECIL GRAHAM. None! That is why it interests me. My own business always bores me to death. I prefer other people's.

LORD DARLINGTON. Have something to drink, you fellows. Cecil, you'll have a whisky and soda?

CECIL GRAHAM. Thanks. [*Goes to table with* **LORD DARLINGTON**.] Mrs. Erlynne looked very handsome to-night, didn't she?

LORD DARLINGTON. I am not one of her admirers.

CECIL GRAHAM. I usen't to be, but I am now. Why! she actually made me introduce her to poor dear Aunt Caroline. I believe she is going to lunch there.

LORD DARLINGTON. [*In Purple.*] No?

CECIL GRAHAM. She is, really.

LORD DARLINGTON. Excuse me, you fellows. I'm going away to-morrow. And I have to write a few letters. [*Goes to writing table and sits down.*]

DUMBY. Clever woman, Mrs. Erlynne.

CECIL GRAHAM. Hallo, Dumby! I thought you were asleep.

DUMBY. I am, I usually am!

LORD AUGUSTUS. A very clever woman. Knows perfectly well what a demmed fool I am—knows it as well as I do myself.

[**CECIL GRAHAM** *comes towards him laughing.*]

Ah, you may laugh, my boy, but it is a great thing to come across a woman who thoroughly understands one.

DUMBY. It is an awfully dangerous thing. They always end by marrying one.

CECIL GRAHAM. But I thought, Tuppy, you were never going to see her again! Yes! you told me so yesterday evening at the club. You said you'd heard—

[*Whispering to him.*]

LORD AUGUSTUS. Oh, she's explained that.

CECIL GRAHAM. And the Wiesbaden affair?

LORD AUGUSTUS. She's explained that too.

DUMBY. And her income, Tuppy? Has she explained that?

LORD AUGUSTUS. [*In a very serious voice.*] She's going to explain that to-morrow.

[**CECIL GRAHAM** *goes back to C. table.*]

DUMBY. Awfully commercial, women nowadays. Our grandmothers threw their caps over the mills, of course, but, by Jove, their granddaughters only throw their caps over mills that can raise the wind for them.

LORD AUGUSTUS. You want to make her out a wicked woman. She is not!

CECIL GRAHAM. Oh! Wicked women bother one. Good women bore one. That is the only difference between them.

LORD AUGUSTUS. [*Puffing a cigar*.] Mrs. Erlynne has a future before her.

DUMBY. Mrs. Erlynne has a past before her.

LORD AUGUSTUS. I prefer women with a past. They're always so demmed amusing to talk to.

CECIL GRAHAM. Well, you'll have lots of topics of conversation with *her*, Tuppy. [*Rising and going to him*.]

LORD AUGUSTUS. You're getting annoying, dear-boy; you're getting demmed annoying.

CECIL GRAHAM. [*Puts his hands on his shoulders*.] Now, Tuppy, you've lost your figure and you've lost your character. Don't lose your temper; you have only got one.

LORD AUGUSTUS. My dear boy, if I wasn't the most good-natured man in London—

CECIL GRAHAM. We'd treat you with more respect, wouldn't we, Tuppy? [*Strolls away*.]

DUMBY. The youth of the present day are quite monstrous. They have absolutely no respect for dyed hair. [**LORD AUGUSTUS** *looks round angrily*.]

CECIL GRAHAM. Mrs. Erlynne has a very great respect for dear Tuppy.

DUMBY. Then Mrs. Erlynne sets an admirable example to the rest of her sex. It is perfectly brutal the way most women nowadays behave to men who are not their husbands.

LORD WINDERMERE. Dumby, you are ridiculous, and Cecil, you let your tongue run away with you. You must leave Mrs. Erlynne alone. You don't really know anything about her, and you're always talking scandal against her.

CECIL GRAHAM. [*Coming towards him L.C.*] My dear Arthur, I never talk scandal. *I* only talk gossip.

LORD WINDERMERE. What is the difference between scandal and gossip?

CECIL GRAHAM. Oh! gossip is charming! History is merely gossip. But scandal is gossip made tedious by morality. Now, I never moralise. A man who moralises is usually a hypocrite, and a woman who moralises is invariably plain. There is nothing in the whole world so unbecoming to a woman as a Nonconformist conscience. And most women know it, I'm glad to say.

LORD AUGUSTUS. Just my sentiments, dear boy, just my sentiments.

CECIL GRAHAM. Sorry to hear it, Tuppy; whenever people agree with me, I always feel I must be wrong.

LORD AUGUSTUS. My dear boy, when I was your age——

CECIL GRAHAM. But you never were, Tuppy, and you never will be. [*Goes up C.*] I say, Darlington, let us have some cards. You'll play, Arthur, won't you?

LORD WINDERMERE. No, thanks, Cecil.

DUMBY. [*With a sigh.*] Good heavens! how marriage ruins a man! It's as demoralising as cigarettes, and far more expensive.

CECIL GRAHAM. You'll play, of course, Tuppy?

LORD AUGUSTUS. [*Pouring himself out a brandy and soda at table.*] Can't, dear boy. Promised Mrs. Erlynne never to play or drink again.

CECIL GRAHAM. Now, my dear Tuppy, don't be led astray into the paths of virtue. Reformed, you would be perfectly tedious. That is the worst of women. They always want one to be good. And if we are good, when they meet us, they don't love us at all. They like to find us quite irretrievably bad, and to leave us quite unattractively good.

LORD DARLINGTON. [*Rising from R. table, where he has been writing letters.*] They always do find us bad!

DUMBY. I don't think we are bad. I think we are all good, except Tuppy.

LORD DARLINGTON. No, we are all in the gutter, but some of us are looking at the stars. [*Sits down at C. table*.]

DUMBY. We are all in the gutter, but some of us are looking at the stars? Upon my word, you are very romantic to-night, Darlington.

CECIL GRAHAM. Too romantic! You must be in love. Who is the girl?

LORD DARLINGTON. The woman I love is not free, or thinks she isn't. [*Glances instinctively at* **LORD WINDERMERE** *while he speaks*.]

CECIL GRAHAM. A married woman, then! Well, there's nothing in the world like the devotion of a married woman. It's a thing no married man knows anything about.

LORD DARLINGTON. Oh! she doesn't love me. She is a good woman. She is the only good woman I have ever met in my life.

CECIL GRAHAM. The only good woman you have ever met in your life?

LORD DARLINGTON. Yes!

CECIL GRAHAM. [*Lighting a cigarette*.] Well, you are a lucky fellow! Why, I have met hundreds of good women. I never seem to meet any but good women. The world is perfectly packed with good women. To know them is a middle-class education.

LORD DARLINGTON. This woman has purity and innocence. She has everything we men have lost.

CECIL GRAHAM. My dear fellow, what on earth should we men do going about with purity and innocence? A carefully thought-out buttonhole is much more effective.

DUMBY. She doesn't really love you then?

LORD DARLINGTON. No, she does not!

DUMBY. I congratulate you, my dear fellow. In this world there are only two tragedies. One is not getting what one wants, and the other is getting it. The last is much the worst; the last is a real tragedy! But I am interested to hear she does not love you. How long could you love a woman who didn't love you, Cecil?

CECIL GRAHAM. A woman who didn't love me? Oh, all my life!

DUMBY. So could I. But it's so difficult to meet one.

LORD DARLINGTON. How can you be so conceited, **DUMBY**?

DUMBY. I didn't say it as a matter of conceit. I said it as a matter of regret. I have been wildly, madly adored. I am sorry I have. It has been an immense nuisance. I should like to be allowed a little time to myself now and then.

LORD AUGUSTUS. [*Looking round.*] Time to educate yourself, I suppose.

DUMBY. No, time to forget all I have learned. That is much more important, dear Tuppy. [**LORD AUGUSTUS** *moves uneasily in his chair.*]

LORD DARLINGTON. What cynics you fellows are!

CECIL GRAHAM. What is a cynic? [*Sitting on the back of the sofa.*]

LORD DARLINGTON. A man who knows the price of everything and the value of nothing.

CECIL GRAHAM. And a sentimentalist, my dear Darlington, is a man who sees an absurd value in everything, and doesn't know the market price of any single thing.

LORD DARLINGTON. You always amuse me, Cecil. You talk as if you were a man of experience.

CECIL GRAHAM. I am. [*Moves up to front off fireplace.*]

LORD DARLINGTON. You are far too young!

CECIL GRAHAM. That is a great error. Experience is a question of instinct about life. I have got it. Tuppy hasn't. Experience is the name Tuppy gives to his mistakes. That is all. [**LORD AUGUSTUS** *looks round indignantly.*]

DUMBY. Experience is the name every one gives to their mistakes.

CECIL GRAHAM. [*Standing with his back to the fireplace.*] One shouldn't commit any. [*Sees* **LADY WINDERMERE'S** *fan on sofa.*]

DUMBY. Life would be very dull without them.

CECIL GRAHAM. Of course you are quite faithful to this woman you are in love with, Darlington, to this good woman?

LORD DARLINGTON. Cecil, if one really loves a woman, all other women in the world become absolutely meaningless to one. Love changes one—*I* am changed.

CECIL GRAHAM. Dear me! How very interesting! Tuppy, I want to talk to you. [**LORD AUGUSTUS** *takes no notice.*]

DUMBY. It's no use talking to Tuppy. You might just as well talk to a brick wall.

CECIL GRAHAM. But I like talking to a brick wall—it's the only thing in the world that never contradicts me! Tuppy!

LORD AUGUSTUS. Well, what is it? What is it? [*Rising and going over to* **CECIL GRAHAM**.]

CECIL GRAHAM. Come over here. I want you particularly. [*Aside.*] Darlington has been moralising and talking about the purity of love, and that sort of thing, and he has got some woman in his rooms all the time.

LORD AUGUSTUS. No, really! really!

CECIL GRAHAM. [*In a low voice.*] Yes, here is her fan. [*Points to the fan.*]

LORD AUGUSTUS. [*Chuckling.*] By Jove! By Jove!

LORD WINDERMERE. [*Up by door.*] I am really off now, Lord Darlington. I am sorry you are leaving England so soon. Pray call on us when you come back! My wife and I will be charmed to see you!

LORD DARLINGTON. [*Upstage with* **LORD WINDERMERE**.] I am afraid I shall be away for many years. Good-night!

CECIL GRAHAM. Arthur!

LORD WINDERMERE. What?

CECIL GRAHAM. I want to speak to you for a moment. No, do come!

LORD WINDERMERE. [*Putting on his coat.*] I can't—I'm off!

CECIL GRAHAM. It is something very particular. It will interest you enormously.

LORD WINDERMERE. [*Smiling.*] It is some of your nonsense, Cecil.

CECIL GRAHAM. It isn't! It isn't really.

LORD AUGUSTUS. [*Going to him.*] My dear fellow, you mustn't go yet. I have a lot to talk to you about. And Cecil has something to show you.

LORD WINDERMERE. [*Walking over.*] Well, what is it?

CECIL GRAHAM. Darlington has got a woman here in his rooms. Here is her fan. Amusing, isn't it? [*A pause.*]

LORD WINDERMERE. Good God! [*Seizes the fan—**DUMBY** rises.*]

CECIL GRAHAM. What is the matter?

LORD WINDERMERE. Lord Darlington!

LORD DARLINGTON. [*Turning round.*] Yes!

LORD WINDERMERE. What is my wife's fan doing here in your rooms? Hands off, Cecil. Don't touch me.

LORD DARLINGTON. Your wife's fan?

LORD WINDERMERE. Yes, here it is!

LORD DARLINGTON. [*Walking towards him.*] I don't know!

LORD WINDERMERE. You must know. I demand an explanation. Don't hold me, you fool. [*To **CECIL GRAHAM**.*]

LORD DARLINGTON. [*Aside.*] She is here after all!

LORD WINDERMERE. Speak, sir! Why is my wife's fan here? Answer me! By God! I'll search your rooms, and if my wife's here, I'll— [*Moves.*]

LORD DARLINGTON. You shall not search my rooms. You have no right to do so. I forbid you!

LORD WINDERMERE. You scoundrel! I'll not leave your room till I have searched every corner of it! What moves behind that curtain? [*Rushes towards the curtain C.*]

MRS. ERLYNNE. [*Enters behind R.*] Lord Windermere!

LORD WINDERMERE. Mrs. Erlynne!

[*Every one starts and turns round. **LADY WINDERMERE** slips out from behind the curtain and glides from the room L.*]

MRS. ERLYNNE. I am afraid I took your wife's fan in mistake for my own, when I was leaving your house to-night. I am so sorry. [*Takes fan from him.*

LORD WINDERMERE *looks at her in contempt.* **LORD DARLINGTON** *in mingled astonishment and anger.* **LORD AUGUSTUS** *turns away. The other men smile at each other.*]

ACT DROP.

FOURTH ACT

SCENE—SAME AS IN ACT I.

LADY WINDERMERE. [*Lying on sofa.*] How can I tell him? I can't tell him. It would kill me. I wonder what happened after I escaped from that horrible room. Perhaps she told them the true reason of her being there, and the real meaning of that—fatal fan of mine. Oh, if he knows—how can I look him in the face again? He would never forgive me. [*Touches bell.*] How securely one thinks one lives—out of reach of temptation, sin, folly. And then suddenly—Oh! Life is terrible. It rules us, we do not rule it.

[*Enter* **ROSALIE** *R.*]

ROSALIE. Did your ladyship ring for me?

LADY WINDERMERE. Yes. Have you found out at what time Lord Windermere came in last night?

ROSALIE. His lordship did not come in till five o'clock.

LADY WINDERMERE. Five o'clock? He knocked at my door this morning, didn't he?

ROSALIE. Yes, my lady—at half-past nine. I told him your ladyship was not awake yet.

LADY WINDERMERE. Did he say anything?

ROSALIE. Something about your ladyship's fan. I didn't quite catch what his lordship said. Has the fan been lost, my lady? I can't find it, and Parker says it was not left in any of the rooms. He has looked in all of them and on the terrace as well.

LADY WINDERMERE. It doesn't matter. Tell Parker not to trouble. That will do.

[*Exit* **ROSALIE**.]

LADY WINDERMERE. [*Rising.*] She is sure to tell him. I can fancy a person doing a wonderful act of self-sacrifice, doing it spontaneously, recklessly, nobly—and afterwards finding out that it costs too much. Why should she hesitate between her ruin and mine? . . . How strange! I would have publicly disgraced her in my own house. She accepts public disgrace in the house of another to save me. . . . There is a bitter irony in things, a bitter irony in the way we talk of good and bad women. . . . Oh, what a lesson! and what a pity that in life we only get our lessons when they are of no use to us! For even if she doesn't tell, I must. Oh! the shame of it, the shame of it. To tell it is to live through it all again. Actions are the first tragedy in life, words are the second. Words are perhaps the worst. Words are merciless. . . . Oh! [*Starts as* **LORD WINDERMERE** *enters.*]

LORD WINDERMERE. [*Kisses her.*] Margaret—how pale you look!

LADY WINDERMERE. I slept very badly.

LORD WINDERMERE. [*Sitting on sofa with her.*] I am so sorry. I came in dreadfully late, and didn't like to wake you. You are crying, dear.

LADY WINDERMERE. Yes, I am crying, for I have something to tell you, Arthur.

LORD WINDERMERE. My dear child, you are not well. You've been doing too much. Let us go away to the country. You'll be all right at Selby. The season is almost over. There is no use staying on. Poor darling! We'll go away to-day, if you like. [*Rises.*] We can easily catch the 3.40. I'll send a wire to Fannen. [*Crosses and sits down at table to write a telegram.*]

LADY WINDERMERE. Yes; let us go away to-day. No; I can't go to-day, Arthur. There is some one I must see before I leave town—some one who has been kind to me.

LORD WINDERMERE. [*Rising and leaning over sofa.*] Kind to you?

LADY WINDERMERE. Far more than that. [*Rises and goes to him.*] I will tell you, Arthur, but only love me, love me as you used to love me.

LORD WINDERMERE. Used to? You are not thinking of that wretched woman who came here last night? [*Coming round and sitting R. of her.*] You don't still imagine—no, you couldn't.

LADY WINDERMERE. I don't. I know now I was wrong and foolish.

LORD WINDERMERE. It was very good of you to receive her last night—but you are never to see her again.

LADY WINDERMERE. Why do you say that? [*A pause.*]

LORD WINDERMERE. [*Holding her hand.*] Margaret, I thought Mrs. Erlynne was a woman more sinned against than sinning, as the phrase goes. I thought she wanted to be good, to get back into a place that she had lost by a moment's folly, to lead again a decent life. I believed what she told me—I was mistaken in her. She is bad—as bad as a woman can be.

LADY WINDERMERE. Arthur, Arthur, don't talk so bitterly about any woman. I don't think now that people can be divided into the good and the bad as though they were two separate races or creations. What are called good women may have terrible things in them, mad moods of recklessness, assertion, jealousy, sin. Bad women, as they are termed, may have in them sorrow, repentance, pity, sacrifice. And I don't think Mrs. Erlynne a bad woman—I know she's not.

LORD WINDERMERE. My dear child, the woman's impossible. No matter what harm she tries to do us, you must never see her again. She is inadmissible anywhere.

LADY WINDERMERE. But I want to see her. I want her to come here.

LORD WINDERMERE. Never!

LADY WINDERMERE. She came here once as *your* guest. She must come now as *mine*. That is but fair.

LORD WINDERMERE. She should never have come here.

LADY WINDERMERE. [*Rising.*] It is too late, Arthur, to say that now. [*Moves away.*]

LORD WINDERMERE. [*Rising*.] Margaret, if you knew where Mrs. Erlynne went last night, after she left this house, you would not sit in the same room with her. It was absolutely shameless, the whole thing.

LADY WINDERMERE. Arthur, I can't bear it any longer. I must tell you. Last night—

[*Enter* **PARKER** *with a tray on which lie* **LADY WINDERMERE'S** *fan and a card*.]

PARKER. Mrs. Erlynne has called to return your ladyship's fan which she took away by mistake last night. Mrs. Erlynne has written a message on the card.

LADY WINDERMERE. Oh, ask Mrs. Erlynne to be kind enough to come up. [*Reads card*.] Say I shall be very glad to see her.

[*Exit* **PARKER**.]

She wants to see me, Arthur.

LORD WINDERMERE. [*Takes card and looks at it*.] Margaret, I *beg* you not to. Let me see her first, at any rate. She's a very dangerous woman. She is the most dangerous woman I know. You don't realise what you're doing.

LADY WINDERMERE. It is right that I should see her.

LORD WINDERMERE. My child, you may be on the brink of a great sorrow. Don't go to meet it. It is absolutely necessary that I should see her before you do.

LADY WINDERMERE. Why should it be necessary?

[*Enter* **PARKER**.]

PARKER. Mrs. Erlynne.

[*Enter* **MRS. ERLYNNE**.]

[*Exit* **PARKER**.]

MRS. ERLYNNE. How do you do, Lady Windermere? [*To* **LORD WINDERMERE**.] How do you do? Do you know, Lady Windermere, I am so sorry about your fan. I can't imagine how I made such a silly mistake. Most stupid of me. And as I was driving in your direction, I thought I would take the opportunity of returning your property in person with many apologies for my carelessness, and of bidding you good-bye.

LADY WINDERMERE. Good-bye? [*Moves towards sofa with* **MRS. ERLYNNE** *and sits down beside her.*] Are you going away, then, Mrs. Erlynne?

MRS. ERLYNNE. Yes; I am going to live abroad again. The English climate doesn't suit me. My—heart is affected here, and that I don't like. I prefer living in the south. London is too full of fogs and—and serious people, Lord Windermere. Whether the fogs produce the serious people or whether the serious people produce the fogs, I don't know, but the whole thing rather gets on my nerves, and so I'm leaving this afternoon by the Club Train.

LADY WINDERMERE. This afternoon? But I wanted so much to come and see you.

MRS. ERLYNNE. How kind of you! But I am afraid I have to go.

LADY WINDERMERE. Shall I never see you again, Mrs. Erlynne?

MRS. ERLYNNE. I am afraid not. Our lives lie too far apart. But there is a little thing I would like you to do for me. I want a photograph of you, Lady Windermere—would you give me one? You don't know how gratified I should be.

LADY WINDERMERE. Oh, with pleasure. There is one on that table. I'll show it to you. [*Goes across to the table.*]

LORD WINDERMERE. [*Coming up to* **MRS. ERLYNNE** *and speaking in a low voice.*] It is monstrous your intruding yourself here after your conduct last night.

MRS. ERLYNNE. [*With an amused smile.*] My dear Windermere, manners before morals!

LADY WINDERMERE. [*Returning.*] I'm afraid it is very flattering—I am not so pretty as that. [*Showing photograph.*]

MRS. ERLYNNE. You are much prettier. But haven't you got one of yourself with your little boy?

LADY WINDERMERE. I have. Would you prefer one of those?

MRS. ERLYNNE. Yes.

LADY WINDERMERE. I'll go and get it for you, if you'll excuse me for a moment. I have one upstairs.

MRS. ERLYNNE. So sorry, Lady Windermere, to give you so much trouble.

LADY WINDERMERE. [*Moves to door R.*] No trouble at all, Mrs. Erlynne.

MRS. ERLYNNE. Thanks so much.

[*Exit* **LADY WINDERMERE** *R.*] You seem rather out of temper this morning, Windermere. Why should you be? Margaret and I get on charmingly together.

LORD WINDERMERE. I can't bear to see you with her. Besides, you have not told me the truth, Mrs. Erlynne.

MRS. ERLYNNE. I have not told *her* the truth, you mean.

LORD WINDERMERE. [*Standing C.*] I sometimes wish you had. I should have been spared then the misery, the anxiety, the annoyance of the last six months. But rather than my wife should know—that the mother whom she was taught to consider as dead, the mother whom she has mourned as dead, is living—a divorced woman, going about under an assumed name, a bad woman preying upon life, as I know you now to be—rather than that, I was ready to supply you with money to pay bill after bill, extravagance after extravagance, to risk what occurred yesterday, the first quarrel I have ever had with my wife. You don't understand what that means to me. How could you? But I tell you that the only bitter words that ever came from those sweet lips of hers were on your account, and I hate to see you next her. You sully the innocence that is in her. [*Moves L.C.*] And then I used to think that with all your faults you were frank and honest. You are not.

MRS. ERLYNNE. Why do you say that?

LORD WINDERMERE. You made me get you an invitation to my wife's ball.

MRS. ERLYNNE. For my daughter's ball—yes.

LORD WINDERMERE. You came, and within an hour of your leaving the house you are found in a man's rooms—you are disgraced before every one. [*Goes up stage C.*]

MRS. ERLYNNE. Yes.

LORD WINDERMERE. [*Turning round on her.*] Therefore I have a right to look upon you as what you are—a worthless, vicious woman. I have the right to tell you never to enter this house, never to attempt to come near my wife—

MRS. ERLYNNE. [*Coldly.*] My daughter, you mean.

LORD WINDERMERE. You have no right to claim her as your daughter. You left her, abandoned her when she was but a child in the cradle, abandoned her for your lover, who abandoned you in turn.

MRS. ERLYNNE. [*Rising.*] Do you count that to his credit, Lord Windermere—or to mine?

LORD WINDERMERE. To his, now that I know you.

MRS. ERLYNNE. Take care—you had better be careful.

LORD WINDERMERE. Oh, I am not going to mince words for you. I know you thoroughly.

MRS. ERLYNNE. [*Looks steadily at him.*] I question that.

LORD WINDERMERE. I *do* know you. For twenty years of your life you lived without your child, without a thought of your child. One day you read in the papers that she had married a rich man. You saw your hideous chance. You knew that to spare her the ignominy of learning that a woman like you was her mother, I would endure anything. You began your blackmailing.

MRS. ERLYNNE. [*Shrugging her shoulders.*] Don't use ugly words, Windermere. They are vulgar. I saw my chance, it is true, and took it.

LORD WINDERMERE. Yes, you took it—and spoiled it all last night by being found out.

MRS. ERLYNNE. [*With a strange smile.*] You are quite right, I spoiled it all last night.

LORD WINDERMERE. And as for your blunder in taking my wife's fan from here and then leaving it about in Darlington's rooms, it is unpardonable. I can't bear the sight of it now. I shall never let my wife use it again. The thing is soiled for me. You should have kept it and not brought it back.

MRS. ERLYNNE. I think I shall keep it. [*Goes up.*] It's extremely pretty. [*Takes up fan.*] I shall ask Margaret to give it to me.

LORD WINDERMERE. I hope my wife will give it you.

MRS. ERLYNNE. Oh, I'm sure she will have no objection.

LORD WINDERMERE. I wish that at the same time she would give you a miniature she kisses every night before she prays—It's the miniature of a young innocent-looking girl with beautiful *dark* hair.

MRS. ERLYNNE. Ah, yes, I remember. How long ago that seems! [*Goes to sofa and sits down.*] It was done before I was married. Dark hair and an innocent expression were the fashion then, Windermere! [*A pause.*]

LORD WINDERMERE. What do you mean by coming here this morning? What is your object? [*Crossing L.C. and sitting.*]

MRS. ERLYNNE. [*With a note of irony in her voice.*] To bid good-bye to my dear daughter, of course. [**LORD WINDERMERE** *bites his under lip in anger.* **MRS. ERLYNNE** *looks at him, and her voice and manner become serious. In her accents as she talks there is a note of deep tragedy. For a moment she reveals herself.*] Oh, don't imagine I am going to have a pathetic scene with her, weep on her neck and tell her who I am, and all that kind of thing. I have no ambition to play the part of a mother. Only once in my life have I known a mother's feelings. That was last night. They were terrible—they made me suffer—they made me suffer too much. For twenty years, as you say, I have lived childless,—I want to live childless still. [*Hiding her feelings with a trivial laugh.*] Besides, my dear Windermere, how on earth could I pose as a mother with a grown-up daughter? Margaret is twenty-one, and I have never admitted that I am more than twenty-nine, or thirty at the most. Twenty-nine when there are pink shades, thirty when there are not. So you see what difficulties it would involve. No, as far as I am concerned, let your wife cherish the memory of this dead, stainless mother. Why should I interfere with her illusions? I find it hard enough to keep my own. I lost one illusion last night. I thought I had no heart. I find I have, and a heart doesn't suit me, Windermere. Somehow it doesn't go with modern dress.

It makes one look old. [*Takes up hand-mirror from table and looks into it.*] And it spoils one's career at critical moments.

LORD WINDERMERE. You fill me with horror—with absolute horror.

MRS. ERLYNNE. [*Rising.*] I suppose, Windermere, you would like me to retire into a convent, or become a hospital nurse, or something of that kind, as people do in silly modern novels. That is stupid of you, Arthur; in real life we don't do such things—not as long as we have any good looks left, at any rate. No—what consoles one nowadays is not repentance, but pleasure. Repentance is quite out of date. And besides, if a woman really repents, she has to go to a bad dressmaker, otherwise no one believes in her. And nothing in the world would induce me to do that. No; I am going to pass entirely out of your two lives. My coming into them has been a mistake—I discovered that last night.

LORD WINDERMERE. A fatal mistake.

MRS. ERLYNNE. [*Smiling.*] Almost fatal.

LORD WINDERMERE. I am sorry now I did not tell my wife the whole thing at once.

MRS. ERLYNNE. I regret my bad actions. You regret your good ones—that is the difference between us.

LORD WINDERMERE. I don't trust you. I *will* tell my wife. It's better for her to know, and from me. It will cause her infinite pain—it will humiliate her terribly, but it's right that she should know.

MRS. ERLYNNE. You propose to tell her?

LORD WINDERMERE. I am going to tell her.

MRS. ERLYNNE. [*Going up to him.*] If you do, I will make my name so infamous that it will mar every moment of her life. It will ruin her, and make her wretched. If you dare to tell her, there is no depth of degradation I will not sink to, no pit of shame I will not enter. You shall not tell her—I forbid you.

LORD WINDERMERE. Why?

MRS. ERLYNNE. [*After a pause.*] If I said to you that I cared for her, perhaps loved her even—you would sneer at me, wouldn't you?

LORD WINDERMERE. I should feel it was not true. A mother's love means devotion, unselfishness, sacrifice. What could you know of such things?

MRS. ERLYNNE. You are right. What could I know of such things? Don't let us talk any more about it—as for telling my daughter who I am, that I do not allow. It is my secret, it is not yours. If I make up my mind to tell her, and I think I will, I shall tell her before I leave the house—if not, I shall never tell her.

LORD WINDERMERE. [*Angrily.*] Then let me beg of you to leave our house at once. I will make your excuses to Margaret.

[*Enter* **LADY WINDERMERE** *R. She goes over to* **MRS. ERLYNNE** *with the photograph in her hand.* **LORD WINDERMERE** *moves to back of sofa, and anxiously watches* **MRS. ERLYNNE** *as the scene progresses.*]

LADY WINDERMERE. I am so sorry, Mrs. Erlynne, to have kept you waiting. I couldn't find the photograph anywhere. At last I discovered it in my husband's dressing-room—he had stolen it.

MRS. ERLYNNE. [*Takes the photograph from her and looks at it.*] I am not surprised—it is charming. [*Goes over to sofa with* **LADY WINDERMERE**, *and sits down beside her. Looks again at the photograph.*] And so that is your little boy! What is he called?

LADY WINDERMERE. Gerard, after my dear father.

MRS. ERLYNNE. [*Laying the photograph down.*] Really?

LADY WINDERMERE. Yes. If it had been a girl, I would have called it after my mother. My mother had the same name as myself, Margaret.

MRS. ERLYNNE. My name is Margaret too.

LADY WINDERMERE. Indeed!

MRS. ERLYNNE. Yes. [*Pause.*] You are devoted to your mother's memory, Lady Windermere, your husband tells me.

LADY WINDERMERE. We all have ideals in life. At least we all should have. Mine is my mother.

MRS. ERLYNNE. Ideals are dangerous things. Realities are better. They wound, but they're better.

LADY WINDERMERE. [*Shaking her head.*] If I lost my ideals, I should lose everything.

MRS. ERLYNNE. Everything?

LADY WINDERMERE. Yes. [*Pause.*]

MRS. ERLYNNE. Did your father often speak to you of your mother?

LADY WINDERMERE. No, it gave him too much pain. He told me how my mother had died a few months after I was born. His eyes filled with tears as he spoke. Then he begged me never to mention her name to him again. It made him suffer even to hear it. My father—my father really died of a broken heart. His was the most ruined life know.

MRS. ERLYNNE. [*Rising.*] I am afraid I must go now, Lady Windermere.

LADY WINDERMERE. [*Rising.*] Oh no, don't.

MRS. ERLYNNE. I think I had better. My carriage must have come back by this time. I sent it to Lady Jedburgh's with a note.

LADY WINDERMERE. Arthur, would you mind seeing if Mrs. Erlynne's carriage has come back?

MRS. ERLYNNE. Pray don't trouble, Lord Windermere.

LADY WINDERMERE. Yes, Arthur, do go, please.

[**LORD WINDERMERE** *hesitated for a moment and looks at* **MRS. ERLYNNE**. *She remains quite impassive. He leaves the room.*]

[*To* **MRS. ERLYNNE**.] Oh! What am I to say to you? You saved me last night? [*Goes towards her.*]

MRS. ERLYNNE. Hush—don't speak of it.

LADY WINDERMERE. I must speak of it. I can't let you think that I am going to accept this sacrifice. I am not. It is too great. I am going to tell my husband everything. It is my duty.

MRS. ERLYNNE. It is not your duty—at least you have duties to others besides him. You say you owe me something?

LADY WINDERMERE. I owe you everything.

MRS. ERLYNNE. Then pay your debt by silence. That is the only way in which it can be paid. Don't spoil the one good thing I have done in my life by telling it to any one. Promise me that what passed last night will remain a secret between us. You must not bring misery into your husband's life. Why spoil his love? You must not spoil it. Love is easily killed. Oh! how easily love is killed. Pledge me your word, Lady Windermere, that you will never tell him. I insist upon it.

LADY WINDERMERE. [*With bowed head.*] It is your will, not mine.

MRS. ERLYNNE. Yes, it is my will. And never forget your child—I like to think of you as a mother. I like you to think of yourself as one.

LADY WINDERMERE. [*Looking up.*] I always will now. Only once in my life I have forgotten my own mother—that was last night. Oh, if I had remembered her I should not have been so foolish, so wicked.

MRS. ERLYNNE. [*With a slight shudder.*] Hush, last night is quite over.

[*Enter* **LORD WINDERMERE**.]

LORD WINDERMERE. Your carriage has not come back yet, Mrs. Erlynne.

MRS. ERLYNNE. It makes no matter. I'll take a hansom. There is nothing in the world so respectable as a good Shrewsbury and Talbot. And now, dear Lady Windermere, I am afraid it is really good-bye. [*Moves up C.*] Oh, I remember. You'll think me absurd, but do you know I've taken a great fancy to this fan that I was silly enough to run away with last night from your ball. Now, I wonder would you give it to me? Lord Windermere says you may. I know it is his present.

LADY WINDERMERE. Oh, certainly, if it will give you any pleasure. But it has my name on it. It has 'Margaret' on it.

MRS. ERLYNNE. But we have the same Christian name.

LADY WINDERMERE. Oh, I forgot. Of course, do have it. What a wonderful chance our names being the same!

MRS. ERLYNNE. Quite wonderful. Thanks—it will always remind me of you. [*Shakes hands with her.*]

[*Enter* **PARKER**.]

PARKER. Lord Augustus Lorton. Mrs. Erlynne's carriage has come.

[*Enter* **LORD AUGUSTUS**.]

LORD AUGUSTUS. Good morning, dear boy. Good morning, Lady Windermere. [*Sees* **MRS. ERLYNNE**.] Mrs. Erlynne!

MRS. ERLYNNE. How do you do, Lord Augustus? Are you quite well this morning?

LORD AUGUSTUS. [*Coldly*.] Quite well, thank you, Mrs. Erlynne.

MRS. ERLYNNE. You don't look at all well, Lord Augustus. You stop up too late—it is so bad for you. You really should take more care of yourself. Good-bye, Lord Windermere. [*Goes towards door with a bow to* **LORD AUGUSTUS**. *Suddenly smiles and looks back at him*.] Lord Augustus! Won't you see me to my carriage? You might carry the fan.

LORD WINDERMERE. Allow me!

MRS. ERLYNNE. No; I want Lord Augustus. I have a special message for the dear Duchess. Won't you carry the fan, Lord Augustus?

LORD AUGUSTUS. If you really desire it, Mrs. Erlynne.

MRS. ERLYNNE. [*Laughing*.] Of course I do. You'll carry it so gracefully. You would carry off anything gracefully, dear Lord Augustus.

[*When she reaches the door she looks back for a moment at* **LADY WINDERMERE**. *Their eyes meet. Then she turns, and exit C. followed by* **LORD AUGUSTUS**.]

LADY WINDERMERE. You will never speak against Mrs. Erlynne again, Arthur, will you?

LORD WINDERMERE. [*Gravely*.] She is better than one thought her.

LADY WINDERMERE. She is better than I am.

LORD WINDERMERE. [*Smiling as he strokes her hair*.] Child, you and she belong to different worlds. Into your world evil has never entered.

LADY WINDERMERE. Don't say that, Arthur. There is the same world for all of us, and good and evil, sin and innocence, go through it hand in hand. To shut one's eyes to half of life that one may live securely is as though one blinded oneself that one might walk with more safety in a land of pit and precipice.

LORD WINDERMERE. [*Moves down with her*.] Darling, why do you say that?

LADY WINDERMERE. [*Sits on sofa.*] Because I, who had shut my eyes to life, came to the brink. And one who had separated us—

LORD WINDERMERE. We were never separated.

LADY WINDERMERE. We never must be again. O Arthur, don't love me less, and I will trust you more. I will trust you absolutely. Let us go to Selby. In the Rose Garden at Selby the roses are white and red.

[*Enter* **LORD AUGUSTUS** *C.*]

LORD AUGUSTUS. Arthur, she has explained everything!

[**LADY WINDERMERE** *looks horribly frightened at this.* **LORD WINDERMERE** *starts.* **LORD AUGUSTUS** *takes* **WINDERMERE** *by the arm and brings him to front of stage. He talks rapidly and in a low voice.* **LADY WINDERMERE** *stands watching them in terror.*] My dear fellow, she has explained every demmed thing. We all wronged her immensely. It was entirely for my sake she went to Darlington's rooms. Called first at the Club—fact is, wanted to put me out of suspense—and being told I had gone on—followed—naturally frightened when she heard a lot of us coming in—retired to another room—I assure you, most gratifying to me, the whole thing. We all behaved brutally to her. She is just the woman for me. Suits me down to the ground. All the conditions she makes are that we live entirely out of England. A very good thing too. Demmed clubs, demmed climate, demmed cooks, demmed everything. Sick of it all!

LADY WINDERMERE. [*Frightened.*] Has Mrs. Erlynne—?

LORD AUGUSTUS. [*Advancing towards her with a low bow.*] Yes, Lady Windermere— Mrs. Erlynne has done me the honour of accepting my hand.

LORD WINDERMERE. Well, you are certainly marrying a very clever woman!

LADY WINDERMERE. [*Taking her husband's hand.*] Ah, you're marrying a very good woman!

    CURTAIN

ANTHEM
BY AYN RAND

PART ONE

It is a sin to write this. It is a sin to think words no others think and to put them down upon a paper no others are to see. It is base and evil. It is as if we were speaking alone to no ears but our own. And we know well that there is no transgression blacker than to do or think alone. We have broken the laws. The laws say that men may not write unless the Council of Vocations bid them so. May we be forgiven!

But this is not the only sin upon us. We have committed a greater crime, and for this crime there is no name. What punishment awaits us if it be discovered we know not, for no such crime has come in the memory of men and there are no laws to provide for it.

It is dark here. The flame of the candle stands still in the air. Nothing moves in this tunnel save our hand on the paper. We are alone here under the earth. It is a fearful word, alone. The laws say that none among men may be alone, ever and at any time, for this is the great transgression and the root of all evil. But we have broken many laws. And now there is nothing here save our one body, and it is strange to see only two legs stretched on the ground, and on the wall before us the shadow of our one head.

The walls are cracked and water runs upon them in thin threads without sound, black and glistening as blood. We stole the candle from the larder of the Home of the Street Sweepers. We shall be sentenced to ten years in the Palace of Corrective Detention if it be discovered. But this matters not. It matters only that the light is precious and we should not waste it to write when we need it for that work which is our crime. Nothing matters save the work, our secret, our evil, our precious work. Still, we must also write, for—may the Council have mercy upon us!—we wish to speak for once to no ears but our own.

Our name is Equality 7-2521, as it is written on the iron bracelet which all men wear on their left wrists with their names upon it. We are twenty-one years old. We are six feet tall, and this is a burden, for there are not many men who are six feet tall. Ever have the Teachers and the Leaders pointed to us and frowned and said:

"There is evil in your bones, Equality 7-2521, for your body has grown beyond the bodies of your brothers." But we cannot change our bones nor our body.

We were born with a curse. It has always driven us to thoughts which are forbidden. It has always given us wishes which men may not wish. We know that we are evil, but there is no will in us and no power to resist it. This is our wonder and our secret fear, that we know and do not resist.

We strive to be like all our brother men, for all men must be alike. Over the portals of the Palace of the World Council, there are words cut in the marble, which we repeat to ourselves whenever we are tempted:

"WE ARE ONE IN ALL AND ALL IN ONE.
THERE ARE NO MEN BUT ONLY THE GREAT *WE*,
ONE, INDIVISIBLE AND FOREVER."

We repeat this to ourselves, but it helps us not.

These words were cut long ago. There is green mould in the grooves of the letters and yellow streaks on the marble, which come from more years than men could count. And these words are the truth, for they are written on the Palace of the World Council, and the World Council is the body of all truth. Thus has it been ever since the Great Rebirth, and farther back than that no memory can reach.

But we must never speak of the times before the Great Rebirth, else we are sentenced to three years in the Palace of Corrective Detention. It is only the Old Ones who whisper about it in the evenings, in the Home of the Useless. They whisper many strange things, of the towers which rose to the sky, in those Unmentionable Times, and of the wagons which moved without horses, and of the lights which burned without flame. But those times were evil. And those times passed away, when men saw the Great Truth which is this: that all men are one and that there is no will save the will of all men together.

All men are good and wise. It is only we, Equality 7-2521, we alone who were born with a curse. For we are not like our brothers. And as we look back upon our life, we see that it has ever been thus and that it has brought us step by step to our last, supreme transgression, our crime of crimes hidden here under the ground.

We remember the Home of the Infants where we lived till we were five years old, together with all the children of the City who had been born in the same year. The sleeping halls there were white and clean and bare of all things save one hundred beds. We were just like all our brothers then, save for the one transgression: we fought with our brothers. There are few offenses blacker than to fight with our brothers, at any age and for any cause whatsoever. The Council of the Home told us so, and of all the children of that year, we were locked in the cellar most often.

When we were five years old, we were sent to the Home of the Students, where there are ten wards, for our ten years of learning. Men must learn till they reach their fifteenth year. Then they go to work. In the Home of the Students we arose when the big bell rang in the tower and we went to our beds when it rang again. Before we removed our garments, we stood in the great sleeping hall, and we raised our right arms, and we said all together with the three Teachers at the head:

"We are nothing. Mankind is all. By the grace of our brothers are we allowed our lives. We exist through, by and for our brothers who are the State. Amen."

Then we slept. The sleeping halls were white and clean and bare of all things save one hundred beds.

We, Equality 7-2521, were not happy in those years in the Home of the Students. It was not that the learning was too hard for us. It was that the learning was too easy. This is a great sin, to be born with a head which is too quick. It is not good to be different from our brothers, but it is evil to be superior to them. The Teachers told us so, and they frowned when they looked upon us.

So we fought against this curse. We tried to forget our lessons, but we always remembered. We tried not to understand what the Teachers taught, but we always understood it before the Teachers had spoken. We looked upon Union 5-3992, who were a pale boy with only half a brain, and we tried to say and do as they did, that we might be like them, like Union 5-3992, but somehow the Teachers knew that we were not. And we were lashed more often than all the other children.

The Teachers were just, for they had been appointed by the Councils, and the Councils are the voice of all justice, for they are the voice of all men. And if sometimes, in the secret darkness of our heart, we regret that which befell us on our fifteenth birthday, we know that it was through our own guilt. We had broken a law, for we had not paid heed to the words of our Teachers. The Teachers had said to us all:

"Dare not choose in your minds the work you would like to do when you leave the Home of the Students. You shall do that which the Council of Vocations shall prescribe for you. For the Council of Vocations knows in its great wisdom where you are needed by your brother men, better than you can know it in your unworthy little minds. And if you are not needed by your brother man, there is no reason for you to burden the earth with your bodies."

We knew this well, in the years of our childhood, but our curse broke our will. We were guilty and we confess it here: we were guilty of the great Transgression of Preference. We preferred some work and some lessons to the others. We did not listen well to the history of all the Councils elected since the Great Rebirth. But we loved the Science of Things. We wished to know. We wished to know about all the things which make the earth around us. We asked so many questions that the Teachers forbade it.

We think that there are mysteries in the sky and under the water and in the plants which grow. But the Council of Scholars has said that there are no mysteries, and the Council of Scholars knows all things. And we learned much from our Teachers. We learned that the earth is flat and that the sun revolves around it, which causes the day and the night. We learned the names of all the winds which blow over the seas and push the sails of our great ships. We learned how to bleed men to cure them of all ailments.

We loved the Science of Things. And in the darkness, in the secret hour, when we awoke in the night and there were no brothers around us, but only their shapes in the beds and their snores, we closed our eyes, and we held our lips shut, and we stopped our breath, that no shudder might let our brothers see or hear or guess, and we thought that we wished to be sent to the Home of the Scholars when our time would come.

All the great modern inventions come from the Home of the Scholars, such as the newest one, which was found only a hundred years ago, of how to make candles from wax and string; also, how to make glass, which is put in our windows to protect us from the rain. To find these things, the Scholars must study the earth and learn from the rivers, from the sands, from the winds and the rocks. And if we went to the Home of the Scholars, we could learn from these also. We could ask questions of these, for they do not forbid questions.

And questions give us no rest. We know not why our curse makes us seek we know not what, ever and ever. But we cannot resist it. It whispers to us that there are great things on this earth of ours, and that we can know them if we try, and that we must know them. We ask, why must we know, but it has no answer to give us. We must know that we may know.

So we wished to be sent to the Home of the Scholars. We wished it so much that our hands trembled under the blankets in the night, and we bit our arm to stop that other pain which we could not endure. It was evil and we dared not face our brothers in the morning. For men may wish nothing for themselves. And we were punished when the Council of Vocations came to give us our life Mandates which tell those who reach their fifteenth year what their work is to be for the rest of their days.

The Council of Vocations came on the first day of spring, and they sat in the great hall. And we who were fifteen and all the Teachers came into the great hall. And the Council of Vocations sat on a high dais, and they had but two words to speak to each of the Students. They called the Students' names, and when the Students stepped before them, one after another, the Council said: "Carpenter" or "Doctor" or "Cook" or "Leader." Then each Student raised their right arm and said: "The will of our brothers be done."

Now if the Council has said "Carpenter" or "Cook," the Students so assigned go to work and they do not study any further. But if the Council has said "Leader," then those Students go into the Home of the Leaders, which is the greatest house in the City, for it has three stories. And there they study for many years, so that they may become candidates and be elected to the City Council and the State Council and the World Council—by a free and general vote of all men. But we wished not to be a Leader, even though it is a great honor. We wished to be a Scholar.

So we awaited our turn in the great hall and then we heard the Council of Vocations call our name: "Equality 7-2521." We walked to the dais, and our legs did not tremble, and we looked up at the Council. There were five members of the Council, three of the male gender and two of the female. Their hair was white and their faces were cracked as the clay of a dry river bed. They were old. They seemed older than the marble of the Temple of the World Council. They sat before us and they did not move. And we saw no breath to stir the folds of their white togas. But we knew that they were alive, for a finger of the hand of the oldest rose, pointed to us, and fell down again. This was the only thing which moved, for the lips of the oldest did not move as they said: "Street Sweeper."

We felt the cords of our neck grow tight as our head rose higher to look upon the faces of the Council, and we were happy. We knew we had been guilty, but now we had a way to atone for it. We would accept our Life Mandate, and we would work for our brothers, gladly and willingly, and we would erase our sin against them, which they did not know, but we knew. So we were happy, and proud of ourselves and of our victory over ourselves. We raised our right arm and we spoke, and our voice was the clearest, the steadiest voice in the hall that day, and we said:

"The will of our brothers be done."

And we looked straight into the eyes of the Council, but their eyes were as cold blue glass buttons.

So we went into the Home of the Street Sweepers. It is a grey house on a narrow street. There is a sundial in its courtyard, by which the Council of the Home can tell the hours of the day and when to ring the bell. When the bell rings, we all arise from our beds. The sky is green and cold in our windows to the east. The shadow on the sundial marks off a half-hour while we dress and eat our breakfast in the dining hall, where there are five long tables with twenty clay plates and twenty clay cups on each table. Then we go to work in the streets of the City, with our brooms and our rakes. In five hours, when the sun is high, we return to the Home and we eat our midday meal, for which one-half hour is allowed. Then we go to work again. In five hours, the shadows are blue on the pavements, and the sky is blue with a deep brightness which is not bright. We come back to have our dinner, which lasts one hour. Then the bell rings and we walk in a straight column to one of the City Halls, for the Social Meeting. Other columns of men arrive from the Homes of the different Trades. The candles are lit, and the Councils of the different Homes stand in a pulpit, and they speak to us of our duties and of our brother men. Then visiting Leaders mount the pulpit and they read to us the speeches which were made in the City Council that day, for the City Council represents all men and all men must know. Then we sing hymns, the Hymn of Brotherhood, and the Hymn of Equality, and the Hymn of the Collective Spirit. The sky is a soggy purple when we return to the Home. Then the bell rings and we walk in a straight column to the City Theatre for three hours of Social Recreation. There a play is shown upon the stage, with two great choruses from the Home of the Actors, which speak and answer all together, in two great voices. The plays are about toil and how good it is. Then we walk back to the Home in a straight column. The sky is like a black sieve pierced by silver drops that tremble, ready to burst through. The moths beat against the street lanterns. We go to our beds and we sleep, till the bell rings again. The sleeping halls are white and clean and bare of all things save one hundred beds.

Thus have we lived each day of four years, until two springs ago when our crime happened. Thus must all men live until they are forty. At forty, they are worn out. At forty, they are sent to the Home of the Useless, where the Old Ones live. The Old Ones do not work, for the State takes care of them. They sit in the sun in summer and they sit by the fire in winter. They do not speak often, for they are weary. The Old Ones know that they are soon to die. When a miracle happens and some live to be forty-five, they are the Ancient Ones, and the children stare at them when passing by the Home of the Useless. Such is to be our life, as that of all our brothers and of the brothers who came before us.

Such would have been our life, had we not committed our crime which changed all things for us. And it was our curse which drove us to our crime. We had been a good Street Sweeper and like all our brother Street Sweepers, save for our cursed wish to know. We looked too long at the stars at night, and at the trees and the earth. And when we cleaned the yard of the Home of the Scholars, we gathered the glass vials, the pieces of metal, the dried bones which they had discarded. We wished to keep these things and to study them, but we had no place to hide them. So we carried them to the City Cesspool. And then we made the discovery.

It was on a day of the spring before last. We Street Sweepers work in brigades of three, and we were with Union 5-3992, they of the half-brain, and with International 4-8818. Now Union 5-3992 are a sickly lad and sometimes they are stricken with convulsions, when their mouth froths and their eyes turn white. But International 4-8818 are different. They are a tall, strong youth and their eyes are like fireflies, for there is laughter in their eyes. We cannot look upon International 4-8818 and not smile in answer. For this they were not liked in the Home of the Students, as it is not proper to smile without reason. And also they were not liked because they took pieces of coal and they drew pictures upon the walls, and they were pictures which made men laugh. But it is only our brothers in the Home of the Artists who are permitted to draw pictures, so International 4-8818 were sent to the Home of the Street Sweepers, like ourselves.

International 4-8818 and we are friends. This is an evil thing to say, for it is a transgression, the great Transgression of Preference, to love any among men better than the others, since we must love all men and all men are our friends. So International 4-8818 and we have never spoken of it. But we know. We know, when we look into each other's eyes. And when we look thus without words, we both know other things also, strange things for which there are no words, and these things frighten us.

So on that day of the spring before last, Union 5-3992 were stricken with convulsions on the edge of the City, near the City Theatre. We left them to lie in the shade of the Theatre tent and we went with International 4-8818 to finish our work. We came together to the great ravine behind the Theatre. It is empty save for trees and weeds. Beyond the ravine there is a plain, and beyond the plain there lies the Uncharted Forest, about which men must not think.

We were gathering the papers and the rags which the wind had blown from the Theatre, when we saw an iron bar among the weeds. It was old and rusted by many rains. We pulled with all our strength, but we could not move it. So we called International 4-8818, and together we scraped the earth around the bar. Of a sudden the earth fell in before us, and we saw an old iron grill over a black hole.

International 4-8818 stepped back. But we pulled at the grill and it gave way. And then we saw iron rings as steps leading down a shaft into a darkness without bottom.

"We shall go down," we said to International 4-8818.

"It is forbidden," they answered.

We said: "The Council does not know of this hole, so it cannot be forbidden."

And they answered: "Since the Council does not know of this hole, there can be no law permitting to enter it. And everything which is not permitted by law is forbidden."

But we said: "We shall go, none the less."

They were frightened, but they stood by and watched us go.

We hung on the iron rings with our hands and our feet. We could see nothing below us. And above us the hole open upon the sky grew smaller and smaller, till it came to be the size of a button. But still we went down. Then our foot touched the ground. We rubbed our eyes, for we could not see. Then our eyes became used to the darkness, but we could not believe what we saw.

No men known to us could have built this place, nor the men known to our brothers who lived before us, and yet it was built by men. It was a great tunnel. Its walls were hard and smooth to the touch; it felt like stone, but it was not stone. On the ground there were long thin tracks of iron, but it was not iron; it felt smooth and cold as glass. We knelt, and we crawled forward, our hand groping along the iron line to see where it would lead. But there was an unbroken night ahead. Only the iron tracks glowed through it, straight and white, calling us to follow. But we could not follow, for we were losing the puddle of light behind us. So we turned and we crawled back, our hand on the iron line. And our heart beat in our fingertips, without reason. And then we knew.

We knew suddenly that this place was left from the Unmentionable Times. So it was true, and those Times had been, and all the wonders of those Times. Hundreds upon hundreds of years ago men knew secrets which we have lost. And we thought: "This is a foul place. They are damned who touch the things of the Unmentionable Times." But our hand which followed the track, as we crawled, clung to the iron as if it would not leave it, as if the skin of our hand were thirsty and begging of the metal some secret fluid beating in its coldness.

We returned to the earth. International 4-8818 looked upon us and stepped back.

"Equality 7-2521," they said, "your face is white."

But we could not speak and we stood looking upon them.

They backed away, as if they dared not touch us. Then they smiled, but it was not a gay smile; it was lost and pleading. But still we could not speak. Then they said:

"We shall report our find to the City Council and both of us will be rewarded."

And then we spoke. Our voice was hard and there was no mercy in our voice. We said:

"We shall not report our find to the City Council. We shall not report it to any men."

They raised their hands to their ears, for never had they heard such words as these.

"International 4-8818," we asked, "will you report us to the Council and see us lashed to death before your eyes?"

They stood straight all of a sudden and they answered: "Rather would we die."

"Then," we said, "keep silent. This place is ours. This place belongs to us, Equality 7-2521, and to no other men on earth. And if ever we surrender it, we shall surrender our life with it also."

Then we saw that the eyes of International 4-8818 were full to the lids with tears they dared not drop. They whispered, and their voice trembled, so that their words lost all shape:

"The will of the Council is above all things, for it is the will of our brothers, which is holy. But if you wish it so, we shall obey you. Rather shall we be evil with you than good with all our brothers. May the Council have mercy upon both our hearts!"

Then we walked away together and back to the Home of the Street Sweepers. And we walked in silence.

Thus did it come to pass that each night, when the stars are high and the Street Sweepers sit in the City Theatre, we, Equality 7-2521, steal out and run through the darkness to our place. It is easy to leave the Theatre;

when the candles are blown out and the Actors come onto the stage, no eyes can see us as we crawl under our seat and under the cloth of the tent. Later, it is easy to steal through the shadows and fall in line next to International 4-8818, as the column leaves the Theatre. It is dark in the streets and there are no men about, for no men may walk through the City when they have no mission to walk there. Each night, we run to the ravine, and we remove the stones which we have piled upon the iron grill to hide it from the men. Each night, for three hours, we are under the earth, alone.

We have stolen candles from the Home of the Street Sweepers, we have stolen flints and knives and paper, and we have brought them to this place. We have stolen glass vials and powders and acids from the Home of the Scholars. Now we sit in the tunnel for three hours each night and we study. We melt strange metals, and we mix acids, and we cut open the bodies of the animals which we find in the City Cesspool. We have built an oven of the bricks we gathered in the streets. We burn the wood we find in the ravine. The fire flickers in the oven and blue shadows dance upon the walls, and there is no sound of men to disturb us.

We have stolen manuscripts. This is a great offense. Manuscripts are precious, for our brothers in the Home of the Clerks spend one year to copy one single script in their clear handwriting. Manuscripts are rare and they are kept in the Home of the Scholars. So we sit under the earth and we read the stolen scripts. Two years have passed since we found this place. And in these two years we have learned more than we had learned in the ten years of the Home of the Students.

We have learned things which are not in the scripts. We have solved secrets of which the Scholars have no knowledge. We have come to see how great is the unexplored, and many lifetimes will not bring us to the end of our quest. But we wish no end to our quest. We wish nothing, save to be alone and to learn, and to feel as if with each day our sight were growing sharper than the hawk's and clearer than rock crystal.

Strange are the ways of evil. We are false in the faces of our brothers. We are defying the will of our Councils. We alone, of the thousands who walk this earth, we alone in this hour are doing a work which has no purpose save that we wish to do it. The evil of our crime is not for the human mind to probe. The nature of our punishment, if it be discovered, is not for the human heart to ponder. Never, not in the memory of the Ancient Ones' Ancients, never have men done that which we are doing.

And yet there is no shame in us and no regret. We say to ourselves that we are a wretch and a traitor. But we feel no burden upon our spirit and no fear in our heart. And it seems to us that our spirit is clear as a lake troubled by no eyes save those of the sun. And in our heart—strange are the ways of evil!—in our heart there is the first peace we have known in twenty years.

PART TWO

Liberty 5-3000... Liberty five-three thousand... Liberty 5-3000....

We wish to write this name. We wish to speak it, but we dare not speak it above a whisper. For men are forbidden to take notice of women, and women are forbidden to take notice of men. But we think of one among women, they whose name is Liberty 5-3000, and we think of no others. The women who have been assigned to work the soil live in the Homes of the Peasants beyond the City. Where the City ends there is a great road winding off to the north, and we Street Sweepers must keep this road clean to the first milepost. There is a hedge along the road, and beyond the hedge lie the fields. The fields are black and ploughed, and they lie like a great fan before us, with their furrows gathered in some hand beyond the sky, spreading forth from that hand, opening wide apart as they come toward us, like black pleats that sparkle with thin, green spangles. Women work in the fields, and their white tunics in the wind are like the wings of sea-gulls beating over the black soil.

And there it was that we saw Liberty 5-3000 walking along the furrows. Their body was straight and thin as a blade of iron. Their eyes were dark and hard and glowing, with no fear in them, no kindness and no guilt. Their hair was golden as the sun; their hair flew in the wind, shining and wild, as if it defied men to restrain it. They threw seeds from their hand as if they deigned to fling a scornful gift, and the earth was a beggar under their feet.

We stood still; for the first time did we know fear, and then pain. And we stood still that we might not spill this pain more precious than pleasure.

Then we heard a voice from the others call their name: "Liberty 5-3000," and they turned and walked back. Thus we learned their name, and we stood watching them go, till their white tunic was lost in the blue mist.

And the following day, as we came to the northern road, we kept our eyes upon Liberty 5-3000 in the field. And each day thereafter we knew the illness of waiting for our hour on the northern road. And there we looked at Liberty 5-3000 each day. We know not whether they looked at us also, but we think they did. Then one day they came close to the hedge, and suddenly they turned to us. They turned in a whirl and the movement of their body stopped, as if slashed off, as suddenly as it had started. They stood still as a stone, and they looked straight upon us, straight into our eyes. There was no smile on their face, and no welcome. But their face was taut, and their eyes were dark. Then they turned as swiftly, and they walked away from us.

But the following day, when we came to the road, they smiled. They smiled to us and for us. And we smiled in answer. Their head fell back, and their arms fell, as if their arms and their thin white neck were stricken suddenly with a great lassitude. They were not looking upon us, but upon the sky. Then they glanced at us over their shoulder, as we felt as if a hand had touched our body, slipping softly from our lips to our feet.

Every morning thereafter, we greeted each other with our eyes. We dared not speak. It is a transgression to speak to men of other Trades, save in groups at the Social Meetings. But once, standing at the hedge, we raised our hand to our forehead and then moved it slowly, palm down, toward Liberty 5-3000. Had the others seen it, they could have guessed nothing, for it looked only as if we were shading our eyes from the sun. But Liberty 5-3000 saw it and understood. They raised their hand to their forehead and moved it as we had. Thus, each day, we greet Liberty 5-3000, and they answer, and no men can suspect.

We do not wonder at this new sin of ours. It is our second Transgression of Preference, for we do not think of all our brothers, as we must, but only of one, and their name is Liberty 5-3000. We do not know why we think of them. We do not know why, when we think of them, we feel all of a sudden that the earth is good and that it is not a burden to live. We do not think of them as Liberty 5-3000 any longer. We have given them a name in our thoughts. We call them the Golden One. But it is a sin to give men names which distinguish them from other men. Yet we call them the Golden One, for they are not like the others. The Golden One are not like the others.

And we take no heed of the law which says that men may not think of women, save at the Time of Mating. This is the time each spring when all the men older than twenty and all the women older than eighteen are sent for one night to the City Palace of Mating. And each of the men have one of the women assigned to them by the Council of Eugenics. Children are born each winter, but women never see their children and children never know their parents. Twice have we been sent to the Palace of Mating, but it is an ugly and shameful matter, of which we do not like to think.

We had broken so many laws, and today we have broken one more. Today, we spoke to the Golden One.

The other women were far off in the field, when we stopped at the hedge by the side of the road. The Golden One were kneeling alone at the moat which runs through the field. And the drops of water falling from their hands, as they raised the water to their lips, were like sparks of fire in the sun. Then the Golden One saw us, and they did not move, kneeling there, looking at us, and circles of light played upon their white tunic, from the sun on the water of the moat, and one sparkling drop fell from a finger of their hand held as frozen in the air.

Then the Golden One rose and walked to the hedge, as if they had heard a command in our eyes. The two other Street Sweepers of our brigade were a hundred paces away down the road. And we thought that International 4-8818 would not betray us, and Union 5-3992 would not understand. So we looked straight upon the Golden One, and we saw the shadows of their lashes on their white cheeks and the sparks of sun on their lips. And we said:

"You are beautiful, Liberty 5-3000."

Their face did not move and they did not avert their eyes. Only their eyes grew wider, and there was triumph in their eyes, and it was not triumph over us, but over things we could not guess.

Then they asked:

"What is your name?"

"Equality 7-2521," we answered.

"You are not one of our brothers, Equality 7-2521, for we do not wish you to be."

We cannot say what they meant, for there are no words for their meaning, but we know it without words and we knew it then.

"No," we answered, "nor are you one of our sisters."

"If you see us among scores of women, will you look upon us?"

"We shall look upon you, Liberty 5-3000, if we see you among all the women of the earth."

Then they asked:

"Are Street Sweepers sent to different parts of the City or do they always work in the same places?"

"They always work in the same places," we answered, "and no one will take this road away from us."

"Your eyes," they said, "are not like the eyes of any among men."

And suddenly, without cause for the thought which came to us, we felt cold, cold to our stomach.

"How old are you?" we asked.

They understood our thought, for they lowered their eyes for the first time.

"Seventeen," they whispered.

And we sighed, as if a burden had been taken from us, for we had been thinking without reason of the Palace of Mating. And we thought that we would not let the Golden One be sent to the Palace. How to prevent it, how to bar the will of the Councils, we knew not, but we knew suddenly that we would. Only we do not know why such thought came to us, for these ugly matters bear no relation to us and the Golden One. What relation can they bear?

Still, without reason, as we stood there by the hedge, we felt our lips drawn tight with hatred, a sudden hatred for all our brother men. And the Golden One saw it and smiled slowly, and there was in their smile the first sadness we had seen in them. We think that in the wisdom of women the Golden One had understood more than we can understand.

Then three of the sisters in the field appeared, coming toward the road, so the Golden One walked away from us. They took the bag of seeds, and they threw the seeds into the furrows of earth as they walked away. But the seeds flew wildly, for the hand of the Golden One was trembling.

Yet as we walked back to the Home of the Street Sweepers, we felt that we wanted to sing, without reason. So we were reprimanded tonight, in the dining hall, for without knowing it we had begun to sing aloud some tune we had never heard. But it is not proper to sing without reason, save at the Social Meetings.

"We are singing because we are happy," we answered the one of the Home Council who reprimanded us.

"Indeed you are happy," they answered. "How else can men be when they live for their brothers?"

And now, sitting here in our tunnel, we wonder about these words. It is forbidden, not to be happy. For, as it has been explained to us, men are free and the earth belongs to them; and all things on earth belong to all men; and the will of all men together is good for all; and so all men must be happy.

Yet as we stand at night in the great hall, removing our garments for sleep, we look upon our brothers and we wonder. The heads of our brothers are bowed. The eyes of our brothers are dull, and never do they look one another in the eyes. The shoulders of our brothers are hunched, and their muscles are drawn, as if their bodies were shrinking and wished to shrink out of sight. And a word steals into our mind, as we look upon our brothers, and that word is fear.

There is fear hanging in the air of the sleeping halls, and in the air of the streets. Fear walks through the City, fear without name, without shape. All men feel it and none dare to speak.

We feel it also, when we are in the Home of the Street Sweepers. But here, in our tunnel, we feel it no longer. The air is pure under the ground. There is no odor of men. And these three hours give us strength for our hours above the ground.

Our body is betraying us, for the Council of the Home looks with suspicion upon us. It is not good to feel too much joy nor to be glad that our body lives. For we matter not and it must not matter to us whether we live or die, which is to be as our brothers will it. But we, Equality 7-2521, are glad to be living. If this is a vice, then we wish no virtue.

Yet our brothers are not like us. All is not well with our brothers. There are Fraternity 2-5503, a quiet boy with wise, kind eyes, who cry suddenly, without reason, in the midst of day or night, and their body shakes with sobs they cannot explain. There are Solidarity 9-6347, who are a bright youth, without fear in the day; but they scream in their sleep, and they scream: "Help us! Help us! Help us!" into the night, in a voice which chills our bones, but the Doctors cannot cure Solidarity 9-6347.

And as we all undress at night, in the dim light of the candles, our brothers are silent, for they dare not speak the thoughts of their minds. For all must agree with all, and they cannot know if their thoughts are the thoughts of all, and so they fear to speak. And they are glad when the candles are blown for the night. But we, Equality 7-2521, look through the window upon the sky, and there is peace in the sky, and cleanliness, and dignity. And beyond the City there lies the plain, and beyond the plain, black upon the black sky, there lies the Uncharted Forest.

We do not wish to look upon the Uncharted Forest. We do not wish to think of it. But ever do our eyes return to that black patch upon the sky. Men never enter the Uncharted Forest, for there is no power to explore it and no path to lead among its ancient trees which stand as guards of fearful secrets. It is whispered that once or twice in a hundred years, one among the men of the City escape alone and run to the Uncharted Forest, without call or reason. These men do not return. They perish from hunger and from the claws of the wild beasts which roam the Forest. But our Councils say that this is only a legend. We have heard that there are many Uncharted Forests over the land, among the Cities. And it is whispered that they have grown over the ruins of many cities of the Unmentionable Times. The trees have swallowed the ruins, and the bones under the ruins, and all the things which perished. And as we look upon the Uncharted Forest far in the night, we think of the secrets of the Unmentionable Times. And we wonder how it came to pass that these secrets were lost to the world. We have heard the legends of the great fighting, in which many men fought on one side and only a few on the other. These few were the Evil Ones and they were conquered. Then great fires raged over the land. And in these fires the Evil Ones and all the things made by the Evil Ones were burned.

And the fire which is called the Dawn of the Great Rebirth, was the Script Fire where all the scripts of the Evil Ones were burned, and with them all the words of the Evil Ones. Great mountains of flame stood in the squares of the Cities for three months. Then came the Great Rebirth.

The words of the Evil Ones... The words of the Unmentionable Times... What are the words which we have lost?

May the Council have mercy upon us! We had no wish to write such a question, and we knew not what we were doing till we had written it. We shall not ask this question and we shall not think it. We shall not call death upon our head.

And yet... And yet... There is some word, one single word which is not in the language of men, but which had been. And this is the Unspeakable Word, which no men may speak nor hear. But sometimes, and it is rare, sometimes, somewhere, one among men find that word. They find it upon scraps of old manuscripts or cut into the fragments of ancient stones. But when they speak it they are put to death. There is no crime punished by death in this world, save this one crime of speaking the Unspeakable Word.

We have seen one of such men burned alive in the square of the City. And it was a sight which has stayed with us through the years, and it haunts us, and follows us, and it gives us no rest. We were a child then, ten years old. And we stood in the great square with all the children and all the men of the City, sent to behold the burning. They brought the Transgressor out into the square and they led them to the pyre. They had torn out the tongue of the Transgressor, so that they could speak no longer. The Transgressor were young and tall. They had hair of gold and eyes blue as morning. They walked to the pyre, and their step did not falter. And of all the faces on that square, of all the faces which shrieked and screamed and spat curses upon them, theirs was the calmest and the happiest face.

As the chains were wound over their body at the stake, and a flame set to the pyre, the Transgressor looked upon the City. There was a thin thread of blood running from the corner of their mouth, but their lips were smiling. And a monstrous thought came to us then, which has never left us. We had heard of Saints. There are the Saints of Labor, and the Saints of the Councils, and the Saints of the Great Rebirth. But we had never seen a Saint nor what the likeness of a Saint should be. And we thought then, standing in the square, that the likeness of a Saint was the face we saw before us in the flames, the face of the Transgressor of the Unspeakable Word.

As the flames rose, a thing happened which no eyes saw but ours, else we would not be living today. Perhaps it had only seemed to us. But it seemed to us that the eyes of the Transgressor had chosen us from the crowd and were looking straight upon us. There was no pain in their eyes and no knowledge of the agony of their body. There was only joy in them, and pride, a pride holier than is fit for human pride to be. And it seemed as if these eyes were trying to tell us something through the flames, to send into our eyes some word without sound. And it seemed as if these eyes were begging us to gather that word and not to let it go from us and from the earth. But the flames rose and we could not guess the word....

What—even if we have to burn for it like the Saint of the Pyre—what is the Unspeakable Word?

PART THREE

We, Equality 7-2521, have discovered a new power of nature. And we have discovered it alone, and we alone are to know it. It is said. Now let us be lashed for it, if we must. The Council of Scholars has said that we all know the things which exist and therefore the things which are not known by all do not exist. But we think that the Council of Scholars is blind. The secrets of this earth are not for all men to see, but only for those who will seek them. We know, for we have found a secret unknown to all our brothers.

We know not what this power is nor whence it comes. But we know its nature, we have watched it and worked with it. We saw it first two years ago. One night, we were cutting open the body of a dead frog when we saw its leg jerking. It was dead, yet it moved. Some power unknown to men was making it move. We could not understand it. Then, after many tests, we found the answer. The frog had been hanging on a wire of copper; and it had been the metal of our knife which had sent the strange power to the copper through the brine of the frog's body. We put a piece of copper and a piece of zinc into a jar of brine, we touched a wire to them, and there, under our fingers, was a miracle which had never occurred before, a new miracle and a new power.

This discovery haunted us. We followed it in preference to all our studies. We worked with it, we tested it in more ways than we can describe, and each step was as another miracle unveiling before us. We came to know that we had found the greatest power on earth. For it defies all the laws known to men. It makes the needle move and turn on the compass which we stole from the Home of the Scholars; but we had been taught, when still a child, that the loadstone points to the north and that this is a law which nothing can change; yet our new power defies all laws. We found that it causes lightning, and never have men known what causes lightning. In thunderstorms, we raised a tall rod of iron by the side of our hole, and we watched it from below. We have seen the lightning strike it again and again. And now we know that metal draws the power of the sky, and that metal can be made to give it forth.

We have built strange things with this discovery of ours. We used for it the copper wires which we found here under the ground. We have walked the length of our tunnel, with a candle lighting the way. We could go no farther than half a mile, for earth and rock had fallen at both ends. But we gathered all the things we found and we brought them to our work place. We found strange boxes with bars of metal inside, with many cords and strands and coils of metal. We found wires that led to strange little globes of glass on the walls; they contained threads of metal thinner than a spider's web.

These things help us in our work. We do not understand them, but we think that the men of the Unmentionable Times had known our power of the sky, and these things had some relation to it. We do not know, but we shall learn. We cannot stop now, even though it frightens us that we are alone in our knowledge.

No single one can possess greater wisdom than the many Scholars who are elected by all men for their wisdom. Yet we can. We do. We have fought against saying it, but now it is said. We do not care. We forget all men, all laws and all things save our metals and our wires. So much is still to be learned! So long a road lies before us, and what care we if we must travel it alone!

PART FOUR

Many days passed before we could speak to the Golden One again. But then came the day when the sky turned white, as if the sun had burst and spread its flame in the air, and the fields lay still without breath, and the dust of the road was white in the glow. So the women of the field were weary, and they tarried over their work, and they were far from the road when we came. But the Golden One stood alone at the hedge, waiting. We stopped and we saw that their eyes, so hard and scornful to the world, were looking at us as if they would obey any word we might speak.

And we said:

"We have given you a name in our thoughts, Liberty 5-3000."

"What is our name?" they asked.

"The Golden One."

"Nor do we call you Equality 7-2521 when we think of you."

"What name have you given us?" They looked straight into our eyes and they held their head high and they answered:

"The Unconquered."

For a long time we could not speak. Then we said:

"Such thoughts as these are forbidden, Golden One."

"But you think such thoughts as these and you wish us to think them."

We looked into their eyes and we could not lie.

"Yes," we whispered, and they smiled, and then we said: "Our dearest one, do not obey us."

They stepped back, and their eyes were wide and still.

"Speak these words again," they whispered.

"Which words?" we asked. But they did not answer, and we knew it.

"Our dearest one," we whispered.

Never have men said this to women.

The head of the Golden One bowed slowly, and they stood still before us, their arms at their sides, the palms of their hands turned to us, as if their body were delivered in submission to our eyes. And we could not speak.

Then they raised their head, and they spoke simply and gently, as if they wished us to forget some anxiety of their own.

"The day is hot," they said, "and you have worked for many hours and you must be weary."

"No," we answered.

"It is cooler in the fields," they said, "and there is water to drink. Are you thirsty?"

"Yes," we answered, "but we cannot cross the hedge."

"We shall bring the water to you," they said.

Then they knelt by the moat, they gathered water in their two hands, they rose and they held the water out to our lips.

We do not know if we drank that water. We only knew suddenly that their hands were empty, but we were still holding our lips to their hands, and that they knew it, but did not move.

We raised our head and stepped back. For we did not understand what had made us do this, and we were afraid to understand it.

And the Golden One stepped back, and stood looking upon their hands in wonder. Then the Golden One moved away, even though no others were coming, and they moved, stepping back, as if they could not turn from us, their arms bent before them, as if they could not lower their hands.

PART FIVE

We made it. We created it. We brought it forth from the night of the ages. We alone. Our hands. Our mind. Ours alone and only.

We know not what we are saying. Our head is reeling. We look upon the light which we have made. We shall be forgiven for anything we say tonight....

Tonight, after more days and trials than we can count, we finished building a strange thing, from the remains of the Unmentionable Times, a box of glass, devised to give forth the power of the sky of greater strength than we had ever achieved before. And when we put our wires to this box, when we closed the current—the wire glowed! It came to life, it turned red, and a circle of light lay on the stone before us.

We stood, and we held our head in our hands. We could not conceive of that which we had created. We had touched no flint, made no fire. Yet here was light, light that came from nowhere, light from the heart of metal.

We blew out the candle. Darkness swallowed us. There was nothing left around us, nothing save night and a thin thread of flame in it, as a crack in the wall of a prison. We stretched our hands to the wire, and we saw our fingers in the red glow. We could not see our body nor feel it, and in that moment nothing existed save our two hands over a wire glowing in a black abyss.

Then we thought of the meaning of that which lay before us. We can light our tunnel, and the City, and all the Cities of the world with nothing save metal and wires. We can give our brothers a new light, cleaner and brighter than any they have ever known. The power of the sky can be made to do men's bidding. There are no limits to its secrets and its might, and it can be made to grant us anything if we but choose to ask.

Then we knew what we must do. Our discovery is too great for us to waste our time in sweeping the streets. We must not keep our secret to ourselves, nor buried under the ground. We must bring it into the sight of all men. We need all our time, we need the work rooms of the Home of the Scholars, we want the help of our brother Scholars and their wisdom joined to ours. There is so much work ahead for all of us, for all the Scholars of the world.

In a month, the World Council of Scholars is to meet in our City. It is a great Council, to which the wisest of all lands are elected, and it meets once a year in the different Cities of the earth. We shall go to this Council and we shall lay before them, as our gift, this glass box with the power of the sky. We shall confess everything to them. They will see, understand and forgive. For our gift is greater than our transgression. They will explain it to the Council of Vocations, and we shall be assigned to the Home of the Scholars. This has never been done before, but neither has a gift such as ours ever been offered to men.

We must wait. We must guard our tunnel as we had never guarded it before. For should any men save the Scholars learn of our secret, they would not understand it, nor would they believe us. They would see nothing, save our crime of working alone, and they would destroy us and our light. We care not about our body, but our light is...

Yes, we do care. For the first time do we care about our body. For this wire is as a part of our body, as a vein torn from us, glowing with our blood. Are we proud of this thread of metal, or of our hands which made it, or is there a line to divide these two?

We stretch out our arms. For the first time do we know how strong our arms are. And a strange thought comes to us: we wonder, for the first time in our life, what we look like. Men never see their own faces and never ask their brothers about it, for it is evil to have concern for their own faces or bodies. But tonight, for a reason we cannot fathom, we wish it were possible to us to know the likeness of our own person.

PART SIX

We have not written for thirty days. For thirty days we have not been here, in our tunnel. We had been caught. It happened on that night when we wrote last. We forgot, that night, to watch the sand in the glass which tells us when three hours have passed and it is time to return to the City Theatre. When we remembered it, the sand had run out.

We hastened to the Theatre. But the big tent stood grey and silent against the sky. The streets of the City lay before us, dark and empty. If we went back to hide in our tunnel, we would be found and our light found with us. So we walked to the Home of the Street Sweepers.

When the Council of the Home questioned us, we looked upon the faces of the Council, but there was no curiosity in those faces, and no anger, and no mercy. So when the oldest of them asked us: "Where have you been?" we thought of our glass box and of our light, and we forgot all else. And we answered:

"We will not tell you."

The oldest did not question us further. They turned to the two youngest, and said, and their voice was bored:

"Take our brother Equality 7-2521 to the Palace of Corrective Detention. Lash them until they tell."

So we were taken to the Stone Room under the Palace of Corrective Detention. This room has no windows and it is empty save for an iron post. Two men stood by the post, naked but for leather aprons and leather hoods over their faces. Those who had brought us departed, leaving us to the two Judges who stood in a corner of the room. The Judges were small, thin men, grey and bent. They gave the signal to the two strong hooded ones.

They tore the clothes from our body, they threw us down upon our knees and they tied our hands to the iron post. The first blow of the lash felt as if our spine had been cut in two. The second blow stopped the first, and for a second we felt nothing, then the pain struck us in our throat and fire ran in our lungs without air. But we did not cry out.

The lash whistled like a singing wind. We tried to count the blows, but we lost count. We knew that the blows were falling upon our back. Only we felt nothing upon our back any longer. A flaming grill kept dancing before our eyes, and we thought of nothing save that grill, a grill, a grill of red squares, and then we knew that we were looking at the squares of the iron grill in the door, and there were also the squares of stone on the walls, and the squares which the lash was cutting upon our back, crossing and re-crossing itself in our flesh.

Then we saw a fist before us. It knocked our chin up, and we saw the red froth of our mouth on the withered fingers, and the Judge asked:

"Where have you been?"

But we jerked our head away, hid our face upon our tied hands, and bit our lips.

The lash whistled again. We wondered who was sprinkling burning coal dust upon the floor, for we saw drops of red twinkling on the stones around us.

Then we knew nothing, save two voices snarling steadily, one after the other, even though we knew they were speaking many minutes apart:

"Where have you been where have you been where have you been where have you been?..."

And our lips moved, but the sound trickled back into our throat, and the sound was only:

"The light... The light... The light...."

Then we knew nothing.

We opened our eyes, lying on our stomach on the brick floor of a cell. We looked upon two hands lying far before us on the bricks, and we moved them, and we knew that they were our hands. But we could not move our body. Then we smiled, for we thought of the light and that we had not betrayed it.

We lay in our cell for many days. The door opened twice each day, once for the men who brought us bread and water, and once for the Judges. Many Judges came to our cell, first the humblest and then the most honored Judges of the City. They stood before us in their white togas, and they asked:

"Are you ready to speak?"

But we shook our head, lying before them on the floor. And they departed.

We counted each day and each night as it passed. Then, tonight, we knew that we must escape. For tomorrow the World Council of Scholars is to meet in our City.

It was easy to escape from the Palace of Corrective Detention. The locks are old on the doors and there are no guards about. There is no reason to have guards, for men have never defied the Councils so far as to escape from whatever place they were ordered to be. Our body is healthy and strength returns to it speedily. We lunged against the door and it gave way. We stole through the dark passages, and through the dark streets, and down into our tunnel.

We lit the candle and we saw that our place had not been found and nothing had been touched. And our glass box stood before us on the cold oven, as we had left it. What matter they now, the scars upon our back!

Tomorrow, in the full light of day, we shall take our box, and leave our tunnel open, and walk through the streets to the Home of the Scholars. We shall put before them the greatest gift ever offered to men. We shall tell them the truth. We shall hand to them, as our confession, these pages we have written. We shall join our hands to theirs, and we shall work together, with the power of the sky, for the glory of mankind. Our blessing upon you, our brothers! Tomorrow, you will take us back into your fold and we shall be an outcast no longer. Tomorrow we shall be one of you again. Tomorrow...

PART SEVEN

It is dark here in the forest. The leaves rustle over our head, black against the last gold of the sky. The moss is soft and warm. We shall sleep on this moss for many nights, till the beasts of the forest come to tear our body. We have no bed now, save the moss, and no future, save the beasts.

We are old now, yet we were young this morning, when we carried our glass box through the streets of the City to the Home of the Scholars. No men stopped us, for there were none about from the Palace of Corrective Detention, and the others knew nothing. No men stopped us at the gate. We walked through empty passages and into the great hall where the World Council of Scholars sat in solemn meeting.

We saw nothing as we entered, save the sky in the great windows, blue and glowing. Then we saw the Scholars who sat around a long table; they were as shapeless clouds huddled at the rise of the great sky. There were men whose famous names we knew, and others from distant lands whose names we had not heard. We saw a great painting on the wall over their heads, of the twenty illustrious men who had invented the candle.

All the heads of the Council turned to us as we entered. These great and wise of the earth did not know what to think of us, and they looked upon us with wonder and curiosity, as if we were a miracle. It is true that our tunic was torn and stained with brown stains which had been blood. We raised our right arm and we said:

"Our greeting to you, our honored brothers of the World Council of Scholars!"

Then Collective 0-0009, the oldest and wisest of the Council, spoke and asked:

"Who are you, our brother? For you do not look like a Scholar."

"Our name is Equality 7-2521," we answered, "and we are a Street Sweeper of this City."

Then it was as if a great wind had stricken the hall, for all the Scholars spoke at once, and they were angry and frightened.

"A Street Sweeper! A Street Sweeper walking in upon the World Council of Scholars! It is not to be believed! It is against all the rules and all the laws!"

But we knew how to stop them.

"Our brothers!" we said. "We matter not, nor our transgression. It is only our brother men who matter. Give no thought to us, for we are nothing, but listen to our words, for we bring you a gift such as had never been brought to men. Listen to us, for we hold the future of mankind in our hands."

Then they listened.

We placed our glass box upon the table before them. We spoke of it, and of our long quest, and of our tunnel, and of our escape from the Palace of Corrective Detention. Not a hand moved in that hall, as we spoke, nor an eye. Then we put the wires to the box, and they all bent forward and sat still, watching. And we stood still, our eyes upon the wire. And slowly, slowly as a flush of blood, a red flame trembled in the wire. Then the wire glowed.

But terror struck the men of the Council. They leapt to their feet, they ran from the table, and they stood pressed against the wall, huddled together, seeking the warmth of one another's bodies to give them courage.

We looked upon them and we laughed and said:

"Fear nothing, our brothers. There is a great power in these wires, but this power is tamed. It is yours. We give it to you."

Still they would not move.

"We give you the power of the sky!" we cried. "We give you the key to the earth! Take it, and let us be one of you, the humblest among you. Let us all work together, and harness this power, and make it ease the toil of men. Let us throw away our candles and our torches. Let us flood our cities with light. Let us bring a new light to men!"

But they looked upon us, and suddenly we were afraid. For their eyes were still, and small, and evil.

"Our brothers!" we cried. "Have you nothing to say to us?"

Then Collective 0-0009 moved forward. They moved to the table and the others followed.

"Yes," spoke Collective 0-0009, "we have much to say to you."

The sound of their voices brought silence to the hall and to beat of our heart.

"Yes," said Collective 0-0009, "we have much to say to a wretch who have broken all the laws and who boast of their infamy!

"How dared you think that your mind held greater wisdom than the minds of your brothers? And if the Councils had decreed that you should be a Street Sweeper, how dared you think that you could be of greater use to men than in sweeping the streets?"

"How dared you, gutter cleaner," spoke Fraternity 9-3452, "to hold yourself as one alone and with the thoughts of the one and not of the many?"

"You shall be burned at the stake," said Democracy 4-6998.

"No, they shall be lashed," said Unanimity 7-3304, "till there is nothing left under the lashes."

"No," said Collective 0-0009, "we cannot decide upon this, our brothers. No such crime has ever been committed, and it is not for us to judge. Nor for any small Council. We shall deliver this creature to the World Council itself and let their will be done."

We looked upon them and we pleaded:

"Our brothers! You are right. Let the will of the Council be done upon our body. We do not care. But the light? What will you do with the light?"

Collective 0-0009 looked upon us, and they smiled.

"So you think that you have found a new power," said Collective 0-0009. "Do all your brothers think that?"

"No," we answered.

"What is not thought by all men cannot be true," said Collective 0-0009.

"You have worked on this alone?" asked International 1-5537.

"Many men in the Homes of the Scholars have had strange new ideas in the past," said Solidarity 8-1164, "but when the majority of their brother Scholars voted against them, they abandoned their ideas, as all men must."

"This box is useless," said Alliance 6-7349.

"Should it be what they claim of it," said Harmony 9-2642, "then it would bring ruin to the Department of Candles. The Candle is a great boon to mankind, as approved by all men. Therefore it cannot be destroyed by the whim of one."

"This would wreck the Plans of the World Council," said Unanimity 2-9913, "and without the Plans of the World Council the sun cannot rise. It took fifty years to secure the approval of all the Councils for the Candle, and to decide upon the number needed, and to re-fit the Plans so as to make candles instead of torches. This touched upon thousands and thousands of men working in scores of States. We cannot alter the Plans again so soon."

"And if this should lighten the toil of men," said Similarity 5-0306, "then it is a great evil, for men have no cause to exist save in toiling for other men."

Then Collective 0-0009 rose and pointed at our box.

"This thing," they said, "must be destroyed."

And all the others cried as one:

"It must be destroyed!"

Then we leapt to the table.

We seized our box, we shoved them aside, and we ran to the window. We turned and we looked at them for the last time, and a rage, such as it is not fit for humans to know, choked our voice in our throat.

"You fools!" we cried. "You fools! You thrice-damned fools!"

We swung our fist through the windowpane, and we leapt out in a ringing rain of glass.

We fell, but we never let the box fall from our hands. Then we ran. We ran blindly, and men and houses streaked past us in a torrent without shape. And the road seemed not to be flat before us, but as if it were leaping up to meet us, and we waited for the earth to rise and strike us in the face. But we ran. We knew not where we were going. We knew only that we must run, run to the end of the world, to the end of our days.

Then we knew suddenly that we were lying on a soft earth and that we had stopped. Trees taller than we had ever seen before stood over us in great silence. Then we knew. We were in the Uncharted Forest. We had not thought of coming here, but our legs had carried our wisdom, and our legs had brought us to the Uncharted Forest against our will.

Our glass box lay beside us. We crawled to it, we fell upon it, our face in our arms, and we lay still.

We lay thus for a long time. Then we rose, we took our box and walked on into the forest.

It mattered not where we went. We knew that men would not follow us, for they never enter the Uncharted Forest. We had nothing to fear from them. The forest disposes of its own victims. This gave us no fear either. Only we wished to be away, away from the City and from the air that touches upon the air of the City. So we walked on, our box in our arms, our heart empty.

We are doomed. Whatever days are left to us, we shall spend them alone. And we have heard of the corruption to be found in solitude. We have torn ourselves from the truth which is our brother men, and there is no road back for us, and no redemption.

We know these things, but we do not care. We care for nothing on earth. We are tired.

Only the glass box in our arms is like a living heart that gives us strength. We have lied to ourselves. We have not built this box for the good of our brothers. We built it for its own sake. It is above all our brothers to us, and its truth above their truth. Why wonder about this? We have not many days to live. We are walking to the fangs awaiting us somewhere among the great, silent trees. There is not a thing behind us to regret.

Then a blow of pain struck us, our first and our only. We thought of the Golden One. We thought of the Golden One whom we shall never see again. Then the pain passed. It is best. We are one of the Damned. It is best if the Golden One forget our name and the body which bore that name.

PART EIGHT

It has been a day of wonder, this, our first day in the forest.

We awoke when a ray of sunlight fell across our face. We wanted to leap to our feet, as we have had to leap every morning of our life, but we remembered suddenly that no bell had rung and that there was no bell to ring anywhere. We lay on our back, we threw our arms out, and we looked up at the sky. The leaves had edges of silver that trembled and rippled like a river of green and fire flowing high above us.

We did not wish to move. We thought suddenly that we could lie thus as long as we wished, and we laughed aloud at the thought. We could also rise, or run, or leap, or fall down again. We were thinking that these were thoughts without sense, but before we knew it our body had risen in one leap. Our arms stretched out of their own will, and our body whirled and whirled, till it raised a wind to rustle through the leaves of the bushes. Then our hands seized a branch and swung us high into a tree, with no aim save the wonder of learning the strength of our body. The branch snapped under us and we fell upon the moss that was soft as a cushion. Then our body, losing all sense, rolled over and over on the moss, dry leaves in our tunic, in our hair, in our face. And we heard suddenly that we were laughing, laughing aloud, laughing as if there were no power left in us save laughter.

Then we took our glass box, and we went on into the forest. We went on, cutting through the branches, and it was as if we were swimming through a sea of leaves, with the bushes as waves rising and falling and rising around us, and flinging their green sprays high to the treetops. The trees parted before us, calling us forward. The forest seemed to welcome us. We went on, without thought, without care, with nothing to feel save the song of our body.

We stopped when we felt hunger. We saw birds in the tree branches, and flying from under our footsteps. We picked a stone and we sent it as an arrow at a bird. It fell before us. We made a fire, we cooked the bird, and we ate it, and no meal had ever tasted better to us. And we thought suddenly that there was a great satisfaction to be found in the food which we need and obtain by our own hand. And we wished to be hungry again and soon, that we might know again this strange new pride in eating.

Then we walked on. And we came to a stream which lay as a streak of glass among the trees. It lay so still that we saw no water but only a cut in the earth, in which the trees grew down, upturned, and the sky lay at the bottom. We knelt by the stream and we bent down to drink. And then we stopped. For, upon the blue of the sky below us, we saw our own face for the first time.

We sat still and we held our breath. For our face and our body were beautiful. Our face was not like the faces of our brothers, for we felt not pity when looking upon it. Our body was not like the bodies of our brothers, for our limbs were straight and thin and hard and strong. And we thought that we could trust this being who looked upon us from the stream, and that we had nothing to fear with this being.

We walked on till the sun had set. When the shadows gathered among the trees, we stopped in a hollow between the roots, where we shall sleep tonight. And suddenly, for the first time this day, we remembered that we are the Damned. We remembered it, and we laughed.

We are writing this on the paper we had hidden in our tunic together with the written pages we had brought for the World Council of Scholars, but never given to them. We have much to speak of to ourselves, and we hope we shall find the words for it in the days to come. Now, we cannot speak, for we cannot understand.

PART NINE

We have not written for many days. We did not wish to speak. For we needed no words to remember that which has happened to us.

It was on our second day in the forest that we heard steps behind us. We hid in the bushes, and we waited. The steps came closer. And then we saw the fold of a white tunic among the trees, and a gleam of gold.

We leapt forward, we ran to them, and we stood looking upon the Golden One.

They saw us, and their hands closed into fists, and the fists pulled their arms down, as if they wished their arms to hold them, while their body swayed. And they could not speak.

We dared not come too close to them. We asked, and our voice trembled:

"How did you come to be here, Golden One?"

But they whispered only:

"We have found you...."

"How did you come to be in the forest?" we asked.

They raised their head, and there was a great pride in their voice; they answered:

"We have followed you."

Then we could not speak, and they said:

"We heard that you had gone to the Uncharted Forest, for the whole City is speaking of it. So on the night of the day when we heard it, we ran away from the Home of the Peasants. We found the marks of your feet across the plain where no men walk. So we followed them, and we went into the forest, and we followed the path where the branches were broken by your body."

Their white tunic was torn, and the branches had cut the skin of their arms, but they spoke as if they had never taken notice of it, nor of weariness, nor of fear.

"We have followed you," they said, "and we shall follow you wherever you go. If danger threatens you, we shall face it also. If it be death, we shall die with you. You are damned, and we wish to share your damnation."

They looked upon us, and their voice was low, but there was bitterness and triumph in their voice.

"Your eyes are as a flame, but our brothers have neither hope nor fire. Your mouth is cut of granite, but our brothers are soft and humble. Your head is high, but our brothers cringe. You walk, but our brothers crawl. We wish to be damned with you, rather than blessed with all our brothers. Do as you please with us, but do not send us away from you."

Then they knelt, and bowed their golden head before us.

We had never thought of that which we did. We bent to raise the Golden One to their feet, but when we touched them, it was as if madness had stricken us. We seized their body and we pressed our lips to theirs. The Golden One breathed once, and their breath was a moan, and then their arms closed around us.

We stood together for a long time. And we were frightened that we had lived for twenty-one years and had never known what joy is possible to men.

Then we said:

"Our dearest one. Fear nothing of the forest. There is no danger in solitude. We have no need of our brothers. Let us forget their good and our evil, let us forget all things save that we are together and that there is joy as a bond between us. Give us your hand. Look ahead. It is our own world, Golden One, a strange, unknown world, but our own."

Then we walked on into the forest, their hand in ours.

And that night we knew that to hold the body of women in our arms is neither ugly nor shameful, but the one ecstasy granted to the race of men.

We have walked for many days. The forest has no end, and we seek no end. But each day added to the chain of days between us and the City is like an added blessing.

We have made a bow and many arrows. We can kill more birds than we need for our food; we find water and fruit in the forest. At night, we choose a clearing, and we build a ring of fires around it. We sleep in the midst of that ring, and the beasts dare not attack us. We can see their eyes, green and yellow as coals, watching us from the tree branches beyond. The fires smoulder as a crown of jewels around us, and smoke stands still in the air, in columns made blue by the moonlight. We sleep together in the midst of the ring, the arms of the Golden One around us, their head upon our breast.

Some day, we shall stop and build a house, when we shall have gone far enough. But we do not have to hasten. The days before us are without end, like the forest.

We cannot understand this new life which we have found, yet it seems so clear and so simple. When questions come to puzzle us, we walk faster, then turn and forget all things as we watch the Golden One following. The shadows of leaves fall upon their arms, as they spread the branches apart, but their shoulders are in the sun. The skin of their arms is like a blue mist, but their shoulders are white and glowing, as if the light fell not from above, but rose from under their skin. We watch the leaf which has fallen upon their shoulder, and it lies at the curve of their neck, and a drop of dew glistens upon it like a jewel. They approach us, and they stop, laughing, knowing what we think, and they wait obediently, without questions, till it pleases us to turn and go on.

We go on and we bless the earth under our feet. But questions come to us again, as we walk in silence. If that which we have found is the corruption of solitude, then what can men wish for save corruption? If this is the great evil of being alone, then what is good and what is evil?

Everything which comes from the many is good. Everything which comes from one is evil. This have we been taught with our first breath. We have broken the law, but we have never doubted it. Yet now, as we walk through the forest, we are learning to doubt.

There is no life for men, save in useful toil for the good of all their brothers. But we lived not, when we toiled for our brothers, we were only weary. There is no joy for men, save the joy shared with all their brothers. But the only things which taught us joy were the power we created in our wires, and the Golden One. And both these joys belong to us alone, they come from us alone, they bear no relation to all our brothers, and they do not concern our brothers in any way. Thus do we wonder.

There is some error, one frightful error, in the thinking of men. What is that error? We do not know, but the knowledge struggles within us, struggles to be born. Today, the Golden One stopped suddenly and said:

"We love you."

But they frowned and shook their head and looked at us helplessly.

"No," they whispered, "that is not what we wished to say."

They were silent, then they spoke slowly, and their words were halting, like the words of a child learning to speak for the first time:

"We are one... alone... and only... and we love you who are one... alone... and only."

We looked into each other's eyes and we knew that the breath of a miracle had touched us, and fled, and left us groping vainly.

And we felt torn, torn for some word we could not find.

PART TEN

We are sitting at a table and we are writing this upon paper made thousands of years ago. The light is dim, and we cannot see the Golden One, only one lock of gold on the pillow of an ancient bed. This is our home.

We came upon it today, at sunrise. For many days we had been crossing a chain of mountains. The forest rose among cliffs, and whenever we walked out upon a barren stretch of rock we saw great peaks before us in the west, and to the north of us, and to the south, as far as our eyes could see. The peaks were red and brown, with the green streaks of forests as veins upon them, with blue mists as veils over their heads. We had never heard of these mountains, nor seen them marked on any map. The Uncharted Forest has protected them from the Cities and from the men of the Cities.

We climbed paths where the wild goat dared not follow. Stones rolled from under our feet, and we heard them striking the rocks below, farther and farther down, and the mountains rang with each stroke, and long after the strokes had died. But we went on, for we knew that no men would ever follow our track nor reach us here.

Then today, at sunrise, we saw a white flame among the trees, high on a sheer peak before us. We thought that it was a fire and stopped. But the flame was unmoving, yet blinding as liquid metal. So we climbed toward it through the rocks. And there, before us, on a broad summit, with the mountains rising behind it, stood a house such as we had never seen, and the white fire came from the sun on the glass of its windows.

The house had two stories and a strange roof flat as a floor. There was more window than wall upon its walls, and the windows went on straight around the corners, though how this kept the house standing we could not guess. The walls were hard and smooth, of that stone unlike stone which we had seen in our tunnel.

We both knew it without words: this house was left from the Unmentionable Times. The trees had protected it from time and weather, and from men who have less pity than time and weather. We turned to the Golden One and we asked:

"Are you afraid?"

But they shook their head. So we walked to the door, and we threw it open, and we stepped together into the house of the Unmentionable Times.

We shall need the days and the years ahead, to look, to learn, and to understand the things of this house. Today, we could only look and try to believe the sight of our eyes. We pulled the heavy curtains from the windows and we saw that the rooms were small, and we thought that not more than twelve men could have lived here. We thought it strange that men had been permitted to build a house for only twelve.

Never had we seen rooms so full of light. The sunrays danced upon colors, colors, more colors than we thought possible, we who had seen no houses save the white ones, the brown ones and the grey. There were great pieces of glass on the walls, but it was not glass, for when we looked upon it we saw our own bodies and all the things behind us, as on the face of a lake. There were strange things which we had never seen and the use of which we do not know. And there were globes of glass everywhere, in each room, the globes with the metal cobwebs inside, such as we had seen in our tunnel.

We found the sleeping hall and we stood in awe upon its threshold. For it was a small room and there were only two beds in it. We found no other beds in the house, and then we knew that only two had lived here, and this passes understanding. What kind of world did they have, the men of the Unmentionable Times?

We found garments, and the Golden One gasped at the sight of them. For they were not white tunics, nor white togas; they were of all colors, no two of them alike. Some crumbled to dust as we touched them. But others were of heavier cloth, and they felt soft and new in our fingers.

We found a room with walls made of shelves, which held rows of manuscripts, from the floor to the ceiling. Never had we seen such a number of them, nor of such strange shape. They were not soft and rolled, they had hard shells of cloth and leather; and the letters on their pages were so small and so even that we wondered at the men who had such handwriting. We glanced through the pages, and we saw that they were written in our language, but we found many words which we could not understand. Tomorrow, we shall begin to read these scripts.

When we had seen all the rooms of the house, we looked at the Golden One and we both knew the thought in our minds.

"We shall never leave this house," we said, "nor let it be taken from us. This is our home and the end of our journey. This is your house, Golden One, and ours, and it belongs to no other men whatever as far as the earth may stretch. We shall not share it with others, as we share not our joy with them, nor our love, nor our hunger. So be it to the end of our days."

"Your will be done," they said.

Then we went out to gather wood for the great hearth of our home. We brought water from the stream which runs among the trees under our windows. We killed a mountain goat, and we brought its flesh to be cooked in a strange copper pot we found in a place of wonders, which must have been the cooking room of the house.

We did this work alone, for no words of ours could take the Golden One away from the big glass which is not glass. They stood before it and they looked and looked upon their own body.

When the sun sank beyond the mountains, the Golden One fell asleep on the floor, amidst jewels, and bottles of crystal, and flowers of silk. We lifted the Golden One in our arms and we carried them to a bed, their head falling softly upon our shoulder. Then we lit a candle, and we brought paper from the room of the manuscripts, and we sat by the window, for we knew that we could not sleep tonight.

And now we look upon the earth and sky. This spread of naked rock and peaks and moonlight is like a world ready to be born, a world that waits. It seems to us it asks a sign from us, a spark, a first commandment. We cannot know what word we are to give, nor what great deed this earth expects to witness. We know it waits. It seems to say it has great gifts to lay before us, but it wishes a greater gift for us. We are to speak. We are to give its goal, its highest meaning to all this glowing space of rock and sky.

We look ahead, we beg our heart for guidance in answering this call no voice has spoken, yet we have heard. We look upon our hands. We see the dust of centuries, the dust which hid the great secrets and perhaps great evils. And yet it stirs no fear within our heart, but only silent reverence and pity.

May knowledge come to us! What is the secret our heart has understood and yet will not reveal to us, although it seems to beat as if it were endeavoring to tell it?

PART ELEVEN

I am. I think. I will.

My hands... My spirit... My sky... My forest... This earth of mine....
What must I say besides? These are the words. This is the answer.

I stand here on the summit of the mountain. I lift my head and I spread my arms. This, my body and spirit, this is the end of the quest. I wished to know the meaning of things. I am the meaning. I wished to find a warrant for being. I need no warrant for being, and no word of sanction upon my being. I am the warrant and the sanction.

It is my eyes which see, and the sight of my eyes grants beauty to the earth. It is my ears which hear, and the hearing of my ears gives its song to the world. It is my mind which thinks, and the judgement of my mind is the only searchlight that can find the truth. It is my will which chooses, and the choice of my will is the only edict I must respect.

Many words have been granted me, and some are wise, and some are false, but only three are holy: "I will it!"

Whatever road I take, the guiding star is within me; the guiding star and the loadstone which point the way. They point in but one direction. They point to me.

I know not if this earth on which I stand is the core of the universe or if it is but a speck of dust lost in eternity. I know not and I care not. For I know what happiness is possible to me on earth. And my happiness needs no higher aim to vindicate it. My happiness is not the means to any end. It is the end. It is its own goal. It is its own purpose.

Neither am I the means to any end others may wish to accomplish. I am not a tool for their use. I am not a servant of their needs. I am not a bandage for their wounds. I am not a sacrifice on their altars.

I am a man. This miracle of me is mine to own and keep, and mine to guard, and mine to use, and mine to kneel before!

I do not surrender my treasures, nor do I share them. The fortune of my spirit is not to be blown into coins of brass and flung to the winds as alms for the poor of the spirit. I guard my treasures: my thought, my will, my freedom. And the greatest of these is freedom.

I owe nothing to my brothers, nor do I gather debts from them. I ask none to live for me, nor do I live for any others. I covet no man's soul, nor is my soul theirs to covet.

I am neither foe nor friend to my brothers, but such as each of them shall deserve of me. And to earn my love, my brothers must do more than to have been born. I do not grant my love without reason, nor to any chance passer-by who may wish to claim it. I honor men with my love. But honor is a thing to be earned.

I shall choose friends among men, but neither slaves nor masters. And I shall choose only such as please me, and them I shall love and respect, but neither command nor obey. And we shall join our hands when we wish, or walk alone when we so desire. For in the temple of his spirit, each man is alone. Let each man keep his temple untouched and undefiled. Then let him join hands with others if he wishes, but only beyond his holy threshold.

For the word "We" must never be spoken, save by one's choice and as a second thought. This word must never be placed first within man's soul, else it becomes a monster, the root of all the evils on earth, the root of man's torture by men, and of an unspeakable lie.

The word "We" is as lime poured over men, which sets and hardens to stone, and crushes all beneath it, and that which is white and that which is black are lost equally in the grey of it. It is the word by which the depraved steal the virtue of the good, by which the weak steal the might of the strong, by which the fools steal the wisdom of the sages.

What is my joy if all hands, even the unclean, can reach into it? What is my wisdom, if even the fools can dictate to me? What is my freedom, if all creatures, even the botched and the impotent, are my masters? What is my life, if I am but to bow, to agree and to obey?

But I am done with this creed of corruption.

I am done with the monster of "We," the word of serfdom, of plunder, of misery, falsehood and shame.

And now I see the face of god, and I raise this god over the earth, this god whom men have sought since men came into being, this god who will grant them joy and peace and pride.

This god, this one word:

"I."

PART TWELVE

It was when I read the first of the books I found in my house that I saw the word "I." And when I understood this word, the book fell from my hands, and I wept, I who had never known tears. I wept in deliverance and in pity for all mankind.

I understood the blessed thing which I had called my curse. I understood why the best in me had been my sins and my transgressions; and why I had never felt guilt in my sins. I understood that centuries of chains and lashes will not kill the spirit of man nor the sense of truth within him.

I read many books for many days. Then I called the Golden One, and I told her what I had read and what I had learned. She looked at me and the first words she spoke were:

"I love you."

Then I said:

"My dearest one, it is not proper for men to be without names. There was a time when each man had a name of his own to distinguish him from all other men. So let us choose our names. I have read of a man who lived many thousands of years ago, and of all the names in these books, his is the one I wish to bear. He took the light of the gods and he brought it to men, and he taught men to be gods. And he suffered for his deed as all bearers of light must suffer. His name was Prometheus."

"It shall be your name," said the Golden One.

"And I have read of a goddess," I said, "who was the mother of the earth and of all the gods. Her name was Gaea. Let this be your name, my Golden One, for you are to be the mother of a new kind of gods."

"It shall be my name," said the Golden One.

Now I look ahead. My future is clear before me. The Saint of the pyre had seen the future when he chose me as his heir, as the heir of all the saints and all the martyrs who came before him and who died for the same cause, for the same word, no matter what name they gave to their cause and their truth.

I shall live here, in my own house. I shall take my food from the earth by the toil of my own hands. I shall learn many secrets from my books. Through the years ahead, I shall rebuild the achievements of the past, and open the way to carry them further, the achievements which are open to me, but closed forever to my brothers, for their minds are shackled to the weakest and dullest ones among them.

I have learned that my power of the sky was known to men long ago; they called it Electricity. It was the power that moved their greatest inventions. It lit this house with light which came from those globes of glass on the walls. I have found the engine which produced this light. I shall learn how to repair it and how to make it work again. I shall learn how to use the wires which carry this power. Then I shall build a barrier of wires around my home, and across the paths which lead to my home; a barrier light as a cobweb, more impassable than a wall of granite; a barrier my brothers will never be able to cross. For they have nothing to fight me with, save the brute force of their numbers. I have my mind.

Then here, on this mountaintop, with the world below me and nothing above me but the sun, I shall live my own truth. Gaea is pregnant with my child. Our son will be raised as a man. He will be taught to say "I" and to bear the pride of it. He will be taught to walk straight and on his own feet. He will be taught reverence for his own spirit.

When I shall have read all the books and learned my new way, when my home will be ready and my earth tilled, I shall steal one day, for the last time, into the cursed City of my birth. I shall call to me my friend who has no name save International 4-8818, and all those like him, Fraternity 2-5503, who cries without reason, and Solidarity 9-6347 who calls for help in the night, and a few others. I shall call to me all the men and the women whose spirit has not been killed within them and who suffer under the yoke of their brothers. They will follow me and I shall lead them to my fortress. And here, in this uncharted wilderness, I and they, my chosen friends, my fellow-builders, shall write the first chapter in the new history of man.

These are the things before me. And as I stand here at the door of glory, I look behind me for the last time. I look upon the history of men, which I have learned from the books, and I wonder. It was a long story, and the spirit which moved it was the spirit of man's freedom. But what is freedom? Freedom from what? There is nothing to take a man's freedom away from him, save other men. To be free, a man must be free of his brothers. That is freedom. That and nothing else.

At first, man was enslaved by the gods. But he broke their chains. Then he was enslaved by the kings. But he broke their chains. He was enslaved by his birth, by his kin, by his race. But he broke their chains. He declared to all his brothers that a man has rights which neither god nor king nor other men can take away from him, no matter what their number, for his is the right of man, and there is no right on earth above this right. And he stood on the threshold of the freedom for which the blood of the centuries behind him had been spilled.

But then he gave up all he had won, and fell lower than his savage beginning.

What brought it to pass? What disaster took their reason away from men? What whip lashed them to their knees in shame and submission? The worship of the word "We."

When men accepted that worship, the structure of centuries collapsed about them, the structure whose every beam had come from the thought of some one man, each in his day down the ages, from the depth of some one spirit, such spirit as existed but for its own sake. Those men who survived those eager to obey, eager to live for one another, since they had nothing else to vindicate them—those men could neither carry on, nor preserve what they had received. Thus did all thought, all science, all wisdom perish on earth. Thus did men—men with nothing to offer save their great number—lost the steel towers, the flying ships, the power wires, all the things they had not created and could never keep. Perhaps, later, some men had been born with the mind and the courage to recover these things which were lost; perhaps these men came before the Councils of Scholars. They were answered as I have been answered—and for the same reasons.

But I still wonder how it was possible, in those graceless years of transition, long ago, that men did not see whither they were going, and went on, in blindness and cowardice, to their fate. I wonder, for it is hard for me to conceive how men who knew the word "I" could give it up and not know what they lost. But such has been the story, for I have lived in the City of the damned, and I know what horror men permitted to be brought upon them.

Perhaps, in those days, there were a few among men, a few of clear sight and clean soul, who refused to surrender that word. What agony must have been theirs before that which they saw coming and could not stop! Perhaps they cried out in protest and in warning. But men paid no heed to their warning. And they, these few, fought a hopeless battle, and they perished with their banners smeared by their own blood. And they chose to perish, for they knew. To them, I send my salute across the centuries, and my pity.

Theirs is the banner in my hand. And I wish I had the power to tell them that the despair of their hearts was not to be final, and their night was not without hope. For the battle they lost can never be lost. For that which they died to save can never perish. Through all the darkness, through all the shame of which men are capable, the spirit of man will remain alive on this earth. It may sleep, but it will awaken. It may wear chains, but it will break through. And man will go on. Man, not men.

Here on this mountain, I and my sons and my chosen friends shall build our new land and our fort. And it will become as the heart of the earth, lost and hidden at first, but beating, beating louder each day. And word of it will reach every corner of the earth. And the roads of the world will become as veins which will carry the best of the world's blood to my threshold. And all my brothers, and the Councils of my brothers, will hear of it, but they will be impotent against me. And the day will come when I shall break all the chains of the earth, and raze the cities of the enslaved, and my home will become the capital of a world where each man will be free to exist for his own sake.

For the coming of that day shall I fight, I and my sons and my chosen friends. For the freedom of Man. For his rights. For his life. For his honor.

And here, over the portals of my fort, I shall cut in the stone the word which is to be my beacon and my banner. The word which will not die, should we all perish in battle. The word which can never die on this earth, for it is the heart of it and the meaning and the glory.

The sacred word:

EGO

Thank you for reading!

5	2	1	6	4	8	3	7	9
3	6	9	5	1	7	4	8	2
4	7	8	2	9	3	5	1	6
1	4	6	7	8	9	2	5	3
2	5	7	1	3	6	9	4	8
9	8	3	4	2	5	7	6	1
6	9	4	3	5	1	8	2	7
7	3	2	8	6	4	1	9	5
8	1	5	9	7	2	6	3	4

The next issue is coming out this fall.
See more at:
AdventuresBookZine.com